THE
LIARS

NAOMI JOY

HEAD
ZEUS

An Aria Book

First published in the UK in 2019 by Aria,
an imprint of Head of Zeus Ltd

This paperback edition published in the UK in 2020 by Head of Zeus
An Aria book

9 7 5 3 1 2 4 6 8

A CIP catalogue record for this book is available
from the British Library.

ISBN (PB): 9781838930684
ISBN (E): 9781789543759

Printed and bound by CPI Group (UK) Ltd, Croydon, CR0 4YY

MIX
Paper from
responsible sources
FSC® C020471

Aria
c/o Head of Zeus
First Floor East
5–8 Hardwick Street
London EC1R 4RG

www.ariafiction.com

THE
LIARS

NAOMI JOY is a pen name of a young
PR professional who was formerly an
account director at prestigious Storm
Communications. Writing from experience,
she draws the reader in to the darker side
of the uptown and glamorous, presenting
realism that is life or death, unreliable and
thrilling to page-turn.

For my mum, Jackie, and my sister, Charlotte.

TRAGEDY STRIKES TWICE FOR DAVID STEIN

MULTI-MILLIONAIRE PR GURU DAVID STEIN
OUT OF HIDING FOR DAUGHTER'S INQUEST

Olivia Stein, David Stein's only daughter, died of a cardiac arrest following a 'massive' cocaine overdose, a coroner ruled today. Discovered 'slumped over' at home by her father, it was also revealed Olivia's blood alcohol level was a significant factor in her death.

The coroner told the inquest, 'It is well known that cocaine mixed with alcohol is far more dangerous than taking either drug in isolation. The large quantities found in Olivia's blood, in addition to her underlying heart condition, ultimately caused her sudden and untimely death.'

Her father, David Stein, who tragically lost his wife and business partner Kate Watson to an overdose almost twenty years ago to the day, said Olivia 'had tried hard to manage her addictions in recent months.' He went on to say she 'dreamed of taking over his Public Relations firm one day' and that he had 'no reason' to believe Olivia's overdose was intentional.

Her death is not being treated as suspicious.

1

Ava

When I think about Olivia, the first memory that hits is the way she smelt the morning after she died. It hadn't been rank or overly pungent, she hadn't been dead long, but the early scent of death – cold, lingering and sickeningly sweet – is always what I think of first. Next, I think of the jaunty angles of her stiffening limbs, the way her head had lolled off the sofa, hanging heavy towards the floor, her neck bent double, her black eyes rolling deep into her skull. She'd looked uncomfortable, like she'd been dropped by a puppet-master who'd suddenly snipped her ties. I find myself wondering about her thoughts, too: what had she considered as she'd taken her final breaths? Had she known she was going to die? Sometimes I try to imagine myself in her place that night, heart beating out of my chest, palms sweating, blood pooling in my lungs, travelling up my windpipe, seeking out the light. I've often wondered if her final position – lying stretched out across the sofa – had indicated she'd been reaching for her phone. It had only sat a few centimetres from her fingertips. Olivia was a kind, beautiful and fiercely intelligent young woman; she hadn't deserved to die in such an undignified way.

I clamped my hands over my face, desperate to halt my mind's furious slideshow, and pressed my fingertips into my forehead, leaving prints behind. I took a sharp breath in, then felt the warmth of my exhalation against my palms. I was sitting alone in the dead quiet of the office, the open-plan space beyond my own glass-walled room completely still. By day, this floor was a hive of activity, by night it was a graveyard. 'Everything OK?' David's voice made me jump, his question accompanied by a firm rap on my open door. David is my ultimate boss, the CEO of Watson & Stein Partners – W&SP, for short – and Olivia's father. I was surprised he was still in the office and I glanced at the clock as it ticked past ten. I should have left hours ago. His cat-like eyes narrowed; I was taking too long to respond. He spoke again. 'You shouldn't be working this late.'

'I know, I'm just—'

'Reading about the inquest?'

I looked at him apologetically. He knew. 'Yes,' I replied, avoiding eye contact. David moved into the room and sat silently across from me. The darkness outside had transformed the glass walls surrounding us into black mirrors and David's face flashed and reflected in every pane. I studied his angular features for a moment, running my stare along his razor-sharp jaw, his carved and cavernous cheekbones, his prominent brow bone and deep-set eyes. No wonder I often felt on edge round him, his face wasn't exactly 'friendly'. But his looks weren't the only thing that made me nervous. He had a terrifying majesty about him. An aura. He was the kind of man you're warned about: dangerous, controlling, more money than sense. I suppose I've always found David a little unnerving but, sat before me now, I noticed the vulnerability in him for the first time too, the fragility. His grief was palpable.

I looked at him cautiously, unsure what to say next. I must have uttered the phrase, *I can't imagine how you're feeling*, a million times since Olivia died. He was probably sick of it. Instead, I let silence fill the space between us, the only sound in the room the monotonous whirr of my computer fan. He didn't seem to mind the quiet. In fact, he looked deep in thought, his focus on the middle distance. He smoothed a hand down the neat crease of his left suit trouser, ironing it out.

'I tried so hard to help her,' he said quietly, pinching the pleat back in line. 'The best rehab, the best doctors, the best therapies... but nothing worked against—'

He stopped speaking abruptly, unwilling to say the name of the substance that killed his daughter. Cocaine. The stuff had been prolific and readily available at the W&SP offices before Olivia died but, once she was gone, David was determined to cleanse the office of the toxin. *Too little, too dead.* He'd brought a private firm in to search people's desks one morning, had fired those caught with it in their possession on the spot. The purge had worked and those unable to get through the day without snorting lines in the toilets had left the company. Personally, I'd never understood the appeal. For me, drugs fell firmly in the same category of *No thanks* as skydiving, fairground rides, helicopter tours and shark cage diving. I would never understand how an activity with an above-average possibility of death could be considered fun.

David looked to the floor to compose himself and chewed the inside of his cheek. I imagined the mottled look of it, a line of flesh missing due to his obsessive gnawing. It took me back to the morning I'd told him Olivia hadn't turned up for our nine o'clock catch up. He'd looked at me askance that day – I'd only been working at Watson & Stein Partners for three months – and cocked his head to one side as if to say: *Who are you and what are you doing in my office?*

'Have you tried her phone?' he'd asked after he'd assessed me.

'Yes,' I'd replied patiently. 'Fifteen times so far...'

He'd started to chew his cheek, just as he was doing now, as I'd waffled on.

'I just thought maybe someone should check in on her. Do you have a key to her place?'

A shadow had fallen across the room. He'd asked if I'd wanted to go with him. I'd stuttered. *No*, my gut instinct had screamed, *why would you want me to go with you?* But I'd suppressed that urge, reasoning it could only be a good thing to get some face time with David.

'Sure,' I'd replied. 'If she's up to it, we can have our catch-up there. I'll grab my things.' I wish I'd listened to my gut.

Now I can't think of Olivia without light-red froth splattered all over her face, without urine soaking her bottom half, without chunks of cakey vomit caught in her hair.

'You'd known her for a long time. Do you think she wanted to die?' David asked, his voice distant. I took a moment before replying. I wondered if part of him wanted me to say yes, but it wouldn't be the truth.

'No,' I answered. 'But I don't think she was scared of death, fear never held her back.'

I guess that was the problem.

My mind traced back to a happier time, to university, where Olivia and I had first crossed paths. I remember being in awe that she would smoke without a second's thought of lung cancer, enjoy carefree one-night stands unconcerned about the existence of antibiotic-resistant gonorrhoea, pontificate on the meaning of life rather than the meaning of essays and deadlines and exams. For me, the experience was quite different: nothing short of a baptism of fire in growing up. It was where I was first kissed, *properly*, by a heavy-jawed boy on a rugby scholarship, unearthing the taste of vomit as I'd tucked into the crevices of his mouth. The taste of regurgitated food had hit me more than the kiss itself and later I was sick too: all over a row of yellow weeds in someone's garden on my way back to halls. I'd gone back the next morning. Little pieces of ham and pea had frosted into the soil, and I'd snuck in through the gate to try and clear up my mess. Olivia had laughed, kindly, when I'd told her about it. *Puke is biodegradable, silly, you should have left it. It's why graveyards are so green: the bodies feed the flowers.*

'She flew too close to the sun; just like her mother.' David moved his focus back towards my watery hazel eyes. 'Neither of them ever *listened*.'

A memory gripped me: Olivia holding my hands in hers, pleading with me to keep her relapse quiet. She'd been horrified a rumour might get out at work and back to her father. He'd put thousands towards rehabilitating her. 'Please,' she'd begged, tears in her eyes. 'He'll kill me if he finds out.'

At that moment, my phone vibrated into action, the sound not dissimilar to a pneumatic drill as it clanged against the glass-topped table in front of me. I hit the cancel button before it had the chance to ring again, but David had already clocked the panic on my face.

'Let me guess... boyfriend?'

'How did you know?'

'Well, you're here, stupidly late, reading about the inquest. You obviously don't feel you can talk to him about what happened... if you did, you'd be at home.'

I was surprised he was passing comment on my private life; he'd never shown any interest in it before. David and I had grown closer in the months following Olivia's death; I hadn't imagined us becoming *friends* exactly, but here we were, tearing down the barriers of our professional relationship with surprising ease. I tried to figure out why: perhaps the inquest into Olivia's death had reminded David of what we'd shared together that morning not so long ago.

I hesitated for a moment, then had a thought. I decided to let David in.

'Truthfully, I want to leave him.' I splayed the fingers of my right hand across the desk, then curled them into a fist. 'But our rental agreement is too expensive to break out of and I have nowhere else to go.'

I glanced down at the new message that flashed across the screen. It joined a cluster of other unopened snippets of vile abuse.

Don't bother coming back tonight, I don't want to smell him on you aga—

I know you're with him, I know exactly what you're doing, I always—

This can't go on. You have to stop work. It's him or—

I barely recognised the man I once knew in these messages. If I went home now, he'd be sat alone at our sad two-person dining table, his spine curved into a dramatic C as he hunched over his mobile phone, typing furiously. I'd walk in and, at first, he'd choose not to notice. Then he'd tell me he hadn't eaten: *You should have been back in time to cook.* He'd pour himself a protest bowl of brown cereal, a child's brand he'd never dared to progress from, and I'd watch him fill it to the brim with milk. He'd wait until the chunks of puffed rice were white and water-logged, the milk the colour of a filthy puddle, then dig in. I'd sit quietly on the sofa, waiting. Then it would begin, the angry ping-pong of accusations.

Were you with him tonight?

I was working. There is no 'him'.

Give me your laptop, your phone. I want to go through them.

That's really not necessary.

And your underwear. I want to check it.

I'd do as he said, just to make him stop, and hand over my personal effects like a refugee at the Mexican border. He'd try to hide his fury as I brought him what he'd asked for, to keep control, but his wobbling spoon would give

7

him away. Spilt milk would dribble down past his chin, the hair on his jaw soaking it up, the rest running down to the table, a cloudy pool forming below which I'd have to clean up in the morning.

'Look,' I said, rising to hand David my phone.

'Ava, this is…' I watched as his eyes scanned across the screen, his paternal instinct kicking in. 'Unacceptable. You can't stay with this man.'

'I don't have a choice,' I replied.

'You have to let me help.'

I looked at him nervously, part of me worried I'd taken a step too far. I hadn't let anyone know had bad things were before now.

'I should go,' I said, gathering my coat from the stand in the corner.

'To him?' David looked agitated.

I shrugged past him. 'Like I said…' Then turned to him before I left. 'Thank you for checking in on me, it feels good to have someone to talk to about Olivia. I miss her so much.'

He stood, cheeks sunken, grasping for a line of appropriate words.

'Do you mind if I pop back in the morning? We need to talk about your situation. I want to help.'

I smiled, reluctant to believe him, scared of getting my hopes up. Charlie, my boyfriend, had cut me off from everyone when we moved to London and, though I'm sure any one of my friends would have offered to help in much the same way as David was now, none of them actually had the means. My mother would only have encouraged me to give things another go. So I hadn't bothered asking. David

Stein was the opposite: he had the means all right, I just had to give him the motivation.

I arrived back at the rabbit hutch of a flat I shared with Charlie and slotted my key silently into the lock. I'd been in and out of hotels this week, trying to keep my distance from him, but my funds were running low and I had no option but to come back here tonight. I winced as the front door creaked when I opened it and took a moment to check it hadn't woken him. When I was happy the coast was clear, I went inside.

I tiptoed quietly into the hallway and my eyes immediately picked up a trail of destruction that snaked its way through to the kitchen. It was clear that Charlie's dinner had felt his wrath tonight, and I breathed a sigh of relief that it wasn't *me* plastered all over our kitchen walls. Working late certainly had its advantages. A bowl of tomato pasta had redecorated our notice board and, if I wiped away the red stains, I'd uncover a semi-complete shopping list, a few coupons, a wedding invitation and a joint calendar beneath the mess. A fitting metaphor for our relationship, I mused.

I craned my neck round the door and observed that Charlie's dinner had, after the moment of impact, run sloppily down the length of our kitchen's formerly white side wall. It was currently settled in a relatively neat pile over the skirting board, a pool of it stuck to the tiles below.

As I lingered in the hallway I smelt cleaning products, strong and bleachy, emanating from the lounge. The hospital scent curled up in the back of my throat, so chemical it made me reluctant to investigate further, but I pressed on.

Charlie was passed out, small mercy, the TV on mute, still flickering. He was clutching a half-swigged bottle of vodka in his clammy hand, the sterile liquid slow-leaking across the cheap wooden floor below. My first thought wasn't of pity, or sorrow, or sadness, but relief. For a moment I thought he might be dead, he didn't sound like he was breathing, but then I watched, disappointed, as he grunted in his slumber and came back to life, his chest undulating in shallow peaks and troughs. I looked him up and down: yellow sweat-stains covered his T-shirt and clumps of white saliva pooled in the corners of his pale lips. He disgusted me, but at least I wouldn't have to face him until morning.

I padded into the bedroom, locked the door, and moved over to the window to shut out the night. At that moment, the moon emerged from behind a cluster of bruised clouds, revealing its hard, white surface. Its luminescent rays flared through the window and covered me completely, exposing me, its innocent snow-white face disappointed. *Why did you do it?* It asked wistfully. I felt a terrible sense of guilt and closed the flimsy blind with a quick flick of my wrist, shutting out the accusation. I crawled into bed, gathered the covers up round my shoulders and turned away from the window but, as I drifted off into a fitful sleep, I could still feel the moon as it glared through the cracks in the blinds. *You can't hide forever, Ava. I know what you did. I know your secret.*

2

Jade

I shot my eyes up from my monitor: nearly eleven o'clock. Well, well, well, guess what the cat dragged in: the *usually* perpetually early and perpetually perfect Ava. Late night, was it?

Others in the office had clocked her tardy arrival too and I watched my colleagues, Josh (6'3, Superman, the future Mr Jade) and Georgette (6'0, Essex, bitchy) eyeball her as she walked in, head bowed, and closed the glass door to her office. She didn't often do that, not that the transparent panes afforded her any more privacy than usual. I strained my eyes, squinted, and read Georgette's lips.

'What do you think all that's about? Olivia?'

I almost guffawed from my desk. Of course. If anyone could make an inquest into someone else's death all about them, it was Ava. Clearly she was still milking Olivia's passing for all it was worth. My see-through stockings stuck to my legs, clammy and irritated. Well, I'd managed to make it into work on time and I'd worked with

Olivia for eight years compared to Ava's paltry one. In fact, Olivia and I had been extremely close colleagues; we'd both joined W&SP around the same time and had spent the years working our way up the slippery ladders of power side-by-side. Ava had joined last year and, as Olivia and Ava had known each other at university, she'd slotted right into our clique – perhaps a little too well. Then Olivia passed away, turning our threesome into a double act, and it wasn't long before everything turned into a competition between Ava and me: who'd known Olivia better, who'd been more affected by her death, who'd been best placed to take on her clients, who'd step up to try and fill her shoes. Looking back, I was even jealous that Ava had been with David the morning they'd found Olivia's body; it had only brought Ava closer and pushed me further away.

'Psst! George!' I whispered sharply to Georgette, motioning for her to come over.

'What?' she mouthed at me from across the room.

'Come here!'

She moved away from her conversation with Josh and back over to our shared desk. As she clip-clopped my way, I was dismayed by her outfit: a T-shirt dress comprised entirely of aquamarine sequins. I decided not to comment on how inappropriate it was – mermaids should never inspire one's office attire – and made a mental note to bring it up another time.

'Wot?' George cawed, her overly contoured face and the near-monobrow she'd created with a few overzealous licks of her brow brush appearing dead opposite me, inches away, like a full-size, full-on jack-in-the-box.

'Pathetic!' I exclaimed in a whisper, leaning over the desk so we were closer still. 'Absolutely pathetic.'

Georgette didn't exactly spring out of her box to agree. 'Seeing your workmate the morning after an overdose is probably gonna mess you up for a while, right? The inquest will only have brought it all back.'

I refused to comment, keen to deflect her from talking about Olivia's death. It brought back awful memories for me too; it wasn't just Ava.

Georgette covered my silence. 'Josh was just saying he feels really bad for her too.'

My heart sank and my eyes turned a darker shade of green. 'He said that?'

Josh was mine. Well, perhaps that was going a bit far. Josh would be mine, one day. I knew that sounded disgustingly desperate: a grown-up woman with a tragic crush. But I couldn't help it. He'd always been mine. It should have been me he was feeling bad for. I'd known Olivia, and him, for years longer than Ava.

I was just about to dive into planning how I could turn the tide and make Josh feel sorry for me instead when I noticed someone unusual approaching in my peripheral vision. My expression clouded and my mouth dropped open to form a perfectly round 'o'. David Stein – company CEO who never came onto this floor, ever – had burst magnificently through the double doors and was striding across the office, his dark hair flecked with grey, his expression drawn and steely. Instinct told me exactly where he was headed: Ava.

Georgette followed my stare and swung her chair round to witness the scene unfolding behind her. I flicked my focus over to Ava, oblivious to who was coming her way, and watched, hypnotised, as she gathered the long twist of her hair in one hand, tying the thousands of shades of slightly different blonde tighter and tighter together. In one effortless motion she curled her hair up on top of her head and stuck a pen through it, then David knocked on her door and her pen-bun loosened and fell, as though in shock, each strand of her hair catching the spring light as it did so, rippling like a sandy avalanche as it came to rest against her back. Georgette spun back round, happy shock on her face. George loved office drama, in fact, I'd wager procuring office gossip and disseminating the information was her number one skill. And it wasn't the worst thing to be good at in a place like this: information was everything at W&SP.

'What's David Stein want with Ava?' George whispered, turning towards me for just a moment. 'You think this is 'cos of the inquest?'

I shrugged, lost for words, and watched as Ava motioned for him to come in, then greeted him with a kiss on the cheek. Well, well, well. Although we were all reeling, Ava didn't look surprised to see him at all. Had they arranged a meeting? Without me?

My green eyes flashed for the second time in as many minutes – first Josh and now David. My body felt like one of those lightning receptors on top of the Shard or the Empire State Building, just after one billion angry God-like volts had struck. Except I couldn't survive it. Strike after strike of jealousy coursed through my veins, splitting them open until I was nothing but a heap of clothes on the floor, smoke pouring out of them. 'Where did she go?' they'd ask. Would anyone care?

In that moment I made a rash decision: I had to act, I couldn't just stand on the outside looking in. Ava didn't own the rights to Olivia's death, and it wasn't fair she was using Olivia's passing to get ahead. Not if I couldn't use it, too.

I got up from my desk, ignoring Georgette's bleats – 'Jade, no, Jade, what are you doing, Jade, come back here!' – and pushed forward to her office.

I *hated* her for having an office. I'd been at the company for eight years and all David Stein had rewarded me with was an area a few metres apart from the communal bullpen, opposite a woman who dressed like a toddler and painted her face like a clown.

I knocked twice at Ava's closed door, my angry breath forming furious bullseyes of condensation against the glass, and watched as her face fell when she saw it was me. In that moment, the resentment I had for her swelled and I could scarcely believe what I once saw in her as a friend. We used to have lunch together, talk about the ways we could change the company for the better. We'd been a sisterhood at one point. A unit. A team. But ever since Olivia had died and David had taken Ava under his bony wing, favouring her over me in almost every conceivable way despite her vastly inferior experience, the barriers between us had started to stack up and, rather than help me, she relished in every opportunity to kick me back. To make matters worse, David had put us both up for the same job, a glittering promotion which I deserved tenfold over her: Team Head.

So, here I was. Fighting for my career.

I didn't wait for her to beckon me in.

'Is everything OK?' I asked, pushing my way into their clandestine one-to-one. 'The news about the inquest was pretty tough reading yesterday,' I said matter-of-factly, closing the door behind me. 'Olivia would have hated everything being so public.'

'Jade, could you give us a moment?' Ava asked curtly, brushing me off.

There she went again, acting as if there was no way I could possibly have been affected by Olivia's death. It was like she didn't even remember what we went through together.

'It's just—'

'We're fine, thank you Jade,' she repeated, raising her voice.

Before I could speak again, David spat out a rhetorical question aimed at me.

'Jade – do you mind?'

His words hit like a punch to the gut and my cheeks blazed. Embarrassment opened its mouth and swallowed me whole. I hadn't expected David to be so rude. Had Ava been busy poisoning him against me? Nevertheless, I didn't need telling twice and I left in a hurry, floored once again by how Ava had managed to turn an inquest into a way to get ahead at work. I skulked, defeated, back to my desk.

'Jade, what were you thinki—'

I cut Georgette off. 'I don't want to talk about it.'

I sat down, staring straight ahead at nothing in particular, unblinking, thinking. I was supposed to be Team Head this year. That was the plan. That had always been the plan. But since Ava had turned up it was as though my years of loyal servitude to this company had all been for nothing: not now a blonde-haired damsel-in-distress with less experience than a toilet brush and the constitution of a ferret had entered the fray. No, I couldn't let it happen. I had to do something, I had to stop this situation running away from me, I had to reverse the trend, put myself back into the ring. Play dirty, just the way Ava was with me.

I wasn't sure how much time had passed when I became aware of Georgette calling me from across the desk.

'You gonna answer that?'

My phone was ringing, but my thoughts were still a million miles away, and I sat staring at the black hole of my screen, wondering what my therapist would make of this latest development. *Why do you think you react so strongly to female competition, Jade? Comparing yourself to someone else isn't very helpful. We're all different. You must rise above it. Tread your own path.*

I imagined myself opposite her now, explaining exactly why she'd been wrong in our last session: *Your clichés don't stack up. The whole point is that there's only one path: the path to the top. And Ava and I are both on it. If I want to get to the end before her, I can't be 'different': I have to be better. And you know how they'll decide who gets there first? By comparing us. By weighing us up, side by side. Evaluating myself against her couldn't be more relevant. In fact, you know what? You're fired. You just don't get it.*

'Jade!' Georgette barked, making me jump. 'What's up with you today? Honestly,' she huffed, handing me the phone.

I shook myself back to the present and took the receiver from her tan-stained grasp, checking the caller ID. I recognised the number immediately. On the other end of the line was W&SP's most important client: Kai, marketing head of AthLuxe, a high-end new range of activewear that was completely impractical for anything actually, you know, active. Ava and I were both on the account and we'd been jostling to assert seniority on it ever since we landed the business – together, unbelievably, back when we were on good terms. Ava had been especially quick to position herself as the main point of contact with Kai, but now that she was holding a more important meeting in her office, he'd had to resort to calling me. This was good, though. Impressing Kai was of the utmost importance. Him having a high opinion of me would be crucial to securing the job as Team Head and I intended to blow his bloody brains out with how fantastic this call was about to be. This was my chance to win him over. I cleared my throat, said a silent prayer.

'Morning, Kai, how can I help?' Kai didn't answer my question right away, instead he began our conversation with an expletive-fuelled rant about not being able to get through to anyone but me. I brushed off the implication. 'Ava's not taking calls due to a personal issue,' I explained. I heard a sharp intake of breath, followed by a dramatic pause for effect. Kai told me once he'd attended drama school instead of a regular secondary and I knew better than to interrupt this moment. He was quite fond of practising what he'd learnt there.

'I'm sorry.' He paused again, and I imagined one hand flying to his forehead, mouth open wide. 'Did I hear you correctly?'

This time, Kai's outrage was exactly the reaction I'd hoped for. No client likes to be told they're second best to anything, let alone 'personal issues'.

'I know, and I'm sorry. But I'm more than happy to take your calls while Ava's... incapacitated. What did you want to go through today?' I skimmed my notes for something to say, some area of the launch I could usurp from Ava and stamp my authority on instead: front-row guests, ticket sales for select members of the public, media attendees, coverage, security to protect all of the above. I started with the most interesting. 'How about front-row attendees?'

'Well, yes, I suppose. I was hoping for an update on that. Go ahead.'

It had worked; my question and utmost professionalism had placated him and, even though this wasn't my area, I felt confident blagging as I trotted through Ava's documents, reading her notes as though they were my own. I listened with an attentive ear as Kai weighed up paying A-list celebrities versus cheaper bit-part reality stars and advised him that we shouldn't pay up for anyone he wasn't completely comfortable with. He agreed: we should hold out for top-end media and absolute stars only. And AthLuxe shouldn't have to pay. I smiled as I told him to leave it with me. I would make his wish come true.

3

Ava

'I've had an idea.'

The clipped and confident tones of David Stein filled the room as he walked into my office. Well, he didn't just *walk*, obviously, he strode, like a bony gladiator, a few silver streaks visible in his stubble. Perhaps he hadn't slept well and hadn't had time to shave. Or perhaps he'd been lying awake all night thinking about how to help me. I glanced out nervously through the glass, expecting to see a few pairs of raised eyebrows, but my colleagues knew better than that: they tended to whisper rather than stare. Except Jade Fernleigh, of course, who looked like she was performing a one-woman re-enactment of the eruption of Mount Vesuvius over at her desk.

'So,' David said. 'You need somewhere to stay while you sort out this mess with Charlie.'

'Right,' I answered, touched by how quickly he'd come to my aid. He looked at me fondly and smiled, our eyes locking inappropriately like potential suitors across a busy bar in downtown Chicago, jazz dancing in our ears, bourbon sticking to our teeth.

'Listen, I know you'll have your reservations, but hear me out.'

He hesitated as we both heard a knock at the door at the same time.

It was Jade, red faced and short of breath. Was she running from the ruins of a collapsing city or just desperate to muscle in on a meeting she thought should include her? It was difficult to tell. She let herself in and said something about Olivia's inquest. David and I exchanged a look. I tried to give her an opportunity to excuse herself but, when she kept on blabbering, David snapped.

'Jade, do you mind?' he growled, irritated. He waited until she'd closed the door to speak again. 'What was that all about?'

'She's harmless,' I said, trying to defuse the situation.

He shook his head. 'She's a loose cannon. I'll have to have a word. Anyway, where was I?'

'You were saying I was about to have my reservations...'

'I think you should move into Olivia's place.'

My body clenched at the sound of her name, the all-too familiar four-syllable arpeggio whistling in my ears, every fibre of my being rejecting the suggestion. 'I can't do that, David,' I replied, horrified he'd even suggested it.

'It's Pimlico,' David said. 'Near the office. And it's just sitting there at the moment, dormant, waiting for someone to breathe some life back into it. I think it's time to move on now that the inquest is over. It's been months. She'd have wanted you to, honestly, as long as you need.'

My first thought, of course, was the way her body had smelt the morning we'd found her three months ago. Then guilt, the things he didn't know, the rumour mill in the office. David picked up on it as the thoughts flashed across my face.

'What's the matter?' He crossed his arms, slotting them into the perfect grooves either side of his chest.

'The last time I was there was the day we…' I trailed off.

'So, bring some happiness to the place again, it needs it. Plus, it would do you good to confront that memory, don't you think?'

I couldn't think of anything worse. I wrapped my arms round my chair, as if David might have to prise me from it like a limpet from rock.

'The place is worth millions, Ava, it wouldn't exactly be a hardship.' His molars set to work on the inside of his cheek. He thought I was being ungrateful.

'People will gossip,' I said quickly, thinking of anything to stop him suggesting I go back to the building I thought about every night before I fell asleep. 'What if Charlie follows me back there? He'd break in, he'd destroy everything. At least in a hotel he can't do that.'

'So I'll put in a CCTV and alarm system and hook it all up to the police. When I'm done with it, Olivia's will be far safer than a hotel. Anyone can get a keycard to a hotel room if they say the right things or pay the right people.'

I didn't answer. David waited patiently for me to accept. 'I wouldn't be able to forgive myself if something happened to you. At least at Olivia's I know you'll be safe.' He put one hand deliberately on the desk and moved the other to my cheek, pushing the hair that had fallen loose round my shoulders behind my ear. 'I couldn't save Olivia, but I can try to save you, Ava.' I shivered, his sensitivity taking me by surprise. 'I'll go with you. I can help you settle in, if you like,' he said softly.

I took a deep breath in, feeling myself about to accept. Did I have a choice? This was what I wanted, wasn't it? 'All right,' I said, forcing a smile.

'You just need to get over the hurdle of seeing the place again.'

I nodded and went to stand up, pressing my palms into the table in front of me.

'You must let me pay you rent,' I said. 'Just tell me how much or take it out of my paycheque if you like.' I rose to standing, leaving two sweaty handprints behind on the wood.

David shook his head.

I moved to the door but David didn't budge. His arms folded determinedly. I recalled an article I'd read a few years ago which valued him into the hundreds of millions. I knew he wouldn't take the money, but I wanted to offer, I didn't want to feel doubly indebted to him. 'I'm serious, I don't want you to feel I'm taking advantage of your kindness.' I reached out to him, pressing a hand to his arm. The lady doth protest.

'Look, Ava, darling, I don't need your money, and I don't want it.' I smiled at him. *Thank God.* 'Come for a drink with me tonight,' he said after a moment's pause. 'To celebrate.'

I stuttered and, just as I considered spinning David a lie, some reason why I was far too busy or far too tired to go with him, I realised he hadn't really asked me to go for a drink: he'd told me.

'OK,' I agreed, playing his game. 'I'd love to.'

As David's eyes silently interrogated me, I felt the light from my computer screen intensify until I was bathed in it, the stark brightness exposing every twitch and every tell in my expression. I held his gaze. If I broke eye contact it would be over. The light burned whiter still; *I know what you've done*, it hissed, and the heat crawled up my neck, my heel bouncing up and down like a manic wind-up toy. Then, just as soon as it began, it was over: the bright-white died and David's lips returned to a satisfied line as he left.

4

Jade

My phone rang and Ava's name flashed up on the caller ID.
I stole a look into her office; she was rubbing her forehead
as if distinctly irritated.

'Yes?' I asked impatiently. 'I had a missed call from Kai,
he said he was going to try your phone instead. Did you
speak to him?'

I grinned. I started to line up the pens scattered round my
desk in order. 'I did. He was worried about the attendees we
had in place for the front row. I said I would handle it: top
media and A-list only.' I felt smug; finally it was *me* calling
the shots on the account. I pulled the final pen in line: a row
of plastic fingers.

'What?' she asked, her voice agitated. 'Why would you
agree to that? You know we can't afford A-list at this
launch; his budget is about five pounds.'

My confidence in my decision ebbed but I persevered,
trying my best not to be put off by Ava's condescension.

'He told me he wouldn't pay them anything, actually, he just wants people there who care about the brand.'

'Excuse me?' she asked, seemingly flabbergasted. I held the receiver tighter in my hand. Had I done something wrong?

'Jade, what were you thinking? AthLuxe hasn't launched yet. No one knows the brand exists, let alone *cares* about it. And, even if it were established, everyone is paid, Jade. Always. No matter the celebrity, no matter their status. Surely you know that? Haven't you done a launch like this before?' *Truth be told, no.* She continued as I shrank in my seat, grateful no one else could hear this conversation. 'Why are you even getting involved in this area, anyway? This isn't what you're supposed to be doing,' she ranted, exasperated. 'Stay in your lane, Jade. You're making a fool of yourself—'

'And where *exactly* does it say you're in charge of telling me what to do?' I snapped. 'You act so high and mighty but if you'd done your job by taking Kai's call instead of holding some secretive meeting with David then none of this would have happened. This is on you.'

Georgette's eyes sparkled as they appeared above her monitor.

Ava paused. *I was onto her.* Then she hit me with a threat I wasn't expecting: 'I don't think David would see it like that.' The way she delivered the line, with such cold, callous precision, hit me right where it hurt. I puckered my lips, reaching for a comeback, but it was too late and Ava carried on as I flailed. 'Anyway, I don't want to get petty here, it's not about who's telling who what to do: it's about what we agreed. You knew not to get involved with attendees but you did it anyway. Now I'm going to have to spend the rest of my day fixing your mess.'

'Well…' I mumbled.

'Which I could really do without.' I could taste the glee in her voice, sticky-sweet, delighted to receive the ammunition I'd just handed her on a silver serving platter. 'I'll call Kai later, explain that you made a mistake—'

My eyes widened. 'No!' I blurted desperately. 'I'll do it, I'll call Kai,' I said firmly, trying to claw back a couple of scraps of my dignity. 'I'll fix it, I promise.'

She faltered. Let me back in. 'OK,' she said, like a parent talking to a toddler. 'But if it's not done tomorrow, I'm taking over, understand?' And with that she hung up on me, the dial tone left ringing in my ear.

I was furious with myself, my inability to stand up to Ava once again rearing its nervous little head. Why did I let her talk to me like that? Rolling over for Ava must be one of my specialist skills. She *wasn't* better than me, but proving it seemed impossible sometimes.

'What was that about?' Georgette yapped as soon as I put the phone down, her painted brows arched impossibly high.

'Nothing, it's nothing. Just leave it,' I said, knowing full well she'd do anything but.

I put on my headphones to make it clear I didn't want to talk. I watched Ava running her fingers through her hair and scowled. Good PRs see glass. Bad PRs see other people. When I got the job as Team Head – a positive mental attitude is half the battle – my first order of business would be to move into her crystal-cut room and watch how *she* dealt with being stuck on the outside looking in. I watched her closely as she picked up her phone, her expression changing from fierce to friendly in a millisecond, and a series of dark thoughts crossed my mind. Ava and I had always had an understanding not to get personal at work – there were certain topics we knew were off limits – but now we were competing against each other, was she shifting the goalposts and leaving me in her wake? As if it wasn't enough to convince David I deserved the job on my own merit, now I had to worry about Ava burying me in order to make sure she won.

I pressed my nails into my palms as I plotted my next move: I had to play Ava at her own game and, if she was busying wrapping David round her little finger, I needed to ensnare a Stein of my own. Which was far easier said than done, of course, especially as I'd been desperately head-over-heels for the other Stein in this office ever since he first flew through W&SP's imposing double doors and landed on my team all those years ago. We'd worked together back then as I'd shown him the ropes and helped him to fit in.

I looked over at my target now, his laid-back laugh and dimpled cheeks radiating warmth across the room. *My* Stein was Josh Stein, David's adopted son, man of my dreams and, following a successful six years at the company, now a major influence on promotion-related decisions. And his star was only set to rise: now that Olivia was no longer around, David would elevate Josh up through the ranks, grooming him to take over the firm eventually. Nepotism was alive and well here at the offices of W&SP, that's for sure. If I could just marry into the family, I'd be golden... So, enough dilly-dallying, enough procrastinating, enough 'waiting and seeing'. I'd officially run out of time. Now being with Josh was more important than ever before and I had no time to waste getting on with it. I lost myself in thought as I planned phase one of my operation. First, I'd sidle up to his desk, cranking my pencil skirt just a *fraction* higher, and bend down next to him, resting on my heels, my elbows on his desk. I'm sure I'd heard that putting yourself in a naturally suggestive pose, i.e. at waist height gazing up, would make your target subconsciously think of you as a potential sexual partner. I'd open with something relaxed. *How's life? How's it going? How's tricks?* That was the one, I decided. *How's tricks?* Offbeat and stand-out. He'd remember it. Next, I'd ask him for help with something – Josh liked to fix things. I'd tell him my Wi-Fi signal won't reach my bedroom and that I... get bored at night. Was that too forward? *Yes!* OK, I wouldn't say that. I'd figure something out.

I picked up my pocket-size mirror and checked my make-up was still in place. The office bustled in the reflection: Georgette was now at the printer smacking it through a malfunction like a renegade pony, and a meeting was taking place in the area behind me, which seemed to be mostly gesticulations and impassioned facial expressions rather than anything productive. I angled my mirror back towards my face and studied my own image. My eyes were my only notable feature: green, a striking, contact-lens worthy shade. I was always being asked if the colour was real. 'It's Celtic!' I'd say, citing the 13 per cent Irish ancestry I'd uncovered thanks to a dubious DNA test I'd taken three years ago. From the bottom of my razor-sharp black fringe, they shot out now with renewed purpose, like the eyes of a leopard stalking its next meal. I clapped the mirror shut and changed my focus, eyeing my prey over the top of the screen, waiting for the perfect moment to pounce. He'd just finished a conversation with the sales drone next to him (5'5, horsey, obvious) and had turned his attention back to his monitor. I'd checked his diary this morning, no meetings scheduled for the next hour. It was the perfect time. I rehearsed the opening line in my head – *Hey Josh. How's tricks?* – then rose, determinedly, from my chair and flattened my palms against my thighs to smooth out my skirt, pulling it slightly above my knees.

I used the back of my wrist to dab my face free from shine, paying particular attention to my top lip, then strode over, placing one foot carefully in front of the other like I was walking the runway at Paris fashion week, reminding myself to channel confidence, strength and power. Something moved in my peripheral vision, on high alert as I closed in. Ava was standing up behind her desk. If she came out and tried to corner Josh before me my plan would be ruined. Did she know what I was up to? I upped my pace and locked my eyes on him. He was leaning back casually in his chair, his lightweight, long-sleeve jumper hanging perfectly off his sculpted shoulders. The window behind channelled the sunlight onto his back, casting a lemon-yellow halo around his Adonis-like frame. I wondered what he smelt like today? Usually it was a kind of just-washed shower smell with notes of charcoal and sandalwood. I shivered with pleasure as I imagined sucking in a long, slow breath of it. I shot my gaze towards Ava's office, she was sitting back down and, as I met her stare, she clipped her head in the other direction. I'd beaten her. I felt like I'd won an Olympic gold medal. My palms glistened and I wiped them once more on my skirt as I approached him. I was ready to do this.

'Hey tricks!'

I looked at him. He looked at me. The world stood still, the office fell silent, I turned to stone and all I could hear in my head was *hey tricks, hey tricks, hey tricks, hey tricks,* on repeat, swirling, building in speed and sound, like I was being brainwashed by those two stupid words. Was he going to think 'tricks' was the nickname I used for him? Could I start again, please? Rewind that moment? I stammered as if I was suffering the early signs of a brain-altering seizure.

'I mean—'

He smiled at me. It was a lifeline: I'd hit a rock when I was sure I was about to crash over Niagara Falls.

'Can I help?'

His voice was like honey and I was drenched in it, sticking to each silky syllable. I dropped down on my knees and stuck my elbows on his desk, just as I'd planned.

'What do you know about Wi-Fi?'

I gazed up at him adoringly.

'I'm not much of a *texpert* but fire away...'

'Right, yes, well my Wi-Fi won't reach my, um, bedroom area and it just gets sort of weak...'

I traced my finger round his notepad as if to indicate a bad Wi-Fi connection. It made more sense in my head and it didn't look as sexy as I'd intended.

'Have you tried rebooting it?'

He was so assured in his advice, but things weren't quite going according to plan. His suggestion was very Microsoft Windows 98 and it made me seem like the world's most unstoppable of morons.

Of course I've tried that.

'No, I have not tried that.' I blinked slowly a few times, embodying the airhead I had decided to channel into my Josh persona.

'Cool, hope it gets sorted.' I stayed crouched down by his side, not quite ready for my great expedition to be over. 'Was there something else?' He looked right at me, his chair slightly angled in my direction, his muscular legs wide apart.

Bloody hell, stop getting distracted, think on your feet. Is there something else? Of course there is. I love you? That's something else.

'Is your Wi-Fi always OK at home, all working properly? You hear about these boosters and things, you know…'

'Is that a euphemism?' he asked, amused.

Abort.

'Who dared you to ask me that? This has got wind-up written all over it!'

Abort. Abort.

'No! There are just so many problems nowadays!' I was clutching the rock he'd sent me but the swell was building and the falls would claim me soon.

Abort! Abort! Abort!

'Not if you seek professional help. They can get your Wi-Fi back up and running in no time. I think it involves some sort of balloon contraption. Isn't that right, Harry?' Harry (limited potential, 5'10, easily peer-pressured) made some sort of primal mating sound from down the table. I stood up and out of the waterfall, knowing I had to retreat.

'Very good, Josh, you sussed me out!' I rolled my eyes like I was their cool mum or fun teacher, then I stood still for a moment, hoping I would suffer a sudden brain aneurysm to distract everyone from what had just happened. I willed blood to spurt from my nose, suffocating me as I drowned in it, praying I'd fall to the ground, my vision disintegrating. I stole one last look at Josh and watched as his facial expression softened. He smiled at me again.

'You're hilarious, Jade, great dare. Chat later.'

Hilarious? Great dare? Wait a minute, had it worked? Had I not completely embarrassed myself? As he turned back to his computer, I noticed that was my cue to leave and hurried away. Phase one: complete! I could feel Ava's eyes like lasers all over me, analysing the situation, weighing me up, staring me down. I didn't meet her glare and instead kept my focus fixed ahead, contemplating whether it had *really* been a successful mission. It had, just not in the way I'd intended – I guess I'd come off more as a loveable idiot than a sexy, sophisticated single.

Later that day my phone lit up and Instagram delivered the best news of the year: *Josh Stein is following you.* My heart stopped. Josh. Following. *Me?* Bloody hell, how did I not know he had an account?

5

Ava

A calendar reminder popped up on my screen, its short melody startling me slightly.

David, Ava, drinks at The Whive, Sloane Square, SW1W

'Right, yes,' I muttered to myself, remembering what I'd agreed to earlier that day. I picked up my bag and coat and stole a moment in the toilets to apply some much-needed make-up before I left. I carefully drew a black wing across each eyelid, turned each of my eyelashes to thick spider's legs, and dabbed a fingertip of gold shimmer to each of my pale cheeks. I sprayed my white blonde hair with a touch of argan oil, taming any flyaways, and readjusted my bra in the mirror. Why did I feel like I was preparing for a date?

I took a cab from the office and, after surprisingly few traffic jams, arrived at the opulent dining room of The Whive. The building was grand and ancient, frequented by celebrities, and even had a guard outside in a top hat. I knew

David would arrive promptly, he always liked to be ahead of time, so I was glad that I was running early too. I saw the back of his head first: so statuesque. His hair perfectly gelled into position. I'd recognise that head anywhere.

'David.'

He stood as I arrived and greeted me with a kiss on the cheek. I bristled as his hand lingered on my shoulder a few seconds longer than it should have.

'Please, sit.'

I sucked in the dangerously intoxicating smell of him as our movement whipped up the air around us, the sound of classical music playing gently in the background.

He waited for me to make contact with my seat before returning to his own, then stroked his white-cotton napkin back across his lap.

'So, your housing arrangements,' David said, not wasting any time getting to the point. 'You'll be pleased to know you can move in to Olivia's as early as tomorrow night, if you like. The alarm and camera systems have been installed and I'm having the place cleaned in the morning.'

An elaborately etched bottle of sparkling water arrived at the table and I didn't speak until my drink had been poured, using the seconds of silence to gather and steady my thoughts. A plate of charcuterie, fussily presented, was placed between us.

'Wow. So quick,' I said, careful not to sound too excited. Because, truthfully, I could have jumped on him in that moment and kissed him all over and, maybe I would have if I hadn't thought he'd take it the wrong way. My God, was this finally going to happen? I pinched myself. It was! This was it, my escape from Charlie: I could almost taste it.

'I had my PA look up the details of your current rental agreement. She called the company masquerading as you – I hope you don't mind – and terminated the contract. I've paid the remainder of the break clause and, well, it was all pretty straightforward, really. They'll want you both out by the end of the week.' He picked up his knife and fork and rolled a piece of salami until it looked like a fat cigar.

I sat before him, shellshocked. 'David, you really didn't need to do all of that for me. I – I don't know what to say.' Everything was so much easier when money wasn't an object. I spared a thought for other women like me who weren't as lucky to have met a man like David Stein.

'You don't need to say anything, darling. It's my pleasure.' He pierced the meat with his fork and sucked it into his mouth, chewing slowly.

The waiter floated over and topped up my glass, David and I had been at The Whive together for almost two hours now, chatting and drinking and laughing together, and I could feel my guard slipping.

'You've never really told me what happened between you and Charlie,' he said, open-ended, taking another sip of red wine, his long fingers curling round the stem of his glass.

I looked up at him, conflicted. 'I wouldn't know where to begin.'

'You don't have to talk about it if you don't want to,' he said, sensing my reluctance. I thought I detected hurt in his voice.

'It's fine, I'm sorry, it's just difficult to explain. Things are so bad between us now, but they weren't always, I mean, he's always been a little bit controlling, but when we lived in Reading it wasn't as much of an issue.' Our old life in the little two-bed we rented in Berkshire seemed like a lifetime ago. Charlie had loved living there: he'd had a good job, a close circle of friends, an affordable local. 'There'd been signs though. Like the Christmas he'd totalled our car on the way to my parents' house because he thought I'd spent more money on them than him... But those kinds of incidents had been the exception, really, not the rule.' I carried on, the words coming surprisingly easily. 'He always says I "forced" him to move to London so I could follow my dream of working at W&SP. I told him at the time that he didn't have to come, that we could make things work long distance. But that was out of the question. He tried everything in his power to stop me from moving but, somehow, I'd won. I found us a place, I found him a job and, for a little while, everything was OK.' I stopped speaking, not wanting to tell David that while I'd found him a job, Charlie had found drugs and alcohol, and that his paranoia had been out of control ever since. It felt too close to home, too close to Olivia.

'What changed?'

'He was fired, he blamed me for pushing him to work somewhere he hadn't chosen, and now he's refusing to get a new job while we're still living in London. He keeps trying to break me into moving back to Reading but I won't, so I've been trying to distance myself from him so that when I end it... it's not such a shock for him. He's very volatile. I'm not sure how he'll react to finding he no longer has a place to live.' I paused to take a breath, feeling guilty for worrying about Charlie.

'Well, he can move back to Reading now, just as he's been so desperate to.'

Talking about all of this felt cathartic, it made me realise how long I'd bottled it up for. I didn't talk to anyone about my problems with Charlie. I supposed part of me felt like I'd brought them on myself. I cast my mind back to all the times I'd tried to cheer him up, tried to motivate and inspire him into being a better person. For his birthday a few weeks ago, I'd practically cleared my bank account buying him a set of expensive shirts and ties, hoping they'd spur him into replying to a few job ads. I'd had it in my head that if he just started working everything could be OK again. I still remember how the material had felt: rich, expensive and so tightly woven I'd wanted to wrap myself up in one and sit, quaffing Champagne, singing 'Happy Birthday' and eating chocolate cake.

He hadn't felt the same way. 'How much did you spend on these? What a waste of money! How unoriginal are you?! I mean, really – buying me a shirt and tie for the dead-end office job you wish I had. Couldn't you have bought me something I might have actually liked?'

I'd left the flat crying and when I'd got back later, I'd found the shirts ripped in two, the ties streaked with toilet bleach. He'd deliberately left the spoils of his outburst in an open bin bag outside the front door for me to find. It had been the final straw. I'd spent so much money on them and he'd chosen to destroy my gift rather than letting me return it and replace it. From that day on I knew our relationship wasn't worth fighting for.

'So, while I'm working, he sits at home drinking, smoking, getting high, whatever, and inventing all the fantastical ways in which I might have betrayed him that day. He's currently quite preoccupied with the idea that I'm having an affair.'

'Do your parents know how bad things are? Your friends?'

'I haven't seen my parents for a year, and Charlie cut ties with all of our friends when we moved. Another couple of ways of testing me. I guess I've been in denial about the mess I'm in...' That was a lie, I knew exactly how messy my situation was. I just hadn't been able to get myself out of it. Until now.

'Well, enough's enough, Ava. Let's do it tonight, shall we? Let's break up with Charlie.' He grinned at me, this mission exciting him, and he called the waiter over to ask for a pen and paper. 'We can write to him. If you call, or text, it only gives him the chance to reply, and you don't want to give him that.'

'What do I say?' I was enjoying the game, getting into it.

'That you never want to see him again.'

David's hand lingered close to mine and I smelt the alcohol on his breath. I averted my eyes as he moved his hand closer still, until his reedy little finger touched mine, a spark of uneasy electricity running between us.

I wrote under David's watchful gaze – *Charlie, I should have done this a long time ago* – but the letter was pure fantasy. I couldn't break up with Charlie like this, I needed to do it face to face. He wouldn't accept it otherwise.

'Where will you stay tonight?' David asked after we'd finished writing.

'At home. I'll pack my things when I get back, then leave tomorrow morning before he wakes up. I'll post the letter back through the box as I go.'

David nodded, pleased with the plan, and wrapped my hand up in his.

I swallowed hard: lying to David was becoming a habit I couldn't seem to break.

My eyes stuttered open, the room ringing with the ear-splitting sound of my morning alarm. My head was pounding – that would be thanks to that second bottle of Rioja – and I thrust my arm sleepily out of my cotton fortress and into the world beyond to silence its scream. The temperature change was stark. I jabbed the off button then recoiled, reeling my rogue limb back into safety, not ready for the outside yet. Not ready to find out which Charlie I was going to face this morning. Sometimes he woke up still angry and drunk from the night before. I turned onto my side and my shoulder, still recovering from a past dislocation, settled at an awkward angle. I groaned and brought it back into position, I couldn't deal with my body falling apart, not today, not as well as everything else. I took a few deep breaths, trying to push it from my mind, the delicious fibre-filled comfort enveloping me, begging me to sink back into it for a moment longer. It was still dark outside, the sun only just crowning on the horizon. I turned ninety degrees as my bed yawned with me and we sank back into sleep together. That same high-pitched ringing filled my drowsy head fifteen minutes later. I turned it off again and reluctantly pressed myself up to a seated position, resting my head back against the bed's wooden headboard, steeling myself to face the day. I swung my feet to the floor and wrapped myself in my old dressing gown, stamped with worn-out teddies and worn-through sleeves and, as I went to unlock the bedroom door, heard the unmistakable symphony of Charlie rattling around in the kitchen. I pulled the handle towards me and walked barefoot to the kitchen, hanging back, watching him. His raven-coloured hair was sticking up in a number of directions and he was bobbing up and down as he moved, muttering urgently to himself. He'd finally cleared up his pasta wall-art, and I deduced he must have done a few early-morning lines to get through it. So this morning I'd face manic Charlie, trying-to-make-amends Charlie, he'd-never-do-it-again Charlie. He talked to the eggs as he cracked them against the side of the frying pan. I backed away from the door, deciding I didn't want to interrupt him and, as I moved, a floorboard betrayed me, squealing under my weight.

'Aha!' He turned round, his eyes wired and wild, a cut across his cheek. He was wearing a half-tucked creased shirt and sweatpants. Why was he wearing a shirt? He raced towards me and gripped my arms with his hands. I stood, glued to the spot, holding my breath. 'Take a seat next door, OK? At the dinner table.' He let me go and turned back to the eggs. 'Everything's got to be absolutely perfect. Go and put on a dress or something. This is important.' He rushed through his sentences, his apparent act of kindness foiled by the order he'd given me. In his mind this kind of gesture was all he had to do to be exonerated, days of abuse cancelled out with a plate of bacon and scrambled eggs. But these transparent displays were never for my benefit. I was merely a passenger in his path to self-forgiveness; my only job was to play along. I traipsed through to the bedroom and got ready for work, picked up last night's clothes from the floor and placed them on the bed. I'd packed a small bag of essentials when I'd arrived home last night, but I'd be leaving the majority of my things here when I left for good today, including last night's outfit. I could hardly pack a suitcase without Charlie realising, could I? I chose my favourite dress from the wardrobe: a simple black number my mum had given me when I'd told her I'd got the job at W&SP. She'd been proud of me that day. Then I walked through to the lounge, took a seat at the dining table and waited. 'Here we are! Coffee, coffee, coffee!' Charlie powered into the room where I sat at our cheap, chipped dining table. *Your joint living and dining area here*, the gummy estate agent had said as she'd shown me round this time last year. *Perfect for one*, she'd told me, assuming I was flat-hunting alone as no one had been with me. When I'd corrected her she'd simply updated the refrain. *Perfect for two as well, perfect for two.* I couldn't wait to leave this life. A cup of thin brown liquid landed before me, then, shortly afterwards, a plate of insipid scrambled eggs atop a single piece of cardboard-thin toast.

'Wow, thank you, what a treat,' I said, not trying as hard as I normally would to inject enthusiasm into my voice. He sat down. His shadow covered the table.

'Isn't this perfect?' he asked, pointing his crooked face at me, lips cracking apart, bloody, as he smiled with spiky teeth. I took a bite. The eggs were awfully dry.

'Perfect,' I agreed.

'OK, Ava, I can't pretend any more.' His hands were shaking, cutlery firing against his plate, ringing out like a warning bell. I slowed my chewing. 'I'm too nervous to eat. I have to get this out of the way now.' He stood up, his body coiled like a tightly-wound spring. 'Last night – and I don't want to get into the whole he-said, she-said thing now.'

I tried desperately not to roll my eyes. It was very much a he-said, he-said 'thing', but I knew better than to correct him.

'Anyway, yesterday I realised something.' He put the emphasis on 'realised' as if he'd had a life-changing epiphany. I put my knife and fork down, my appetite evaporating as he continued to speak. 'You're punishing me.'

I looked at him, confused.

'I realised the reason why you want to be here, in London, with a career and everything, is because we haven't, *I* haven't, taken things to the next level. It occurred to me: wait. Everything would be different, *everything*, if you weren't just my girlfriend, but my wife.' He dropped to one knee and held a ring up towards me that he'd bought, presumably, with my money. He certainly didn't have any of his own. My stomach lurched and I felt an urgent need to be sick. He'd have maxed out my overdraft to buy it.

'If you were my wife we would want to have a family, and family must come first. Don't you agree Ava? That family must come first?' I tried my best to keep the horror from my face, but I couldn't hold back the tide and, as my lip wobbled, I felt tears carve trails down my cheeks.

'Oh! Ava! I knew you'd be happy! I knew I was right about this.' He'd taken them to be tears of joy – what else could I expect – and grabbed my hand, fumbling the ring onto my reluctant digit. It felt wrong, rough, uncomfortable, too loose round the base of my finger.

'I can't believe it,' I managed.

Time slowed, he kept on talking, his monologue diving into plans for our children, how soon we'd have to move away from London if we wanted to get into a decent catchment area, and that I couldn't delay quitting my job.

How on earth was I going to tell him I was about to leave after this? He'd be crushed. Worse. He'd be furious. Murderous.

'I knew this was all that you needed. A bit of *commitment*. This year has just been a test, hasn't it? You were angry I hadn't proposed yet, so you pretended to be obsessed with your career. It's all so clear now that I've worked it out. You're very clever, Ava, but you've got your way now! And, well, here I am at last, ball and chain firmly attached!' He jiggled his ankle out towards me, bruised on one side.

'Charlie, I…' For a moment, for a split-second, I thought about saying that I couldn't do it, that I didn't want to marry him. But I managed to hold myself together. Now wasn't the right time.

'Shall we cheers to our future?'

I lifted my coffee towards his, but he pulled his mug away at the last moment, wanting me to make eye contact with him. *Come on, Ava, you know the rule: it's bad luck if we don't look at each other!*

I forced another smile and dragged my eyes to his. His jaw slid from side to side, front to back.

'Why don't we take a photo? We can send it to your parents: we must tell them the happy news. They'll be thrilled we're moving home.'

I scowled internally at his suggestion. Mum *would* be thrilled. She's been wanting me to get married ever since I left university. It was all she talked about. The idea of me growing up but not 'getting on with things' – her greatest grievance. I felt she deliberately hadn't noticed how much he controlled me, how Charlie had stopped me from visiting her and dad alone almost as soon as we'd got together. She had ignored the way he insisted on muscling his way in on every Christmas, every birthday. The fact she still badgered me to marry him had turned us against each other, and it hadn't been a particular hardship when Charlie had stopped me from seeing my parents after we moved to London. It showed how little he knew me. He thought it was a punishment. His own parents lived in Ireland, separated, and he didn't see them often. He liked the idea that my family were his family, he called my parents 'Mum and Dad'.

'Great,' I agreed, watching him bound through to the bedroom to retrieve my phone. The camera on his was smashed. Of course it was. I sat still in my chair, my hands trembling, trying to make sense of the situation I was in. I was leaving today. No matter what. I'd leave, stay at Olivia's, then wait a couple of days for Charlie to calm down so we could talk. Somewhere neutral. Somewhere public. He was still in the bedroom as my mind whirred through my options, then I felt the wind change. Something wasn't right.

It was the silence that worried me first. Then the rustling. Then the tone of his voice.

'Ava?' he called. The way he said my name, so deliberately, made the air catch in my throat. He'd seen something on my phone he didn't like, I was sure of it. I felt the heavy drumbeat of his footsteps as he slammed his heels into the floor on his way back through to the lounge, each one sending a shudder up my spine. 'What the fuck is this?' He was holding the note I'd written with David last night in his hand. The edge bouncing up and down as fury coursed through his grip. It occurred to me what had happened: after picking up my clothes from the floor it must have fallen from my back pocket and down to the ground, ready for him to find.

'Charlie, no, it's not what you thin—' He stepped towards me and in that moment I considered making a run for it. Would hurling myself out of our third-storey window kill me? I hesitated and reconsidered: better to believe I could talk my way out of this and pray for a miracle.

'Looks like you've made up your mind,' he said, his back teeth gritted together, his willpower turning in somersaults trying to keep his limbs to himself. 'Off you go then.' He whacked the lounge door wide open, smashing it against the wall, the handle crunching deep into the plasterboard behind. 'Go on,' he repeated again, louder. 'Why are you making this difficult? It's easy: you want to go... *so fucking go,*' he hissed: a boa constrictor suffocating me with my own words. I sat silently in my seat, my heel twitching up and down in the nervous way it had grown accustomed to, listening to his breathing as it turned ragged. I knew the signs. This was only the beginning. 'Stand up!' he shouted, spittle flying from his mouth.

I said nothing. I stood on his command.

'Walk!' His nostrils flared as I started towards the door and he splayed his fingers out across the frame theatrically. *After you, mademoiselle,* he implied, goading me. I drew level with his hot, dank breaths and felt his eyes piercing my torso. One more step would bring me out over the threshold but, as I moved my leg forward, his arm flung out like a whip across the doorframe.

'No,' he said, his head twitching in supersonic vibrations. He moved in a blur, shoving me back the way I'd come, one hand over my mouth to stop me screaming, the other against my chest. I tasted the hot, sticky sweat of his palm as he pushed me down into the chair I'd just risen from. Then he let go and the dining table, standing quite happily on all fours, spun like a merry-go-round as he flipped it up on itself, the side of the table cracking against my knee as I failed to move out of the way in time, everything moving too quickly, a deafening roar accompanying his outburst. He picked up and launched a framed photo of us, our baby-faced first year anniversary, directly above my head and I screamed as it smashed it into a thousand jagged pieces round me.

'*I should have done this a long time ago? My job comes first? I no longer love you?*' he barked, reading snippets from the note as rhetorical questions. 'You just said yes to marrying me! What's wrong with you, Ava? Who put you up to this? Was it him? Stein?' I tried my best to shrink into the wall as he drew closer. 'It was him, wasn't it?' I so desperately wanted to say yes; anything to divert his anger. He shouted at me again. 'Ava!' I could smell last night's vodka seeping out of his pores as he pulled me to standing and pressed a hand to my sternum, pinning me against the wall. He started to laugh in hearty, horrible cackles that filled the broken room. 'And to think I was going to forgive you for being unfaithful, wipe the slate clean, use our engagement to start again...' His breath smelt like poison. 'It would be funny if it weren't so fucking tragic.'

6

Jade

I'd hardly stopped looking at Josh's page since he added me. There were just ten photos so far, all uploaded pretty recently, and I'd checked through his friends. It was only *me* he was following from work – *he wasn't even following Ava*. His profile was like fine art, honestly, you could hang these pictures in a gallery and I'm sure people would queue in droves on Saturday and Sunday mornings, flocking like eager little pigeons to see them. Looking into his eyes, even on a screen, was like staring into the purest blues of the ocean and my feelings for him poured over me like waves, lapping at my heels at first, then at my waist, my neck, my eyes. As I continued to study each picture I walked further out to sea. Soon, I would drown.

I knew this was an infatuation, not quite love, but to be honest I wasn't sure what love really felt like. I thought I was in love once, but my ex's grand plans of opening a restaurant turned out to be more important than my grand plans of starting a life together. February 29th. Seven years and four months together. I'd set up everything perfectly: A Cab Sav '08, melt-in-the-mouth lamb shanks, his and hers silver bands, one knee. His eyes had popped out of his head, his jaw had hit the floor, and his feet couldn't have run away fast enough. People had told me not to do it – *it's emasculating, it's desperate* – but whatever, at least I'd found out for sure he didn't want the same things as me, even if it *had* taken him years to figure it out. I'd booked the cheapest plane ticket I could find after he'd rejected my proposal, had sent him a final goodbye in seat 33A, and set off to Sri Lanka. I suppose you could say I'd been having a crisis – world travel the most important thing on my bucket list, even though it had never really featured there before. I'd planned to stay for six months, maybe longer if things went well, but it all ended rather abruptly after just two. Those eight weeks had been beautiful though, lush and smelly, chaotic and exciting, and I'd learnt a lot. Such as: do not go on a group elephant ride alone, they are only designed for *couples*. I did not know this at the time. I'd gone, with my bumbag and my awe for these mighty creatures, and stood alongside five other blissfully happy gap-yah twosomes as we'd stared up at the five almighty elephants ahead of us. Because I was alone and they were all paired up, I'd been matched with the elephant equivalent of the runt of the litter, brought out once I'd paid in the cash for the ride; blind, lame in one leg and suffering from chronic diarrhoea. Imagine elephant diarrhoea, for a second; the smell, the volume, the explosiveness. It was a bit like riding a malfunctioning hoover wildly spraying watery, rancid poo in every direction. All the other elephants had behaved extremely well so there I'd been, taking up the rear, breathing in the rear of my elephant, watching as each of the couples ahead shot nervous *Is she ok?* looks back at me, giggling, then out-performing each other with their revoltingly public displays of affection. So, after that, world travel slipped back down my to-do list and a romantic relationship shot straight back up to the number one spot. Once the ride was over, one of the elephant tamers with kind grey eyes and a shoulder to cry on had comforted me, with alcohol mainly, and we'd spent the night together at my hotel. I'd felt myself falling for him as the sun had set and we'd snuggled together under a blanket beneath the stars. I'd wondered how difficult it would be to get a visa. We could move to Mumbai and make a fortune in the city, then head back to Sri Lanka and help build a better home for his family. But he left before sunrise with my heart in his hands and 16,000 rupees in his pockets.

I pushed open the front door to my home deep in South East London. It sits on a street of identikit post-Second World War terraces, all hastily constructed with crummy brickwork and concrete gardens. A build-up of post had wedged itself under the base of the splintered front door and I bent down to dislodge it, dispersing envelopes in all directions over the hallway. *I'll deal with it later*, I thought, for the umpteenth time. The brown-beige, tobacco-stained paint was peeling in some areas in the hallway, the culprit a decrepit leaky pipe, not quite bad enough to warrant a call-out, but chronic enough to fill the entrance with the smell of a thriving mould colony. It was crazy that this shithole cost me more than a grand a month. I slammed the door to the hallway shut, lit a cigarette and collapsed on the sunken settee in the living room. The evening sun hit my eyes as I tried to relax, inviting itself into my home so insistently it was as if it was trying to alert my attention to something. I cursed myself for not replacing the old curtains and for leaving the windows bare for so long, then slumped off the sofa onto the floor, clearing a space between the discarded dinner plates and empty packets of cigarettes. Basking in the shade, I picked up my phone. *A notification.* A new message on Instagram. I opened it. Josh had sent me a gif of a computer on fire.

My heart stopped.

How's the Wi-Fi?

I smiled deeper and wider than the Grand Canyon. The mouldy pipes and bare windows didn't matter any more: Josh Stein was interested in me and now everything was going to be OK.

That morning I took a hot shower to cool off. I shaved my legs. I scrubbed at the soles of my feet with decades-old pink body scrub. I slathered my limbs in a moisturiser that smelt of tinned pineapple. On went my flesh-coloured tights, pencil skirt and a simple, woollen pullover. I combed through my hair five times on each side, picked out the little specks of dandruff that rose to the top, and looked at myself in the mirror. Perfectly acceptable, I thought. Despite what the girls at school used to call me – *dirty, germy, grubby* – I scrubbed up OK. Not in a way that anyone would go out of their way to compliment me on, not like Ava, but in a way that didn't draw any unnecessary attention. I imagined most people left with a neutral opinion of my appearance, I knew I was non-threatening, disarming, unremarkable. Just the way I liked it. Just the way Josh seemed to, too.

David had called me for a meeting at an exclusive café round the corner from the office and I found him at the back of the room drinking coffee with no milk, a pristine napkin folded off to one side. I plopped myself in the seat across from him, feeling positive. My turn for a one-to-one with the boss.

I *assumed* he'd want to fill me in on whatever he'd spoken to Ava about yesterday and I decided I was willing to forgive him for discussing things with her first.

He asked if I wanted a drink and a skinny waitress with bulbous eyes, made bigger by the thick lenses that magnified them, appeared beside me.

'What do you have?' I asked, wanting to be sure I made the *right* order. One that would impress David.

She spoke fast, with an Italian accent I found impossible to decipher. '*Caffè affogato, caffè lungo, caffè doppio, caffè mocha, caffè Americano…*'

David's fingers were interlaced round his cup. I wondered what he was drinking. Should I ask for the same? Or was that embarrassing? Transparent?

I'd known this place would be fancy, six-pounds-a-coffee fancy, and I cursed myself for not looking up the menu before I'd arrived. I cringed remembering a time I'd once ordered a babyccino at a posh coffee shop thinking it was probably a very small, very Italian, very *sophisticated* little cappuccino.

'Do you have a child with you? No? Then I can't offer you a babyccino. They're for babies.'

I'd shrunk through the floor that day and had resolved never to order something on a menu I wasn't sure about again. Promise broken already.

'The first one,' I said eventually, cutting the waitress off from her list.

'*Caffè affogato,*' she confirmed, I think, or something to that effect. I nodded hastily and she dashed off.

'Jade, thanks for meeting me,' David said, pulling my focus back to the table, his hair slicked back into position. I took a breath, reminding myself it was still of the utmost importance to impress David on my own terms. Ensnaring Josh was one thing, an insurance policy, but David was still the man in charge.

'Yes sir,' I replied, from nowhere, like I'd adopted the vocabulary of a marine, about to follow up my words with a salute. He took a long sip of his coffee, put it back down. He unfurled his serviette and pressed it into his lips. Dry. He folded it back up to a perfect triangle and placed it back by his side. I kept quiet as he carried out his routine, letting my mind wander. What kind of father-in-law would David make? Kind, I think. David adopted Josh when he was a boy and has looked after him ever since as though he were his own. If that doesn't show enormous compassion, I don't know what does. Josh was the son of David's older brother who died, along with Josh's mum, in an horrific fifty-car pile-up on a motorway in the South of France. I'd read about it online. A lorry driver had fallen asleep at the wheel, jack-knifed into the central reservation, and foggy conditions on the day meant that Josh's parents in their 1930s classic Jaguar – with its enormous headlights, sweeping wheel arches, open top, and flimsy, flaky bodywork – had driven headfirst, full-speed, pedal-to-the-metal, into the side of it, not able to see the wreckage ahead of them until it was too late. The fuel from the accident sparked with the flammable cargo the lorry had been carrying, sending Josh's parents' car, the lorry, and a handful of nearby drivers to tragic, fiery deaths. After being adopted by David, Josh had spent his childhood growing up alongside Olivia, the pain of losing parents something they both shared from a young age. He'd hurtled off the rails with her in his late teens; you can still find endless pictures online of the pair of them falling out of nightclubs, dead behind the eyes, hospital thin, just a glimpse of Josh's beauty detectable behind the shaggy hair and dilated pupils. He was hit really hard when she died, maybe he blamed himself for fuelling her destructive lifestyle for so many years. Poor Josh, so plagued by death – he must have felt cursed that those closest to him always met their end in such gruesome ways, plucked from the earth way ahead of their time. Today the story is brighter, though: Josh is David's protégé, grooming him to fill his shoes with a view to eventually running the operation with a partner of his own. I often find myself lost in the fantasy of that partner being me... now more than ever. I imagined we'd change the name of the company to Stein & Fernleigh and do things like smoke a fat cigar together every Friday night in the office, spend the holidays at our home in the country. David would be a peculiar father-in-law, certainly.

Particular in his habits. But generous, I thought. If not troubled. Distracted. Grief-stricken. He'd spend Christmas reflecting, sat in an armchair looking into the fire, his family opening presents round him.

'We need to talk,' he said abruptly, slicing through my daydream, cutting me out of the Christmas-at-the-Steins tableau I'd created.

The worst four words in the world.

'Listen, Jade.' He was cushioning the blow. 'Charlie attacked Ava this morning at their home.' His eyes bored into mine, my imagination running in circles already. *Was she OK? Was he about to offer me the job? How did David know? Why was he telling me?* 'It was nasty.' I looked at him, goldfish-like. *Bob, bob, bob,* my mouth went as I failed to think of a single thing to say out loud. 'And I'm hoping I can rely on you to steady the team until she's back.'

The warmth in the air around us was stifling and I wrestled to remove the woollen jumper I was wearing. *He's literally spelling it out: you are Ava's second in command.*

'OK…' I said after a while. And then I took a risk. 'Do you mean you'd like me to sort out the mistake she made with Kai yesterday? Has she told you about it? Has he?'

'Excuse me?'

'Oh, I'm sorry I didn't…' He looked basically disinterested but allowed me to elaborate. 'It's not really my area but I'm happy to step in. I'm sure I can fix it.'

'Jade,' he said slowly. 'Have you ever heard of the expression "kicking a woman while she's down"?'

He sipped, dabbed and folded.

'I didn't mean it like that…' I swore internally at myself for being too eager to put Ava down.

David interrupted my feeble protestation to speak. 'Let me be clear—' he began, interrupted by the reappearance of the bug-eyed waitress. She was holding an ice cream topped with biscuit crumbs and chocolate flakes, an embarrassing nod to coffee gathering at the base of the glass.

I'd ordered a fucking dessert.

She put it down.

David coughed, crossed his legs, scratched his temple; communicating his disgust with these small adjustments.

'Sorry,' I started to say.

'Let me be clear,' he pressed, cutting over my apology. 'This difficult patch in Ava's personal life won't be affecting her chances of becoming our new Team Head.'

I conjured what little fight I had in me. 'I'm sorry David, it's just, you don't know the full picture. You're not aware of what I'll have to pick up in her absence.'

'Jade, stop talking, you're not doing yourself any favours. If you so much as dare utter another word against her...' Sweat pooled underneath my top and my mind stuttered. I scrambled for the words but I couldn't find the right thing to say.

You have to be cleverer than her, she's making you look stupid! The voice in my head was deafening in its criticism and I tried to block it out. I had to say something, anything, to make this better. David was getting up, he'd had enough and wanted to leave. I should have taken it in my stride, acted like it wouldn't have been a problem, made him think I *already* steadied the team – with or without Ava.

'I'll make sure everything is under control while she's gone.'

'OK. Thanks Jade.'

His voice was laced with indifference and I tried to summon something else to say that might still save the conversation. 'I hope she feels better soon.'

I was too late, though. A second later and he was already out of earshot. I sat, dumbstruck, as my sparkler fizzled out and dots of ash covered the cream.

I pumped my way back towards the office, my head thick with conspiracy theories. What was really going on between Ava and David? What was her angle? What was his? Were they an item? A couple? ... Frankly, I couldn't think of anyone worse as a mother-in-law. I let my brain work through the puzzle, the idea of Ava and David together reminding me of something Charlie had told me once. *You think she's Little Miss Perfect? She'd sleep with your dad if she thought it would further her career...* My dad happened to resemble a kind of inflatable Chairman Mao, so it was quite the statement, and it had stuck with me. Was she sleeping with him to get ahead? Really? Like someone from the eighties?

I stopped dead on the pavement, an unsuspecting shopper crashing into my backpack as I did, and thought about Charlie. I'd met him (6'1, complicated, emotional) on multiple occasions, mostly on wild nights out before Olivia had died. Ava would always moan about how controlling he was when he was high, that he was high more often than he was sober, and that she wasn't sure how much more she could take. I'd seen it first hand, too, thought it interesting that despite his prolific experience with illegal substances he wasn't particularly good at handling the stuff. She was right, it made him twitchy and panicked and paranoid. I remember how he'd whisper to me about his suspicions that Ava was cheating on him, his Irish accent always so aggressive when he spoke about her. *I know it, she's changing. She looks at me differently. We aren't as close as we used to be.* I'd actually stuck up for Ava at the time, which had infuriated him. *Don't lie to me too, I know that you know. You've probably seen her kissing him in the office. I know they're together when she tells me she's working late. I guess you girls will always stick together, but if I find out that you knew and didn't tell me, I'll never forgive you.* Back then I hadn't doubted Ava but now I'm nowhere near as sure. Maybe Charlie had been onto something?

Perhaps he'd been right all along.

7

Ava

Everything had happened so quickly. I'd woken up to what I'd thought was a mirage of black and yellow human-sized insects; but what turned out to be a heavy police response to three separate 999 calls from our adjoining neighbours. I'd been taken to hospital for a medical assessment and then to the station so the police could take a statement. So much for breaking up with Charlie, letting him calm down, then seeing him in a couple of weeks to end things amicably. After this I never wanted to lay eyes on him again. At the station I'd called David, the only person who truly knew what was going on, and he'd driven down immediately to be with me. He'd assured me I could take a couple of days to recover, not to worry about work, and that I could use the time off to move into Olivia's old place and get settled. He'd moved me out of the station and towards his car with his arm round my waist. We'd driven fast to Olivia's. *No need to pick up your things*, he'd said. *Everything is taken care of.* His little finger touched my leg every so often as he manoeuvred the gear stick.

I put one foot carefully in front of the other as I climbed the stairs to my new home, David behind me, the sights and sounds of last time I was here almost deafening in their clarity. 'Beautiful day, isn't it?' David observed, small-talking to fill the gap in our conversation. He was right; the sky was a bright spring blue and, as I reached the top step, I paused to soak it in, moving aside to let him pass, more methodically than I normally would, the bruise on my knee hindering fast forward progress. I tried to keep my breathing level. He put his fingers round my waist, marionette-like, as he tucked round me to unlock the front door. He pushed it wide and I hid behind him slightly, half-expecting to see her here all over again.

'Hi,' a voice called from somewhere inside. I detected an Eastern European accent. 'I am Oxana. I clean for you.' David ignored her and held my hand as he helped me navigate my way inside. Oxana ran a pair of judgmental eyes up from my feet, over my middle, then into my eyes. I could tell what she was thinking: *Is David's new hobby taking in strays?* I felt her stare cast its way over the swelling on the side of my face.

I smiled a lot to persuade her that I was fine, and started jabbering about how I worked with David, that he was doing me a favour letting me crash here for a few nights. I'm not sure it was her I was trying to convince and she clearly didn't understand, or care about, a word I'd said. She moved aside, letting David and me pass, her movement accompanied by the shuffling and swinging of her box of bleach and cloths. Then I heard the door click shut and I realised we were alone. At least, I had to keep telling myself that, because, as I stood there, I couldn't help but feel Olivia all around me: in the walls, in the artwork that lined the hallway, in the ornate and precise gold work in the ceiling that piped and snaked its way in and out of floral patterns. I looked down at the black and white marbled floor and, even though I knew it wasn't there, could hardly look at it without imagining Olivia's blood stained all over the tiles. David let go of my hand and turned to me.

'Why don't I show you round?'

'Sure,' I agreed, following him into the kitchen like a puppy on a lead. 'It's absolutely stunning, David. Thank you again for letting me stay.' He swivelled to face me, lifted his hand, and ran his fingers through the hair hanging loose in front of my face. He tucked it back behind my ear in a movement he'd become far too fond of. I made a mental note to start wearing it in a ponytail more often.

'As long as you need, darling,' he assured me as his fingers finished their loop. 'So, what would you like me to show you first?' We spent the next hour going through each room. There was so much to remember that I wish I'd been taking notes because I was just too tired to memorise everything, my face sore, turning from swollen to bruised as we completed the grand tour. When David noticed me stifle a yawn, he decided to finish up and, as he strode towards the front door to leave, told me I didn't need to understand the intricacies of the security system anyway.

'Did the police find Charlie?' I asked, nervous about my impending loneliness.

'Don't worry, Ava, I've got people on it. We'll deal with him.'

He said it in a way that suggested his 'people' were mafiosi types who'd torture him to death.

I raised my eyebrows. 'What does that mean? What about the police?'

He raised his brows back, arched, finely sculpted, not a hair out of place. 'He won't be bothering you again. Let's just leave it at that.' My imagination went into overdrive. Would David really hurt Charlie? Why would he do that? Was he just trying to impress me? I was torn and, to be honest, the more I thought about it the more I realised I didn't care. Whatever happened to Charlie he'd brought on himself. Reasonably confident in the fact that Charlie wasn't going to find me here, I turned my attention back to David. I wanted him to leave now, the sky was turning dark blue, the air outside chilly. I thanked him, deliberately crossing my arms in front of my body so when he kissed me goodbye our contact wasn't as close. 'See you tomorrow,' I'd said.

'Take all the time you need.' And, as the door clicked shut, a conflicted part of me wished I'd asked him to stay. As I stood by myself in the cavernous hallway, I thought about leaving. How could I do this? How could I stay here after what I'd done? But then I considered the alternatives now I had nowhere else to go: a hostel, a shelter, the street? Or I could give up my job and go back to Reading to be with my parents. No, I couldn't face any of those options: I'd fought too hard to keep my job to throw it all away now. I'd be doing what Charlie had wanted all along. Now I had a beautiful house to live in, I couldn't take the place of someone at a shelter or a hostel who needed it more than me. This was it. This was my home now. And it was good; Olivia's gave me a chance to reset. To save up for somewhere new. To start again.

But, as I paced through the house, I was struck by its noise. It felt alive, somehow. Whips and whirs and wails called out to me from every room. I slipped off my shoes and walked barefoot towards the lounge, trying to ignore the sounds. I reflected that my old life was tormented by monsters, my present haunted by ghosts.

8

Jade

My computer whirred into action and a procession of music and lights excitedly alerted me to the eighty emails I'd received already this morning. My meeting with David had focused my mind. I could see Ava's game plan, it was obvious – it was *too* obvious – but breaking David would take Ava a long time and there was no guarantee he'd fall for it. It meant I still had a chance and that I therefore had serious, life-changing, business to attend to. My mission with Josh was now more important than ever. *He'd direct-messaged me.* Now I had to construct the perfect reply, preferably channelling the opposite of the technophobe lunatic he kept meeting in person.

I typed out numerous drafts in the notes section of my phone and, after endless iterations, whittled the list down to a four-strong shortlist.

Wi-Fi is dead to me.
Hey, Josh, what brings you here?

Look at you sliding into my DMs!
Hey Tricks!

The last one was an off-the-cuff throwback to our conversation yesterday. *Ha, ha, ha, I called you tricks? Remember me? The idiot?* But perhaps it was a bit much. Bloody hell. How could I reply to this demigod? I had to say *something*, though. I sucked in a deep breath and checked the clock on my computer screen. I'd been drafting and redrafting this reply for the best part of two hours. At some point Georgette must have appeared, as she was sat next to me now, clad today in a plum coloured pair of dungarees. I despaired.

I rattled off a few emails, checked my pocket mirror and laughed half-heartedly at the punchline of a story Georgette was telling to one of her minions who'd wandered over for the latest gossip.

'Turned out, he was a porn star!'

Cue: 'Hahahaha!'

Wait a minute, I thought, Georgette was fantastic at this sort of thing, she'd probably know *exactly* what to write to Josh... Plus, it couldn't hurt to hear what people in the office were saying about Ava's absence.

'Excuse me?' I stared daggers at Georgette's minion. 'Do you have anything work related to discuss or is this just a chit chat? Sorry to be the fun police, but we *do* all have things to be getting on with. Launch night really isn't that far away now.'

The girl was wearing a push-up bra – attention-seeker – and subtly rolled her eyes at Georgette before scurrying off.

I leant in towards my desk-mate; she smelt of hairspray

more than usual and a vast number of grips were putting in a serious shift to keep her sky-high ponytail in position. Her stare was currently fixed on her screen, pretending she was working. 'George?'

She didn't look away from her monitor as she answered. 'Yeah?'

'What are people saying about Ava not being in today?'

'I thought you didn't want to chit chat, *babe.*'

'This is different.'

She pressed a button on her keyboard with the bright pink talon on her index finger, lowered her voice and bent down slightly, hiding her face from the rest of the office behind her computer screen. I followed suit and leant in as far as my seat would allow. I knew I could always win George over with the opportunity to gossip.

'I got this message from her this morning: *Things are really bad with Charlie, I have to take a couple of days off, call me with anything urgent. Please keep an eye on Jade.*' She looked at me faux-apologetically. 'Sorry, obviously you two aren't the best of friends at the moment…'

'Evidently,' I agreed. 'Do you believe her?' I asked.

I considered spilling the beans about my meeting with David, about how *he* was the first to know, but quickly thought better of it. I couldn't risk David's wrath and I certainly couldn't trust Georgette to keep anything I told her quiet.

She smiled at me wickedly. 'Why, what do you know? You think she's hiding something?'

'I think she's playing a very clever game, George, that's all I'll say.'

'With who?' George pressed, leaning in further. 'With

Charlie? You think this is all for sympathy?' she asked, putting words in my mouth. 'You know, apparently he *proposed* and that's what set this whole thing off.'

My eyes widened at that piece of information but I stayed silent, reluctant to comment. Georgette changed the subject. 'Talking of blossoming romances and all that, I heard you asked for Josh's help with your Wi-Fi yesterday?' She pointed her talon at me. 'Listen. Don't ever go over there to talk to him again without running the plan by me first. What you did sounded really, really cringe.'

I shuddered at the thought of my great operation doing the rounds this morning.

'I really do have a problem with my Wi-Fi though.'

She smirked, then dismissed me, bored of our catch-up, turning all her attention to plucking the skin round a loose cuticle.

I realised then I couldn't trust Georgette with my reply to Josh, she was far too willing to stab her sources in the back and, even if I pretended I was texting someone anonymous, that news would reach Josh in thirty seconds flat and he'd think I was being unfaithful. I was on my own with this one. I turned away from George, still fiddling with her fingernail, unlikely to attempt to talk to me while her attention was elsewhere.

I tried to conjure a cooler, calmer, prettier, better, version of myself as I turned my focus back to my reply to Josh. *You'll never be pretty*, the voice in my head said.

I silenced it.

I looked through my drafts again.

Look at you sliding into my DMs!

That was the one. Casual. Smiley. Flirty. Not like me at all. It was perfect. I pressed send and breathed in deeply through my nose and out through my mouth. Just like they taught you at yoga. *Let your rib cage expand… and contract.*

9

Ava

I stood at the door, psyching myself up to walk into the lounge and confront my fear. I half-expected to see her there again, just like last time, and, as I talked myself into standing in that same spot, goose bumps formed and rose along my arms as though my body was trying to jump out of its skin. After too long procrastinating I decided I'd had enough and, in one quick motion, I strode into the room, blinked my eyes up and stared at Olivia's resting place.

The sofa was new: ivory and faux-leather with navy blue scatter cushions dotted along it. It was the exact opposite of the one that had been here before and for that I should be thankful, I suppose. But it didn't stop me from recalling a disturbing new memory about that morning, one I thought I'd forgotten; as the ambulance staff had lifted Olivia from the sofa, the black fabric of the previous settee had stuck to her legs. Even once she'd been pulled free, dark marks had persisted along the backs of her thighs, sticking to her, reluctant to let go. The smell of sickening sweetness clumped in my throat, underscoring how nauseated I felt about being back here and I stumbled out into the hallway, the black and white marble cold underfoot, my head awash with colours and sounds and smells. I willed myself to be calm. It was dark now, the moon rising through the sash windows as I stood, breathing deep, the gold-work in the ceiling sparkling as glints in the material were picked up by street lights outside. Everything would be picture-perfect – this place was incredible – if it weren't for the toe-curling memories. I headed upstairs, trying to convince myself that I'd feel OK if I just kept going. I'd confronted the memory, survived, and now I just had to move on. But panic set in when I thought of sitting on that too-white sofa: it was too new, too perfect, and it wouldn't be there at all if Olivia hadn't – if I hadn't...

Would she be happy I was here? I wasn't as sure as David had been about that. I was sure she'd be much happier if *she* were still here instead.

I wondered if I should just shut the door to the living room and pretend it didn't exist. Perhaps I would do that for a few days, then try again. I hurried back down the stairs, pulled the door to the lounge shut with a surprising slam. Silence followed and I felt the weight lift from my shoulders.

I managed a few hours of difficult sleep, expecting Olivia would turn up at any minute to throw me out. I kept shooting up in bed, spine like an arrow, my heart palpitations so off-rhythm I wondered if she'd somehow possessed my body and planned to kill me from the inside out. I dreamt I'd worn a rival brand's clothes to the AthLuxe launch and, instead of turning up at our catwalk

I'd been dropped at a different venue. I hadn't been able to leave, bodies closing in on me, it was raining inside and I couldn't open my eyes properly to see through the haze... I dreamt my mother had set up an arranged marriage for me but, when the guests arrived, I realised it was actually my funeral she'd been planning. She'd worn white. I'd floated overhead, observing.

My alarm ripped through the stillness just after six and, for a moment, I forgot entirely where I was and what had happened but, as my eyes adjusted to the room, it all came flooding back. The first waves of relief swelled through me: I didn't have to wake up and face Charlie, I'd survived my first night in this house, I was still alive. I hit snooze and stretched out like a whippet across the ginormous memory-foam mattress, tired after a night spent wide awake.

I began daydreaming about work as I dozed – this time pondering the more realistic possibilities of facing an empty front row – when the celestial call bell sounded for the front door. My pulse raced as I rolled onto my side to see who it was, slipping my feet into the perfectly plump slippers on the floor. I pressed the answer button.

'Yes?' I asked tentatively, half expecting to hear Charlie's voice. Or David's.

But it wasn't either.

'Hi, chef here.'

'Chef?'

'Right. David Stein sent me?'

What?

I grabbed the cream satin robe that hung on the back of the bedroom door and galloped down the spiral staircase, careful not to trip on the gold rods which lined each step on the way down. I opened the door suspiciously, still not entirely trusting, surprised to be greeted by a man who more closely resembled a bodybuilder than a chef.

'Morning, Miss,' he grunted. He didn't just look like a movie tough guy, he sounded like one too. 'I'm here to cook.'

'Right, well you'd better come in then!'

I held the door open and he walked inside carrying a brown crate of ingredients under one of his enormous arms. I was pleased to see it was full of eggs and spinach and bread – I reasoned that no axe-murderer would be prepared enough to turn up with props. I let myself relax. I directed him through to the kitchen and gestured for him to put his crate down on the marbled island in the centre.

'David suggested Eggs Florentine. That all right for ya?'

I nodded enthusiastically and left him to his preparations but, as I took the flight of stairs back up to the bedroom, wondered for a moment if things were going too far. David was bending over backwards for me and, though I hadn't asked for him to go so above and beyond, my guilty conscience was banging away at me. *You know what you're doing, you know he likes you.*

I slipped off the silky robe and chose an outfit for the day, gasping as I opened the wardrobe doors at the sight of an entirely full closet. I felt like Belle from a *Beauty and the Beast* office re-make. I settled on a two-piece tuxedo with black satin lapels, a crisp shirt, heels, and a simple gold necklace. I reasoned that David must have hired someone to do all of this and made a mental note to politely thank him later, the things he was doing to help me get back on my feet were completely overwhelming. I transferred my stuff from my scruffy handbag to the monochrome shoulder bag he'd also bought for me to use and double checked I had everything: contactless, wallet, keys, phone...

Where was my phone?

I looked towards the bedside tables, pulled the duvet cover back from the bed, checked again in my bag and rummaged through yesterday's pockets – zilch.

Where had I left it? Back at the flat? I dreaded the thought of Charlie getting hold of it. *I'll have another look at work*, I thought, then picked up my bag and jogged down the stairs to breakfast. The smell of golden muffins, eggs and fresh spinach pervaded my senses as I stepped into the kitchen.

'Smells incredible,' I said towards the chef with quads that would rival an Olympic cyclist. There was something of a juxtaposition about a man with such muscular strength chopping and seasoning and sautéing. I liked it, though. It made him interesting. He smiled back.

'How long have you known David?' I asked, busying myself filling up the kettle.

'Oh, we go way back,' he replied, spooning a poached egg from a pan he must have found on his own. Maybe he used to cook for Olivia, too. 'Do you cook for David?'

He chortled as he answered, 'Now and then.' He whistled as he tore off a bunch of spinach and walked over to the sink to wash it. 'Do you work with him then? Is that right?'

'Yes. He's helping me through a rough patch. Hopefully I won't be here, inconveniencing him, for too long.'

The kettle pinged to signal it was ready. I cut a slice of lemon and a hunk of ginger from the things the chef had brought along, and added them to a cup along with the boiling water.

'Do you want one?' I offered.

'No, none for me.'

'What should I call you, anyway?' I asked, embarrassed that I'd handled this conversation totally backwards. 'I'm Ava.'

'People call me Sheff,' he answered. 'I'm from Sheffield, so it's kind of my nickname and my job. Sheff, like, with an S.'

I nodded an agreement as I moved the hot water up to my lips and blew ripples across the surface. A few moments later Sheff plated up the most divine breakfast, packed up his things and left. I wolfed it down then set off for work, ready to face the day with a delightfully full stomach.

10

Jade

I walked confidently into the meeting room and sat down opposite Ava. She was back at work after just one day away, wearing the blue-black bruise across her face like a badge of honour, acting as though she deserved the same treatment as a war hero returning from front-line action. I didn't smile at her: I wanted her to know I wasn't backing down, that I wasn't prepared to stand for her asking members of our team to 'keep an eye on me', and that I certainly wasn't about to give her special dispensation for her inability to choose a suitable partner. So here we were: head to head.

Ava had called this meeting an 'emergency catch-up' and she didn't even look up from her notes when I walked in, so we sat in an uneasy silence each waiting for the other to break the ice. Then Josh walked in and cut the tension. I smiled nervously, my shoulders hunched in, my heart thudding against my chest. I looked up at him; he was smiling at me too. I melted. It was as though a huge section of a polar ice cap had just broken off and fallen into the sea, and my legs momentarily lost their solidity. I was glad I was already sitting down. When I turned my attention back to the table, Ava was watching me closely.

'Right, I want to sort our roles for the launch. There's been a bit of confusion over who's doing what and I'd like to take this opportunity to clarify everything.' She delivered her opening monologue staring right at me.

The glass walls of her office were a thin veil to the rest of the floor and no doubt a few people would be keeping their eyes on this meeting, interested to observe the dynamics between this awkward threesome play out. Most of the office knew the headlines: I was into Josh, Ava and I were currently at each other's throats, and there was little hope of the three of us working together to pull off a successful launch. But there was plenty they didn't know: that Josh liked *me* now, that Ava was playing in the gutter to get the promotion to Team Head over me, that I wasn't going to go down without a fight.

Ava continued her opening monologue and I breathed in deeply, the smell of my just-smoked morning cigarette clinging to my clothes.

'The first collection is the biggest deal for any new brand and we need the entire evening to run without a hitch…'

I'd *have* to give up smoking soon, I wasn't sure Josh approved of it, and Kai certainly wouldn't if he ever found out. In fact, he'd be *extremely* reluctant to put a full-time smoker at the helm of an activewear account, wouldn't he? Imagine the negative headline it could create. I berated myself for my own shortcomings. I'd only started smoking to fit in with all the cool girls at the office, but now they'd all switched their twenty-a-day for superfood smoothies and spirulina shots and I'd been left puffing on the toxic sticks I was now addicted to.

'I want everyone to be happy with their assigned jobs and I certainly don't want any more slip-ups.'

She said it like Josh and I were keen for slip-ups. God, she was insufferable. Josh didn't look that bothered, though, and moved his large left hand round his water bottle, lifting it to his mouth. I imagined what it would feel like to be that bottle, so safe in his grip, so close to his lips.

'I'll handle Kai and the front row business,' Ava continued as I imagined myself as a drinks vestibule. 'Josh, obviously you'll look after the media—'

I couldn't be bothered to listen to her any more.

I zoned out her waffling *rah-rah-rah*, and instead thought about what Josh might message next. Maybe he'd suggest dinner? Or drinks? Dinner would be more his style. He'd probably wear a crisp white shirt with the top couple of buttons undone, a glimpse of his dark chest hair visible, a hint of his impressive pecs beneath. I bet he'd want to go to a steak restaurant... and I'd order the same as him to show how well matched we were. Oh God, I hope he doesn't like blue cheese sauce, it *has* to be Béarnaise on a steak, surely?

'... Is that OK, Jade? So you'll manage the security team and ticket sales?'

'Pardon?' I was still lost in the thought of having to eat blue cheese sauce.

Ava looked up from her notepad, slightly exasperated at having to repeat herself.

'You'll do security?'

77

No. Security wasn't OK at all, I needed to be close to Kai, I couldn't miss out on valuable face time with him in the run up to this promotion. Security? Was she serious?

'Right, and I'm supposed to sit back and let you take all the credit for this launch, am I? While you're swanning around with Kai and the front row, you'd like me kicking out the riff-raff and autograph hunters with a few bulked-up idiots in ill-fitting suits?'

My reply even took *me* by surprise. Usually I didn't just blurt out what my head was thinking, but my meeting with David had put me on edge, ignited the urgency of the competition between us. An awkward pause followed as Ava recovered from my right hook.

'Well, no, not at all, Jade, that's why we're here talking about it. Is there something you'd rather manage?'

I coughed loudly and looked down at my notepad. An idea formed.

'Well, Jade?' Ava pressed, testily.

'It's just, I've already started sorting the front row out with Kai. We spoke on the phone yesterday and he specifically asked me to be his liaison on the night and to keep up the conversation with attendees. You were out of the office yesterday, Ava, you missed quite a lot, and I think it would be weird if I handed over to you now. I don't think Kai would go for it.'

It was as though I was having an out of body experience. The first time I thought of the lie I'd just told was when I was hearing it along with everyone else. What was I doing? Could I really get away with this?

Josh shuffled awkwardly in his seat as the tension in the room mounted.

'So why have you waited until now to say anything?' Ava asked, her voice thick with irritation. 'Who have you confirmed? How much of the budget have you spent? Why haven't you consulted anyone else about this? Why haven't you at least sent me a heads up, a recap, why did you wait until now to say anything? Don't you think it's quite important?'

'Well, *if* you'd let me get a word in, Ava,' I retorted.

Her face was a picture. I stuck the knife in. 'Are you sure you're OK, by the way? Kai was wondering if your breakup is affecting your work? Do you need some more time off?'

She rapped each of her fingernails quickly on the desk and the bruise on her face darkened.

'I'd prefer you didn't talk about my personal life with clients, Jade, it's not why they pay us and it's certainly not very prof—'

'Sorry, Ava.' I cut her off. 'But *you* were the one who brought your personal life into this. *You* were the one who decided to date some lunatic. *You* were the one who had to take time out to deal with it all, so we may as well talk about how it's affecting the launch. Josh and I need to know if we can't rely on you.'

She interrupted me. I could see water building in her eyes. *The truth hurts.* She put on a brave face. 'So, if I were to call Kai, he'd verify your story? He'd be happy that everything was under control?'

I curled my toes inwards, gathering the material of my tights in the space between. 'Be my guest,' rattled off my alter ego with surprising ease. She didn't say anything, which was remarkable really.

'So, *I'll* look after Kai and the front row, and *you'll* manage the security and ticket sales,' I clarified, staring her down. 'I'll send you an update on what Kai and I have agreed after this. I'm sure you'll be happy.'

I knew I was playing with fire as Ava called an end to the meeting, asking Josh to stay behind. She could easily call Kai today, ask a set of roundabout questions to clarify what the situation was, at which point he'd confirm he hadn't spoken to me yesterday about being his liaison. If she did that I'd be rumbled, which was why I had to get in there and call him first. Write the history I'd already delivered as fact.

I exaggerated my hips swaying from side-to-side as I left the room, hoping Josh was watching, and hurried back to my desk.

As I waited for Kai to answer his mobile, I observed Ava and Josh talking animatedly within the glass walls I'd left behind. Clearly they were discussing me, but what Ava didn't know was that Josh was on *my* team now. I picked up a couple of pills from the pot on my desk and swallowed them down just before Kai answered: I needed all the calm I could get.

'Kai, how are you?' I asked breezily when he answered the phone. 'I've just been speaking to the team about launch night. Ava's keen for us to pay a few of the higher-end celebrities to ensure we get at least a few attendees one hundred per cent confirmed for the night—'

He started ranting again about not wanting to pay anyone.

'Yes, I know, and I agree, but it *is* better to pay a few so we can be sure at least some famous people will turn up. If there's some other event on that week that conflicts with us it could be a disaster.'

'Was this Ava's idea?' he asked. 'You didn't mention this yesterday.'

I gritted my teeth. 'I've had a chance to think about it. And Ava agrees. We've also decided that I'll be your liaison for the night.'

'OK then,' he said. So that was that.

'Perfect, I'm glad you agree. I'll send an email to clarify the finer details now.'

I checked my watch. Four hours forty-one minutes since I'd written *Look at you sliding into my DMs!*

Which day, I wondered, would Josh most like to meet for dinner, if he asked? I knew he took part in some sort of American Football practice on a Wednesday, usually went for drinks with his friends on Thursday. Would he cancel these for our dinner? I didn't know what he did on a Friday. Maybe Friday, then. I looked at my phone. No reply. I turned it to loud so I'd hear as soon as it came in.

Four hours forty-two minutes.

Just then, just as I was counting down the seconds, the loudest and clearest of notification tones erupted, like a volcano dormant for millennia. It had arrived. *It had arrived!* I breathed in deeply through my nose, out through my mouth, expanded my rib cage, steadied myself, opened my eyes properly.

You excited for the summer party?

The summer party! How had I let this slip my focus? Why hadn't Georgette reminded me? I had so much weight to lose before then!

'George!' I called across the desk. 'Summer party. We haven't spoken about it: how long do I have to lose three stone?'

'Babe, it's in two days.'

'What?' I blabbed, almost ejecting my stomach through my mouth in shock.

'What's the big deal? You weren't bothered when I asked you about it the other day.'

Everything had changed now that Josh and I were talking, now that there was a chance the party could end in our first kiss!

'What are those weird tea things you use? Would they work in time?'

'The laxatives?'

'They're laxatives?'

'Yeah. You just shit yourself for a week basically. They do work, though.'

'Gracious. No. That sounds awful.'

'Just be happy in your own skin then babe, embrace your curves and that. It's cool now anyway.'

Yes, all very well for you in your tiny size tens to tell me to embrace my flab. I knew what George meant, of course: plus-size models are all over billboards on the tube nowadays. But it seemed to be all or nothing, no one represented the awkward in between phase, did they? The women not big enough to be plus size and not small enough to be 'thin'. Where was the slightly flabby model with a doughy, but fair, midriff? Where was the model who'd just let herself go a bit? Where was the model who put on a stone at university that went entirely to her face and double chin? She wasn't there. And you want to know why? Because no one wanted to be, or be with, that girl. You had to aspire to be either massive, or tiny, seemed to me. And Josh would prefer me tiny. I contemplated the laxa-teas again, but had visions of a bathroom-related incident at the party and decided firmly against it. I flicked back to Josh's message and typed an excited reply.

I guess! It's come round so quick hasn't it? David always pushes the boat out… I'm sure it will be an amazing night.

He replied immediately and I almost had an aneurysm from the amount of good news in one morning: first I'd cut down Ava and now I was winding in Josh!

Can I look forward to seeing you in something a little sexier than work clothes?

My heart was pounding furiously, a heady mix of endorphins and adrenaline racing round my body. My desire to tell someone was intense. But I couldn't, I had to keep it secret, I didn't want this to become one of the many rumours at work.

Wait. What was wrong with my work clothes? Didn't he like my pencil skirt collection?

11

Ava

The day had been manic so far and I hadn't eaten since my incredible breakfast this morning. The emergency team meeting with Josh and Jade had come to an abrupt close with Jade storming out and it had left the pair of us more than a little shell-shocked.

'Do you believe her story about Kai?' I asked Josh once the door had shut behind her.

Josh and Jade had never been close despite her rabid fascination with him. The story going round was that she'd tried, and failed, to hook up with him when he'd first joined the agency a couple of years after her and that, after her rejection, she'd harboured a secret crush ever since.

'Why wouldn't I?' he answered.

He was being annoyingly diplomatic. I could usually count on Josh to stick up for me. He'd always been one of the better members of the team, despite the fact that he could have coasted here given his surname.

'Well, since when has Kai been keen to spend any more time with Jade than absolutely necessary?'

Josh shrugged.

Despite Josh's apparent faith in Jade, I *knew* she was lying about the phone call with Kai. The problem was proving it. It would mean calling Kai, explaining and exposing Jade's pathetic in-fighting, and that would make the entire agency look bad. So I didn't have much choice but to let her get away with it. Wasn't life unfair? Yes, we were competing for the same job, but I couldn't understand why she was using such dirty tactics.

A shadow of doubt crossed my mind.

'The two of you need to work out whatever it is you have going on. I'm not getting involved.' Josh drummed his fingers rhythmically on his leg, tapping out a beat from the annals of his mind. Then he fixed his beautiful blues on me. 'Rise above it, Ava. Don't let it get to you.'

I left the meeting room in a huff and closed the door to my office. I didn't often do that but I needed time to process what had just happened. Josh believed Jade. Had something changed between them that I was unaware of? I ran my fingers through my hair and stared blankly at the notepad on my desk, deep in thought. A chill ran down my spine as I considered the secrets we shared together, the tenuous bonds we'd promised we'd never break. I hadn't realised things were so bad between us. I had to talk to her. Keep your friends close, I thought; but keep Jade Fernleigh closer.

The working day had ended well over an hour ago but the office was still busy spitting out its remaining occupants.

As I tidied my desk of the day's detritus, I heard the unmistakable buzz of my mobile phone and it occurred to me how quiet things had been without it. It was muffled, coming from my desk drawer, and I slid my fingers under the handle to investigate. Sure enough, there it was: sitting pretty, screen illuminated, vibrating happily round its hiding place. I sighed, I hadn't remembered putting it there, but I'd been awfully preoccupied recently, and my phone had been driving me mad. It certainly wasn't beyond the realms of possibility. An unknown number was calling and I prayed it wasn't Kai. I couldn't face another lecture about security or press protocols right now: I'd been up to my eyeballs in launch preparations all day.

'Hello, Ava speaking,' I trotted out on autopilot. My greeting was met with silence, but I could hear the caller's muffled breathing. 'Hello?' I tried again, a note of panic in my voice this time. Beads of sweat formed across my brow and my mouth dried.

'Ava,' Charlie's clipped Irish accent growled out of the receiver and gripped tight round my neck. He was drunk, I could tell by the lazy lilt to his voice. It was my turn to be quiet. 'Ava,' he said again, the signal cutting in and out. 'I nee—'

'What do you want, Charlie?' I spoke in no more than a whisper. I knew he'd pick up on my fear and use it against me, but I couldn't hang up, I was frozen. His heavy breathing continued and I wondered where he was, if he'd moved back to Reading after being kicked out of our flat, or was still hanging around somewhere nearby. But he said nothing more and the call dropped. I needed to get another phone, I didn't want that to happen again. Next time Charlie called his words would be full of malice and hatred, accusations of cheating and lying and sleeping around behind his back would roll down the receiver. Every time he was drunk, or high, he'd turn puce and paranoid and hurl out the same old rubbish. I was so tired of this. In one quick and decisive motion I cracked the phone against my desk, breaking the screen and rendering it useless. I wouldn't put it past Charlie to have installed a tracker in it or something and, as I hurried out of the office, I saw Jade in the corridor, heading my way. I reached out to stop her, to ask her if everything was OK after our meeting this morning but, as my hand landed on her knitted cardigan she pushed me away and walked straight by, refusing to speak to me, refusing to even *look* at me. I stood in the stairwell, shocked, then put her to the back of my mind: I had bigger problems than Jade Fernleigh's grudge. I took a turning at the ground floor and used the back exit just in case Charlie was waiting for me outside.

I lost myself in the crush of commuters on the Victoria line, steam from our tightly packed bodies condensing on the windows. I thought of my parents; I really needed to call and tell them what was happening, but it was almost as if too much had gone on in such a short space of time to unleash it all at once. I hadn't spoken to them for ages and one thing had led to another and another and another and now it was all just a bit ridiculous. I resolved to tell them a simplified version of events when I got home: things had been getting worse between Charlie and me, we'd had a fight, I'd moved out. Perhaps I'd leave out the bits about living in my dead colleague's apartment – which happened to be owned by my company's CEO – for now. Mum would be disappointed enough as it was.

I watched the sign for Pimlico station fly past the tube carriage windows as the train grinded to a very noisy halt at the platform and enjoyed the rush of air against my skin as I exited the station. My cheeks glowed from the summer humidity as I walked briskly back to the place I now called home.

My ears pricked up as I sensed someone closing in on me, like the air had compressed against my back, but, just as I turned my head slightly to my shoulder to steal a glance behind me, a man hurtled past on a bike, almost knocking me off my feet. I pushed forward, willing my legs to carry me as fast as they physically could, checking obsessively round me as I fit the key into the lock and let myself in.

A crumpled letter sat ominously on the doormat as I pushed open the door. I knew immediately who it was from. His horrible texts had turned into dropped calls, hate mail in the post, eyes in the darkness. I needn't have left through the back exit; he'd already found me. I picked up the paper.

Is this where you came when you were working late? Is this where you came when you pretended to go away with your friends? Is this where you will come to betray me with him over and over again with my ring on your finger?
Come back to me.
It's not too late.
Please call.
All my love,
Charlie

12

Jade

Josh and I were messaging during work hours now, mere metres apart, playing it cool, not looking at each other. There was something so sexy about keeping it a secret: our burgeoning relationship like the sweetest forbidden fruit. I wondered if we'd be able to keep our hands off each other at the office party. His latest text was still tattooed across my mind. I'd been flirting with him about summer holidays and bathing suits and he'd said:

I'd like to see that though... you know, you in a bikini. Maybe you could send something?

It had left me with quite the problem, however, as now the only logical next step was to acquiesce to his request. I had to show him 'me in a bikini' otherwise the conversation would die.

I rushed out after work to buy what I'd need to make any bikini of mine look acceptable. I prowled up and down the aisles of a nearby beauty store like a cougar with tunnel vision. I flung instant tan, hair removal cream, bronzer, a shiny leg brush – what the hell was that?! – and even one of George's 'brow brushes' into my basket. Who set the rules on which parts of us were supposed to be hairy now? And how had I missed the memo about eyebrows? At least I'd found out in time. I needed to have the photoshoot of my life. This was no time to look unremarkable, or ordinary. I had to look good. I had to look my absolute, glittering, best. The cashier racked up my items, showing me glimpses of her chewing gum as she opened her mouth comically wide with each bite.

'D'ya 'ave a loyalty card?'

I handed it over, paid on my debit card and hurried out of the store. I saw my bus pulling into the bay at the other side of the road and dashed like a maniac across four lanes of traffic to catch it, dodging in and out of cars and buses like a hare on a country road.

I pushed away the post clogging the entrance hall. *No time for that tonight*, I thought for the gazillionth time, and ran upstairs, stripping off as I did so to make the most of every available minute. *Apply to clean, cool skin and leave to dry for five minutes after applying. The tan is instant, so use a mitt to ensure the product doesn't stain your hands.* Obviously I'd forgotten a mitt. But it would be fine, I'd just wash my hands between each limb's application.

First, I jumped in the shower with the hair removal cream covering almost every inch of my body: I didn't want to take any chances. And, as the box round me heated up, so too did the rancid smell of rotten fish corpses currently smothering me from head to toe. How could they sell something that smells so horrific? I waited for the seemingly endless eight-minute application time to pass. Eventually, my timer sounded and I used the tiny scraper tool provided with the packet to start shovelling off the lotion. It took quite a lot of force to dislodge the hair, so much so that when I jumped out of the shower my body looked as though it had been through a tumble dryer: red raw and streaky where the hair remover had achieved varying degrees of success in clearing me of my patchy brown body fuzz.

I grabbed the shiny leg brush. Maybe this would help remove the dregs? The thing was ridiculous – a little eraser-sized tool – designed, presumably, for the legs of a Milanese catwalk model and I dutifully scrubbed away at my calves, reasoning that the fronts would be the only part in shot, but, even after fifteen minutes, couldn't notice even the slightest bit of shine. I chucked the stupid thing in the bin and proceeded with the rest of my preparations. I rubbed the instant fake tan over each leg, ensuring both received a generous coat, moved up to my belly, spreading it over the lumps and bumps that existed even though I wished so much that they didn't – I bet Ava's stomach didn't look like this – then washed my hands after every inch of me had transformed from ghostly to golden. I scolded myself as the product stubbornly refused to remove itself completely from my palms and realised I'd forgotten to wash between limbs. *Curses!* I ran into the bedroom: nail varnish remover. That ought to do it. I picked up a cotton pad and poured the alcoholic solution all over it before transferring it to my hands. *Not much better.* Oh dear. Well, that was that: my hands *could not* be in the shot.

I set up some subtle mood lighting in the bathroom with a few strategically placed candles and lamps that I'd brought from all over the house to sit in the hallway outside. I flipped the camera round so I could see what it was capturing. I started off sitting on the toilet, looking up. *Snap!* I studied it. Not the right mood, really, sitting on the toilet, it implied all the wrong things. I moved to the bathroom floor, balancing the phone against the hideous pink floral tiles which encased the sewer-green bathtub and lay down side-on to the lens. Eurgh, you could really see the bits you miss cleaning when you got down on the bathroom floor. I really had to clean behind the toilet more. I bent my knees and pushed my bottom to the ceiling. The phone's flash illuminated – *Snap!* – and I studied the image: cellulite, double chin, a flash of full-frontal frightfulness. Disgusting.

I stood up, sucked in my gut as much as possible and angled the camera to a diagonal. *Snap!* It grabbed the bottom of my face and my body up to the top of my thighs. Too much midriff. Too bad I couldn't wear a pencil skirt: the garment really worked to hold everything in place. God, I really needed to lose weight. I grabbed my phone and tried another angle. I faced the camera head-on, my shoulders closing in, pushing my voluptuous chest together, cropping out my lower body entirely. I let the bikini top come a little loose as I squeezed my breasts tighter together still. *Snap!* OK, getting there. Sort of. The plus part of being fat was it made your boobs look good, I supposed. *If you were into cow's udders,* cackled the voice within me. I studied the image close up. Could I really send this? I was having doubts. I read his message again. No, he wanted this and, besides, this was sexy, this was fun, this was exactly the kind of thing I needed to do to bring Josh and me closer together. I needed to take a risk, take a chance. It wasn't just our future relationship that depended on him liking me, but my job, too.

After half an hour procrastinating, scrubbing feverishly behind the toilet, I sent it.

13

Ava

David had invited me to meet him for a drink at The Whive again this evening and, as the doorman greeted me with familiarity, I wondered if this place was fast becoming my local. I wondered what people at work would think if they saw me here and I worried about everyone getting the wrong impression about our sudden friendship. I took a moment in the entranceway to pull my hair up into a ponytail.

David was sat in the same seat as last time: a deep leather chair with intricately carved wooden armrests. His expression was downcast, his stare fixed to the floor, his shirt collar over-starched and upright, stiff, his hand locked round a tumbler of amber-coloured liquid. As he saw me approach, he feigned a smile, shielding his real expression from me. I guessed he'd been thinking about Olivia and my heart broke for him: how sad it must be to bury your only child.

'Thank you for coming,' he said, by way of greeting. Unusually for David, he didn't get up, didn't kiss my cheek, didn't pull my chair out.

'Is everything OK?' I asked tentatively.

'I'm just—' His voice broke between the words. 'Excuse me—'

'You don't need to excuse yourself. I can't imagine what you're going through.' I cringed at my enthusiastic use of my favourite refrain. 'Olivia and I had only reconnected again for a few, too short, months, and the impact she had on me was incredible. I just wished we'd kept better touch after university.'

He smiled with damp eyes and stared off into the distance. I remembered how the body-bag they'd brought for Olivia had been too small, the end of it flapping loose in the wind as she'd been wheeled into the back of the ambulance that morning.

'Why didn't you tell me you were engaged, Ava?' His eyes met mine, wiggles of red streaking the white. My expression changed and my brain whirred. *Had he been upset about Olivia or upset about my engagement?* His stare was intense and accusatory.

'How did you—' I asked, slightly taken aback.

'Charlie,' he cut in.

'When?' I asked.

'Does it matter?'

He shot back the rest of his drink, pressing a napkin to his mouth afterwards, breathing in through the cotton.

I was surprised by the tension between us.

'It's not what you think,' I said slowly. 'It wasn't as though I accepted. He ambushed me.'

'So why didn't you tell me?'

'I—' I struggled to find the right words to say. The phrase *Because it's none of your business* sprung to mind but didn't seem appropriate. Even if it was the truth. 'I didn't tell you because it wasn't important... it meant nothing, it was just one of Charlie's games.'

He considered my answer for a moment. 'Don't lie to me again,' he said firmly, then relaxed. 'Not while you're under my roof.'

I was taken aback, colour rushing to my cheeks, burning pink as he told me off. 'Of course not, I just, sorry, it all happened very quickly. Charlie asked me to marry him, I *didn't* say yes, then seconds later he found the break-up note,' I said, slipping back into the role of subservient woman far too easily.

'Is there anything else you'd like to tell me?' His sadness had been replaced by something more sinister. He knew something. He played with the edges of his serviette, fiddling, took his cheek between his teeth.

My pulse quickened. Telling him my secrets hadn't been part of the deal. And he didn't know the half of it.

'You told me Charlie was convinced you were seeing someone,' he started to say when I wasn't forthcoming. '*Is* there anyone else?'

I'd let my guard down to tell David about Charlie's accusations and now he was using them against me. Was this the kind of tight leash he put on Olivia, too?

'Like I said, Charlie's been obsessed with that theory for as long as we've been in London. He won't leave it alone.' I paused for a moment. 'Where is he?'

'Do you care?'

I lowered my voice. 'He left a note.' I pulled Charlie's poison from my pocket. I wanted David to understand how nothing Charlie said was true, that he was unhinged and unstable. I also wanted to fall under his favour again, and I knew he liked me vulnerable. 'I'm scared, David. Look. He's found me.'

A flash of fury crossed David's face and his brow tightened as he unfurled the crumpled note. But he was happy I wasn't keeping this from him and I watched his pupils skip excitedly over the words.

'I destroyed my phone, too, I was worried he'd put a tracker on me or something.'

'Should I put some protection on you? I could stay in the spare room for a while, if you like?'

It hadn't occurred to me he'd offer to stay.

'No, no, that's not necessary,' I said hurriedly, now regretting telling him about the note altogether. 'I just want this whole thing to blow over with as little fuss as possible. I know him; he'll get bored soon. No reaction is the best reaction.' Great, in order to deter David from getting too involved I'd talked myself into a corner: now I wouldn't even be able to go to the police with my concerns. *If you're that worried Ava, I should stay, just until he's found. Or longer, if you want.*

David shook his head.

'You must let me know if he tries anything else. And I'll send a new phone to the house.'

'Thank you,' I said, relaxing. 'And thank you for all the clothes you left me. They're beautiful. I feel like the luckiest woman alive.'

He tried hard not to smile too wide. 'I knew you'd like them. They used to be Olivia's, I had them all dry-cleaned before you moved in.'

My heart stopped and my gut convulsed. I'd been wearing a dead woman's clothes all day. My skin started to itch and the material of her tux clung horribly to my skin.

'Why would you want me to wear her things?'

'She'd have wanted them to be worn, don't you think? She took great pride in her outfits. She wasn't one of those people who'd want her clothes tucked away, turning musty and moth-bitten in the wardrobe.'

I felt sick, violated, lied to, but still I sat there, with no choice but to pretend I was OK with it.

'Are you all right?' he asked, as though nothing were the matter.

'Fine, I'm fine.'

'Did I get this wrong? Should I send new things?'

'No, David, it's fine.'

'Darling, you can talk to me if anything's wrong, you know that, don't you?'

No, I don't.

I imagined myself then as David's doll, plucked from a disordered supermarket shelf to live in his gorgeous townhouse: wardrobe full of dressing-up clothes, beautiful four-poster bed to lie in at night, perfect white picket fence encasing the perimeter. I thought of his hands reaching in, moving me from room to room, undressing me for bathtime, redressing me for dinner, plastic food on the table, a mini-comb for him to brush through my hair at night. And, just like a doll, I needed him in order to survive. My life depended on him wanting to play with me, to keep me in his house, to find me interesting, pretty. I had to keep it up: at least until I didn't need him any more.

'Of course I do. I told you about Charlie, didn't I? I hadn't told *anyone* about him.' David's mood shifted, happier now, and he changed the subject.

'Are you looking forward to the summer party?'

I matched his incredible change of pace by feigning excitement too but, to be honest, I couldn't think of anything worse than getting drunk at a work do while things with Charlie were still fresh and things with David were so weird.

'I can't wait to see what you've organised this year,' I said, avoiding answering the question directly.

'You won't be disappointed, although it's a shame Josh can't make it. I've had to send him to Monaco... I've set him up with a new business lead that's just perfect—'

David's mobile rang and he answered it mid-sentence.

He cupped his hand over the receiver. 'I have to take this,' he whispered. 'I'll see you at the party.'

I took it as my cue to leave and The Whive's heavy timber door swung shut behind me as I left the restaurant, and the bill, behind with David. It was coming up to ten o'clock and the sun had finally given up for the day, the headlights and streetlights outside dazzling and slightly disorienting as my eyes took some time to adjust. I negotiated the bustling crowds outside Sloane Square tube station, picking my way through the rush of post-theatre tourists gathered in the square, trying to work out how to get back to their Chelsea hotels. For a moment, I thought I saw Charlie's face in the crowd, and froze, ready to confront him. But he was gone just as soon as he'd appeared.

Sitting in the bedroom, hand clasped round the landline, I ended the call with my mother – I'd finally found the time to fill her in on my car crash week – and her wiry, worried voice rattled round in my mind. *This all seems like a lot of change. Are you sure you don't want to give things with Charlie another go? Aren't you a little old to be starting all over again? I read an article the other day, Ava, it said you should be starting to try for a baby as soon as you turn thirty. It was never a problem in my day, but now, well, it's as if you girls have all forgotten what God put you on this Earth to do.*

My instinct had been right: she didn't care about me, she cared about what her friends were saying about me. She would never have helped me leave Charlie. Though my relationship with David was taking a turn for the controlling, I still owed him a lot. He'd helped me when no one else could. However, I was determined to stand on my own two feet before long: I didn't want to feel indebted to anyone ever again.

I walked through to the bathroom and turned the chrome-finish tap as far as it would go. I set the temperature to medium-hot and steamy water poured into the giant tub, sat solidly on four silver legs. I scattered in Epsom salts and watched as they fell, gathering at the base of the bath, diffusing their magical healing powers into the water. The cupboards held all kinds of bubbles; I picked lemon and black pepper then stood over the water and fed it a generous amount.

The bathroom mirrors steamed up and I hardly recognised myself in the reflection – my cheek was back to a normal size again, but a few faint purple marks persisted, tracing the outline of my bruises, reminding me how lucky I was to have escaped without worse. I tentatively placed a toe in the warm water, now brimming with frothy bubbles that filled the room with a sweet, lemony scent. Satisfied with the temperature, I closed off the taps and stepped in, pausing every so often as a new part of my skin acclimatised to the heat. Finally submerged, I rested my head against the back edge of the tub, letting the water cover me, lapping its way up my neck. I told myself to relax, enjoy, let the bubbles and the bathwater transport me to a zen-like mindset, but every time I closed my eyes I imagined Olivia lying in this very spot, her hands gripped round the edges. A barrage of horrific images streaked through my mind, blue lips, shallow breath, wild eyes. I sank beneath the bubbles quickly, covering myself completely in the water. What must it feel like to drown on your own blood? If I opened my mouth now and took a huge breath in, I'd certainly get an idea...

I slipped under the water, my mouth wide, my hair ballooning behind me.

1, 2, 3, 4... I counted, daring myself to do it: to breathe in. But I couldn't. I emerged, panting heavily, sending tidal waves over the lip, deciding against suicide – things were finally looking up, plus, I'd already put my mother through enough today. Not that she wouldn't have revelled in the drama of a deceased daughter; she'd probably rather have me dead than single. I thought of our conversation moments ago. She'd told me she and Dad would come down tomorrow morning. I'd insisted it wasn't necessary – it wasn't, my call had been a mere courtesy – and groaned at the thought of having to explain myself all over again.

As I lay in the bath and thought of home, I didn't notice the creak of the front door as it opened, nor the careful footsteps as they padded around downstairs.

14

Jade

10 p.m. I'd been attempting to watch TV, but the TV and I both knew I wasn't paying it much attention. Mainly I'd just been staring directly at the soulless, colourless screen of my phone, willing it to light up. I was hungry now, starving. I guess the adrenaline was wearing off. He didn't like it. My attempt at a sexy photoshoot had failed.

10.15 p.m. I rattled up a festival of food in the kitchen, stopping every minute or so to check for signs of life from my iPhone. It was on loud but, just in case it malfunctioned and didn't make a noise, I kept checking. Did chorizo ever go off? I flung it into the oven and turned the heat to 240°C. A good cooking would kill the germs. There was some old penne in the cupboard, not quite enough, and the dregs of a packet of spaghetti. I bundled them together in a pan and added a heavy pinch of salt. The saltier the water, the better. I checked my phone again. Nothing. Hmm... no sauce... There was milk in the fridge, could milk be a sauce if I put butter with it? Too risky. Plain was fine. Great start to the diet.

10.45 p.m. Beep beep! My heart jumped for a moment as I thought the alert was from my phone. Dinner was ready and I bashed the timer on the oven. Bloody hell – I'd completely forgotten about the pasta. It was all gloopy and dense due to the amount of water it had absorbed. I persevered and drained it anyway, the steam from the boiling water giving me a mini-facial as I poured it into the colander. I chopped the somewhat charred chorizo and added it to the bowl with a knob of butter. I took my sloppy dinner to the kitchen table and ate it in silence, my phone propped up against the fruit bowl, currently housing exactly zero pieces of my five-a-day: just a letter reminding me to book an appointment with my counsellor and an empty packet of sweets. I barely took my eyes off the screen. Why did I send him that picture? Our fledgling relationship had been a thing for about five minutes and I was already undressing for him. It was truly tragic.

11 p.m. Pub closing time now. I guessed if he'd gone out for a drink and things had got a little out of hand that he'd be starting to head back now. Twenty minutes, maybe thirty, before he got home. If he was drunk whilst looking at my picture it would be better, his inhibitions lowered for starters. I let myself get excited at the prospect of a late night steamy sexting sesh. Or he was laughing at it with a group of gorgeous friends.

11.30 p.m. OK, so maybe he's home and he's just thinking about what to say back…

12 a.m. I should turn my phone off now and go to sleep. Sleeping is more important than a text. If he replies now, do

I want to look like I waited up all night for it?

Desperate.

12.10 a.m. Depends what it says, I guess.

Desperate.

12.30 a.m. I fell asleep for a couple of minutes, woke up with a start and checked my phone. Nothing. The backlight woke me up further and I started browsing... not much news at the moment.

Desperate.

1 a.m. Tears were building behind my eyes, that telltale lump growing in my throat. I buried my head deep in my pillow and let them free, crying myself to sleep, soaking my pillow in sadness.

Desperate.

15

Ava

My parents had arrived moments earlier, the doorbell sounding like the *ping!* of a microwave oven about to spit out its dubious contents.

'Is this really it? *This* place?' My mother's shrill and judgemental voice behind the door.

I opened the barrier between us and stood before them. Mum's face almost disappeared in on itself as she sucked on her own bitterness, the entranceway chandelier sparkling in the reflection of her pale blue eyes. The only reason she'd been so desperate to see me was she thought she'd find me at my lowest ebb today, she'd probably wanted to feed on my weakness, use it to make her feel stronger.

'Hello,' I said, trying my best to keep my voice level.

'Well,' she started. She didn't greet me properly, not even with the air-kiss I'd been expecting, but a thick waft of her liberally applied perfume clung to me as she pushed past. My dad stuck out his hand for me to shake.

Not much had changed in the year we'd been apart, then.

'What on earth are you doing living in a place like this?' she gasped, her petite stature emphasised by the cavernous hallway surrounding her. 'You didn't mention you'd moved into a luxury townhouse on the phone...'

I wasn't allowed to be any more, or less, well off than she was. That was the rule. Either would be judged, either would be too different, too foreign.

'I'm not here for long and it's the CEO's house, not mine. He's letting me stay for a while, just until I get back on my feet.'

'Gracious, for a moment I thought you'd turned to escorting, darling.' She flicked her expensive pashmina from her wiry neck with a quick twist of her hand. 'Heavens. Are you sure peasants are welcome inside? I expect you'll want us to take our shoes off...'

Mum always insisted on people taking shoes off at her house – a three-bedroom semi on a tidy street in Reading – so quite why she was so put out about the thought of it here was beyond me. You'd think she'd appreciate a well-kept home – she always made sure there were fresh-cut flowers in the hallway at hers – but instead she was taking it as a personal attack. Of course, my mother didn't follow up with any questions about my work, or why the CEO had been so kind to me. She rarely asked questions about my career. She simply didn't care for it.

'Can I take your coats?' I asked helpfully as they pulled jackets from limbs. Mum was wearing a beige roll-neck, adorned with a carefully considered heart-shaped silver jewellery set – bracelet, necklace *and* earrings – her hair set in tight blonde ringlets.

'Very good,' my dad said. 'Could I get a brew? I've been

gasping for one since the station but the prices are just *murder* down here.'

Mum looked sideways at Dad. She didn't want to talk about money, not in a house like this. He felt her bony elbow in his side.

'Sure,' I said. 'Mum?'

'I'd prefer an Earl Grey.' I shot her a slightly bemused look. I'd never seen her drink a cup of Earl Grey in her life. 'Do you have lemon, though? I like to add just a little to the cup, sharpens the taste. But honey, or sugar, would do. What do you have?'

Mum and Dad looked as startled and apprehensive as two antelopes dropped unwittingly into a lion enclosure as they sat, side by side, joined at the hip, on the ivory sofa in the living room. I hadn't asked them to sit there and chills had run over every inch of my skin as I'd brought two steaming cups of strong Yorkshire tea through to the living room, then Mum's special Earl Grey. I'd added honey to the cup instead of lemon as a sort of peace-offering, hoping she'd calm down if she had something to complain about.

'No lemon, darling?' she asked predictably, smiling wide.

'Afraid not.'

'Goodness me, you'd think you'd have *lemon* in a place like this! But that's OK, I suppose it is *awfully* fussy of me. I'm sure it will be *fine* as it is.'

We cradled our cups in awkward silence. Mum broke the ice. 'Have you spoken to Charlie?' A quick pause.

'No.'

She clinked her shimmering pink fingernails against the

mug. 'It's just, don't you think darling, that you should give it another go?' It was the first time we'd seen each other for a year and, surprise surprise, her preoccupation was with my marital status, not with me. My hair was a different length, I'd probably lost a stone in weight, but she hadn't seemed to notice. She still looked the same, of course, a tidy tailored blazer over well-cut jeans, leather boots sticking out of the bottom, a logo on each side. Mum liked to buy brands: hated the thought that people might suspect she could only afford the plain alternative. I ignored her question.

'My only plan is to work as hard as I can at W&SP.'

'Wasp?' Dad asked.

I peeked at him, surprised by his complete absence of knowledge about my life. 'The company I work for.' Dad nodded and took a large gulp of his tea, milky residue left dripping from his moustache.

I've often wondered if Dad was my mother's first choice of husband. You'd think a prim and proper thing like Mum would marry up, that she wouldn't *dream* of turning up to dinner parties and events with someone as untidy as him. She would have paired perfectly with an executive type in a black suit and checkered tie, briefcase in one hand, eighties mobile phone in the other. Dad was, if anything, the opposite of that. His eyebrows were long and curled inwards, his hair shaggy at the back, his shirt buttons carelessly undone at the bottom, a bit of hairy belly poking through. I couldn't imagine Mum marrying for love: she just wasn't that type of woman. But their decades-long marriage was the strange piece of evidence to the contrary. Now he sat, flat-cap still on, about to open the local paper and read it for, what was probably, the second or third time today in order to avoid 'London news' or, indeed, mine.

'We can't stay long,' Mum said, sipping her tea like a sparrow, her needly hands creeping out from under her blazer.

'I have to get back to the dogs,' Dad said over the top of his paper.

'Is there someone else?' Mum asked, hopefully.

I shook my head.

'Oh, Ava.' My mother looked down at the floor. 'It's a shame. You were always such a pretty girl.'

16

Jade

I'd woken up full of hope that I'd missed Josh's reply overnight but my worst fears were realised as I'd stared at the flowery stock-photo screensaver on my phone. *No new messages.* It had taken a Herculean effort to get myself dressed and ready for work and I felt I'd almost deserved a little round of applause from my colleagues for making it in just twenty minutes late, even if I was still covered in fake tan and heavy make-up from last night's photoshoot. Kai called early, just as I'd sat down at my desk, my eyes still puffy from crying all night, my head far from ready to face the day. I looked across the floor into Ava's office. Empty. Why wasn't she in yet? Was she going to take another day off? Another example of special treatment for special Ava? *Jade, could you just pick up the pieces?*

Kai's voice was ratty. 'I called earlier but Georgette said you were running late.'

'My train was delayed.'

'I thought you walked to work?'

'Sometimes I take the train.'

'You told me last week it took longer to take the train than to walk, that you enjoyed the exercise.'

What was this, the bloody Spanish inquisition? Did he remember every detail of every conversation we'd ever had? Jeez!

I opened an email whilst I was still on the phone to him. Ava's junior had been tasked with booking Kai a hotel room for launch night. Kai lived in Oxfordshire but, when he came down to the city, had extremely exacting standards.

I knew from reviewing the booking that she'd booked the wrong one.

'Has Ava sent through your hotel details yet?'

'No, has it been done?'

'She hasn't turned up for work today but I'll chase her on it now.'

'What's going on with her lately? I've barely heard a peep.'

I left his question alone, let him sow the seeds of doubt about Ava by himself.

'Anyway, best get going, as you can imagine her absence leaves Josh and me a little in the lurch.' I opened up my email and jabbed CTRL+N into the keyboard.

Ava. Kai's wondering where his hotel booking is...

I fired off another email, taking out my frustration on her that Josh hadn't replied to my picture yet.

Why am I having to chase you on this, Ava? We really can't afford these kinds of mistakes.

I smirked, enjoying every moment of being on top for once.

Next I rounded on Georgette, she'd messed up this morning too. She was supposed to be on my side in this.

'George,' I whispered harshly, attracting her attention and that of a few others round us. 'Never tell a client, especially not Kai, that I'm running late – do you *realise* how bad that makes us all sound?'

Pairs of eyes bobbed up from their screens and stared over at me and Georgette: public humiliation was always enjoyable viewing in an open plan office and, after all, George needed to learn.

'What was I supposed to say, Jade? You weren't here,' she fought back.

'Off the top of my head?' I asked, raising my voice and standing up. 'How about... "Oh, sorry Kai, she's on the other line I'll get her to call you in a mo", or... "She's at a breakfast meeting with Kate Moss, she's schmoozing her to attend the launch, not sure when she's due back..." or "Unfortunately she had an urgent doctor's appointment, her spleen exploded this morning",' I countered, heat rising from my body.

'Fine,' she replied haughtily, ducking her head back behind her monitor, keen to end our altercation.

I put on my best disappointed teacher voice. 'If you picked up your effort level overall, small things like this phone call wouldn't be such a big problem, George. Stop slacking and you could start being successful here. At the moment you're taking too many notes from Ava's book.'

A few team members stifled their giggles: Georgette had learned her lesson this morning, that was for sure. I got up from my desk and moved towards the double doors to the office kitchen area; my stomach rumbling at the thought of the turkey and avocado sandwich I had brought for lunch in the fridge. As I closed in on it, Josh strode through, one hand on each door, throwing them apart before him. He didn't even look at me as he marched to his desk. I felt the lump in my throat building again, a little round rock bobbing up and down in the sea, and I aborted lunch in favour of the women's toilets. I slammed down the seat cover and sat, crying, too much for what the situation really was.

You're hideous! That photo you took was revolting, you really think he's interested in you? You've shown too much of yourself. You're revolting. You should have realised when it took hundreds of attempts to get just one acceptable shot. He much preferred you plain. Why on earth did you pimp yourself up like that? The voice in my head was so loud and I couldn't drown it out. *You are delusional. You spent more than a hundred quid to look that bad. You used gallons of fake tan, a shiny leg brush, an eyebrow pencil, and, even still, despite all of that stuff, that horrible picture you ended up sending him was the best you could do!* I rocked back and forth, the insults running riot. I breathed in through my nose, expanded my rib cage, out through my mouth. In through my nose, out through my mouth. In through my nose... I started to feel better. Calmer. I had to rationalise it. *He hasn't seen it yet.* Breathe in. *It hasn't even been twenty-four hours.* Breathe out. *Yes, give it a day before you start to worry.*

I grabbed reams and reams of toilet roll and patted my damp face with them. As I stumbled out of the cubicle my reflection stared back at me: what a mess. Wisps of hair had escaped from the slicked-back bun I'd had it in, my mascara ran in wavy lines down my face and a significant amount of lipstick was smudged across my right cheek. I rushed to the sink and splashed water against my cheeks, squeezing a mound of soap into a cupped hand and rubbed furiously, teasing the clumps of mascara from each eyelash. When I was happy I looked slightly less alien, I walked briskly to the kitchen, keeping my head down, opened the fridge, retrieved my sandwich, and ambled back to my desk. I shook a couple of pills into my hand and, as I swallowed them down, glanced over at his desk. He was gone.

My new-ish housemate was prowling back and forth in the kitchen when I arrived home. I rented the spare room in this run-down, two-storey terrace – no one normal had the money to buy these days – and I was irritated that this one had managed to hang around for quite so long. I was usually so adept at dispatching any would-be lodger, that the spare room should have featured a revolving door.

I overheard her talking about me as I moved inside.

'It's sad, really, I wish I could set her up… I just don't know anyone else with a BMI over 25!'

I imagined the person on the receiving end laughing.

All I wanted to do was head straight for the wine fridge and pour myself a pint of pinot. *She* would disapprove. *She* would tell me it wasn't good for me. But I barged past her and opened it anyway.

'Straight for the wine tonight, Jade? Bad day? It's no good for you, you know that don't you…'

I didn't listen to her about the booze. I finished half the bottle sitting on the battered couch by myself, then she came in and started.

'Why do you always do this, Jade? You jump straight to the worst conclusion and then straight for the wine! You think he's embarrassed by you? That he's realised you're not good enough? That his messages were just a terrible mistake?'

I'd made an error of judgment in telling her about Josh.

What was wrong with me? Why couldn't I have just kept it a total secret? A notification buzzed in. *Finally*. But it wasn't from Instagram.

Ms Jade Fernleigh, your appointment is confirmed for 10.00 Wednesday. Please call should you wish to rearrange.

I screamed. I screamed for a full minute. I hurled my phone across the room. It smashed her favourite vase. She screamed too and sprinted over to it, assessing the damage, picking up the pieces. My tears were so stupid. I knew that really. I knew it was crazy to get this worked up over a message, over a man. I just, I *really* wanted it to happen; for one of my relationships to work out for once.

She went to bed; she wasn't speaking to me. I took repeated swigs from the bottle on the floor, gearing myself up for sleep, repeating to myself that he wasn't going to text between the hours of midnight and 6 a.m. It had been over twenty-four hours now, so that meant it was over. Completely over and done with, for good. Stop thinking, I thought. Clear your mind. Nothing matters. Not the job, not Josh, not Ava. I drank some more, thinking it would help me forget, drowning it all out. I repeated the pattern. Stop thinking, stop it. Just a couple more sips… Clear your mind. One last swig.

17

Ava

My parents had left without fanfare, my mother annoyed she hadn't been able to convince me to change my mind about Charlie, my father annoyed he'd been dragged away from home, away from his routine. *Waste of a day*, I imagined him tutting to mum as they made their way back round the M4. As soon as they'd left I'd gone to sit in a nearby coffee shop: the house had reeked of Mum's too-sweet perfume and my head was sore from the smell.

As I arrived home later that evening, I was surprised to find a new phone had already arrived for me. It sat on the doormat in pristine packaging and I muttered a quick thank you that David hadn't decided to hand-deliver it. Unwrapping my new phone as I made my way through to the kitchen, I noticed the window over the sink was open a fraction, the blind that covered it billowing gently into the room. I hesitated for a moment, a bad feeling creeping up behind me, then started humming – *doesn't humming out loud make you feel better somehow? Nothing bad can happen when you're humming* – I debated whether it was a trap. I decided, on balance, it probably wasn't, and hurried over to the window, slammed the frame down and twisted the lock tight. The rational part of my mind tried to calm me down – maybe Sheff had popped in today at some point and left it like that? – but the irrational part guffawed. *Sure, and the man who's in the house right now broke in because he just wants to talk…*

I moved quickly selecting a glass from the cupboard, desperate to get upstairs and lock the bedroom door. I pushed it roughly into the American-style fridge-based water dispenser. The liquid hit the sides of the glass noisily and bubbled upwards. As I turned to leave, my finger on the light switch ready to send the room into darkness, I spotted something that caused me to drop it: a plain envelope sitting ominously in the middle of the kitchen island. *Ava* scrawled across the front.

Visions of Charlie in the flat streaked through my mind and I heard a smash as thousands of tiny pieces of glass scattered across the floor, my dropped glass drenching my shins in water. I winced as I crunched over the shards and frantically ripped at the envelope. Another note.

Ava, your security arrangements leave a lot to be desired. What's the point of a fancy CCTV camera outside if you're just going to leave the kitchen window unlocked? Next time you do that I'll be here, waiting for you to come home. For now, I just want you to call me back. Please. We need to talk.

All my love,
Charlie.

My hand shook as I held the note and read it over and over again, hoping the words before me would change. The tone was different: no more, *I still love you*, or, *it's not too late*. This was threatening, plain and simple. A last-ditch attempt to get me to speak to him. I looked up again at the window over the sink. That was how Charlie had broken in. I held my new phone heavy in my hand and debated calling 999. Then I heard a noise, a slow and deliberate creak that called out from somewhere behind me: from somewhere deep inside the house. I spun round quickly. What if Charlie was still here? I stood stock still, listening out for the slightest confirmation I was right, but my ears were greeted only by the sound of my quickening breath and the thud of my own terrified heart. My body trembled, my feet covered in cold water, and I dropped the note back on to the countertop. I crept into the hallway, balanced on tiptoes, listening out for anything that would give his position away.

Another crack. It was coming from the lounge. I hurried silently to the closed door and pressed my ear against it. I didn't want to go in, but there it was again. The sound. The creaking. I braced myself to barge through the door, but realised I was woefully ill-equipped for a duel and raced back into the kitchen, grabbing the largest carving knife from the block on the side. I dashed back to my previous position, mouth dry, senses heightened to fever pitch, knife wobbling erratically by my side. I wasn't actually going to stab him, was I? And what if it wasn't Charlie but something darker, someone more dangerous: Olivia angry with me for wearing her clothes, sleeping in her bed, stealing her father's affections. I counted to three under my breath, then crashed through the door, a cacophony of sound and shouts following as I prepared to face the worst.

My eyes darted all over the darkness, over every shape, every silhouette in the room, but nothing. The crack called out again. I thumped the light on. Empty. The radiator next to the door whirred and crackled sheepishly. My rage grew and I took advantage of the adrenaline racing laps round my body to zoom from room to room, flinging open doors and cupboards as I searched, shouting and grunting as I braced myself to confront anything I came into contact with. I caught sight of myself in the dark windows, my eyes wild, my hair loose, the knife glinting in my hand. What was this place turning me into?

Eventually, I concluded my search and, even though the house was clear, I still felt deathly afraid. I walked slowly upstairs to the bedroom, blade in hand, and closed the door behind me. I used the last of my energy to manoeuvre the chest of drawers up against it and tucked the knife under my pillow. How long could I go on like this?

I tossed in the cotton covers that night, moonlight seeping through the gaps in the shutters, calling to me. *I know what you did. Does anyone else? Does anyone else know the real reason you and Jade fell out? The real reason you're both terrified of the other: the secrets you could spill, the lives you could ruin, the truth you could out.*

18

Jade

The sun, blinding, invited itself into my front room at an unnatural hour.

What had happened last night?

My mind was foggy and I was slow, disoriented, maybe a little drunk still. I saw the wine bottle, smashed vase, abandoned phone. I groaned. Then thought: Maybe? Could there be a message? Judging by the upturned bottle, I was probably completely out of it last night, I could easily have missed it. I stumbled on my hands and knees like an injured ape, quickly, towards my phone, praying I hadn't damaged it, frantic to get past the lock screen. Nothing. I navigated to my inbox, the text confirming my appointment still there, laughing at me. Sneering. *You? You thought Josh Stein was seriously interested in* you? *You haven't been to the dentist for* five years. *Your teeth are a horror show, like a portrait of someone from the 1600s before the invention of toothpaste. You didn't brush them last night, did you? No. Didn't think so. You just let the wine rot, rot, rot away at them.*

I dragged myself into the shower, clawed at the knots in my hair and cleared away all the fake tan and failure that still clung to my body. I shook a couple of pills into my cupped hand. They weren't making me feel any better recently. Maybe I should up my dose? My housemate was quiet, I didn't want to see her this morning anyway, best let what happened between us yesterday blow over.

The enormous clock in the grand reception area of Watson & Stein Partners confirmed my suspicion that I was running appallingly late. I could tell Georgette had been talking about me; probably wondering where I was, discussing how often I came in late, how I didn't work hard enough, how there was no way I'd get the job ahead of Ava.

I spent most of the afternoon staring at the computer's time and date settings, watching the second hand meander round the clock face, willing six o'clock on so I could leave and down a case of wine.

Reception I.D. sprang up on my phone and I turned the dial volume down to one so it didn't break my head open with the noise of its violent ringing.

'What?' I asked impatiently.

'There are flowers for you here, in reception.'

My ears pricked up. *Could he...?*

'I'll be down in two.' I found a new lease of life and my legs leapt into action carrying me downstairs to receive the delivery. Bright oranges, pinks and yellows blossomed out of the wrapping and I searched for a note.

'Was there a card?' I directed my question at the perfectly-proportioned socialite on reception.

'Umm... Maybe this is it?' She produced a note which had clearly fallen off the side. It said FAO: Jade Fernleigh. I traced my finger round the rough section the sellotape had pulled from the packaging and matched the two up. I ripped open the card, my excitement barely containable.

Dear Ava,

Hopefully Jade can look after these whilst you're away. I know you're going through a rough time at the moment so please take as long as you need to recover.

Also, I didn't thank you properly for the thoughtful birthday gift you sent, so these flowers are extra special – my favourites!

Kai x

She'd sent Kai a birthday present. Was this a joke? The receptionist was looking at me, waiting for me to tell her what the note said.

'Ah, that's nice,' I said, looking wistfully at the disgusting card in front of me.

She chirped back, sensing gossip. 'Who are they from?'

I tapped the side of my nose twice and gave her a knowing look.

'Tease,' she called as I walked away.

I called the lift from reception and, when the doors closed, tore the card into tiny pieces and stuffed them into my cardigan pocket. I'd dispose of them later.

The lift doors opened and I strode into the kitchen area, pulled a pint glass from the cupboard and filled it with water. I cut the stems one by one and placed each of them in the glass. I walked quietly back to my desk with it and set the flowers down, obscuring what would normally be my view of Josh.

He wasn't in the office today, but as soon as he got back I wanted him to be jealous. I wanted him to think there was someone else.

19

Ava

Tonight was the annual summer party, a lavish affair at the expense of our clients' generous marketing budgets. Georgette appeared at my office door and let herself in, a package under her arm and a bottle in her hand. 'Here's that nail varnish you wanted to borrow.' Then, the real reason for her visit: 'Urgh, she's driving me *mad* today.'

She nodded towards Jade with her angular chin. Georgette's vulpine features matched her prickly personality and, save for the fact being close to George had taught me it was useful to have her on side – she'd steal all your secrets and scream them from the rooftops left to her own devices – I knew she played both sides: she'd repeat anything I said about Jade back to her, and vice versa.

'What's happened now?' I took the nail varnish from Georgette and applied careful strokes of the gold shimmering gel to each fingernail.

'She's sulking. In fact, she's been sulking for *days*. You know, I've been starting to wonder if she's bipolar or something. She goes from high to low like a fucking yo-yo.'

I nodded along with Georgette's attempts at a diagnosis for Jade's personality but kept my concentration fixed on applying the nail varnish. The colour was perfect for tonight, it made me feel powerful and feminine and indestructible and a night away from Olivia's and out with lots of people was exactly what I needed. I was trying my best to be positive. One day at a time.

Georgette continued her rant, 'What do you think she's gonna wear tonight? Probably some rank tunic dress or ill-fitting pencil skirt as per.'

I giggled along for her benefit.

'How about you?' she asked. 'Because *this* arrived downstairs this morning and I can't help feeling it might just be something *gawjus* for this evening.' She handed me the large box she'd been carrying, *Westwood* splashed across the front. 'Don't look so frightened,' she shrieked. 'Jesus! You'd think you'd been sent it by a ghost.'

I couldn't bring myself to laugh along this time and snatched it from her, feeling faint. I made some excuses and eventually she left – the only reason she'd come in here was to watch my reaction to receiving the package she'd probably already looked inside. What she didn't know was who probably used to wear it.

The great dining room of Taften Manor, David's revered country house, had transformed into the ultimate summer retreat, runs of creeping ivy snaked their way up the walls, gathering in the centre of the ceiling and twisted round the base of an enormous, champagne-coloured chandelier.

Rich, white linen covered each table, topped with gold crockery and cutlery at every place setting, a stunning floral centrepiece tying it all together.

'Isn't it perfect?' David's hand was in the small of my back as he appeared by my side.

His touch was firm and assured and it made me jump: why wasn't he more guarded in his affection? Did he really want everyone to whisper about us?

I moved away from his grasp. 'It's wonderful, David, the place looks truly stunning.'

His eyes made their way down my body. He was pleased I was wearing the dress he'd sent.

'I could say the same about you...' he remarked under his breath.

He forced me to twirl for him, taking my hand above my head and twisting me round. The dress he'd chosen was a flashy flesh-hugging number with a plunging neckline and slight train. There were cut-outs at the waist and slashes down the arms. I felt like I was wearing an expensive cage.

I tried to divert his attention from looking at me like that.

'Is there a seating plan?'

'Don't worry about that, darling, you'll be in good company.'

My pulse was racing, my breath shallow. Was I reading this situation correctly? Had David taken me away from Charlie just so he could control me instead? Where was his conscience in doing that? I couldn't work him out: it wasn't like he was forcing himself on me exactly, or being aggressive, it was just that he wanted to get too close. Wear his clothes, live under his rules, dance to his drum... The other half of me argued: Wouldn't a normal person be absolutely thrilled if someone bought them a designer party dress to wear, gave them somewhere beautiful to live, helped them out of a horrible relationship? What was wrong with me? I shouted down the doubts and told myself he was just being friendly. Perhaps too friendly for someone who was supposed to be my boss, but still: I'd spent more time with David than anyone else in recent weeks. He was the only one who'd really known what I'd been going through and maybe he realised that. He just wanted to help pick me up. I told myself David was probably like this with all of his close pals; I imagined people saying things like, 'Oh, don't mind David, he might shower you with gifts but he's completely harmless: a heart of gold that man.'

As more staff arrived, we moved to the adjoining drawing room for a Champagne and canapé reception. Dark wood panels clad each wall, interspersed with full-length bookcases which required little ladders to reach the top shelves. As I popped a tiny blini in my mouth, I made out Georgette standing in a conspiratorial clump of women in the corner. Long limbs stretched out of shimmering dresses, cheekbones sharpened with contour, imperfections ironed out with heavy make-up. They were bent in towards each other, giggling. Then George, the loudest, their leader, motioned for me to come over. I wished they hadn't caught me looking.

'Hi girls,' I said as I neared their exclusive little group. 'You all look gorgeous.'

It was true. George had chosen extra-thick false lashes to accompany her outfit tonight, and the other girls in the group must have got ready together they were so homogenous in their beauty. They almost looked like triplets, with identical caramel-coloured locks, petite bird-like figures and grey-blue eyes. No wonder George was head of the pack, she was the only one with any personality.

'Nothing compared to you, Ava,' Georgette cooed. 'That dress is stunning. We're all dying to know who sent it... go on, who's the secret admirer?'

Oh dear, I thought. By morning the entire office would be gossiping about my non-existent new relationship. I decided to lie. 'I bought it myself, actually.'

'Jade seemed to think it had come from David.'

I looked Georgette dead in her glitter-lidded eyes and she angled her neck towards Jade, blowing her nose next to the drinks table by herself.

'But I should know better than to listen to a word she says about you. Sorry.'

I thought on my feet, reasoning she'd already seen who had sent the Westwood package to the office and that, on balance, Jade probably had nothing to do with it.

'David has a contact who sent it to me, but that's all.'

Georgette changed the subject quickly, she'd already got all the information she needed and she wasn't about to let anything get in the way of a good story.

'Told you she'd be wearing a tunic dress,' she giggled. 'Though I'm not sure why she's so attached to it: it makes her look like a fucking inpatient.' The rest of the group spluttered with laughter behind her.

At that moment, a woman announced that we should all take our seats in the main hall and I was able to extract myself from Georgette's clutches to follow the crush of people funnelling through the double doors to the main room.

Jade's emerald eyes were all over me as David sat down and kissed my cheek. She'd be hating this, cursing me a hundred times over for sitting at the top table without her. I hoped she hadn't seen him touch me earlier. I hoped no one had.

He rose to speak and the room hushed.

'I'd like to welcome you all to my favourite home and thank each and every one of you for another fantastic year of W&SP PR.'

Polite applause rippled around the room. The elephant in the room, of course, was Olivia. I noted he'd said a fantastic year of PR, not a fantastic year. 'I think we've actually managed to get through this one without a dogging scandal!'

The applause made way for nervous laughter and someone shouted out *Don't speak too soon!* from somewhere near the back. We'd had an incident last year: one of our restaurant clients' car parks had sprung up on a load of forums as the number-one dogging hotspot in the UK. Before we knew it, the car park was heaving with topless creeps and the story had made national news. Then, the mummy trolls had come for the restaurant, reservations went down by 80 per cent – you'd have thought the doggers would have booked a few tables to help us out, but no – and the brand's Twitter page crashed due to the amount of people writing to us expressing their outrage. We'd all suspected there was a high likelihood the most vocal mummies 'worried about it happening in their area' were also the most prolific doggers, the ones who'd turn up first wearing masks. Beware the loudmouth trolls: they were always the biggest hypocrites.

David chuckled in response which instantly lightened

the mood, staff round the room noticeably relieved that it didn't appear their boss was about to launch into a fifteen-minute speech about his personal loss.

'I've been talking to a few colleagues about the scandals we *have* faced this year, however... and I'd like to share a couple we've managed to keep out of the headlines with you tonight.'

His audience was eating out of the palm of his hand and he certainly had a way of connecting with people: he was so charismatic and captivating. Growing 'oooh' sounds began one after the other as David took a pregnant pause before diving in.

'In January, we learnt that our new client, kids' clothing store Gracie & Maine, had unwittingly hired a convicted paedophile to run its flagship store in Cambridge.'

A group at the back of the room familiar with the story squawked in recognition.

'We had to introduce the concept of background checks to them, and stop a vigilante group from coming down with reality TV cameras to catch the guy in the act. Apparently, they'd been stalking the shop for weeks trying to get images of him looking sideways at the kids. Disgusting. Then, in April, the CEO of not-for-profit client Hollywell Health stole three million pounds from the company's books, then used it to pay for numerous plastic surgery procedures. A team of W&SPs managed to limit that potential bombshell to just an eighth of a page in the regional paper, and are doing their best to keep her brand new double Gs out of Page 3.'

His delivery was smooth and I admired how naturally public speaking came to him.

'And, finally, my favourite: it came to our attention earlier this year that a randy manager at hotel client, Lokal, had installed a network of cameras in each guest bathroom on the property.'

'What?! I stayed there!' a bloke shouted from towards the front of the crowd.

'I doubt he was spying on you, Trevor.'

Trevor was the caretaker, bless him, and the years hadn't been particularly kind. Gentle laughter flowed round the room and the people either side of Trevor put their arms round him.

'Ironically, the hotel's *existing* security cameras caught him watching back the footage in his office. But, that's not the best bit, he'd watch his videos in a giant pink tutu and eat packets of sliced ham at the same time. Don't worry: ham is off the menu tonight, I wouldn't want anyone to get too carried away...'

Applause fired up again and David reiterated his thanks to everyone before taking his seat.

'That was brilliant.' I beamed, meaning it.

He smiled, his lips curling at the edges. 'I'm glad you thought so, darling.'

20

Jade

She was practically dribbling as David gave his opening speech, salivating over every word, wearing a dress that barely covered her, giggling like a stupid schoolgirl by his side. I bet she'd begged to sit there next to him, all saucer-eyed and drop-mouthed in his office after work.

I dug my fingernails into my palms so hard I felt blood running down my wrist before the pain of them puncturing my skin. Tonight was going to be long. Josh wasn't here, hadn't texted to tell me why he couldn't make it, and still hadn't replied to my picture. It really was over and done with; love affair in ashes before we'd even lit the match. He was probably sleeping with someone else.

I didn't talk to the nobodies either side of me. I wasn't here to make friends, I'd been here for Josh, but now that was in tatters there was no point in me being here at all. Once again, thanks to Ava, I was on the back foot. It was so infuriating, just when I'd had a foothold on the job, she'd found a way to outdo me. Again.

I picked my way round melon and Parma ham, shut down any conversation that came my way, and thudded a bottle of red in front of me as if to mark my territory.

I think my propensity for ending second-best stemmed from the fact I was yet to actually *experience* what coming first felt like. I could only imagine the head-high jubilation of it all, that feeling of self-satisfied smugness, the elation of taking joy from others' loss. I *longed* for how that felt. I'd always been the girl behind the winner, vowing to work harder, telling myself I'd be her one day. But, if you haven't done something before you're an adult, *when* you're an adult it's so much harder to achieve: riding a bike, swimming, making friends, learning a language. I'd been second-best growing up too, the unnecessary third-wheel to my parents' perfect bicycle of a relationship. They were a pair of distant academics who preferred study, and each other, to me. I still wondered why they even had a child. My mother once told me my father had tried to move us back to Hong Kong, where he was from, when I was little but that I'd been 'such a fussy infant', falling ill whenever we journeyed to visit relatives on his side, 'for attention'. Then there was my only boyfriend: perpetually indifferent about my presence in his life, then actively disinterested when I suggested spending the rest of it together. At school, in every subject, there was always some girl with her hair in pigtails better than me. In anything sporty I was always bottom of the lot, ditto music, ditto drama. And now work. The only thing that had changed, in fact, was the way I viewed it: when I was younger I didn't think it would always be like this, I was remarkably stoic about it, zen. *My time will come.* Now I was running out of time and, frankly, I was just angry.

The tedious four-course dinner service finally came to a close and I decided to prop myself up at the bar. My aim: to drink a sufficient amount of red wine to get through the next half an hour of 'dancing' before the first taxis arrived.

Though I'd managed to avoid her so far this evening, my luck was about to run out, and I clocked Georgette tottering towards me in a shiny pink ball gown, boobs first. Was Barbie really an acceptable look for anyone over the age of nine?

'Having a good night?' she hiccupped, before yelling at the barman two feet away from her that she wanted a G&T with *fresh* limes. She probably thought that request was classy. I thought about shouting an order for a G&T with stale limes to make her feel stupid. *The staler the better.*

I rolled my eyes and drank some more.

'What happened to Josh, babe? Thought you was gonna get lucky tonight?'

Her eyes were practically cross-eyed she was so drunk. I wasn't sure Barbie would approve of that. How did she know about Josh?

'He's not here. Not that I'd ever tell *you* about my love life, you're like a walking foghorn.'

I wanted her to feel the hate I felt.

'Why are you always such a bitch?'

Her retort took me by surprise and I balked at her assertion, almost spraying her with a fountain of red wine.

'You can't speak to me like that!'

'I'm serious, you treat everyone like shit but expect us all to kiss your arse. Well, not me, not any more.'

She made a sort of 'humph' noise and waddled off to rejoin her cackling bunch of hags. I'd make her regret that comment on Monday morning.

Luckily, David didn't make a habit of asking juniors what they thought of their seniors, so her 'real' opinion of me shouldn't affect my chances of securing the job. I'd probably have to fire her if I did get it though, I couldn't have someone with that little respect for my authority on the team.

My eyes danced lazily from person to person, following a number of my dimly lit colleagues as they navigated behaving appropriately at a work function whilst being peer-pressured to drink copious amounts of booze, when I noticed something interesting towards the back of the room. I moved my position slightly to get a better angle: it was Ava and David, dancing, close. I watched them intently as her twirls, spins and giggles turned dopey, slow and clumsy. She probably hadn't eaten all day to fit into that dress so it had only taken a couple of sips of wine to get her white-girl-wasted. They were dancing away from the main pack and I shifted in my chair so I could follow them as they moved towards the far corner of the room. Then I watched, jaw to the floor, as he pressed her against the wall and kissed her. Both her arms hung floppily by her sides. She whispered something in his ear.

Whatever she'd said had an immediate impact and David practically dragged her out of the dining room and through a door away from the crowds. I had to follow. I had to see what happened next.

I picked my way through the dancefloor, avoiding a drunk girl with knots in her hair, pivoting round her half-full glass as she held it at a precarious forty-five-degree angle, ducking round men who, eight pints down, had decided incessant jumping up and down was an acceptable dance move, and navigated round the centipede-like lines of women dragging each other out towards the toilets.

My head was spinning as I reached the door David and Ava had exited moments earlier. I pushed it open casually and pulled my phone out, ready to look like I was making a call if I found them on the other side. Nothing. I looked left and right quickly, assessing which way they might have gone, deciding that left, ironically, felt right, and marched up the corridor towards a small flight of stairs. The focus of my mission had sobered me up slightly and the floor no longer moved up and down like I was on a treacherous ferry crossing. Round the corner I spotted a lift and, above it, the number was changing as it made its way up the building: one, two, three, four, five. *Five.* I heard a robotic voice. I jabbed my finger into the call button. I wasn't about to stop now. I waited a lifetime for the lift to arrive and, as soon as the doors opened in front of me, pushed my body in through the tiny gap, smashing the button for floor five. *Come on, come on, come on.* The machine creaked and groaned then, finally, arrived. The doors parted as though two lethargic snails were at the controls and I made out two bodies shuffling down the musty corridor in front of me.

Crap.

I moved fast, powering my way out of the gap as soon as it was big enough and pressed my body against the wall to the right of the lift, hoping the archway ahead would sufficiently shelter me from their view. A robotic proclamation, *Doors opening*, followed, as slow as the lift itself, sounding out about a minute after the doors had actually opened. I held my breath. *Dear God, please don't let him turn round and walk back here.* I waited, not wanting to take any chances, and observed my surroundings. The corridor wasn't unusual, it featured the same red carpet as the ground floor: a deep, regal colour flecked with gold. The stone arch I was cowering behind looked ancient, though, and was probably an original feature.

I heard shuffling in the distance: David and Ava were on the move again so I took a chance and poked my head tentatively round the arch. My instinct was right. She was in his arms, being carried like a newlywed, nuzzled against his neck. My phone was still in my hand. The door was open to a room beyond. I raised my mobile and flicked to camera mode. I zoomed in. He turned his body towards me, his eyes on the door, moving sideways to slip her body through the gap more easily. I took a picture. Blackmail. I had it.

21

Ava

A phone rang, loud and obnoxious, vibrating its way around a hard surface nearby. My body stiffened as something moved next to me. It groaned. The vibrations softened, surrounded by flesh, then stopped. A clatter reverberated round the room as the phone slammed back down on the hard surface. Silence. Where was I? My brain stuck in neutral. Who was next to me? Too scared to look. What was that smell?

An acidic, tangy, aroma floated nearby and my hand twitched, seeking out the source, an alien limb more interested than I was to figure out the puzzle. I kept my eyes clamped shut; I desperately didn't want to have to wake up and face whatever reality was before me. My fingers dabbed a wet puddle not far from my face and I knew right away: vomit. I couldn't ignore this any more. In one quick motion I sat up and my eyes, ears, smell, touch and taste fired simultaneously; all five senses assaulted by the scene before me.

A shaft of light burned through a small gap in the red curtains, dust dancing in its path. It illuminated my dress from the night before, folded neatly and placed on a chair in the corner of the room. I sat on a lavish four-poster bed with antique wooden posts and gentle cottons overhead. Two thick metal hoops hung off the headboard; I could only imagine what for. David lay next to me, dozing quietly, so incongruous in this setting I almost didn't recognise him. What was he *doing* here? What was *I* doing here? Wait. Was this his bedroom? The only sound was his breath in and out. The smell of my pool of sick mixed with the stale stench of sleep and clung to my nostrils. My mouth was dry and sore and tasted more of regret and shame and confusion than anything else. I reached down. Where was my underwear? Why did I feel like I'd done something very, very stupid?

Colours and pictures started to come back to me and I remembered dancing with David to 'Sweet Child O' Mine' in the dining room. I recalled his stubble, the whisky on his breath, his eyes on my chest, how he'd been close to me. Had he asked to kiss me? It had been dark, his hands had been on my back, hungrily moving south. I hadn't wanted this.

'David?' I called timidly, my voice a whisper, breaking slightly over the second half of his name. My throat was like sandpaper.

'Yes, darling?' He didn't open his eyes.

'What are we doing here?'

He raised an eyebrow in his slumber and his eyelid lazily followed. 'What do you *think* we're doing here, darling?'

His voice was different. It was almost like he was mocking me.

'I was sick,' I said, my way of explaining this situation couldn't be what it looked like.

'Urgh, clean yourself up, then come back to bed.'

His eye closed again and he rolled onto his side.

Like a robot I obeyed him and padded into the bathroom, my stomach cramping as I tried to repress a wave of nausea. A huge bathtub looked out over fields of lavender and the dregs of an empty tube of bubble bath dripped to the floor. His and hers sinks stood in the corner. But we weren't his and hers. That was never the plan. He was an incredible, powerful, brilliant man and, sure, we'd grown closer recently but *this* was never what I wanted. Not ever. I didn't even remember drinking very much last night, I'd promised myself…

I cupped my hands under the steady flow of the tap and dabbed my face back to life with the freezing water. I studied my reflection in the mirror: puffy, pale, possessed. I didn't look like myself at all.

I sat on the toilet for a moment, about to pee, the cramps getting worse, when a realisation dawned on me.

I had to check, before I washed away the evidence for good.

I angled my fingers into the toilet bowl and held them underneath myself for a moment.

Then I moved them to my nose.

Sniffed.

The smell was unmistakable.

My knees gave way and I sank to the floor, my morality in tatters, clutching the toilet bowl. What had I done? A ball of emotion built inside me but I had to try to control it. I couldn't cry. I had to get out of here.

'Ava?' David's voice. 'Are you OK in there?'

I stood up, forgetting completely that I needed the loo, and straightened the T-shirt I was in – was this his? – pulling it down at the front over myself. I tentatively opened the door and took a step out.

'Oh dear,' he chuckled. 'Why so shy?'

'No, I—'He interrupted my stuttering.

'I don't want to undermine your attempt at modesty but I can see your lovely little bottom in the mirror behind you, darling. Perhaps some underwear would help?'

My cheeks burned under his scrutiny. He thought this was funny. I shuffled over to the pile of clothes and pulled out the white underwear I'd worn last night. It was miniscule, chosen simply because it was the only piece I owned that wouldn't have shown under the delicate silk of the gown I'd worn last night.

'Perhaps you should have worn something a little less, well, see-through, if you were planning on being coy this morning?' He pursed his lips, he was enjoying this. He was one of those people that thought your choice of clothing meant you were fair game.

'Come back to bed.'

He was lying on his back, his chest bare, super-lean, his lower body covered with the bed sheets. Was he naked under there? One hand supported his head as he watched me struggle with the answer to his question.

'I was sick,' I said again.

'In the bed?' He looked to his side and saw the puddle of congealed sea bream and boiled new potatoes in a perfect puddle and sprang out from the covers. Which answered my question; he was naked, all right.

'Oh, God! Revolting. I'm getting in the shower.'

He strode across the floor with the bravado of a matador-slaying bull. 'Perhaps you need one too, judging by that mess?'

I stayed exactly where I was, shocked, unable to conjure a single memory of how I had got here. I went over the sequence of events once more: we'd been dancing, his breath had smelt like whisky, his hands had been all over me. I could remember that. Then nothing. *Nothing.* If I could just recall how we'd got to this point then maybe I wouldn't feel this uneasy. He must have told me something that had changed everything, shifted the entire way we looked at each other, otherwise why would I have done this?

'Get in here!' His voice called out, a haunting wail above the splatter of the rain shower in the walk-in cubicle that occupied the breadth of the bathroom. If I'd really wanted this six hours ago then why did I feel so repulsed by this man now?

My mind was slow and I didn't answer. I sat dejectedly on the floor in my stupid pants and borrowed shirt and went through the situation in my head again: David was my boss. I had an enormous amount of respect and admiration for him. He'd helped me immensely. But he was older than my dad. Up until last night I'd never considered him as someone I'd wanted to sleep with but, for whatever reason – probably alcohol, or guilt, maybe – I'd changed my mind. I couldn't imagine David had forced himself on me, he was a lot of things but was he really capable of that? Either way, there wasn't a lot I could do about it now and for the next couple of hours my priorities were to get back to the house, the house David owned, and try a hell of a lot harder to remember what had happened. Then I could think about what to do next.

This man was in charge of my job and the place I called home. I definitely couldn't accuse him of anything I wasn't one hundred per cent sure about.

He got out of the shower, annoyed I hadn't joined him, and gathered our belongings, then we travelled back to London together in his chauffeur-driven Mercedes. I wore one of his dressing gowns over my T-shirt and underwear and counted my blessings that no one else from the office had stayed overnight. How was I supposed to tell David I wasn't interested in him like this? Why had I let things get to this point? I'd moved into his house, I'd accepted every offer of help, I'd turned up wearing the dress he'd bought for me: it was obvious, wasn't it, that I'd led him on. This was all my own fault.

As I dove into feelings of shame and self-loathing the car made good progress, the fields and greenery giving way to the skyrise buildings and dusty greys of the city after just half an hour. We made idle chit-chat and I did my best to hide my fear from him. I didn't want to make him feel uncomfortable, I'd already rejected him once this morning.

He pressed the intercom button that connected him with the chauffeur.

'Can you put the shield up?'

A black pane of glass whirred into action and erected itself between us and the driver.

'I wanted some privacy for a moment,' he said.

I nodded and evaded his eye contact, staring down into my lap instead.

'I had a wonderful time last night, darling. Did you?'

I looked from side to side, my eyebrows creased in confusion.

I know what you've done.

'Yes,' I said shakily, trying to hide the truth.

'You seem very... quiet.'

'I – I'm not sure I'm ready for this. I'm sorry.'

I smiled at him, my voice wretched.

'Ah,' he said, closing up. Protecting himself.

'Can I just take the weekend to think about everything? You know my head's not on straight at the moment, I didn't really expect all this to happen so quickly.' Or at all. 'I have so much on my mind.'

He put his hand over mine. 'I'm sorry, darling, I didn't want to complicate things for you. Take all the time you need.'

We rolled up outside the marbled pillars of Olivia's home and I started to feel trapped. Not just by him, but by Charlie – whose latest note was probably waiting for me inside – and by all the bad decisions I'd made recently. Perhaps it would just be easier to run away from it all while there was still a chance I could get out unscathed. I'd been so wrong to think David's help would come without strings attached and it was too late now: I was stuck in them, both arms twisted and tied up against my back, his ropes cutting deep into my neck.

22

Jade

It was Monday morning and I'd spent the weekend studying the picture I'd taken of Ava and David. I knew it basically by heart now, could describe it so perfectly I reckon I could have drawn it from scratch if someone had asked. Red carpet, white door with shiny silver bolts, David's hands round her body, moving her through the gap, fuzzy shadows in the bedroom beyond. Her dress wasn't sitting nearly as pretty as it had earlier in the night and had slipped to reveal much more of her cleavage than she'd probably anticipated. Her skin didn't look human, so full of booze it had turned the colour of old tequila. Her head hung back, mid-cackle perhaps, excited for her night with the boss. David was expressionless.

It was dynamite.

If David offered her the job, I'd leak this picture to the office: let them decide if they wanted to work at a place where you had to sleep with the CEO to get ahead. David would drop Ava in minutes and I'd be ready, then, to take her place. This photo was the perfect insurance policy and it couldn't have come at a better time.

23

Ava

Wrapped up in one of my oldest and comfiest sweatshirts, I'd spent the weekend thinking long and hard about Friday night. I'd ignored the solitary call I'd had from home and had disconnected myself from strangers on social media. I'd been lonely for the best part of a year now but this weekend had felt the lowest of all: the one person on my side I could no longer trust. The one person who'd been able to help me get out of my mess with Charlie had landed me right in the thick of another. What was I supposed to do now?

On the one hand, I loved my job, had great prospects at W&SP, was being protected and helped by David, he'd been kind enough to give me somewhere to live, cared about me, listened to my problems; but, on the other, we'd slept together, I hadn't remembered a second of it, and now he was clearly hoping to make things more serious between us. But did I really want to leave my job over it? I didn't want to walk away from everything I'd built at W&SP, and I wasn't ready to give up on being Team Head over a mistake: not yet anyway.

Late on Monday I headed up to the fourth floor – David's office – and knocked on his door. I knew what I needed to do. My thud was heavy, purposeful, and I felt like I was standing at the gates of Mordor. *I know what you've done. I know what you've done.* His plastic PA wasn't on duty, thankfully, so hopefully my visit would remain under wraps. The door swung open and I stepped into the dim light inside, breathing in a heady mix of tequila and black coffee, rails of cigarette smoke, the timeless scent of new leather. He sat, as I imagined he always did, at the far, far end of the room. His hair was gelled back in its classic style, his fingers methodically tapping away the burnt-out end of his asbestos-stick, yellowed from years of nicotine abuse. He didn't often smoke round me and there was something really jarring about watching him do it indoors. Wasn't it illegal? I supposed laws didn't really apply to people like David.

He hadn't looked at me yet, his eyes fixed on something outside the floor-length window next to his desk, the window he used to keep a watchful eye on the city below from the safety of his towering fortress.

'David?' I approached him and sat in the spare seat opposite.

'Ava.'

'Is now a good time? To talk I mean?'

'As good as any.' He smiled to put me at ease. It didn't.

'First of all, I want to apologise. I was disgustingly drunk at the party and, honestly, I'm so ashamed of my behaviour, being sick, ending up in bed with you, it's not how I would ordinarily behave.'

'Please, don't apologise, we've all been young Ava. Even me.'

I resisted the urge to tell him what happened had nothing to do with being young.

'Secondly, I wanted to ask if we could try to go back to the way things were. No special treatment, no exceptions because of the other night. Just normal. I think I can do that if you're open to it as well?'

'Of course.' He looked downcast, ominous, then he pressed his hand to his desk phone and punched in a number. 'You can come through, now.' There was movement from his bathroom and I turned my head to face the direction of the sound.

'Do we have company?' I asked, looking round. 'Do you want me to leave?'

At that moment a woman with a chest full of silicone emerged from David's bathroom, her hair tied half-up in a bun, half-down flowing over each of her tiny shoulders. I got up to greet her, sure that I'd seen her before. My mind whirred, trying to place her face, when I matched it up with the cleaner who'd been in my flat. But why hadn't he told me she was here? What had she overheard?

'Hi...' I stuttered.

'Ava, this is Oxana.' She didn't even look at me.

'Will you be long?' she asked David, her thick accent rounding her words. Who was this woman? Was something going on between them? She had to be more to him than just an occasional cleaner. The thought that they were romantically linked relaxed me. Perhaps I didn't mean that much to him, after all. Oxana floated, barely disturbing the air round her, and disappeared through a door on the other side of the office.

'Oxana is a… friend, from Russia. She's here in London for a few days and has some business to attend to.'

Clearly, I thought.

24

Jade

Sorry for my radio silence. The past week has been crazy. I flew to Monaco and had a tonne of work to do afterwards. Forgive me? And that picture... I've been waiting for things to calm down to enjoy it properly. You're hiding some serious talent beneath those black dresses – you know that, don't you?

I was practically hyperventilating as I read his message, my nostrils gloriously flared, desperate to suck in as much of the air surrounding me as possible. Maybe he'd spotted the flowers on my desk, or was responding to the fact that I'd barely looked at him since I sent the picture. Either way, my plans had worked.

I couldn't wait to write back, my head drunk and dizzy from each exceptional word before me. *Note to self: Don't go so bloody crazy when he doesn't text back in the future. There's probably just a major work emergency on his hands, that's all, it's not that he doesn't like you.* I hit reply. It was a miracle I hadn't given in and double-texted so I did away with the 'make him wait an hour rule' that Georgette had been telling me about and ploughed on.

> I totally understand, it sounds like things have been really busy. I'm glad you liked the pic ;-)

> I felt pretty silly throwing on my old bikini and taking it straight after work, it was so rushed!

I only had to wait a couple of moments before he replied again. Bloody hell, it's so easy when people just *text back!*

> If you think you can do better, I'm more than happy to sit back and be your judge.

Bugger. Another photoshoot. I wish I hadn't thrown away my shiny leg brush.

I'd woken to a picture-perfect example of a stunning summer day and the sun, glorious and gold, transformed my usually dreary commute; I whistled as I walked, letting the blossom-scented air fill my lungs, blowing out the cobwebs that had formed from taking the train too often. I stopped to listen to chaffinches sing as they flew from tree to tree, gazed at frantic little squirrels chasing one another up fences and back down again. I sucked in the smell of flowers and grass and *life*. I shimmied, skipped and clicked my way through a veritable performance of a walk. And

I could hardly help it! For I was pumped full with love! Fit to burst with bliss! Wasn't it just *amazing* how a bit of sunshine could wake up the world?

Before I took a seat at my desk, I located my phone in the depths of my rucksack and snuck into the far cubicle of the women's toilets. I sat on the plastic toilet lid and flicked through the messages I'd exchanged with Josh last night after I'd sent him a heavily filtered flurry of sexy selfies. I'd finally hit my stride around pictures 835–850 when I'd discovered if you pulled your flesh to one side with a hand out of shot it could hide all manner of sins. I almost just wanted to check the messages were real, that I hadn't dozed off and dreamt the whole thing.

You should wear green more often, it would bring out those unreal eyes of yours.

My wardrobe is black, black and black I'm afraid. I like to be professional, you know, it's an art lost on lots of people in this office.

I think you'd look good in green... why don't you buy something green for me?

Like what?

Like... underwear?

Right OK. But can I choose? Because I have lots of stipulations to do with the kinds of things I like to wear.

Since when did you set the rules, miss?

Since just now, I guess… handsome.

After that he'd sent me a picture: it was one I'd already seen on his Instagram account – he had his top off, each ab bulging at the camera, his body sweaty and solid from the workout the accompanying caption told me he'd just finished. His hair was wet, blacker than black, and he had a white towel slung haphazardly round his waist. He'd stuck his tongue out and closed one eye as though his face needed to detract from the sheer perfection his body couldn't hide.

I guess you can get away with sending me an old photo, even if lots of other people have enjoyed it already, but next time I want one for my eyes only!

You're gonna need to give me a copy of this rule book so I can keep up with your demands. Now where were we…

We'd chatted all night, hot and heavy, sexy and steamy, all the juicy details, everything I'd wanted from him after I'd sent that first picture. If only I was able to float back in time to that night where I'd wept uncontrollably into my pillow and could stroke my hair, rub my back and whisper in my ear that it wasn't over, that the best was yet to come. Alas, time travel was still a few years away and, remember, you couldn't have the rainbow without the rain… I was almost nauseating myself coming out with stupid phrases like that. I'd have shot someone at point-blank range, gladly, for wheeling out that kind of crap a couple of days ago.

Who am I?

It's positively ghastly how delirious I have become!

I flushed the loo even though I hadn't been, in case someone was waiting outside and spread a rumour about me not flushing, and, after playing around pinning my hair back in various updos, decided to start the working day. Josh wasn't in yet and I took my seat across from Georgette. She looked a little worse for wear.

'Morning!' I said, brightly.

'What's got into you?' she croaked.

'It's such a beautiful day!'

'Did you get laid or something? You're acting so weird.'

I smiled to myself and turned on my computer, rearranging a couple of the picture frames that sat on my desk, I sprayed myself theatrically with a free sample of perfume I'd been offered on my way to work, dousing myself in notes of peach and pearl.

I sensed him before I saw him, the swing of the double doors and a second later his inch-perfect body sauntered through. Did he look a little tired? *Ah!*

I must have audibly squealed with delight as I watched him take his seat because Georgette was sniggering at me.

'You're a freak today, honestly, you're scaring me.'

It was so thrilling! I hurried to the toilets again to hide my manic grin and wrote Josh another message.

Just had to steal away for a few minutes to calm myself down after seeing you walk in. Who knew it was possible to enjoy a morning at work after no sleep the night before...

You'd best calm down. We have a meeting with Kai soon and I know you want to keep this our dirty little secret.

Kai was coming in today to update Ava, Josh and me on some developments with the launch. How were we going to keep our hands off each other?

Today was such a good day, I had Josh back on my side and Ava's blackmail ready to go. The man was mine, the job was mine and our final-round interviews were just round the corner. I was within touching distance of everything I'd ever wanted.

I took a sip of my double caramel macchiato and checked my calendar for the day ahead. A sudden silence descended on the office and I broke away from my computer screen to see that Kai had made it to us half an hour ahead of schedule; things always went quiet when clients arrived. I watched over my flowers as he walked over to Josh and shook his hand. What I wouldn't give to shake that big, gorgeous hand. That was when I realised: the flowers.

Crap!

What if Kai recognised them and asked why they were on my desk, not Ava's?

I needed to move them.

I needed to dispose of them immediately. I lurched forward, my eyes fixed on Kai and Josh to make sure they weren't about to come over to grab me for the meeting when, clumsily, predictably, I knocked the pint glass over, punching it instead of picking it up, hitting it with such force the bottom of the glass tipped back in my direction. I watched in horror as water spilled all over my desk spreading entrails of broken-off stem and loose petal all over my notepad, printouts for the meeting, newspaper clippings, my phone... I didn't have time to worry about my phone because the flowers were still half on my desk, half on the floor and, as I bent down to pick them up and hide them, I saw Kai and Josh moving towards me: their next stop. No time for a clean-up operation. I grabbed the flowers in an iron grip, breaking most of them as I clutched them tight, and threw them under the table, covering the surplus pairs of shoes I kept under here in broken flower debris. Georgette was staring at me like I'd just had an epileptic fit.

'I'm *so* clumsy today it's ridiculous!' I said, by way of explanation, then stood up, just in time to meet Kai and Josh halfway between Josh's desk and mine to ensure they didn't spot my impromptu flower arrangement.

'Hi Kai, so nice to see you, how are you today? How was your journey in?' I was speaking at a hundred miles an hour, my face red, my palms pollinated.

Kai threw his hands up at the elbow.

'Horrible! Trains into London make me feel like a caged hen, honestly, it's probably against human rights or something to make everyone stand that close together! And the *smell* of some people! Especially in the summer! Don't we deserve air con?'

He gagged for dramatic effect then sashayed into the meeting room ahead of us.

Josh and I smiled coyly at one another behind his back.

Kai took a seat at the head of the table and Josh and I sat either side: we'd be staring right into each other's eyes for the entirety of the meeting.

'Jade, do you have the print-outs for Kai?' Josh asked, perfectly reasonably.

I improvised. 'Sorry, Georgette just flung a pint of water over them but I've asked someone to print some more, shouldn't be too long now. I'll just pop out to see how she's getting on.'

I rushed away and as good as throttled the junior on my team – I wasn't sure of her name (5'1, bouncy ponytail, legs like Bambi). I barked instructions at her: print this document, bind a copy for me, clean up the flowers under my desk, make sure my phone is OK, actually do that first, clean my phone, then sort the documents. She looked like I'd just shot her in the arm but she persevered and set off to carry out my orders. I hoped she didn't mess up, it was the last thing I needed.

Kai, Josh and I talked for two minutes or so before Ava appeared at the doorway in a pair of tight leather trousers. I looked at her in disgust, why on *earth* would she wear something that provocative to the office? How inappropriate!

I tried to make a joke out of it to make Kai feel less uncomfortable.

'The playboy mansion called, Ava, they want their trousers back!'

Her face fell, she looked embarrassed. *Good.* But a metaphorical tumbleweed drifted past as neither man jumped to agree with me. Instead, Kai shot up to greet her and they shared a series of air kisses.

'I think they're fabulous, darling, I'd love a pair but I'd need to saw off your legs to pull them off!'

Kai was impossibly well-groomed. He sported a shock of dyed ginger hair but, unlike most redheads, his skin was tanned. The look suited him and made his hair striking, a talking point, a compliment.

'Thanks. How are you? Love the top, is it Moschino?'

'Yes! Their capsule collection. Cashmere.' Kai looked smug and moved his shoulders back and forth to show off his expensive garms.

A wolf in sheep's clothing.

As Ava went to take a seat she fired a look at me: *keep your opinions to yourself.*

I didn't hold her stare and busied myself clicking the projector into the meeting room laptop. At that moment the baby deer stumbled in on her new-found walking legs and placed the print-outs and my phone in a bowl of rice in front of me.

'I tried to get rid of all the flowers but they—'

I cut her off before she could incriminate me any further. 'You can leave now.' It was as though I'd shot her in the other arm as she limped out of the meeting room, offended, and closed the door clumsily behind her. Did she want a standing ovation for doing her job? Draining the water from my phone using rice was a nice touch, sure, but telling her that would only have unnecessarily inflated her ego. I prayed the photo of Ava and David I'd risked life and limb to take would be retrievable. Kai kicked off the meeting before I could dwell on it any further.

'Thanks for being here today everyone. Ava, as head of the project, I'd love to get an update from you first and then you can fill me in on how these two are getting on.'

Head of the project?

These two?!

I rolled my eyes at Josh and he gave me a look back. I knew *exactly* what he was thinking, the little devil.

'Thanks Kai. From my point of view, everything's going

fab. But we can each present our own portions on front row, media attendees, security and ticket sales...'

I found it impossible to concentrate when Ava spoke, seriously, it was a real problem. Her voice was so sing-song that it was too easy to zone out of and think about other things. Josh was looking at Ava but I knew he was thinking about me. I wondered if I could reach his foot under the table...

'Jade did you want to kick off?' All eyes were on me. I blinked them up from locating Josh's feet under the table and re-focused.

I went through my front row round-up with pinpoint precision, presenting background information on each attendee that went above and beyond what Kai was looking for. I even managed to land a few blows on Ava's reputation.

As I finished up I summarised: 'Everything is accounted for, I've confirmed a further ten attendees *without* needing to pay them and I'm confident the entire front row will be full on the night.'

I was half expecting a round of applause but, before anyone could clap, Ava chimed in with a question. I smiled sweetly at her, all innocence and light.

'Sorry to jump in Jade, but I heard a rumour this morning about a show planned in the warehouse building just behind us. I think it's Macdonald, or McQueen, I'm not sure, they're keeping it all pretty top secret. I'm sure you're already aware but I just wondered if you'd spoken about it with the attendees? It's only that I don't want them to cancel at the last minute and leave us in the lurch. Have you sorted out contracts with the ones you're planning to pay?'

Bit intense.

'Right, I'll have to check on that.'

I sounded pissed off, and I was – she should have given me a heads up before the meeting started.

'It makes me really nervous that you didn't know about this already Jade,' Kai jumped in. 'Could you find out now? Get someone to send through the details so we can discuss it.'

I sat down to make an angry note in my pad, cutting the paper slightly with my pen, then I emailed Georgette and asked her to send the information through to the boardroom computer.

Kai continued with the next point on the agenda.

'Moving on, I wanted to bring you all up to speed with some pictures of the site so you can get a feel for what the stage will look like now the set's finished.'

He tried to plug his phone into the laptop but error messages flashed back.

'Jade, I sent you the pictures, would you have more luck with this than me?'

'Hmm, I can get the pictures but I'm not really sure how to make this talk to that, to be honest.'

Josh must have thought I was a complete Luddite, first I didn't consider rebooting my fake Wi-Fi problem and now this... I guess I could only hope it added to the loveable moron theme I'd been pedalling.

I unlocked my phone and held it out towards him, desperate for our hands to touch.

'I can help,' Ava interjected, snatching my mobile from my fingers. She clicked it into the end of the USB which connected to the projector and a series of pop ups appeared one after the other. Ava quickly clicked through them. *Trust computer? Open Photos. OK.*

We were all staring at the screen when an image, a thousand times larger than the one I'd become familiar with on my phone, filled the space. It was of me, lying on my dirty bathroom floor, legs lifted, ugly black pants covering my genitalia, my huge, white, flabby, stomach blubbering and gathering in unflattering rolls above each thin-stringed side of my underwear, my right arm cupped round my enormous tits, my right hand covering the nipple closest to the camera, my face in an awkward expression that I'd thought at the time was a sexy kind of 'ahh' face but, magnified to this extreme, looked like I was suffering from trapped wind.

I died. I screamed a kind of noise I don't think I'd be capable of reproducing. I threw myself at Ava, ripping the lead from my phone and knocking her over in the process. She yelped as she fell to the ground and Josh and Kai both lunged to catch her, a contest for who could be most chivalrous. I ran out of the meeting room and sat on the toilet in the far cubicle, where I'd been so happy earlier, and rocked back and forth, trying to stop the voices.

25

Ava

Jade ran out of the room, her face so red it looked like she'd sprinted a four-minute mile, as Kai and Josh helped me up from the floor.

'I'm fine, honestly, no harm done.'

'Should someone go and check on her?' Kai asked, stunned by the last thirty seconds. Josh offered and he paced out of the room but returned seconds later.

'She's in the ladies', but she'll be OK, we shouldn't draw any more attention to it. Let's just pick up where we left off and she can rejoin when she's ready.'

'Where did it *come* from?' Kai pondered as we settled back down.

'I think it auto-loaded the pictures when I plugged it in...' I replied. 'I feel terrible.'

'Forget it,' Kai assured me. 'She'll be laughing about it in a few weeks' time!'

He was wrong; Jade didn't laugh about anything.

I left Josh and Kai discussing the possibility of our entire launch being scuppered by a rival show and went out to find Jade. I had to talk to her, this was exactly the kind of thing that would tip her over the edge. Our relationship was already strained, already pulled to its limit, already stretched to breaking point.

I pushed open the door to the ladies' toilets and went inside.

26

Jade

I heard her heels striking the tiles in the toilets as she stalked towards me. I *hated* her. I hated the way she moved, the way she paused between each step, the overly pleasant way she spoke, and I balked at the thought of having to leave this cubicle to look at her stupid face.

'Jade?' she called. I imagined her pulling a taut expression, her lips thick and puckered, her forehead creased. She'd gone too far this time.

'Jade, let me in. We need to talk.'

I know what you've done, Ava. Thunder rolled inside me and I decided I was ready to face her: my nemesis. The woman I'd delight in taking down when the time was right. I flipped the lock open and flung the door to one side. 'Ava.'

'Jade, I'm sorry, I didn't do that on purpose, the photos they just loaded and… I'm sorry, I'm so sorry.' She looked like she was going to cry.

But I wasn't David, or Kai: I didn't fall for crocodile

tears. 'You know, I'd almost be tempted to believe you if it weren't for everything else you've done,' I snarled.

'What do you mean?'

'You've taken things too far for this promotion. Using Olivia, showing our top client that photo to undermine me and...' I changed my voice to a whisper, deciding to say it, to bring her down. Now was as good a time as any. *Sleeping with David.*'

Her entire expression fell and she took a half-step back, the colour of her skin matching the pale blonde of her hair.

'And was it really worth it? All that effort just to beat me?' I asked, seething.

'What happened with David has nothing to do with you, Jade. I swear.'

At least she isn't denying it. 'And why's that? Because now you're in his bed there's no way I can win against you, is there? No matter what I do I won't get the job...'

She stuttered, lost for words.

'Except, Ava, for the fact that I'm one step ahead of you. I can show people what you've done, what lengths you've gone to. I have evidence. A photograph.'

'What?' She gawped, her eyes wide. 'How?'

'I followed you and David the night of the summer party and took it. You were going into his bedroom together.'

Blackmail.

I continued, 'And I'll use it, you know. If he decides to give you the job. I'll send it to everyone, I'll send it to the press... I'll publicly crucify the pair of you...'

I was huffing and puffing and out of breath, shivering from the adrenaline of winning. *Finally.*

'Jade – you can't, you don't understand. That photo can never come out.'

'OK. So quit, leave, resign, break up with David and get fired, I don't care how you do it.'

She took a long breath in before speaking. 'It's like you've forgotten what we did. What we went through together.'

I couldn't stand the thought of her talking about Olivia; I *hated* talking about Olivia. I turned away. 'I haven't forgotten,' I said firmly. 'I think about it all the time.'

'So you can't go round threatening me, Jade, there's too much to lose.'

'Meaning I'm supposed to sit back and let you take the job, am I? Just like that? Or what, you'll ruin us both?'

'I won't, but clearly you would, given half the chance. I don't know if I even *want* the job, to be honest with you, especially not after this.' She paused then, remembering something. 'This is ridiculous, Jade. We were friends once, what happened to us?'

I wouldn't let Ava trick me into changing my mind, not now everything was falling into place. I'd *known* she'd try to dismantle it. I should have been more prepared for something like this, I had to be stronger. She wanted the job more than anything, I knew that.

Come on, Jade, you're better than this. I felt her take my hands in hers, the soft warmth of her skin tempting me to relent.

'Please, Jade, listen to me: it doesn't have to be this way.'

I climbed into my rickety double bed that night and pulled the four-, maybe five-week-old sheets over my body. They smelt of me, warm and musty, Marlboro Reds mixed with cheap perfume. I was drunk and I'd taken a handful of pills to try and stop me from reliving the nightmare of today on a loop. Josh had sent me a message after the meeting. Hiding behind a screen was clearly his forte.

If it's any consolation... I thought you looked amazing in that picture.

No, it wasn't any consolation. Well, maybe a bit. I was angry, Old-Testament-God angry, with Ava, even though she'd forced me, somehow, to make up with her. Convinced me to swear my loyalty and the things I knew to her all over again. My eyelids drooped and my head was heavy. I considered replying to Josh but, after a couple of drafts, decided I wasn't ready to make peace yet. I wanted him to sweat it out, worry that he'd blown it with me for failing to come to my defence, and, before I had a second to change my mind, the suffocating lure of sleep picked me up and transported me to a different place, my head deep in dream-world, my body exhausted from its earthly exertions.

27

Ava

I sat, heels bouncing, outside his office waiting for his PA to unlock the door to his lair. I was supposed to be here for an interview – the final round before David picked his Team Head – but, sitting here, I wasn't sure I wanted to be part of it any more. What was the point? I'd fought for my job when I'd loved it, when everything had been within my grasp, when my relationship with David was normal, and working at W&SP was the only light in my otherwise stormy life. But everything was different now: David wanted more than I was willing to give, Jade was threatening to sabotage the rest of my career if I didn't roll over, and Charlie's notes were growing in frequency and fury. Every night this week I'd come home to a new note stuffed angrily through the letterbox and finding and disposing of them had become the nightly ritual I hadn't asked for. I'd pick them up off the mat, read the first line, then fold them up into perfect squares and shove them into the depths of the same kitchen drawer.

You think you can do better, don't you? You have to talk to me again, meet me tomorrow at...

I've never met anyone more perfect and beautiful than you, you are my world.

I see you're getting better at keeping your windows locked.

Filthy bitch, you never deserved me.

It was textbook Charlie: terrorising, stalking, making me dread going home every night. But if I left W&SP, moved out of Olivia's, walked away from David, from the job, and from Jade, then all of this would just disapp—

'You can go in now,' announced his assistant, cutting through my train of thought.

One last chance, I thought, as the palm of my hand pushed against cool metal. On the other side of the door I found David sitting, thumbing through notes, in one of the yellow Chesterfield armchairs that formed a seating area away from his desk. He didn't look up as I walked in but extended his arm, signalling for me to take the unoccupied seat next to him.

'Hi,' I said, being friendly and, when he didn't respond: 'Should I come back another time?'

His fingers flicked through sheet after sheet, erratically, but still he didn't answer. Instead he raised one of his palms in my direction as though instructing me to be quiet, as though he hadn't just called me in here, as though I hadn't been waiting outside for the last ten minutes for him to finish whatever he was doing... I hadn't signed up to be part of David's power play, so I tried not to let him get to me and relaxed into the chair, sighing quietly.

'Is something wrong?'

My sigh had annoyed him.

'No,' I replied apologetically. He paused and stopped shuffling the papers between his palms then he looked right at me, deep behind my eyes.

'Listen, Ava, I owe you an apology. Clearly the other night has made you uncomfortable. I'm sorry if I misread the signals, truly, I hope you can forgive me.'

He was admitting fault. I hadn't been expecting that. I didn't know how to respond – I wasn't sure what signals I'd given him because I couldn't remember anything. I looked into his sad expression, the wriggly lines that snaked across his face. He was tired. Could I forgive his behaviour? Were there mitigating circumstances given the death of his daughter?

I wasn't sure. I kept quiet.

'So, as an apology, I'd like to offer you the job. Ava Wells: youngest Team Head in the history of Watson & Stein Partners. Sounds good, doesn't it?'

I was taken aback. 'What? Just like that?' My mind rushed to Jade. Was saying no to this job even an option?

'You've proven yourself here, haven't you? Besides, there was never really a contest in my mind. It was always going to be you, Ava.'

'Wow, I don't know what to say,' I stammered. 'Thank you.'

He smiled a devious narrow-lipped grin that made me realise there was more to come.

'Can I talk you through the added responsibility?'

I shuffled nervously in my seat. 'As you know, your new role means you'll be reporting directly to me.' He took a beat. 'And I like to know that I can trust my employees. I'm sure you understand that.'

I nodded slowly, massaging the knuckles on my left hand with my right.

'Can I ask you a few questions?'

'OK...'

'Are you a trustworthy person, Ava?'

I faltered. *I know what you've done.*

'Honest?' he added.

'Yes,' I replied, hurriedly. 'I like to think so.'

'Could you quickly explain your living situation to me?'

I curled my chin into my neck. Was he being serious? He looked up at me, pen poised, waiting for my answer.

'I live in one of your properties—'

'Alone?'

'Yes...'

He stopped talking and took a note.

'And you understand that property is rigged with CCTV, right?' I realised where this was going. 'Do you want to change your answer, Ava? Before I write this down?'

'You're seeing Charlie, aren't you, on the CCTV? He comes every night and leaves me a note. I don't let him in, though.'

'Why didn't you tell me things were this bad?'

'Because I didn't want to upset you.'

'Upset me? You've upset me by not telling me the truth, Ava, can't you see that? I thought we'd been through this already... that I'd been clear with what I expect. You just told me you were trustworthy and honest, but you've been keeping things from me... again.'

The only way to deal with David was to play a different role, to transform into the woman he wanted to look after.

'It's not that, David. It's just, listen—' my character's voice broke '—I had to deal with Charlie for so long by myself that trusting you with everything is taking some getting used to.'

I reached for his hand and felt him relent as our skin touched.

'So you're not seeing anyone, then.'

I gulped.

'You're being honest with me now, are you? And there aren't any secrets between us, correct?'

I know what you've done.

I couldn't bring myself to verbally confirm what he wanted to hear so I squeezed his hands with mine and nodded.

'You're a wonderful man.'

'If Charlie's notes are scaring you, Ava, I can move in. I can look after you.'

I looked away, unable to explain that him moving in was a worse thought than Charlie stalking around outside.

'You remind me of her, you know,' he muttered. An invisible weight crushed me as I battled my own demons about Olivia's passing. I welled up, enormous tears blotting my vision. 'I just want to look after you.'

They fell, heavy, splashing my forearms. 'I know, David. And I'm so grateful for that.'

But my words were feeble and false. I kept my hand locked round his.

'We'll take it slow, darling, don't worry.'

Were we blurring the lines we'd just agreed to redraw? I felt light-headed and took a breath, trying to steady myself, aware of how horrifically complicated my life had become in such a short space of time.

And David didn't even know the half of it.

28

Jade

The basement meeting room had been chosen to conduct my final round interview and I made my way down the flight of stairs to the lower ground floor. The artificial lights were brighter down here to make up for the lack of sunlight and the art followed a yellow theme along the walls.

I'd planned to wear the smart suit jacket I kept hung on the back of my office chair but, to my horror, I'd discovered too late it had acquired a stripe of paint from where my chair makes contact with the wall behind me so, instead, it was hanging inside out over my forearm to make it clear that I *had* a suit jacket, I just... wasn't wearing it for the most important interview of my life.

I knew I didn't look the part and my knees trembled as I made my way to the meeting room.

I offered my hand to David when I entered but he didn't rise to shake it, keeping his fingers interlaced on the table.

'Thanks for making the time to see me today,' I said, reeling in my rejected limb. I took the seat on the opposite side of the glass table. He didn't have any notes, or an iPad, or a phone, even. It was just him, my ruined suit jacket, and me. I put the jacket on the table – the expanse of empty glass between us felt so awkward that I wanted to fill it with something – but as it sat on top of the table it looked ghastly, informal and ridiculous, and I instantly regretted my decision. I grabbed at the jacket to put it behind me but I was moving too quickly and, instead, I pushed it, sending it to the floor in a crumpled heap. Rather than stand up and make a scene, I tried to lean from my chair and pick it up, but the jacket was too heavy and I was too far from the ground to manoeuvre it with my fingertips.

'Just leave it,' David said, his lip curled. 'This won't take long.'

His hostility unnerved me. I started speaking, trying to win him round. 'I wanted to thank you again for—'

He held up his hand to silence me. 'Do you really want this job, Jade?'

'Well, yes, of course, I've been working towards this for the past eight years.'

'Do you think you're ready for it, though?'

His emphasis was on the word ready.

'More than, yes, definitely.'

He raised his eyebrows slightly and nodded slowly as if that wasn't the answer he was expecting.

'Huh. OK. So, tell me. Why do you deserve this job over Ava?'

I felt my stomach tense. He wanted me to turn on her. Now was my chance. Had he asked the same of her? Had she already spilled the secret we both shared?

'Well, she's perfectly good at her job, but I've been here

for longer and I know more about this company than she ever will.'

He looked impressed and I was sure a smile flashed across his face for a moment.

'And are you trustworthy, Jade? Honest?'

I looked sideways for a second.

'I like staff I can depend on – *loyal staff*. I can't stand for betrayal, or deceit, or dishonesty. Especially not at this level.'

I thought of the photo on my phone in my bag. The blackmail I was going to use. The insurance policy I had to help me get the job. Ava had already out-maneuvered me. I couldn't use it, not after this speech.

'I understand,' I said shakily.

'And what do you think Olivia would say? Who do you think she'd endorse for this role?'

I shuddered. I hated thinking about Olivia. Her voice rose in my head. She wouldn't want either of us as Team Head.

'I wish we could ask her,' I said after a while, forcing a smile.

He paused, his eyes crawling over me, picking through the webs that covered my words.

'You were with her, weren't you, the night she died?'

My intestines wriggled like worms inside me and I felt rotten from the inside out. I cast my mind back.

'Ava and I, we'd been partying with her.'

I didn't want to say too much.

'Yes,' he said. 'But why didn't you tell the police you took her home?'

Six o'clock glowed on my computer screen and, off the back of the most stressful interview of my life, my feelings of guilt and paranoia were intensifying. I wasn't sure if I'd managed to convince David we *had* told the police we'd taken Olivia home that evening. I'd blabbed about not being sure why that detail hadn't ended up on record. But I knew he knew something. I should warn Ava.

The office bar opened on a Wednesday night and, usually, I'd avoid it but I wondered if tonight I should make an exception. Ava often went and it would give me a chance to speak to her. I cracked open my pocket mirror and smeared concealer over the stress spots that had cropped up all over my chin, no doubt a result of my earlier meeting, smudged a dollop of peppermint balm over my lips and pulled my fingers through my frazzled hair. I wished I'd washed it this morning, it was lacking its usual sheen today. I changed my footwear from my work-appropriate black leather flats and slipped into four-inch shiny court shoes. I wanted to look the part, at least.

A creeping smell of solvents filled my senses and I looked across the desk to see Georgette applying a topcoat of glitter to her nails.

'Coming down to the bar, Jadey?' She didn't look up but had spotted me in her peripheral vision as she stuck her tongue out, zoning in on the edges of her ring finger. I thought about Ava, about what I had to tell her, and imagined her having the perfect answer for me that would entirely set my mind at ease: *Don't worry, Jade, he's only asking about the night Olivia died because some new evidence has come to light. The police are looking at a specific timeframe, but it wasn't until long after we'd left her. I explained to him that the reason it wasn't in our initial statement was because that timeframe hadn't been of interest. Now it is. Please don't worry.*

'Sure, I'll be there,' I answered. 'Do you have any perfume I could borrow?'

Georgette threw me a bottle, the word *Fantasy* emblazoned across the front. Perhaps it would help mine come true, I thought, as I doused myself in it.

And then my phone lit up. Josh.

Please talk to me.

I looked over at him. He'd put his phone back down already and was talking to the girl who sat next to him: her veneers didn't quite fit inside her mouth. She wasn't his cup of tea at all. Another message pinged through.

You look great tonight.

I'd been making him sweat since photogate. He hadn't stuck up for me, or come to my defence, and I'd let him know I wasn't happy. He'd apologised. He'd grovelled. And maybe tonight I was willing to forgive. I thought about how things might go if I managed to sort everything with Ava. My job came first, of course. But maybe I was worrying about nothing... Perhaps Josh would come up to me when the bar started to empty, fix his beautiful stare on me and lean in close to ask if I was walking to the tube. I'd say yes and he'd suggest stopping at a cosy bar we passed on the way... we'd duck inside and enjoy a few too many... then he'd call a cab to take us home... but we'd kiss on the pavement outside and, as the cab arrived, he'd ask me if I wanted to go back to his place. Things would get heavy in the backseat... then we'd crash into his flat a little later, not bothering to turn on the lights, kicking off our shoes and undressing each other as we made our way to his bedroom... he'd kiss me, hard, the smell of alcohol on his breath turning me on... The next day we'd call in sick at different times and spend hours cuddling in bed getting to know each other... we'd realise we'd forgotten to eat all day as the sun set. Josh would order pizza which we'd feed one another, pausing between slices to giggle about what our colleagues would make of all this... After that night I wouldn't leave his flat ever again and the next day he'd ask me to move in with him... then, in five years' time, when I was the Queen of the office, still managing to run the entire consumer department whilst kicking off a side business in soaps, or ornaments, we'd reminisce fondly on this night in the bar. Josh and I would joke about it: *If we hadn't gone to drinks that night, then none of this would have happened!*

Georgette and I headed down to the bar together, a cloud of her cheap perfume following us like a low-lying fog.

'Here you go, sweetie,' Georgette said gleefully as she handed me a huge glass of red wine. 'Just what you need after the week you've had.'

I looked at her suspiciously. What did she know? 'What do you mean?' I asked.

Georgette got right to the point. 'Babe, I know about the picture in the meeting. I saw it, I'm sorry.'

I felt the walls round me start to close in. She changed her tone, 'You looked hot anyway! Who was it for?'

'I don't want to talk about it,' I said quietly. If she'd seen it, everyone knew.

'Boo, boring! Come on… spill!'

Her eyes were hungry.

If I didn't give her any clues she'd just make something up, so I kept it vague.

'OK. Well, it was for a guy I'm seeing, I've been seeing, for a bit, he's really into sexy pictures… he's… younger.'

'Oooh! How exciting!' She didn't believe me. 'What's his name?'

I looked at her. As *if* I would tell you that, *babe*.

'Was he the one that sent you flowers the other day? Everyone was talking about those, your *mystery delivery*.'

I should have spun her a story about those already. I was on the ropes.

'He's really thoughtful,' I croaked.

'Rich, too, by the looks of it, they weren't cheap. I spotted red roses in there! He must really like you.'

'I guess so. Anyway, I don't want people to know about it, I'm trying to keep it private.' Georgette rubbed my arm and assured me my secret was safe with her. We both knew it was anything but.

I left Georgette with David's plastic PA who'd trotted over to us with a bottle of Champagne and told us proudly it was all she drank. It's always the cheapest, trashiest people who make up stupid rules like that to try and convince you they're in some way refined or distinguished. After two glasses I bet she couldn't tell the difference between Bollinger and Lambrusco. I sat in one of the large, leather armchairs in the bar area, crossed my legs like a schoolgirl and pushed my dress between my thighs, covering my modesty. *For a change.* I pondered whether I should write something back to Josh. He hadn't turned up at the bar yet and I was desperate to see him in person: to turn our offline relationship on. Maybe it was the wine talking as I spun my fingers across the screen, but I wanted to be forward, I wanted to be bold, I wanted this, *us*, to be a thing. I didn't want to have to keep hiding it.

> Why don't you come to drinks tonight... then maybe we could grab one after? I'd like to hear exactly how sorry you are in person.

I felt good about it. I didn't think about how I would feel if he said no, that part wasn't really in my plan. I knocked back the last mouthful of my wine and shuffled between the now packed-out bar area to replenish my glass. Damn: all out. I'd have to head to the storeroom. I jogged down the stairs to the basement. It was eerily quiet down there and the lights were the kind you had to motion-activate. The darkness of the corridor before me filled the glass in the doorway, a blacked-out window into what lay beyond. I opened it timidly, hoping it would set the motion detectors off without me stepping into the blackness to do so. It took a couple of seconds but, sure enough, the corridor illuminated one row of lights at a time and led me, like emergency floor lighting would on a plane, to my destination. I strode to the end, past the basement meeting room from earlier, and punched in the store room code, waiting for the lock to click open. I leant against the door, using all my weight to open it. It was on a slow-close hinge which made it almost impossible to manoeuvre in a hurry. The wine was stored behind the door to the right of the store room entrance. As I walked into the refrigerated room, goose bumps dotted my bare arms and I bustled round the racks as quickly as possible. In a bizarre twist, the red wines were stored in a fridge-like contraption, keeping them warmed from the cool air designed for the white wines and champagnes round them. I traced my fingers across the bottles... Cabernet Sauvignon: no, bad memories. Malbec: too heavy. Pinot Noir: too fruity. Merlot... hmm, OK, Merlot it was. I clutched the bottle in my hand and slammed the warm fridge door shut. As I made my way back out into the store room, I heard something from the back of the room, behind the rows and rows of client stock. I dismissed it at first but, as I turned towards the door, I heard it again, a kind of muffled chitter-chatter that drew me in like a fish on a line. What was so secret it had to be discussed down here? My curiosity piqued, I tiptoed towards the sound, increasing my speed as I passed each section and the noises grew louder. I heard laughter, kissing, closeness, contact. I peered through the shelves and then I saw her – *Ava*. Hair messed up, cheeks flushed, eyes clamped shut, the top button of her see-through blouse undone, her arms round his back, her mouth attached to his as he pushed her against one of the shelves full of AthLuxe apparel. I dropped the wine bottle I was holding and it smashed as it hit the wooden floor, expensive Merlot splashing upwards, covering my shiny court shoes and the bottoms of my legs in deep red stains, then dribbling down to the floor, spreading out, seeping between the cracks. Their heads spun round at the sound. Ava smiled apologetically and bit her bottom lip. Josh barely moved, he didn't even bother to let her go.

Perhaps he'd wanted me to find out.

Perhaps they'd both been fucking with me this entire time.

29

Ava

The red wine kept spreading, its pool of damage continuing to gain new ground, ensuring the maximum possible impact.

I wondered how long she'd been stood there, watching us, before she'd dropped the bottle and fled.

'I guess our secret is out,' Josh said as he kissed my neck and laughed nervously.

I felt ill.

No one was supposed to find out about us. Not yet.

30

Jade

I ran out of the store room, the lights only detecting my motion when it was too late, illuminating the path I'd already trodden through the empty blackness of the corridor. I kept running, up the stairs and out through the double entrance doors of the building, not bothering to pick up my bag from upstairs, just one thing on my mind: home.

Densely packed bodies filled each carriage and the noise and warmth was stifling. It wasn't a particularly hot day today, but it felt humid and the air was close and sticky. Any other day and I would have waited for the next train but today there was no choice. A man in a pinstripe navy suit bore the brunt of my urgency and I practically knocked him off his feet as I forced my way on board. 'Easy love!' He gave me a horrible look. I didn't meet his eyes, I didn't apologise, I just turned round and pressed my head against the tube door praying the journey would be over soon.

I kept my head down as I hurried along the platform at Denmark Hill, my short-sleeve dress exposing my pasty limbs, entirely out of place among the glowing tans of everyone surrounding me. I started to cry: just as I thought we'd settled our differences, just as I thought we'd levelled the playing field, she was at it *again* and now we were back to square one. She'd taken David first, and now Josh. *My Josh*. A low growl erupted from within me as I thought about how disgusting she was. She'd do *anything* to get ahead. A man edged away from me as a noise that started deep in my gut gained in volume. People were staring now, they thought I was a freak, and I broke out into a run when we reached my stop. I jogged like a woman possessed, barely stopping for a break and, eventually, closed in on my front door. It was then that I realised: I didn't have my bag. Or my keys. I cried as I threw myself against the wood that separated me from inside and my shoulder crippled under the pressure, causing me to sink down. I beat my fists against the door, crying for someone to open up.

But no one was there.

I couldn't go back to the office, obviously, and I quickly played through a scenario where I returned, battered and freezing as the double doors opened in front of me. The entire bar area would fall silent, eyes firing from all angles. They already knew. I'd grab my things, the only noise my sniffling and scuffling, like a rat on the tube tracks at night, the office doors barely closing behind me before a raucous cackle broke out and people started talking about me in shrieking staccato.

The thought knocked the wind out of me.

Instead, I formed a rash plan. I raced to the bin, picked up the black sack I'd stuffed full of the week's decaying meals and emptied it out onto the pavement. The smell was horrific: fishy, mouldy, cheesy. It smelt like death, honestly, but I didn't care, I breathed it in, focused only on my plan. I wrapped my left arm in the bin liner, round and round, the sticky, slimy bin juices rubbing against my skin, and stood in front of the ground floor windows. I thought of Ava's puppet-doll grin when I'd discovered her and, at that moment, lifted my arm above my head, then brought it down with monstrous force, crashing it against the window in one fell swoop. The glass smashed, giving way too easily, and I peeled my arm back, now covered in jagged shards, blood oozing from various points. I picked out the wedges one by one, enjoying the pain, then ripped the bin bag from my arm. I'd made a big enough hole that I was able to climb in through the window, but my dress snagged on the glass as I ambled through the gap, cutting me again as it did so, my legs not faring much better as I pushed my way inside: the world's worst cat burglar.

The streets of SE5 didn't blink an eye, it was one of the few places in London where a crazy woman breaking noisily into a ground-floor flat would pass without comment.

'What on earth?'

My housemate appeared in the lounge. *Shock, horror, outrage!*

'I thought you were a burglar! Why did you break the bloody window down?'

I didn't say anything to her. I had nothing to say. My whole world had come crashing down and nothing mattered any more. Everything I'd wished for, everything I was so excited about had vanished – in an instant – and if I hadn't caught them, I would still be living the lie he'd had me believe. I'd seen them together, heard them together, the smell of the heady Merlot filling the scene as it had smashed to the floor. What was it with me and red wine? Like a spectre of bad luck that accompanied my worst memories. I'd tasted the dryness of the air as some other-worldly presence had grabbed at my voice box and silenced me. I'd touched the cool metal of the door handle as I'd fled. This memory would never leave me, not now it was stained across each of my senses. I lay down amongst the broken glass underneath the window without curtains, cut from head to toe, stinking and disgusting, pain coursing through my veins.

31

Ava

I first realised I liked Josh one freezing February night earlier
this year. I'd been working late just to avoid going home,
drinking coffee to keep me alert, watching the snow fall
outside, the tap-tap-tap of my fingernails on the keyboard
the only sound. My head had still been full of grief and guilt
following Olivia's untimely death and Charlie had been
bombarding me with texts all day. At first he'd wanted to
apologise for throwing the dinner I'd made last night in the
bin just as I'd been about to serve, then, when being soft
didn't work, his tone had changed.

Don't bother coming home tonight. None of your things
will be here in the morning.

He'd been sending more and more threats like that and I
was growing sick of them, and him. Josh had been working
late that night too, he'd recently returned to the agency
following Olivia's overdose, and had decamped from his

desk to my office when everyone else had gone home for the night. We'd grown closer during his time off, comforting each other over text, sharing stories about Olivia, and, as soon as he'd returned, it was like we were magnets. He'd stretched out across the black sofa in my office that night, his frame taking up most of it, even the stark overhead spotlights unable to expose a flaw in his beautiful face. He'd summoned me over to watch something on his laptop, some stupid video, and we'd sat side-by-side, our bodies touching gently together. 'You have the cutest laugh.' That's what he'd said to me before I'd bitten my thumb between my teeth and feigned some protestations to the contrary. It hadn't been difficult, or awkward, he'd just slowly, but purposefully, leaned in, bringing his hand underneath my chin, pulling us closer together as if he had me on a string and kissed me softly on the cheek. Then he'd walked me to the tube, pulling our hoods right over our faces so we wouldn't be recognised, walking through the snowy streets hand in hand, glove in glove, like we had nothing to hide. He knew from the outset that things weren't going to be straightforward between us and, sure enough, it hadn't been easy even before David had burst in and complicated things.

My intention had been to keep things simple. I didn't tell Josh everything I was going through so that with him I could just be me, the me I was before Charlie had twisted and tortured me out of shape. And doing that brought feelings out of me I wasn't sure I'd ever feel again: freedom, confidence, levity and love. When I was with him it was as though he'd taken all the bitterness that had built inside me and replaced it with candy floss. Even today, at my lowest ebb, just being near him made me feel better. I was a kid at a fairground and I'd won the biggest, brightest, cuddliest teddy bear. He'd agreed it was a good idea to keep our relationship low-key, at least until things settled down with Charlie, until the Team Head had been announced, until I'd got my own place, and until we'd told David. He didn't mind, he was happy to take things at my pace. So, I hadn't told Josh all the gory details about Charlie's abuse. I hadn't told Josh about Charlie's 'proposal'. I hadn't told Josh about the night of the summer party. I hadn't told Josh that I suspected David thought of me as more than just a friend. I hadn't told Josh that David had offered me the Team Head role as though I were being inducted into the top level of his mafia club. Maybe I was. And I hadn't told Josh how desperate things were, nor how much I needed David's financial help. Instead, I'd made my living arrangements seem very casual – 'David's offered me Olivia's place while I sort myself out, it's just for a few weeks, isn't that kind of him?'

I'd made our relationship appear platonic, paternal and mutual – 'David's been a rock for me, really, he's helped a lot.'

After waking up with David following the summer party, I hadn't known what to do. I'd almost convinced myself that I must have done something wrong and therefore had no right to throw around accusations I couldn't definitively prove. David was Josh's only living relative: saying anything against him would be devastating. That's why I'd kept quiet.

But now Jade knew about us and the rumours would start soon afterwards. I had to talk to her again, explain myself... if that was even possible. She'd be devastated. And then I'd have to talk to David.

I felt physically sick about the prospect of coming clean. This was all such a mess.

The vague plan I'd had in my head had been so different and I wondered if there was any chance of us getting there now. Would we ever just be Josh and Ava?

Part of me wasn't willing to give up on the dream, I wasn't ready: he was such a brilliantly happy, hilarious, hunky human and I loved him. And he loved me.

32

Jade

My dry eyes fluttered a few times, the world a blur before me. Glass crunched under my weight as I rolled over onto my side. I stank, but I didn't care. I was frozen, my hands blue from sleeping next to an open window, yet I felt nothing. All I wanted was wine. My wrists braced as glass cut into the palms of my hands and I pushed myself upright. I crawled on my hands and knees like a sick family cat to the kitchen and pulled a bottle of Sauvignon Blanc from the fridge. The clock on the oven ticked four minutes past six.

I heard the clip-clop of heels striking wood. My housemate flew into the kitchen.

'Really?'

I didn't look at her, just took the wine, a handful of pills, and made my way back to the lounge. I took the blanket I'd never washed from the sofa, lay down on the floor and closed my eyes to shut her out.

'You can't do this to yourself, Jade. You need to face the

music. So you found out the guy you like is an asshole? Well then, welcome to the real world.'

Shut *up*.

'He *was* technically single.'

Shut up.

I brought the blanket up over my face, the odour of dust surrounding me, sick of this, sick of her, sick of Josh. Sick of everything and everyone. Bubbles burbled deep in my stomach.

'Whatever happened, wine at six in the morning is not the answer, not going to work is not the answer. Get up, get in the shower, clean up this mess and get out!'

I lost it. I screamed using all the firepower left in my body. Screaming over everything she said, screaming over her judgmental stare, screaming over my pain, through the cold. When I had nothing left and my body gave in, I sank back onto the floor, wiping the spittle away that had lashed out with my roar. She stood in the corner of the room, snarling. Why wouldn't she just leave? I picked up the bottle, unscrewed the cap and stared at her as I downed a third of it in one go. That's what I think of your fucking advice.

My phone chimed.

Where did you go last night?

33

Ava

We're still in the early days of our relationship, the *early,
early* days. The kind you should look back on when you're
tired and old and grumpy and fantasise about returning
to. Josh, at least, was living in the rose-tinted world of
young love and, if it weren't for the obvious, I'd be right
there with him, living the kind of happiness only families
in cereal commercials seem to achieve. Sometimes, for one
soaring, blissful minute, I'd be able to hit the mute button
on our relationship remote control and eliminate all the
unnecessary noise and, in that moment, my only focus
would be on him, our love, our future. I lived for those
quiet moments.

We lay together now, flushed flesh on crisp cotton, and I
stared at him as he dozed beside me. After David's threats
about honesty and integrity I'd felt apprehensive about
returning to Olivia's place tonight and, when Josh had
asked me to stay over at his, I'd accepted. I wished I could
stay here every night. I wished I could make this bubble last.

I decided I'd tell David I'd gone back to be with my parents for the evening – that I'd completely forgotten it was my mum's birthday and that I'd had to head home at the last minute. I knew lying to him wasn't the smartest idea but it was temporary, just until I could figure out my next move.

I delicately traced a line with my finger from the base of Josh's neck, following the ripple of each vertebrae along his strong, smooth spine. He wriggled a little then grabbed my hand, like a snake that had snapped its jaws over a mouse, and held me down.

'What have I told you about tickling me while I'm sleeping?' He hated it when I stroked him, but I couldn't help it! He was so perfect!

'What does today have in store for you, beautiful?' His face was sleepy but his husky-blue eyes sparkled with life.

'Hmm, let's see: Jade is doing everything possible to derail the AthLuxe launch, Kai's one mistake away from firing us all, and David currently has no idea how close we are to losing his biggest new client.'

I nuzzled my face into Josh's neck and let the warmth from his body seep into mine. I didn't want to go to work, I just wanted to forget about everything and lie here with him all day long.

'Pretty bad, isn't it? Jade's turned into a nightmare, it's like she's a different person.' He pulled me closer and wrapped his arms round me. 'We'll be OK, Ava, as long as we have each other.'

I shut out the noise and bathed in his words.

'I should talk to her today,' he said reluctantly.

I groaned. 'Do you want me to come?'

'I think it's better if I speak to her alone, then she won't feel so ganged up on, you know?'

'Do you think she'll tell Georgette? If she does, half the office will know by lunchtime.'

He interlocked my fingers with his and laughed as if our mistake was nothing more than a blip, a blunder, a boo-boo.

'I'm sorry. This is all my fault for not being able to control myself at work. I just can't resist—' He brought me on top of him, manipulating my body with little effort, my legs either side of his hips. Then he pushed the chunk of my hair that had fallen in front of my face behind my ear. I shivered. It reminded me of David. It reminded me how little Josh knew.

'We should tell David sooner rather than later,' he said, reading my mind, sending the light and love and laughter from his bedroom, replacing it with unwelcomed reality.

'Maybe we should do it tomorrow? I know you have that meeting in Croydon today.'

'Perfect,' he answered.

And, just like that, another secret wedged itself between us. Another lie, another riddle I'd spun to survive but wasn't sure how to resolve. I had to get to David before Josh, but I momentarily lost myself in the thought of simply running away, putting millions of miles between myself and London and W&SP's poisonous hive.

34

Jade

The dregs of beer, flat and foamy, made their way down my dehydrated throat. Malty and warm, the taste of desperation, reminding me of my first experience using alcohol for escapism. In the school holidays, when I was back at home and the house was sleeping, I would sneak downstairs late at night and steal a couple of cans from my parents' entertaining stash. I'd bring them upstairs to my room and drink alone, the alcohol helping me get through those six long, lonely weeks. I'd never been very good at making friends. My parents chalked the drinking up to a 'teenage phase' and never considered there was anything wrong with me: they didn't have any friends, either.

I went to take another sip of my breakfast as I lay on the sofa – more often my bed than the dingy double upstairs – hopeful, but there wasn't a drop left. Saved from myself, just as well, this was no time for drunken escapism: I needed to plan, I needed to plot. I dropped the empty shell on the floor and its aluminium exterior clanged against its peers before settling in place on the floor amongst the myriad of cans and cigarette packets.

My rage was incandescent. Not only had Josh lied to me, played me all along, but he'd reduced me to a horrific sexy-photo-taking *idiot* like so many other clueless, brainless people who go too far and do things they don't want to do to win men over and even though I'd done all of that for him, Ava was still on top. He'd still chosen her. She could have him. That cheating, low-life, scumbag, chinless prick.

I looked forward to the day he screwed her over too. You'd find me sitting in the front row with a box of popcorn cheering for an encore, clapping like a Seaworld seal. I dragged my reluctant body upstairs and changed into my go-to tunic dress, the smell of it – vinegary – wrapped round me as I pulled it down over my head, the underarms still damp.

I took the bus into work, selecting a seat on the top deck towards the back. It occurred to me as I tasted the beer on my tongue that I'd neglected to brush my teeth. I shoved my finger into my mouth and scraped it roughly along each line, pausing to shovel out a build-up of plaque nestled away in a crevice towards the back. I watched as a young couple took the two spare seats ahead of me. I eyed the backs of their heads angrily as the man tucked himself under the woman's chin and slid his hand inside her coat. I scowled. Commuting was no time for affection. This was probably a new relationship; few established couples feel the need to shove their happiness in other people's faces. I thought about her poor colleagues who'd have to endure the story of her latest escapades with 'gorgeous'... hmm, he looked like a Michael. *Gorgeous Mike.* It sounded like an oxymoron. I bet that's what her workmates thought. They'd be right. What kind of lothario uses his date's shoulder as a pillow? I bet he was the kind of modern-day man who'd force her to get rid of a spider in the bath, leave her to put up the shelves in the spare room, but also expect her to cook and clean and wash and iron. I had half a mind to follow her into work and set the record straight. This guy was the worst. About as house trained as an alpaca, with similarly shaggy, unkempt hair... which *she'd* probably had to tie up in that ridiculous man-bun this morning because he couldn't even do *that* himself.

As I stared daggers at them, imagining how much her colleagues must hate her, I pulled out my phone from my rucksack and clicked into my gallery, scrolling through until I landed on the picture of David and Ava. I zoomed in, examining it from different angles, staring into the haunted pallor of her face. I guess this was what she'd look like dead. I smiled. I'd enjoy showing this to Josh.

The bus sat in traffic and the windows steamed up. I leant my head against the mist and let the condensation wet my hair. I thought about the day ahead, about the satisfaction of wiping the joy from her face. You know, there should really be a limit to how long you have to work with someone you don't like. The first few months are fine, then every day starts to wear you down, you stop pretending to hide your distaste for one another and, before long, you're lying awake at night fantasising about ways to kill them. Where I was with Ava now, I was ready to actually do it.

Payback.

That shouldn't be it though.
You need to go further, grander, end this once and for all.
You need to taste her blood.

35

Ava

Kai's number illuminated my desk phone and I picked up, trying to pull my head from the doom.

'Ava, I've been thinking about goody bags for launch night.'

None of this was important any more.

'Uh huh...' I replied testily.

'Shouldn't we have separate ones for the VIPs? Maybe I should write a personal note to each celebrity saying, you know: welcome to the collection, thanks so much for your commitment and love for our new activewear line, if you have any questions don't hesitate to contact me directly, here's my number...'

I raised an eyebrow. Who had commitment and love for an activewear brand for God's sake? What kind of questions was Kai expecting to receive on his help-with-activewear hotline? This was all such complete and utter rubbish and it was all I could do not to smash the receiver down into the phone. But I didn't, and Kai's shallow and vacuous ramblings continued.

'I'm just thinking, you know, it's going to be great once we get these A-listers on side. Perhaps I could take them for dinner? Give them some merchandise, then call the paparazzi to take photos of us leaving. Or I could do it all on my Instagram? Is that something you could arrange?'

Kai just wanted to bag himself a celebrity pal and five minutes of parasitic fame. His plan was transparent and tragic in equal measure. Unfortunately, though, I couldn't tell him that.

'I think that's a great idea, who would you like to go for dinner with first? A Kardashian?' I was being sarcastic, but his delusion managed to cloud reality and he didn't realise I'd checked out, that I was saying yes to any and every thing because I just didn't care any more.

'I love the Kardashians! I'd like to choose the venue, though. And I'll have to get a stylist for the night. Wait, no, a glam squad.'

Clients were, save for a few exceptions, utterly hopeless. Some of the skill in my job was knowing that but making them feel like they weren't.

'Was there anything else?'

There wasn't, and Kai left the call just as I spotted Josh grab his coat and head out to his meeting in Croydon. He didn't smile at me as he left, not that I was expecting him to, and I turned my attention back to my emails. The one at the top burned hollows through my retinas.

Ava. My office please. David.

The one-line email was only five words long but it turned my world upside down. He knew. He knew about Josh and he was about to fire me. One of my hands developed an involuntary spasm and I considered that if I'd been any older I might have suffered a stroke thanks to the stress. Again, I thought about running, but some stupid part of me wanted to face up to what I'd done: the part of me naive enough to think perhaps I could talk David into forgiving me.

I rose from my desk and took my first steps up to his office. They were the hardest. My nerves were suffocating and the butterflies in my stomach felt more like giant, ugly moths. The last time I'd spoken to him he'd told me in no uncertain terms where his boundaries were: no lies. And no one else. Now I was about to tell him that not only was I seeing someone, that it was pretty serious, and that the man in question was his adopted son and sole living relative.

His PA snarled at me as I sauntered past her, ignoring her as she bleated, 'Excuse me, you can't just walk in, I have to check he's ready for—'

Too late. I closed David's office door on her, her mouth still moving, her body halfway to standing. She wasn't a very good gatekeeper; her reaction time was appalling. I didn't dare breathe him in. The smell of him alone was so intimidating it made me want to run and not look back. I kept the air circulating through my mouth instead. My hand rested on the door handle for a beat after it clicked shut, the contact with the metal strangely comforting. I took a quick, short breath and turned to face him.

He looked up from his desk. 'Ava.'

His voice lurked from the other end of the room and I watched him remove a pair of reading glasses from his face.

'Thanks for coming up.'

I hadn't prepared any small talk. 'No problem,' I replied. It was all I could manage.

I took the seat across from him and sat on my hands like a schoolgirl about to be expelled. As I waited for him to speak, I found myself observing the photos on his desk and Olivia's face beamed out at me from the frames: Spade in hand, ice cream smeared across her delighted, chubby cheeks on a pretty beach somewhere. Next to it a black and white family portrait, Olivia in the middle on her knees smiling seriously into the camera, David and his wife on either side in casual nineties attire: acid-wash Levis and giant patterned shirts. The last was a more recent picture, a selfie I'd seen on her social media: hollowed out yellow eyes, painfully thin arms, heavily overlined lips, blonde hair in waves over her right shoulder. That one killed me. She was crying out for help, the sadness emanating from her so blatant it was impossible to ignore. But we had. *We all had.* It made me want to weep. It made me want to travel back in time, wrap her in my arms and tell her that I was going to help her get better. But I couldn't, of course. What was done was done. I swallowed the lump in my throat.

'You probably know what I'm about to ask,' he said ominously. My mouth was completely dry, every muscle tense. 'Where were you last night, Ava? Who were you with?' I stopped breathing. 'I checked the cameras to make sure you got home safely. And last night you didn't appear. You didn't tell me you were going anywhere...' He spoke slowly. 'So, tell me now. Who were you with? Where were you? This isn't a great start to your first day as Team Head, darling.'

My hands were clasped together like a corpse. 'With Josh,' I managed to croak out after a pause. I could only bear to look at his face for a second as a toxic combination of anger, jealousy, confusion, bewilderment and rejection ripped across it. I felt him steady himself, noticed his breathing turn a little ragged. I don't think I'd ever heard David *breathe* before, everything he did was always very purposeful: he didn't like to be surprised. I looked at the floor, at the sea of wriggling worms I'd spilt all over it.

'What?' His eyes flashed dark, almost black.

'We're together,' I managed to say, my focus on a tiny speck of fluff beneath his desk. My voice was meek, wretched, every fibre of my being desperate to escape. I should have run when I had the chance. In return David's stare was blank, save for a microscopic glint of something in his eye. Had he suspected it?

'Right,' he pursed his lips. 'Like to keep it in the family do you, darling?'

I felt like I'd been kicked in the head and the room spun in messy circles, Olivia's face jeering at me. *I thought we were friends, Ava!*

'I feel terrible about this, I really do.' I fought back tears.

'You used me. You used me to get away from Charlie and what, Josh was your insurance, was he? Your back-up plan? When he finds out what you've done, the lengths you've gone to, he's, well, I guess you haven't told him. Just as well.' His fist connecting with the desk was furious and final. A picture frame fell from its position due to the force of the impact and scattered shards of sparkling glass across the floor. I jumped back in my seat, quivering, fear across my face.

'Get out,' he sneered, fire licking from the corners of his mouth.

The streets were empty as I jumped off the train at Pimlico station. Hot summery rain battered me from all angles, slapping against my face like it was teaching me a lesson and I walked as fast as my feet would allow through the back roads to Olivia's house. There was only one thing I could do now.

The wind was picking up and a warm gust caught my hair, throwing it behind my shoulders, thunderous rain following like a flood; drenching me completely. I focused my attention back on the pavement ahead of me, willing it to shorten so I could reach the front door faster. In my peripheral vision standing out in the rain, I gradually became aware of a figure. Still. Tall. Obscured by the shadows. Waiting. There was no mistaking who it was.

Josh.

My heart sank as that powerful, striking face beamed at me through the drizzle. What was he doing at Olivia's? We'd agreed he wouldn't come here until things were ironed out with David.

'Good timing!' he shouted over the elements. *The opposite, actually.*

'Croydon was depressing,' he said, the normality of his conversation making me feel a thousand times worse. We'd never get back to this. Inside, I wrapped my arms as far round his back as they would go, holding him close, not caring about the rain on his trench coat, or the make-up running down my face. He kissed me on the forehead and I pulled back, looking into his eyes.

'What are you doing here?' I asked.

'David called, he wanted to meet me here... He's coming over in a bit.'

We broke apart, pulled wet overcoats from limbs, my legs almost giving way under the weight of his words.

'How was your afternoon?' he asked. 'You seem a little down.' He ran a hand through my sodden hair and lifted my chin up, forcing me to sink into his perfect proportions. 'Does David know already?'

I paused for a moment, not quite knowing what to say.

'My mum's not well.'

'What? Oh God, I had no idea, I'm so sorry.' He angled his head slightly and looked deeper into my eyes. Could he see right through me?

'I need to drive home tonight to see her. You'll have to tell David on your own, I'm sorry.'

I convinced myself I was doing an OK impression of togetherness on the outside but inside my body was running riot. Light head, fast heart, shallow breath. The hallmarks of an imminent anxiety attack.

'Can you wait half an hour?' he asked, hopefully. 'I've ordered pizza...'

If only things were that simple. My knees knocked as he went through to the kitchen and my head flipped the world a quarter turn, my ears ringing so loud it was as though it would drown everything out and break my head in two. But something pulled me back from the brink. My survival instinct, perhaps. My next step.

My escape. I rushed upstairs and flung everything I could into a suitcase. Most of this stuff probably used to be Olivia's, but I didn't care. I didn't have anything of my own any more. I didn't know what my next step was, I just knew I had to leave. I wasn't applying any kind of considered thought process to what went in the bag. If I happened to pass it on my journey round the bedroom, it was going in. If I didn't, it wasn't. I could go home tonight, maybe, then head for the coast. Or overseas? Amsterdam? Spain? America? I sensed Josh close in on the bedroom door and a shadow fell across the room.

'Is everything OK?' I jumped out of my skin as his voice cut through my planning. I took a short, shaky breath, 'Yes, yes, of course. I just need to get back.'

He eyed up my suitcase, clothes pouring out of the top, obviously overfilled, never going to close.

'How long are you planning to be away for?' He shot me a look. A look that said *I know you're lying to me, but I don't know why, I want to trust you because I love you, but you're freaking me out*. I couldn't bear to think what his face would look like when David told him the truth; when David told him what we'd done together. David was obsessed enough with loyalty and honesty, and Josh was just the same. How had I ever thought it would be possible to get myself out of this? I tore myself away from his stare.

'As long as I'm needed, I guess.'

Under his watchful eye the weight of my regret grew heavier and the faster I tried to move against it to leave, the harder it resisted. I felt like I was trapped in a ball pit, each movement dropping me deeper, using every ounce of adrenaline to build up the energy to thrash free, only to find it was futile. I chucked out some clothes from on top so the case would close, then zipped it up and pushed past him, running down the stairs in my race against time.

'Call me when you get home, OK?' His voice came from behind me as he followed me down the staircase.

'Sure,' I said, standing on the threshold of the front door. I looked at him from over my shoulder. 'Apparently the traffic's really bad. It will probably take me ages to get back. Don't wait up.' It took a second for me to realise I was crying. I wasn't going to call him tonight. I wasn't going to call him ever again.

'Don't cry, Ava, everything's going to be fine. As long as we're honest with each other, OK?'

The words hit me like acid and the floodgates well and truly opened.

He spun me round to face him and pulled me close, stemming the flow of tears with kisses and promises that he'd join me at the weekend if I was still at home, rocking us gently back and forth in our embrace, making leaving him even harder than it already was.

'I'll miss you,' I sniffed, pressing my fingers into my eyes.

'I'll miss you, too.'

For one, bright, beautiful moment I let myself believe that we'd be reunited one day. I'd write him a letter explaining everything, he'd be angry but would forgive me after a few days of frostiness and we'd move on, eating pizza together again like nothing had ever happened. David would let me back, perhaps I'd have to work a little harder for a few months to prove myself, but then he'd promote me and everything would get back on track. Back to normal. And it would be feasible, I guess, if I hadn't done what I'd done. If

Olivia was still alive. Because even if we got over this secret, there was another, monstrous one waiting to take its place. *I know what you've done*, the wind howled as it picked up, throwing a new flurry of rain to the ground. Something flickered in Josh's eye as I pulled apart from him, but it was just that; a flicker. Gone before I could interpret what it meant.

'I love you,' I said, feebly, almost to myself, as I headed for my old, battered car.

I texted Mum before I set off, just in case Josh somehow managed to get hold of my parents. If he did, they'd deduce between them that I needed some space and would, hopefully, leave me enough time to escape.

I'm heading away for a few days, work stress, just need a bit of fresh air. Might come and visit afterwards. Ava.

It had taken two hours just to get out of the clutches of central London, but I was finally closing in on the countryside and the roads had shifted from wide, four-lane motorways to thin, slithery trails. The rain had abated and the sun was setting, the sky a watercolour of pinks, greys and reds. I imagined the air outside smelt damp and dewy. I'd decided to drive towards Oxford and stop at the first hotel I liked the look of. My head was still thick and woolly from blubbering through my goodbyes to Josh and, although the panic hadn't completely subsided, I knew that was just because my body didn't have the energy to sustain it. I'd spent most of the journey imagining the scenario of

David turning up at the flat minutes after I'd left. He'd tell Josh all about us and Josh would be blindsided, trying his best to make sense of it all. He'd be furious. David would calm him down. He'd reassure Josh that I wouldn't have a job at the agency any more and that he should move on. I imagined Josh saying to David that Charlie had been right about me all along. That I was a cheater. That I was dishonest. That I'd only ever been out for myself. That I'd used them both to get ahead. *She wasn't quite clever enough to pull it off, though, was she?* he'd say to David. David would give Jade the Team Head job, she'd move into my office and, soon enough, they'd forget I'd ever worked there. Every trace of me erased.

A yellow glare filled my rear-view mirror and I looked up, stupidly, blinding myself. It flashed again and again, and I blinked quickly trying to rid my retinas of the misshapen objects temporarily tattooed across them. The car behind was an SUV of some kind. I slowed my pace, perhaps they wanted to overtake?

Wrong.

The beams fired again in my mirror, longer this time, and my heart started to race. I turned off the radio and pushed my foot to the floor, accelerating away with a determined growl of the engine. With the music stopped, the situation felt all the more threatening and I hummed quietly, pretending to myself that everything was fine. I kept one eye on the road ahead, one eye behind. I didn't know what to do. The car flashed its indicator and the driver, who I couldn't make out thanks to their blinding light show, was waving their arm out of the window. They wanted me to pull over. I kept driving for a moment but, when the headlights flashed for a third time and the indicator went on, I decided to comply.

My car's engine spluttered as it idled by the side of the road, the indicator ticking away rhythmically. My breath was short and I wiggled my toes in my trainers as I waited. Was it an undercover officer? Maybe my brake lights were faulty. A problem with my insurance? I heard a car door opening, the leather of my car seat squeaking as I lent closer towards the rear-view mirror, but I could only make out shadows behind the headlights. Perhaps it was just a concerned member of the public letting me know my boot was half-open, or that a pheasant was trapped on the back bumper. The door slammed shut decisively.

I knew I should get out of the car to talk to the stranger, any normal person would, but I felt uneasy and kept my hand locked round the steering wheel in case I needed to make a quick getaway. The figure came into view. My body braced, confused. *What are* you *doing here*?

I didn't understand what was happening until it was too late. My foot searched for the accelerator and my hand flailed, trying to release my seatbelt, but I hadn't managed to make contact with either before the window had smashed next to me and a gloved hand raced to cover my mouth, strong and synthetic, forcing the scream that was hurtling out back inside my body. The engine cut as the key was pulled from the ignition and I grabbed for my attacker's face, hair, anything that might have hindered their progress. But it was futile. My attempts to escape ending with my wrists being bound, the strength of my attacker's one arm completely outmatching my two. Before I could breathe, one hand had clamped round my mouth, the other round my wrist, so hard I could feel my pulse against their grip. Both were steadfast and my eyes darted wildly from left to right inside their sockets. I tried to wriggle free by arching my back and kicking out my legs, bruising them as they came into harsh contact with the car surrounding me. My breathing was frantic, panicked, accompanied by frightened, muffled whimpers. Then, one hand moved away from my mouth and into the attacker's pocket. They grabbed a dirty rag. I only registered this was happening when it was heading back towards me. At that moment, my brain engaged its ill-trained survival instinct and I used everything in me to scream, as loudly as humanly possible, guttural and savage, for anybody nearby. The person moved faster, unnerved by the strength of my cry, and I snapped my head rapidly from side to side, changing tack, gluing my mouth firmly shut – knowing they wanted to muzzle me with the cloth.

My attacker's gloved fingers prised open the corners of my mouth and I resisted as best I could, the smell of the mouldy rag enough to engage my gag reflex. My jaw ached as I fought against the force and I could feel my reserves burning up. Soon I'd be fighting with adrenaline alone. I knew if I didn't break free now I never would. The headlights still burned brightly and streaked across my line of vision as I looked up momentarily, then, I disarmed my attacker for a moment by opening my mouth wide, biting down, quickly, hard, on the hand trying to push the rag inside me. I heard the crunch, the break of fragile bones underneath my determined teeth, but the person didn't let go, stifling a cry before summoning some super-human strength to finally force the wet cloth into my mouth.

I choked as my tongue tried to escape down my throat to avoid touching its surface. They tied the ends of the gag behind my head and pulled it tight, ripping the corners of my lips open, fresh blood spilling from each. Barely able to breathe, tears streaking down my face, I looked up, right into those eyes, silently pleading. *Please don't do this.*

A noxious smell surrounded me and I shook my head frantically, kicking my legs up against the steering wheel once again and away from the poison cloth in their hand. It was a useless protest and my vision soon cut out as the smell covered my face, eyelids twisting against the material, lashes folding inwards. My heart thundered. Adrenaline saturated my body. *Fight, fight, fight.* My breath was shallow and incredibly fast, trying to keep up, forcing my brain away from the darkness and its gaping, black, terror. My body tangled and turned, fighting until the end, until there was nothing.

7 Days Later

PUBLIC APPEAL AGAINST POLICE DECISION
TO RULE AVA WELLS A RUNAWAY

Seven days ago, twenty-eight-year-old Ava Wells was reported missing from her Pimlico home by her boyfriend Joshua Stein. Today, Ava Wells' parents are urging the public to 'stop turning up at their home' and to 'respect the Met's investigation', as concerns mount against the force's decision to downgrade the search in the light of evidence unearthed during their brief investigation.

Ava's last-known moments have been released by the police in their entirety as they defend their move to scale back the operation amidst public pressure, which started on social media but has transformed into a very real-world presence. Detective Inspector Frederick Crow said, 'As has been widely reported in the media already: Prior to her disappearance on the afternoon of June 12th, Ava Wells packed a bag, bought a one-way ticket to Dublin, ordered 1,000 Euros, and drove from her central London home on a route towards Heathrow Airport. Ava's car was left in a short stay car park at the airport and no unusual DNA or fingerprints, other than those who had access to the car, were present. Ava sent a text message to her parents in the hours before her drive to say that she needed to get away. She told her parents she was stressed at work. Ava Wells boarded her flight to Dublin International Airport that same day and we are in touch with Irish officials to pinpoint her exact location.

'We would like to take this opportunity to remind the public that it is an adult's legal right to leave the country without necessarily telling their loved ones why they are leaving. We understand this is an incredibly difficult time, but the Wells family does not doubt that Ava left London willingly, and we ask that the media, and members of the public, respect their privacy. We will continue to work with our counterparts in the ROI to come to a swift resolution on the matter.'

36

Jade

The entire office had descended into chaos as soon as Ava was reported missing. Josh still wasn't at work – everyone knew about their relationship now – Georgette was inconsolably hysterical, Kai was acting like Queen Victoria in her mourning years, and I was left to pick up everything Ava had left behind.

David had hastily organised a meeting with me this morning, he was back in the building after helping the police with their enquiries, and my hands wouldn't stop shaking as I knocked apprehensively on his office door. I prayed his head was full of Ava and that he'd put his investigations into my whereabouts on the night Olivia died on hold.

I'd just about been allowed past by his fire-breathing gatekeeper and her questions had already put me on edge. It was the first time I'd been permitted into his lair and my brain was scrambled, vividly depicting catastrophic events I might have to contend with in the coming minutes. *He might accuse me of something. He might fire me on the spot. He might kill me.* I clamped my right hand into a fist. It was time for fight not flight, and a super-human voice somewhere above me shouted over the negative and repeated phrases of encouragement. I drew that voice to the foreground for once and allowed it to give me the strength to keep putting one foot in front of the other.

This is it. This is the moment you've been waiting for.

It's all going to be yours.

Forget about her.

You're doing the right thing.

Everything in David's office was designed to intimidate. From the throne-like chair he occupied, to the black marble decor that made the room feel like an exclusive members only club in the Far East rather than an office in London. It hadn't been very long since we'd sat face to face in that awful interview, David issuing questions, doling out veiled threats, and his haunted irises were all I could think about as I approached. I persuaded my reluctant feet to keep moving, to take a seat opposite the man who struck fear into me, and timidly shuffled towards him, my hands clenched together, my heeled brogues scuffing against the floor. 'One moment, Jade.'

His words were direct, but his focus was on the screen in front of him as he finished up typing. I sat, then tucked and crossed my feet beneath me. Even the whites of his eyes were tinged yellow today and he squinted slightly as he concentrated. I guess he hadn't had much sleep. I stole a look outside the floor-to-ceiling window to my right while I waited for his next instruction. The height we were at distorted the view of the people below so that from here they looked like nothing more than busy little insects buzzing from A to B. Even though each of them must have had a mission, a purpose, it seemed so insignificant from all the way up here. One group would cross at the traffic lights below, then, just a few seconds later, a new, identical group would take their place. It was hard to care about people when they were that small: such little people with their tiny little problems. Not like mine.

'Nice to see you,' he said, and I snapped my head back towards him, finding the courage to look into that chiselled, cavernous face.

'Jade, with Ava missing I'd like you to accept the position of Team Head. Staff need strong leadership at times like this and I'm looking to you to galvanize everyone.'

David liked to get to the point, his delivery stern and sincere. I floundered for the right thing to say, so often tongue-tied in his presence, today no exception. This was slightly different though; it was jubilation bursting from my chest which I had to hide and it was all I could do not to jump up and down and punch the air with glee. I was so proud of myself! He saw in me a strong and courageous leader, which was *exactly* what I was.

'David, I wholeheartedly accept. Thank you for the opportunity.'

I heard the words back as soon as I stopped talking and realised too late how much I sounded like an over-eager contestant on *The Apprentice*.

Why couldn't I just be normal? He bowed his head; I was dismissed. I had some questions, though, and I tried my hardest to make my tone more assertive.

'Can I just ask, is this position mine now? There's no rescinding the offer if Ava returns?'

'The position is yours.'

David had already turned back to his computer screen.

'I'd like to tell the team today, if that's OK? Then I'll move my things into Ava's office. I'll make sure all her stuff is kept and boxed up.'

I rose from my seat, brimming with confidence and pride. I'd done it, against the odds, I'd actually bloody gone and done it!

'Whatever you think is best,' he replied, but I wasn't sure he'd heard what I said.

I skipped back from David's office as if he'd given me a gold star. My soul was healing at last, this promotion solidifying eight years of blood, sweat and tears, and the feeling of unbridled happiness confirmed to me that it had been worth fighting for. *You might have beaten Ava to the job, but she ran rings round you for Josh. And wasn't he the real prize, anyway?*

I silenced the voice. Things weren't over for Josh and me. So what if our virtual relationship hadn't amounted to anything yet? It would. At least I hoped it would, as soon as he knew the truth about Ava. It was just telling him about her that was the problem. It seemed a touch insensitive to show him the picture of Ava and David together when he was out every day trying to figure out where she'd gone.

As I strutted back to my desk, a foot taller than when I'd left, I thought about the looks he'd given me; there'd never been any malice in his pale, husky eyes or deceit in those thick, dark lashes. He hadn't deserved to be chewed up and spat out by someone like her. But, when the time was right, I would heal him, I would teach him how to love again.

Perhaps all of this was *meant* to happen? I thought, as

I kicked out my padded chair, turned, and let my weight fall into it. The Universe, in her divine wisdom, always did exactly what she was supposed to do – it just sometimes took a while before it all made sense. I picked up a hairband from my desk and fixed my black locks into a high ponytail, scraping the wisps at the back of my neck up into it, not bothered that they'd come loose in a matter of moments. I glanced at the empty seat that used to be Georgette's, still covered in long strands of her dead, dyed hair. She'd barely spoken to me since Ava went missing and had moved her stuff back to the main bullpen with the rest of the team where she used to sit. Their desks were small and cramped, table-top plants grew on top of swollen in-trays, old make-up sat drying out on their tables next to highlighted notes and old client presentations. I didn't care. I mean, I didn't understand why she'd want to go back to that, but I didn't care.

Time to focus on my number one priority. I hammered out an email to the team.

Emergency meeting in the boardroom, reschedule anything, this is important.

I got up and made my way to the meeting room, waiting impatiently for my lazy workers to peel themselves from their seats and join me. What was it about the word *emergency* that they didn't understand? I watched as they moved like elephants through treacle and drummed my fingers against the glass table to externalise my irritation, which was growing by the second as the infuriating tick-tick-tick of the clock on the wall reminded me that precious seconds of my life were being wasted. Finally, once my troops had gathered, I addressed them.

'Right, now that everyone's finally here, I have an announcement to make.' I raised my voice in the style of a drill sergeant addressing a fresh intake of soldiers.

I paused for dramatic effect.

'I am your new Team Head.' Eyes widened, palms twitched, heads spun.

I was caught off-guard for a moment, disappointed that there hadn't been even an attempt at applause or congratulations from my squadron.

I persevered, my disappointment bringing out my inner dictator.

'And I'll be starting right away. This team hasn't had good leadership for a while and it's time to set that back on track. First of all, I'd like to meet with each of you separately.'

The atmosphere turned dark and a girl with dimples and gold rings shuffled from one foot to the other, moving her weight to try to relieve some of the tension in the room.

'Georgette, I'll start with you.' She looked like she was spoiling for World War III. 'The rest of you are free to go.'

Georgette didn't move a muscle, her lack of respect clearly communicated through her refusal to adopt a less casual pose, and, as we waited for the room to empty, she continued her display of defiance, leaning casually against the glass wall, twiddling her pen between her fingers, a sarcastic smirk across her face. The rest of the girls left without so much as a whisper; the movement of bodies, the hum of tension and the anticipation of a mass-exodus at lunchtime so they could gossip, the only silent sounds.

'Take a seat,' I told Georgette, once the door had closed behind us.

'I'd prefer to stand.'

We stood at opposite ends of the room. I thought about a Sheriff busting in and breaking up our duel. But she didn't realise it was the new Jade Fernleigh she was facing: the one who takes first place, rather than waiting forever for someone to give it to her.

'No, you'll sit,' I said again, this time much more deliberately and clearly to put across my meaning; there was no option here, *this* Jade did not put up with dissent in the ranks.

I sat first, to show her, and she followed, reluctantly wrapping her hand round the nearest chair then sliding it out to the side of her, scraping it along the wood floor to cause a set of deliberately piercing vibrations. I winced. She sat in an equally laborious motion and didn't tuck the chair back in, choosing to sit away from the table. It was pathetic, she was acting like a petulant teenager.

'Georgette, do you like your job?' I said, looking down at my notepad, then directly at her. My question was greeted with derision.

'What do you think?'

'There's no need to be obtuse.'

'I'd say I liked it until about five minutes ago,' she scoffed.

'So, you wouldn't be too bothered if you no longer worked here?'

I delivered the question as more of a statement.

'I wouldn't say that...'

I detected a quiver in her voice.

'OK… so you want to keep your job? That's interesting,' I said, just to annoy her. 'The problem is though, I don't believe you, and I don't have any patience for liars.' I'd been taking notes from David Stein's interview technique. The look on her face changed and she took a moment to respond.

'What have I ever done to you, Jade?'

My jaw dropped at her question and I practically spat out my response, losing my cool for a moment. 'You chose *Ava* when you were supposed to work for me! You called me a bitch at the summer party. You take everything anyone says and relay it round the office like a human parrot wearing circus make-up. You're lazy, sluggish, you make too many mistakes, and it's all because you don't respect me and you don't *listen*. Well, that's all about to change.'

I caught myself and controlled my temper.

'What I mean is, I can't stand for sub-par performance in my team. If I can't trust the people who are working for me, how can we do anything constructive?'

Georgette fired back angrily, my rage sparking hers.

'So this is about me liking Ava more than you. Are you twelve years old, I mean, *are you*? Ava's *missing*, Jade. Missing.' She emphasised the syllables unnecessarily. 'I don't know if you noticed in between getting your promotion and acting like you own the place.'

My blood boiled. Ava was a snake. She didn't deserve the attention she was getting for running away. I knew what had happened: after I'd caught her with Josh, she'd known I could turn both David and Josh against her. So she'd run, scared, like a squealing pig from the slaughter, rather than face up to what she'd done. I'd make sure she did though, don't worry about that.

'She's been gone five minutes and just like that you're switching teams. Especially when there's no suggestion anything bad has happened! I don't get why the whole office is up in arms about it! She *ran away*!' I shrieked.

'She's been gone a week, Jade! It's not like her to just disappear, something definitely happened, something awful.'

'How do you know?' I asked, 'Maybe it's exactly like her.'

'Is it really that difficult for you to show even the slightest bit of concern, or respect?'

'We're not here to talk about my respect for Ava, we're here to talk about yours. For me.'

'You can't get me to leave my job, Jade, you don't have the authority,' she said smugly, adjusting the set of gold bracelets on her wrist.

The pit of my stomach burned, embers alight, ready to destroy. 'It wouldn't be hard to build a case against you, George. In fact, I have full access to each and every inappropriate email you've ever sent. I've even gone to the trouble over the years of keeping a folder of them. I've logged every inappropriate outfit you've ever worn, every slip-up you've ever made, every rumour you've ever started.' We stared at one another, unblinking. I carried on. 'I have endless emails about drunken nights out, flirty texts you've exchanged with clients, hideous remarks you've made about other members of staff. Which, put together, smacks to me entirely of inappropriate use of company time... wouldn't you say?'

I didn't know anything about employment law, I just wanted to scare her enough to think that I did. It worked and she shifted uneasily in her seat.

'What do you want?' She masked her nerves with passive aggression.

'Loyalty.' I was steadfast.

'You want me to pledge some sort of allegiance to you? Is this a joke?' She was out of moves and had resorted to ridiculing me.

'Not at all.'

'OK, fine, I pledge allegiance, to the flag, of the United States of Jade.' She put on a pseudo American accent and placed her hand over her heart, the other up towards the ceiling, her bracelets clanging together as she moved it.

'If you're going to be like that, you can leave now.'

She eyed me up. 'What do I have to do then, to *prove my loyalty?*'

She held up her fingers to denote air quotes over the last three words. I'd rattled her.

'First, I'd like you to clear out Ava's office. I'll be moving in there. Keep her things in boxes and move them to the storeroom downstairs.'

'What!' she exclaimed. 'When Ava comes back she'll *want* her office.'

'I *won*,' I snarled, licking my lips, Ava's blood all over them. She looked at me, horrified, like she'd realised something, then left the room. I couldn't clear out Ava's office myself, it sent the wrong message.

I made a note to fire Georgette tomorrow; she was too far gone.

I stormed into the building just before nine the next morning. It was my first full day as Team Head and I was ready for battle. I'd spent the previous night lost in the crowded aisles of Oxford Street hunting for an outfit that could handle the bloodshed I had planned. In the end, though, I'd chosen a top I'd seen Ava wearing before, with horizontal thick black stripes interlaced with thin yellow lines. Teamed with a black pencil skirt I knew it delivered the right message: I'm your Queen now. I wondered if Josh would be back today. I prayed he would, I couldn't go too much longer without looking at that face.

I knew something was wrong the moment my heel struck the slate tiles of the reception area. The too-happy-to-be-here socialite who patrolled it shuffled away from her desk as soon as she spotted me, the daily chirp she greeted each member of staff with notably absent. I ascended the lift in perfect silence with four fellow colleagues all choosing, quite peculiarly, to occupy the same corner, affording me a generous amount of room. Making my way into the kitchen was equally awkward. A woman with white deodorant lines on her black dress and towel-dried hair didn't even wait for the kettle to boil, choosing to make her morning beverage with lukewarm water rather than be in the same room as me. As she hurried past, I clicked the kettle back on and waited for it to bubble back to life. I busied myself pouring a thin layer of milk and a half-teaspoon of sugar into a mug. Someone appeared at the doorway but headed right back out again. I flung a tea bag into the cup, filled it with boiling water and gripped it tight as I made my way through the double doors, the floor falling to a hushed silence as I passed through the threshold. They'd been talking about me. I slowed my pace, anxious.

What had happened? I turned the corner to my new office

and that's when I saw: My photos for Josh had been printed out, zoomed in, blown up and stuck all over its glass walls. I dropped everything, my boiling mug fell to the floor, the thud audible, drenching my brand new outfit. It took me a moment to spin into action as I took in the grotesque images that looked like a macabre house of mirrors, thanks to the way they'd been cut up, distorted and patched together to look their absolute, horrifying worst. Once I started, I moved fast, barely taking a breath, the shock of what had happened nowhere near sinking in, the urgency of removing the evidence the only thing on my mind. Thank God Josh wasn't here to see this. The sheets ripped easily from the tack holding them up and it didn't take long for the wall to be destroyed. I barked at a nearby intern to clear the mess up, incandescent that she hadn't taken the initiative to start already. My arms were twitching slightly, the ferocity of my recent movement combined with my public humiliation rendering me a quivering wreck. I was sweating profusely under my new striped top, my face shiny and blotchy. I closed my eyes, trying to cling onto some sense of authority. I couldn't be seen to stand for this. It was imperative that I sent a strong, brutal message. I opened my eyes again, the reflected faces of my shell-shocked co-workers visible in the glass walls of my new office opposite. Who had done this? How? Even though I didn't know for sure, I had a pretty good idea. I didn't turn round to address my hostile audience as I called for her.

'Georgette, my office.' I wasn't just going to fire her, I was going to annihilate her.

A voice replied after a prolonged pause. 'She left, Jade, she resigned yesterday.'

Defeat.

37

You write a note to explain why she's here. Even though it's quite simple, really.

Betrayal,
Disloyalty,
Lies.
Revenge,
Retaliation,
Demise.

38

Jade

The team were finding it difficult to accept me as their head. The office felt so much smaller and I was tripping over people who hated me every day. Georgette's little stunt had set everything off to a terrible start and, without her to make an example of, I had to look to more creative means to earn the respect of my rebellious recruits. And, apart from all that, client work wasn't going well either. Plans for the AthLuxe launch had veered off course due to the triple departure of Ava, Josh and Georgette. I thought I could handle it but I didn't realise how much weight they'd all pulled and I was sinking in the workload, not helped by the fact that my thoughts were entirely preoccupied. Now that I had the Team Head job, I was beginning to question everything. Did the world really *need* a sports fashion show?

I was speaking to Kai, no idea what time it was, propping my phone up to my ear with my shoulder, trying to read an urgent press release at the same time, a frustrated hand clutching my temples as I half-listened to him rant.

'It's not *good enough*, Jade! We've been talking about this launch for months, and now that it's just round the corner all four wheels have come off the wagon, the fucking horse has had a heart attack, and today you've just told me the hillbilly in the front is on fire!'

It was true that things were bad. 'I think if we could just discuss postponing for a couple of weeks—'

He cut me off. 'Do *not* suggest that to me right now!' He continued with a high voice, presumably meant to imitate my own. *'Don't worry, Kai, the hillbilly's on fire but if we leave him for two weeks he'll burn out and everything will be bloody brilliant again.'* He switched back to his own voice, full of fury. 'I could really do without this, Jade! Just *fix it!*'

'Fine, fine, look, we *are* on top of it, everything will be great, the launch will be fantastic.'

I lifted a glass of water to my lips and shakily swallowed what must have been my fifteenth pill of the day to try and calm myself down. They just weren't working any more, I needed to go to the doctor, sort it out, but I didn't have any *time*. There was no answer to my empty promise and I wondered if he'd just hurled himself out of the fiftieth floor window he sat beside.

'I miss her,' he said eventually. 'I always prefer blondes to head up my teams. Brunettes are terrible luck. My ex was a brunette, he was a witch, and I'm sure he put a hex on me to make sure I could never date another brunette. Now I know that hex extended to work, too.'

I wanted to dive in through the phone line and throttle him. *Yes, my hair colour has everything to do with my ability to do the job, I'll go out and dye it immediately.*

Then I had a thought. Maybe that wouldn't be such a bad idea? I felt like I needed a fresh start, a makeover; Kai would welcome the gesture as much as anything else and, well, there was one pretty important person who I thought might prefer it too.

After work, in the familiar surroundings of my dingy flat, I formulated a plan smoking a cigarette in bed, dotting the ash on the dusty carpet. My housemate was back. I hadn't seen her for weeks, but here she was, live and kicking. I didn't bother going out to greet her and waited for her to barge into my bedroom.

'Jade! You're in the news!' She lingered in the doorway.

'I am?'

'Your company, not *you*. What happened to her, Jade? What happened to Ava?'

I threw the cigarette to the ground and lifted myself out of bed. I marched over to the door, standing face to face with her for a moment, then slammed it shut, the force of the air compressing through the doorway and billowing under my nightshirt.

'First Olivia died and now Ava's missing. What is it about the women you work with? What are you, some kind of curse?' she asked, her voice muffled by the barrier between us.

'I don't want to talk about Olivia. Or Ava. Just, go away, just – leave me alone!'

Eventually, I heard her footsteps move away and I knew I was by myself. I couldn't let her distract me from this evening's plan so, before I could change my mind, I grabbed my anorak from behind the door and threw it on over my pyjama shirt. I stuffed my feet into a friendly pair of battered Converse and raced down the stairs and out of the front door before she could ask me any more questions. It had been raining for days and thick, tropical drops were still descending on the muggy capital, so I tucked my hair under the hood of my raincoat as I took my first steps outside. I jogged down the pavement, my heels sending dirty splashes up my legs as they struck the sodden ground, slowing as I approached the twenty-four-hour newsagent on the corner. I pushed my bare hand against the front door, disgusted to feel wet condensation under my palm as it made contact, and a robotic sound chimed to alert everyone to my dishevelled presence. I scanned the assorted aisles. How did they choose what to stock in places like this, seriously? Spaghetti hoops next to children's books, tin foil next to inflatable lilos, printer paper next to Royal Wedding '11 memorabilia. I honed in on the shop's attempt at a beauty section. Thankfully, they had what I needed. Bleach. I pulled the worn packet from the shelf and hurried to the till, plonking it on the counter in front of a sullen-faced young man.

'Sixteen pound,' he said in a thick accent.

I dug deep in my coat pocket for the twenty-pound note I knew was in there and, once located, thumped it triumphantly on the counter top.

'Four pound.'

His expression remained the same as he dropped four pound coins onto the counter and stuffed the hair bleach into a small carrier bag. I jogged home, jamming my key into the front door to lock it shut and considered how pointless the ritual was – if someone wanted to break in, they'd just hop through the window in the lounge I'd smashed and hadn't bothered to repair with more than a patchwork of newsagent finest bin bags and gaffa tape.

I hurried up to the bathroom, took the packet of bleach in my hand, pulled out the instructions – slightly disconcerted that they were displayed entirely in Greek – and did my best to follow the picture diagrams printed on one side of the flimsy leaflet. I wrestled with the pair of plastic gloves, angry that my hands weren't slim enough for 'one size fits all', and opened the bottle. The smell emanating from the bright blue mixture was fresh, sterile and chemical and I let my brain wander off on a tangent, considering how quickly it would burn a hole in my trachea if I swallowed it. I shook my head, putting the thought of my burning insides to one side, and wiped the mirror in front of me clear with my elbow. It was thick with greasy smears – God knows the last time I'd cleaned it. I applied the bleach first round my hairline, then worked it back into the ends.

I had to wait half an hour for the dye to work, at least, the diagram had a picture of a clock with the number 30 next to it... so I assumed that's what it meant. I sat on the bathroom floor letting the bleach mercilessly attack my scalp, burning grooves across the length of my head. I prayed out loud the packet hadn't meant thirty seconds.

At eighteen minutes I couldn't bear it any longer and jumped into the shower, frantically rinsing my hair free from the chemicals. The powerful smell mixed with the lukewarm water and clouds of off-yellow dirt disappeared down the plughole. After a quick towel-dry I stepped out of the bathroom, paced through to the bedroom and pulled my hair dryer from the side, watching in the mirror as my image transformed before my emerald eyes. I ran my fingers adoringly through my new hair, drying each white blonde strand, clawing through the slightly damp, straw-like texture, smiling.

I didn't stop there.

I opened my make-up drawer, locating an ancient black eyeliner towards the back. I held it aloft and drew shaky, Ava-worthy, strokes to each eyelid, flicking them up at the end just like she did.

I checked the clock: just gone eight-thirty.

Time to leave.

I waited on the pavement outside my destination crouched behind a lumbering 4x4 – a car completely out of place in the middle of the city. *Drive an electric car if you must drive in London for heaven's sake!* I scratched my nail along it slowly. Served them right.

It had taken me over an hour to get here and it was approaching ten o'clock. The rain had taken a brief hiatus but the smell of it on the pavement remained. I looked down at my hands, yellowing at the fingertips, and stuffed them deeper into my pockets. I'd changed out of my nightshirt and anorak into dark jeans and my new black and yellow top. I was pleased: I looked just like her.

Then I saw him, *my Josh*, walking between the rooms of Olivia's house. I was relieved, nothing more than office gossip had led me here. People had been whispering about Josh staying at Olivia's on the off-chance Ava came back. Some thought it was a bit of an overreaction. Some thought he was hiding something. He was on the phone, his eyebrows creased, hitting his fist against his forehead. I wanted to run in there, towards the bright lights and white walls and tell him that everything would be OK and that I didn't believe what people were saying about him.

After hanging back and watching him for a few minutes, I summoned the strength to approach the imposing front door, its marble pillars either side entirely unnecessary, the obvious locks on the front a symbol to any would-be intruder that there was no point targeting this place. I wondered how he'd react to seeing me. Our virtual relationship had stalled when I'd caught him with Ava, then he'd tried to make amends but I'd ignored him, then she'd gone missing and I guess he had a duty to act like the perfect boyfriend for her family, the media, for her. But I knew the truth. It was *me* he'd wanted. The real Josh didn't care where Ava had gone. What would he make of my new look? Excitable, uncontrollable butterflies flew in circles inside me, struggling to remain calm ahead of what could become a really pivotal moment in our relationship. I promised myself I'd remember every detail so we could reminisce about it when we're married. I probably wouldn't tell him I'd dyed my hair moments earlier, though, and made a mental note to fabricate the timeline of my makeover. I lifted a hand from my pocket and rapped my knuckles against the painted black wood of the door, numbing them further. Once I'd delivered three steady strikes, I placed my hand back inside my pocket and waited, rocking between heels and toes. One, maybe two, minutes passed as I stood outside and considered aborting my mission. I soothed myself by blowing out long exhalations, reminding myself why I was here. Then, I heard a noise. 'Got to go, anyway, there's someone at the door, yes, I'll call later.' It was him. A series of bolts retracted and the front door opened revealing the palatial hallway beyond.

'Jade?'

His face was a picture, his eyes seemingly unable to believe the sight of the blonde-haired beauty that shone before him.

'Oh, sorry, I forgot you hadn't seen my hair like this yet,' I explained, offhand.

'No,' he replied, a little impressed maybe. Then the tone of his voice changed. 'How did you get this address?'

'Well,' I started, furious with myself for failing to think of this. 'Ava and I came here once with Olivia. And, uh, someone said I'd find you here.'

'Right,' he answered, then paused awkwardly. I stared at him hopefully. *Come on, I'm not a stalker, Josh, don't make me feel like this.*

'Do you want to come in?'

I exhaled heavily as he stepped aside to let me into the glorious space, modern whites contrasted against accents of black, ornate, Baroque-style gold patterns on the ceiling.

'Wow,' I uttered, stunned by its luxury all over again. 'Sorry if this is a bad time, but I was just on my way back from work and I really need to ask you a few questions about the launch. Is that OK?'

I batted my eyelashes. I wondered if he thought I looked like her.

'Sure,' Josh replied. Just one word.

He was talking to me as though he hadn't seen me naked. It was surreal, but I suppose it wasn't unexpected. His usually sparkling pale-blue eyes were darker than normal and heavy lines protruded from the corners. The police had crawled all over this place in the days after Ava went missing, before abandoning their investigation. He must be exhausted from it all. I noticed a tomatoey stain on his grey T-shirt, not that it stopped me from wanting to wrestle him out of his clothes, he was still gorgeous, even in grief.

'First of all, I just want to say how sorry I am about Ava,' I said, a little entranced by the way his sweatpants hung lower than the black elastic of his boxers. 'She's in the forefront of my mind and I really hope the police find her soon.'

'Thanks.' His one-word answer told me he felt awkward. Maybe he was nervous that I could rumble his perfect boyfriend cover.

'I'm serious. Even though we didn't always see eye to eye I never wanted something like, well, whatever's happened, to happen to her.' It was a case of the lady-doth-protest-too-much and I felt slightly guilty: I didn't care that she was missing, not one iota.

He didn't speak and kept his arms folded as we stood opposite each other in the hallway. He hadn't offered me a drink. Clearly he didn't want me to stay, and a few of the butterflies whizzing round inside me died mid-flight.

I hadn't expected him to be *quite* so stand-offish.

'Anyway, about the launch... I appreciate it's probably the last thing on your mind but Kai is really, really irate and I need your help.' I smiled.

'With what?' he asked, scratching the back of his head.

I hadn't prepared any specifics, I'd just wanted him to talk to me.

'To be honest... everything. Do you think you're coming back to work any time soon?'

I really wanted him to comment on my top, it made me look so much like Ava, but it was as though he was deliberately ignoring my efforts to transform into the girl he wanted me to be.

'I'm not sure. I thought it might be a good distraction from thinking about what's, you know, going on, but I tried to work the other morning and it drove me crazy. Nothing matters whilst she's out there, nothing else is more important than finding her and making sure she gets back safe.'

His voice wobbled.

'I understand,' I said. Although of course I didn't, how much could he have cared about her when he was trying to start a relationship with me at the same time?

'What's the latest?' I asked disinterestedly.

'Nothing. The police are useless,' he sighed.

A moment of silent tension filled the space, both of us playing the roles we'd been assigned in this post-Ava world.

'She went to Ireland. Why would she go to Ireland?' He scratched his head in the same position. His voice was far off. He wasn't really asking *me* that question.

'Are you sure you're OK, Josh? I can't cook you any meals or do any shopping for you can I? I'm here if you need me. Despite everything that happened with us. Despite the mistakes.' I hunched my shoulders in, already shrinking in preparation for the rejection that was about to hit. He looked at me quizzically.

'I'm OK, thanks.'

The blow wasn't quite as lethal as expected, but it still sent my cheeks burning and all I wanted to do now was retreat. I smiled at him and took a couple of steps towards the door. 'Sorry to have bothered you, I shouldn't have come.'

'Don't be silly.' He touched my shoulder as I moved past him, sending shivers all over me as I longed for that touch to linger. 'It was nice to see you, thanks for checking in on me and for offering to help,' he said softly.

I arrived back that night after a tedious journey aboard numerous night buses, the last words he'd said ringing in my ears. I pulled back on my nightshirt which I'd left crumpled up on the floor in my haste to transform into Ava and walked across the hallway to the bathroom. The smell had progressed from *someone's used a pretty harsh cleaning product in here* to *there's been a military-grade chemical attack in this bathroom*, and I chose to brush my teeth in the hallway leaning against the peeling, purple wallpaper. After thirty seconds or so I ran back into the bathroom holding my nose, careful not to breathe in whilst spitting out the foam.

I lay in bed and thought about him. His slight stubble and unkempt black hair. The abs I'd seen poking through the gap between his boxers and his T-shirt. His strong hand as he'd touched me and said, *thanks for offering to help*. I wasn't convinced he was rejecting my offer, he just didn't want to blow his cover, even for me. That was it! Only *I* could see through the bluster, because I *knew* him, I knew what he was like. And I couldn't judge him too harshly, he didn't know the truth about her yet. He probably felt guilty. I resolved to help regardless, his eyes had been crying out for it even if his words had said otherwise.

39

You knew it wouldn't be hard to give the police what they needed to downgrade the investigation almost immediately: a packed bag, a plane ticket, her passport, money... You'd leaked the information to the media to put pressure on the police. They'd look stupid if they had to backtrack, chances were they'd stick to plan A. You'd read all about similar investigations, about the paths they usually took.

Ava had helped you out by contacting her mother. It made it seem even more likely she'd run away.

You'd paid a lookalike to travel on the Aer Lingus flight to Dublin in her place. She'd worn sunglasses and a baseball cap, her bright, blonde hair visible underneath. Passport control don't get too nervous about young white women. She hadn't even been asked to remove her hat.

Most people wouldn't peg you as a diligent planner, as someone who considers all outcomes and eventualities with a path for each. But you are much better at adapting than people give you credit for: you've had to do it your whole life.

40

Jade

I've promoted a woman called Freya to my number two. She was the kind of girl I imagined being hockey captain at school, a waif of a woman with big front teeth and a jolly good attitude. She hadn't been my first choice. My first choice had been an outside hire: no one here met the grade as far as I was concerned, but I didn't have the time to find someone who did. So Freya sat where Georgette used to. And she was OK: she smelt a lot less of hairspray than her predecessor for starters, and kept her mouth shut far better, but there was definitely something curious about my new number two. I'd been watching her for a few days now. Intently. I'd noticed she liked ritual and routine. She brought in the same little tupperware of green leaves and lean meat every day. The same leaves, the same meat. She drank the same-size mug of black coffee at ten, then again at two. She was *neurotic* about it and I'd started to feel an unhealthy combination of jealous and judgemental every time I watched her tuck into her too-virtuous lunchbox.

I wondered if she was scared of food. I couldn't stop wondering *how* scared.

Kai was coming in today and Freya and I were busy prepping for the showdown. It wouldn't be pretty, not enough had been done and we were woefully short of time before launch night. I'd asked the intern to buy us lunch: I wanted to see how solid Freya's restraint was. Could I tempt her away from her usual meal with white bread tuna sandwiches and double-chocolate coated biscuits? Kai stormed in stage right through the double doors, his burgundy shoulder bag swinging dramatically by his side, and headed straight for the boardroom.

'David's joining us,' he announced, as he catwalked past my desk without looking at me. *Crap.* I turned to Freya.

'This is bad.'

'What do you want me to do?' she asked shakily, worry seeping from her every pore.

She was too young to deal with this kind of meeting and, if circumstances were different, I might have protected her from it. But I couldn't deny that having someone weaker in the room would help me look better, her inadequacies would shine through and I could blame the debacle on my sub-par team.

'Just, be yourself, be professional,' I answered. 'You'll be fine,' I promised her freckled face, albeit not very convincingly.

I entered the boardroom. Kai's gaze was fixed on his blackberry, angrily jabbing away at the keys.

'Hello,' I tried. No reply. 'How are you?' I asked, optimistically.

'How do you think I am?' he answered, irate. 'Pretty fucking stressed out would be a start.' He slammed his phone down on the table and crossed his arms. 'What in the name of *God* have you done to your hair?'

I patted the matted mess of blonde that framed my face down at the sides, I hadn't realised bleaching one's hair would make it awfully dry and, I accepted it didn't look as polished this morning as I'd hoped. It had been murder to drag a comb through. Freya tiptoed in behind me and put her notes down as quietly as possible, slipping into the chair furthest away from Kai.

'Time for a change,' I replied, annoyed he hadn't appreciated the gesture of going blonde for him and his hex.

The intern bustled in with sandwiches and biscuits and kept a funeral-worthy expression on her face the entire time as she busily laid out the platters I'd requested. I watched Freya closely, noting she hadn't looked at the food once, instead focusing her energy on re-reading the notes she'd prepared.

'Kai, any food whilst we wait for David?' I asked, holding out a plate of sandwiches towards him. He grabbed a biscuit instead and shooed away the sandwiches.

'Freya?' My face glowed, this was the moment I'd been waiting for.

'I've got lunch, thanks though,' she said.

'Don't be rude.'

'I'm fine, really.'

'I insist.' I was goading her. She took the bait and extended a visibly wobbly hand to the platter, picking the smallest sandwich of the lot. 'Take another,' I demanded.

She obeyed and reluctantly started sucking on the smaller

sandwich, obviously fighting an internal battle to chew and swallow them. I took a couple of sandwiches of my own and we ate in awkward silence while we waited for the boss. Kai's fury and Freya's fear filled the four walls.

The sudden hush of the office was our initial indication that David had arrived and, sure enough, seconds later his imposing figure appeared at the open door.

'Sorry I'm a little late,' he said, entering with the confidence of a man who had no idea what he was about to face. David's expensive suit and mustard tie caused Freya to retreat further into herself and she was practically in the foetal position by the time he'd taken a seat at the head of the table.

'I gather we're in the midst of a crisis...' David ventured, crossing his arms across his chest and sitting back into his seat.

'Correct,' Kai answered. 'Welcome to Shit Creek.'

He was wearing a tie-dye jumper which reached his knees and a pair of tight white jeans. He looked ridiculous and I was sure David would have a hard time taking him seriously.

'Let me jump in here, Kai, if you don't mind,' I said.

I needed to stamp my authority on the meeting, to prove to David that I was the strong and stable leader the team needed, the only problem was I didn't have much to say and I needed to buy some time. 'Freya, do you want to run through what you've been doing the past week first?'

She stammered and stuttered next to me, a single white breadcrumb attached to her lower lip. I hoped she was making me look better.

'Well, OK, I, umm, well, not me directly, but Henny,

sorry, *Henrietta*, has been dealing with the media. *The Mail* have pulled out, the video we had planned for the Facebook Live got shelved because they're covering the other fashion show that's on at the same time as the AthLuxe launch and, um, well, the only actual media we have definitely confirmed is one Kai doesn't want us to go forward with so that's it, really. Sorry.'

'Why don't you start with the good news?' I joked, trying to lighten the thunder on the faces of the two men in the room.

'There isn't any,' she replied, hushed.

'What about the security partner, they've completed all their checks now, haven't they?' I asked.

'Yes.'

'*See*, there are definitely some positives.'

Kai couldn't hold his anger in any longer and cried out in response to my positivity.

'What is the *fucking* point in a security team if no *fucking* media and no *fucking* people are going to show up?!' David didn't move and I eyed him nervously. Kai continued, 'Because, last time I checked, you'd managed to sell just thirteen of our one hundred tickets. The front row is going to be empty because I can't seem to pin you down on who's filling it, the famous people you'd promised would make up the other seats *aren't* any more, I haven't had dinner with anyone influential, no media give a shit about what we're doing, know, or even care, not now another event we knew about *weeks* ago is stealing our thunder!'

'Well, I'm pleased to inform you that we've now sold closer to seventy-five tickets.'

'Well, I'm *not* pleased to inform *you* that *that's* not

fucking good enough! The event is in seven days! And I *don't* want *my* seats filled with normal people! I want the best! *The best!'*

The truth was I'd actually given away the vast, vast majority of those tickets for free to members of staff, reclaiming the money lost from the overall launch event budget, chalking it up to 'journalist entertaining'. If Kai knew, he'd lose it.

'Listen, Kai, calm down: there's still a week to publicise the event, get the tickets sold and create more of a buzz, honestly, events are always like this. It will turn around,' I said, knowing it would be a miracle if it actually did.

'You promised me A-listers. So who's coming, Jade? Who's sitting on our front row? Tell me.' He flung his arms wide, his chest heaving.

'Freya, did you have anything on that?'

She looked at me, scared. It was definitely my job, it had been my job ever since I muscled it off Ava, but I'd well and truly messed up. I'd forgotten to send contracts to our chosen celebrities; now all of the people I'd confirmed had taken the money and cancelled to go to the other show. I'd only realised this morning.

I needed her to play along. Buy me some time so I could figure out what to do.

Her voice wobbled. 'No, I, well, I wasn't talking to talent…' She looked at me. 'I thought you were.'

Disloyalty. So she would have to go, too. It was so hard to find good people.

'Kai, we'll figure out where we're at with that and let you know.'

'Not good enough.'

Kai was raging, he stood up from his chair and pointed his index finger right at me. '*Ava* would have had this all under control.'

I looked away, embarrassed.

'I knew, as soon as you took over, the entire event would crumble. What I don't understand, though, is why you're trying to pretend everything is OK. Do you think you can pull the wool over my eyes forever? Like, what *actually* is your plan when no one turns up next week? In a way I'm dying to know... Mannequins in seats? Photoshop?' He sat back down, huffing. 'We don't pay this agency good money for shit like this.'

He meant shit like me.

David cleared his throat. 'Right. I think it's clear what we need to do.' He kept his arms crossed and locked his eyes onto mine.

'Jade, you're off the project.'

My heart leapt into my mouth. *Off the project?*

His stare moved to Kai.

'Kai – we'll put another senior member of staff in charge of this. Secondly, we have to postpone. If this other event is taking our talent and our media, we have no choice.'

'OK. I suppose you're right,' Kai said, a visible weight lifted from his shoulders. *So if it's David suggesting a postponement, it's revolutionary; if it's me, it's out of the question.*

David continued, 'I'd recommend delaying for a month; that gives the new Team Head time to get up to speed. In fact, I'll go and get her now.' David got up from his chair and strode into the main bullpen. I didn't – couldn't – move a muscle.

Off the project and demoted in the space of a minute?

'Sorry, I have to...' Freya ran out of the meeting room, presumably to stick two fingers down her throat in the toilets.

'I hope you're happy,' I said to Kai, menacingly, when it was just the two of us left in the room.

'Fucking delighted.' He was so bitter.

David and my successor stood at the door. I almost puked. 'Kai, this is Georgette.'

So she'd been playing her own little game behind the scenes, had she? Not officially up for the job of Team Head but ready to step into the wings as soon as I fell. I was almost impressed. My protégé had defeated me. She'd had a makeover, too. Her nails were short and plain and her usually ratty hair had been cropped into a sharp, no-nonsense bob.

'Hi Jade,' she said.

David motioned for her to take my seat and spoke again to Kai, oblivious of the betrayal unfolding before him.

'Why don't the two of you start the handover now. Jade, do you want to come with me?' He wasn't really asking, I knew that.

I got up in silence, giving George a horrible look as I passed.

How had I let this happen? I was so angry with myself. I should have known. *You can't trust anyone.* I needed to gather my thoughts before I explained everything to David. He would understand, wouldn't he? He had to.

David closed the door to the meeting room, leaving Kai and Georgette, *the new Team Head*, together. I could barely believe it. Then, he addressed the floor.

'Can I have your attention, please?' he asked authoritatively.

He already had their attention.

I stood by his side, trying to figure out what he had planned. Was he going to tell everyone what had just happened?

'I'm afraid to announce that Jade Fernleigh, who's been with us for eight years, has just handed in her resignation and I've agreed, reluctantly, to let her go.'

Murmurs rippled round the room and I noticed a couple of people cover their mouths. It felt like I was being publicly hung, hundreds of villagers out in force to see my limp body swing from the gallows.

'Please join me in giving Jade a well-deserved round of applause for her efforts here and to wish her luck on her next adventure.' A meek round of applause splattered out from various pockets across the room. Everyone knew what was going on, this was a show of strength from David pure and simple. And there was nothing I could do to stop it. He turned on his heel and the smell of his expensive cologne was the only thing that remained as I stood rooted to the spot, unsure what to do next. I reflected that my time at the top had been as short-lived as a mayfly's twenty-four-hour life and far from the queen I'd dreamt I could be.

My hands shook, followed by tears flooding my eyes. The floor was quiet save for a few shrieks of cruel laughter and muffled giggling.

After what felt like an eternity, I gathered my thoughts and forced myself to walk over to my desk, picking up the most important things and transferring them to my rucksack. The bag's zip was soon under pressure and I decided to cut my losses, swung it over my shoulder and left. They could fight over what remained. I passed Freya on the way out, her watery eyes and faint whiff of vomit the last memory of my eight years at W&SP.

On my way home, I stopped at the megastore a couple of bus stops away from my flat. I'd completely fucked the job, but an idea was percolating as the bus meandered in and out of its frequent stations picking up benefits cheats, useless, unemployed fat people and unwashed students.

Maybe there was a way back. As I entered the building I took a deep breath in and grabbed a basket from the tall stack at the store's front doors. I flitted round buying ingredients; onion, garlic, mince, potato, tomato, Worcestershire sauce. I hadn't made this meal for years, but I vaguely remembered the recipe. A woman with dentures and a bad perm racked up my items, then asked me if I needed a bag.

'Of course I need a bag,' I replied, testily.

'Chill out,' she said. Words I wasn't expecting to hear from an OAP. I tapped my foot repetitively against the plastic floor as she took a lifetime to peel my bag away from its compatriots.

'Forget it, I don't need one,' I huffed when it didn't part after her sixth attempt.

'Suit yourself.'

She spoke with a slight Jamaican accent and smiled to herself. Had that little stunt been deliberate? Who on earth did she think she was? I picked up my items and balanced them in my arms, swiping my contactless card against the reader.

'Crazy bitch,' I said under my breath as I turned to walk away.

Before I reached the exit, a sturdy hand curled round my shoulder.

'Easy, love, you need to come with me.' I detected a Northern accent, out of place in London.

'What for? I'm in a hurry,' I explained, trying to make forward progress against his grip.

'There's been a complaint, you were abusive to one of our cashiers.'

His grip tightened.

'What the fuck?' I lost my cool and spun round to meet him. 'She wouldn't get me a plastic bag!'

'This way, love.' Another security guard appeared and held my other shoulder.

'Fine, look, fine!' I shrieked, shrugging them off me, still clutching my bagless groceries.

The two burly blokes frogmarched me to a small room at the back of the supermarket. The old Jamaican lady sat in the corner, visibly upset. She gesticulated and shouted in my direction.

'It was her! She's the one that called me a crazy bitch.'

She cradled a little handkerchief in her hand to dab away her tears.

The security guards stayed by the door and a chubby woman sat next to the crazy bitch. I looked her up and down: she couldn't have been more than about twenty, but her lapel badge told me she was: Carly, Store Manager. Each of her ears boasted a grand, silver hoop, and her ill-fitting white shirt was in the midst of a battle to stay closed over her bulging bust.

I felt sorry for the crazy bitch for a moment: having to report to Carly couldn't be pleasant.

'I don't want to have to call the police, but we have a zero-tolerance policy on abuse towards our staff members.' Carly's voice was mock-managerial, she'd probably learnt to speak like that on a training day in Slough. I didn't have time for this.

'Look, I'm really sorry to… what's her name?' I asked.

'Tay.'

'I'm really sorry if Tay thought I called her that, but I didn't actually say those words. I don't want any fuss. I have a family to feed at home…' I hesitated just as the lie left my lips. Would anyone believe someone like me would have a family? 'I really need to get back.'

I waited, expecting to be found out, but when nobody did anything, I spoke again.

'Sorry.'

'OK, well we have to side with our staff member on this one, I'm afraid, so I will be giving you a ban from the store, OK?'

What was the point in asking me if that was OK?

'Which means you won't be able to come back here, OK?'

Thanks for the clarification. 'Right. Can I go?'

'Terry will show you out.'

My second attempt to leave the supermarket was a lot more successful but fury built inside me at the second injustice of the day and frustrated tears fell down my face. I couldn't get anything right; only one person would make me feel better.

When I eventually got home, my housemate was lounging

on the sofa in the windowless living room, daytime TV blaring from the speakers.

Will Carol and Andy have made the right decision? Find out after the break…

I closed the door with my hip, jostling the items in my arms, trying to stop them from falling to the floor.

'Don't ask me why I'm home early,' I shouted out, warning her. The TV's sound stopped.

'Why are you home early?' she asked, following me through the narrow doorway to the kitchen. I threw my shopping down on the side and rooted round in the cupboards for a frying pan and pyrex dish.

'Let me guess…' She was enjoying this. 'You're not ill, so, Ava's back and you refuse to work for her?'

I made the sound of an incorrect buzzer. 'Nuh-nuh. Try again.'

'You blew up the building.'

'Wrong again.'

'Wait, you weren't fired, were you?'

'Ding ding ding.'

She cackled with laughter. 'Why?'

'Because Ava had Kai so far up her arse that I never stood a chance,' I sighed. 'And while I had my hands full dealing with Ava, Georgette was planning a mutiny of her own.'

'Oh! I'm sorry Jadey-wadey.'

She turned her voice all sing-song and went back to the living room to catch the next thrilling instalment of Carol and Andy's daytime dilemma. Ava had made sure she was the only one breaking through the glass ceiling but, just as I'd smashed through to replace her, Georgette had slipped through the cracks I'd created and poured a tonne of concrete behind her. *But no matter. No matter. Concentrate on what's next. Concentrate on the plan.* I fried onions, added the mince, the tomatoes, boiled and mashed the potatoes and smothered a layer on top of the mince mixture. I put the dish in the oven then went upstairs to change. She followed me.

'What are you doing cooking? You never cook,' she probed.

'It's for a friend, we're having dinner together tonight.' I didn't look at her as I busied myself selecting an outfit. *Maybe a skirt and a low-cut top?*

'Aren't *we* friends, Jade? We used to be, didn't we?'

I refused to look at her.

'Jade?'

She moved closer, her ice-cold arms wrapping round me, constricting my breathing.

'Jade?'

I fought and struggled as I pushed my way out of her embrace.

'*Olivia, stop!*' I cried as her dead eyes came to settle across from mine and her blue lips trembled.

'We were friends, weren't we?' I didn't answer. 'Why didn't you help me, Jade? Why did you let me die?' I couldn't take it any more and I screamed, running through her ghostly body and downstairs to the kitchen, grabbing my lukewarm dish on the way out and slamming the door behind me.

I hopped on the bus, a fellow passenger helping me with my oyster card as I struggled to swipe it as well as hold my pie. I occupied one of the priority seats near the front of the bus – *if ever there was a priority journey it was this*

– and let my mind unravel, the spools and cogs turning and twisting as they rewound time. Memories of Olivia flickered before me as though I were looking through a kaleidoscope. I'd tried to block her out of my mind but she'd come to me in person instead and wouldn't leave me alone, especially when I was down, or emotional. If I tried to forget that night, to forget about her altogether, to forget what I'd done, she'd make me remember five times louder. We'd been friends, yes, of course we'd been friends. I should have told her that. Back when we'd worked together, we'd been thick as thieves, she'd been one of the few people in my life who'd liked me. No one ever liked me. She'd been kind to me. She understood what it was like to live with difficult parents, she understood what it was like to feel like an outsider, like someone who didn't fit in. To be honest, she managed it in that cool-girl misfit kind of way: the girl who was beautiful and haunted and aloof, but it was her own demons that held her back from feeling accepted rather than other people rejecting her. Which is what always happened to me. I felt terrible about what I'd done to her. She hadn't deserved it.

And then there was Ava. *Ava* never struggled to fit in. I wiped the ridge of my bottom eyelid that brimmed wet as I thought about how everything had gone from good to bad when Ava joined W&SP, then bad to worse as she'd dug her claws in.

We approached Lupus Street in Pimlico and I hoped Josh was still staying at Olivia's, that he hadn't decided to move out yet. Then I realised something: I hadn't thought of a pithy opening line to greet him with. Oh, God… I needed longer to prepare. Options whizzed past. *Shepherd's pie at night, Josh's delight! No, Jade, just keep it simple.*

News crews lined the street as I paced down the pavement towards Olivia's house, their white satellite dishes transforming the inner-city road into a Hollywood film set.

If Ava wasn't blonde, they wouldn't be making this much of a fuss. So a spoilt white girl ran away from her problems. What's the big deal? I knocked on the familiar door and waited, running through more practice opening lines in my head. *Hi, you ordered a takeaway? Fifteen pounds please Josh.*

The door opened and thankfully Josh spoke first, saving me from myself.

'Jade. Hi again,' Josh said, perplexed. 'You shouldn't be here. They'll take pictures.' He gestured at the vehicles.

'I made you a shepherd's pie.' I held it out towards him. He paused.

'Wow, you shouldn't have.' He wasn't inviting me inside. Why wasn't he inviting me inside?

'I can stay and eat it with you, if you like, if you need some company?' I tried. I held the pie out towards him and, eventually, he took it, uncertain at best.

'OK, sure, thanks.' He stood aside to let me in and my heart flipped in somersaults of joy and jubilation. My plan had succeeded! Finally! Something was going my way! I sauntered in and let Josh lead the way into the kitchen. Last time I'd been here with him I'd only managed to get as far as the hallway so this was already an improvement. The kitchen itself was exactly how I'd pictured it: minimalistic and chic; white and grey and black. It was gorgeous. I'd *love* to cook in a place like this.

I thought of the lounge that must back on to this room and my memories threatened to unfurl. I tried to curtail them but I already knew what was coming. She'd been sat behind me for the entire bus journey, after all, her fingernails dug into the fleshy part of my shoulder.

'Making yourself at home, are you?' asked Olivia, her voice ringing loud in my ears. I knew she was here, of course, but she still made me jump. I mumbled back to her under my breath – *this isn't your house any more* – and, turning round, hoped Josh hadn't heard but, judging by the look on his face: he had.

'Are you OK?' he asked – which was ridiculous because it was *me* who was supposed to be looking after *him*!

'Of course I'm OK!' I said, slightly too defensively. 'Now, sit down Josh, I want to make sure you're eating, you look awfully thin. Where are the plates?'

He gestured to the cupboards behind me and I sprang into action moving them to the marbled island in the centre of the room. I took a spoon from the utensil tin on the side and started serving up great ladles of dinner. *This is exactly what it will be like when we're together for real. Me cooking him supper, us living somewhere modern, and cool.* As I finished serving up Josh's portion, I bent over to inspect his meal. Something didn't look right: pink juices oozed from the mince and the potatoes looked pale and lumpy, the tomato sauce running like dirty tap water from the main dish, pooling sheepishly at the bottom of the plate. *It hadn't cooked. My shepherd's pie was raw. Olivia had distracted me and I'd grabbed it and left…*I snatched his plate towards me and poured his pie back into the dish.

'It hasn't cooked,' I announced to Josh, who'd gone

awfully quiet. I brought the pie over to the oven and started pressing its buttons. The beast whirred into action as I found the setting for the fan.

'It shouldn't be long. Are you OK? Are you starving?'

'I'm fine...' he said, his voice trailing off. 'I'm not so sure about you, though.'

'Why do you keep saying that?' I snapped.

'Well, this is the second time you've turned up here unannounced and, Jade, we barely know each other. Why the sudden interest? Why the food? Why go to all this trouble to check in on me? Do you feel guilty about something?'

'Well, *do* you?' hissed Olivia from somewhere in the distance. His line of questioning accused me of an ulterior motive and I rushed towards him, wrapping my hands round his arms, the feel of his body rendering me speechless for a moment.

'Do you know where Ava is, Jade?'

'What? No. Of course I don't.' I was taken aback by his question. 'She ran away, Josh... no one knows where she is.'

'I don't know Jade, look, I'm sorry, it's just: the police are useless. David has done everything to put pressure on them and nothing seems to be working. So, when you turn up at my doorstep, acting weird, I can't help but wonder...'

I noticed then that the lines under his eyes were deeper and darker than last time I'd stopped by. Poor Josh. This was really affecting him even though he didn't really love her. He was such a caring person.

'Josh, wait a minute – what did you mean when you said we don't really know each other?'

'I didn't mean it like *that* exactly, obviously we've

worked together for a long time but… we're not friends, really, are we?'

I wondered if I'd still have a heart left after this. Josh had no idea how many times he'd trampled on it recently.

'I know things are *weird* at the moment, on hold, but I'd say we were more than friends, Josh. Much more than friends.'

He looked at me like I was crazy and I took a step back.

'The messages, Josh, the pictures, the…' His blank stare said it all and I realised then that it hadn't been Josh on the other end of my texts but someone else. Someone who'd wanted to humiliate and embarrass me.

'What are you talking about? What messages?'

'Oh God,' I spluttered. 'It was her.' I pulled out my phone to show him and clicked into the long conversations we'd shared, the intimate things we'd said, the pictures we'd sent. 'This definitely wasn't you?' I asked, about to dissolve into a pile of nothing. He shook his head. He took my phone.

'What is this?' he murmured, disbelieving what was before him. 'This is serious, this is sick. I'm not even on social media – I thought you knew that about me, I can't stand it.'

'It was Ava,' I said firmly, gripping the kitchen island to stop me falling, dizzy with the extent of her betrayal.

'Ava wouldn't do this,' he retorted with total confidence, passing me my phone. 'What would be her motive?'

I pushed the nausea I felt to the background. 'Josh, think about it. She was the one who put up the photo in the meeting room that day with Kai. She did that because she knew what she'd find. She knew what I'd sent you because she'd already seen it.'

'I just, yeah, that's not what happened, Jade, your photos auto-loaded when she plugged in your phone.'

I started to pace, piecing it all together. 'She wanted to humiliate me. She was doing everything in her power to stop me from getting the Team Head position. It's exactly the kind of thing she'd do. I've been so *stupid*. I can't believe I didn't realise it until now.' I mused and muttered then noticed Olivia standing in the doorway. I shouted at her to leave us alone.

'Slow down…' he said, his eyes pleading with me. 'Wasn't it George who took the job from you? Couldn't it just as easily have been her?' Georgette's smug face smacked me sideways as I thought of the way she'd looked at me as she'd taken my seat. Then of the large pictures that had been printed out and stuck up all over my office on my first day in charge.

'She betrayed me, too.'

'Everyone's out to get you, aren't they?'

He said it like I was imagining things.

For a moment everything fell quiet and I watched as Josh rubbed his tired eyes with the back of his hand.

'Where do you think she is, Jade? Where has she gone?'

I looked at him.

'You actually love her, don't you?'

'Yes,' he answered.

Slashes across my heart.

'What about me?' I squeaked, not looking him in the eye, already knowing the answer. 'Do you even like me?'

'Of course I like you Jade—'

'—just not like that,' I finished.

He looked at me and raised his shoulders to his ears.

'I'm sorry.' His face fell as he let me down.

A short time later smoke billowed out of the top of the oven and, though I'd been sure I'd set the oven to fan, it had somehow switched to grill. The pie was burnt and I binned it. Instead we ate cheese toasties together and shared a bottle of wine. We talked about work, we shared stories about Olivia and, when I returned home in the early hours of the next morning, despite the fact that the love of my life had rejected me, I reflected it had still been the best night of my life.

BOYFRIEND OF MISSING WOMAN
ENTERTAINS LATE NIGHT GUEST

Joshua Stein, boyfriend of missing Ava Wells, was paid a visit by a late-night guest last night.

The woman, identified as Jade Fernleigh, Joshua Stein's colleague at top PR agency Watson & Stein Partners, is reported by sources close to those involved to have an 'unhealthy infatuation' with Josh, and a 'bitter rivalry' with missing Ava.

Our exclusive pictures appear to show the pair sharing a bottle of wine and enjoying a cosy night in at the property where Ava had been living before she disappeared.

'If I was missing, I wouldn't be very happy if my boyfriend spent the time drinking wine with another woman. I think it's suspicious,' said @MaryF1 on Twitter.

Despite these pictures casting a whole new light on the situation, police maintain Ava Wells is a runaway, regardless of there being no word from authorities in Ireland as to her whereabouts.

If you have any more information about the woman in this picture, please ring our newsdesk. And remember: we pay our sources!

41

Jade

I woke up in my own bed, my mind tired, but relaxed. Last night had been good for me. Finding out Josh wasn't behind the messages had knocked me for six, but his honesty had given me a renewed sense of calm.

And then I'd turned on the radio.

'Reports are coming out this morning that Josh Stein is keen to distance himself from Jade Fernleigh, the woman he shared a cosy night in with last night. He said in a statement: "The pictures surfacing this morning have been taken wildly out of context. Jade Fernleigh is a colleague, she is barely a friend, and she stopped by last night to discuss work-related matters. I hope by speaking out I can end these rumours and focus the investigation back on what really matters: finding Ava."

'We'll bring you more updates on the fascinating case of Ava Wells as we get them.'

His statement would only fan the flames. Didn't Josh realise that? Didn't he know anything about the industry we worked in?

I made my way shakily down the stairs, I wasn't sure what time it was but the air was heavy and the sun had revitalised the smell of last night's mince in the kitchen.

Hang on, I thought. Josh knew exactly the effect a statement like that would have on the media.

Had he done it on purpose?

Why was he trying to poison the public against me?

The letterbox rang out as I stood still on the sticky linoleum floor, its tinny timbre reverberating through my ear canal before snaking its way up to my brain. I swivelled my head towards the noise. I didn't like the sound of it. The way it had opened slowly, then banged shut. I turned on my heels and opened the door to the hallway area. The smell of dank, leaking pipes was overwhelmingly strong and I covered my nose with my pyjama sleeve to avoid breathing the mouldy air directly. The blood drained from my cheeks as I saw my face staring back at me from the newspaper front cover just delivered. Dishevelled, scared and hollow: the sixteen-year-old me. The girl I'd tried so hard to bury was back with a bang, this time on the cover of one of the country's most popular tabloids.

I picked up the crisp paper in my hand, the corners shaking as I failed to control my grip. I hadn't ordered this, someone had put it directly through my letterbox.

COLLEAGUES CLOSE TO MISSING AVA WELLS SPEAK OUT

It was as though the headline had sprung out from the page and hit me with a lethal left hook. I was momentarily breathless and took a couple of uneven steps backward before the wall broke my progress. I slumped down, my muscles providing no resistance, sending me to the floor amongst weeks and weeks of unopened letters and overdue bills. I devoured every word.

Colleagues close to Ava Wells, angry at the lack of action in her case, speak out today in an exclusive interview. They highlight what they feel have been 'catastrophic failures' in the Metropolitan Police Force's handling of the investigation, which they believe should be re-classified as a kidnapping or suspected murder.

Their explosive claims will add to the already heavily scrutinised case which now enters its third week without any word from Irish authorities on Miss Wells' whereabouts.

Meanwhile, public pressure mounts on the Government, with many taking to social media to lambast the Prime Minister for further police cuts. Roy Turnbull, a former officer, said, 'The force is squeezed enough focusing on protecting our borders; there's no money and no time for fighting crime at home. It's a disgrace that we can't look after our own.'

A protest will take place outside Scotland Yard this weekend if a major breakthrough in the case isn't made, or more police funding isn't pledged specifically for solving the Ava Wells mystery.

I skimmed over the rest of the words, my ragged breathing keeping me alert, my rough, dry tongue stuck to the roof of my mouth.

Josh had something to do with Ava's disappearance. He must have orchestrated this witchhunt: the timing was too much of a coincidence. I had to see him again. I had to know.

42

Jade

I shifted my weight from side to side, nervous as I waited for him to answer. The news crews recognised me from yesterday and had started to appear from their vans, cameras in tow. I knocked again, harder this time, more urgently.

'Josh!' I shouted. He flung the door open, but pressed his body in the space between, stopping me from coming inside. I made a move forward but, when he didn't budge, got the message.

'Jade, this has to stop. I'm in the middle of something.'

'Why is everyone talking about me Josh? Why is everyone online saying I've got something to do with Ava? What did you do, Josh?'

'Did you, Jade? It's just – your behaviour...'

I swore loudly at him and he looked at me pitifully.

'Jade, I don't think it's a good idea for you to come here again.'

A switch inside me flicked and I stuck my foot in the doorframe so he couldn't close it on me.

'She wasn't so perfect, Josh! She was cheating on you!'

'What? Jade, please, keep your voice down ...'

A sinister grin wrapped its way round my face.

'She was seeing David behind your back! She was, I have the proof!' My voice was high pitched and jubilant.

But he didn't believe me.

'You need to leave,' he said, firmly, pushing the door against my foot.

'Josh. Listen. I just want to talk...' I was fumbling in my pocket for my phone, I wanted to show him the picture of Ava and David together. *Then* he'd believe me. *Then* he'd realise it was she who'd sent me the messages, that it was *her* devious lies that had got her into some other mess...

His forehead tightened and he took a step back inside. At last he was letting me in. I pulled my foot back to join him and, at that moment, he thudded his palm against the door, slamming it shut in my face. With that final, brutal, rejection a tidal wave of emotion ripped through me. I'd lost everything: my job, my future, my Josh.

And now everyone thought I was guilty of kidnapping, or murder.

You are *guilty of murder, Jade.*

I unleashed a flood of fists on Josh's front door, refusing to leave, crying out to him to let me in. I didn't recognise my own voice, shrill and barbaric, as it warbled and wailed.

He was the way back to my job!

He was the way back to happiness!

He was the only one who could help!

After all the energy had left my bruised bones and I could

no longer thump, my voice broken and unable to cry out, I fell down into a crumpled heap, resting my heavy head against the door, my body balanced on the flagstone step below, cold seeping into my bones. I was vaguely aware of the sounds of cameras clicking as I inspected my fists, cut and swollen from their gladiator-worthy effort. I wished I'd been the one who was dead.

'You need to move on from this address, Miss,' someone in dark trousers said. At that point it hit me and I bolted, running away from it all, away from the rejection, away from the pain, away from Josh. All I could do was go back home, to misery, confusion and loneliness. What was I supposed to do now my life had fallen apart?

COLLEAGUES OF JADE FERNLEIGH AND AVA WELLS LEND THEIR VOICES TO MISSING PERSONS CASE

'When Ava first disappeared, the first thing Jade asked me to do was clear out Ava's desk – I think Jade knew she'd never be coming back to it.' Georgette Giani, 31, Team Head at Watson & Stein Partners with experience working with both Jade and Ava, lends her voice to the missing Ava Wells case, who disappeared from her home address a number of days ago. Ms Giani spoke to one of our reporters in an explosive, tell-all interview, waiving her right to anonymity in a quest to shake up the police handling of the case.

'The first question I want to ask is: do you believe Jade Fernleigh is capable of murder?'

'Absolutely. She's capable of anything, she doesn't understand the meaning of the word empathy, she's one of the most selfish and sociopathic people I've ever met. Put it this way, I've never met anyone with such a one-track mind as Jade Fernleigh. The only thing that mattered to her was ruining Ava's life. She wanted to be promoted over her, she wanted to steal her boyfriend, and the thought, even the thought, that she might not be successful at doing so was driving her crazy. It's awful that the police haven't come to question us at work in detail about her, I'm telling you: she did this.'

Freya Hanlin, 22, an Executive at Watson & Stein Partners, also spoke out. 'Jade's behaviour completely changed when Ava went missing. She turned into a megalomaniac, obsessed with her new power as Team Head.'

'Just to clarify for our readers, am I right in saying that Jade was promoted to the Team Head position almost as soon as Ava went missing?'

'Correct. There were other things too, she dyed her hair blonde – Ava's hair was blonde – and she started doing her make-up kind of like Ava used to, she even wore a top that we all knew Ava owned. I don't know if Ava was wearing it the night of her disappearance, but the police need to find out; if so, it could be a major clue.'

43

No, *this* revelation isn't part of your plan. You want the police to believe Ava's gone willingly: no foul play, no investigation, no awkward questions. That's how you like it: that's how you'd planned it. Nothing suspicious, nothing messy.

But you know what has to be done: you have to adapt to the new situation. You have no choice.

She lies in the room next door, drugged and heavy.

She hadn't come without a fight, I suppose you knew she wouldn't. People tend to fight for their lives, even when it's futile.

But taking her had worked. If anyone had seen, they would have spoken to the papers already. The papers make hiding in plain sight so *easy*. They give people like you all the clues you need, parroting to the masses exactly what the police know, what they don't, what they suspect.

She was followed all the way from London, a comfortable distance between the cars. She didn't notice, she's not particularly observant. She didn't watch the roads turn silent and the CCTV non-existent. Didn't clock the familiar number plate.

You loved her, you *thought* she loved you. She was your girl. You should have been together for the rest of your lives, but she ruined it. She ruined everything.

She sleeps now, the girl, blonde-haired and beautiful. She sleeps in the room you set up for her when you realised she'd lied to you. Betrayed you.

You are alone with her now.

You watch her.

You touch her.

You take off her muzzle.

The cuts on her mouth have yellowed and scabbed over. You run your thumb along her plump lips.

You put the cloth back in her mouth, feeling her tongue, and fasten the tie back round her tangled hair.

Smudges of mascara dirty her pale pink cheeks. You brush them away.

Her clothes ripped during the struggle. You run your fingers all over her body. You wonder if she still loves you. Your girl. She smells earthier than you remember.

She doesn't deserve to die so easily. Not until she knows the reason why.

44

Jade

The police were knocking on my door. I knew it was them, I knew they'd come for me like this and the sound of the heavy knock I'd just heard, *rat-a-tat-tat*, said it all. I'd endured more than a fortnight of stories and gossip and rumour about my apparent involvement in Ava's disappearance so in a way I was ready for this. Prepared.

'Miss Fernleigh?' A muffled voice called for me through the wooden barrier between us.

My head was a mess and, as I opened the door just a crack, became increasingly aware of the two-week-old clothes I was standing in.

The main officer noticeably grimaced as the smell of the damp, soggy, pipes escaped from the confined hallway, her chin doubling as she recoiled her head against her neck. I observed her tight little bun and imagined she was the type of person who filled sachets with potpourri and hung them in her wardrobe.

She regained her composure. 'We need to ask you a few

questions about the disappearance of Miss Ava Wells.'

I observed her through the thin slither I'd opened to the outside world and thought how easy it would be to shut her out again and turn away from this problem. I would just close the door, walk back into the lounge, and lie on the sofa.

'Miss Fernleigh, we'd like to question you at the station.' She placed her palm flat against the front door and tried to open it further, but I was too quick and slammed it shut, bolting the top and bottom locks, screaming in my head to drown out the noise of the officers ordering me to let them in.

The cops crashed through the front door seconds later and ripped me from my home, wrestling me from my hovel out into the unfamiliar outside world, hands tight round my wrists, pressure on the back of my neck. The light outside was blinding and I closed my eyes to stop it burning holes in my pupils, stumbling as I failed to negotiate the step down to the pavement. New hands wrapped round me, holding my shoulders, one on my forehead. I peeped out from the darkness as they bent my body into the waiting police car and, through the gaps between limbs and armour, I swear I saw her across the street, her yellow hair glowing in the sunlight, squinting her eyes as she peered through the glare to see me properly. She had a child by her side, tugging at her shirt. She picked him up and stroked his tiny head as they watched me drive away, cuffed and cornered.

45

Ava

My heartbeat felt as though it was in my skull, and pain from the swelling on my brain roared and pressed against the bones in my head as I came round. My eyes were so dry it hurt to open them even the smallest amount. My mouth was full, choking on an enormous gritty surface, the corners of my lips cut and pulled taut, forcing me to contort my face into a maniacal grin. I checked my fingers and toes were still there. They didn't respond immediately and my mind raced to thoughts of paralysis but, after a while, they twitched as the familiar feeling of blood rushed back to revive them. I could tell they'd been bound. Rope burned against my skin as I moved tentatively, testing the barriers of an incredible escape. I dug my fingernails into my hands, cut through the skin and feverishly gathered my own DNA underneath each nail, staining each a rusty brown.

For a second, I felt there was no point in fighting, my mind had assessed the situation like a computer and decided resistance was futile, but then a breath came sharply back into my lungs and changed everything.

I waited for a few moments, emptied and filled my body with as much air as I could, then let the memories of earlier re-form, loading the colours, voices, thoughts and feelings back into my mind, the pictures playing before my closed eyes.

Fear danced round my limp body, but the breath in my lungs willed me to act and encouraged me to fight.

I tested the rope round my wrists again. Too tight. My skin screamed in protest as I tried rubbing myself free for a second time. I opened my eyes.

A solitary window opposite me.

A bed.

A note lay next to my body.

Betrayal, Disloyalty, Lies. Revenge, Retaliation, Demise.

I closed my eyes again, the scratchy, dry pain alleviated slightly as tears pooled in each.

I had to get out of here.

I refocused, channelling my fear into a plan. I took in the dimensions, assessed the movements I'd need to make to escape, observed the chains and ties that held me.

My heart was skipping now, faster, faster, faster, *beatbeatbeatbeatbeat*, as I saw that my clothes were ripped.

In one quick movement, I tried to propel myself to seated, but a chain I hadn't seen pulled taut round my neck, the strength of the metal beating my willpower and my body fell back, like a ragdoll, onto the mattress.

I blinked, it was all I could do.

46

Jade

I waited in the cramped and claustrophobic surroundings of the police station, my hands still cuffed and crossed behind my back, employing my right to remain silent. I sat on a thin, plastic chair and considered that the basic decor surrounding me depicted the harsh reality of the police funding cuts I'd read about earlier that day. I thought about what my colleagues had said about me. The way they'd plotted together to stitch me up. I was surprised the police hadn't seen through the hatred and bitterness that flowed through their empty accusations.

Next to me sat my assigned lawyer, he'd spoken to me earlier but I'd found the movement of his chubby moustache, off-white and fluffy, hypnotic and I hadn't listened to a word.

'Are we ready?' A different officer to those who had brought me here spoke to the lawyer from across the other side of the table. His physique looked sculpted by a finely balanced diet of beer and pie and I decided immediately that I didn't trust him. Us vs. Them.

The lawyer, in his faded grey suit and spotty blue tie, mumbled at me again, 'Remember, you're allowed to give a no comment interview.'

I looked down at the table and my reflection confronted me for the second time that day, this time in metal. The old me, the one I'd left behind, had tried so hard to move on from, sneered back.

'I'm DI Crow.' He was a crow all right, with his hooked nose and too-long fingernails. 'Ready?' he asked.

I didn't move, focusing instead on a dark mass that had gathered in one of the corners of the room, firing tendrils out over the unpainted breeze blocks across the ceiling. I heard him depress a button on the tape recorder that sat on the table between us. I looked at it and thought how sinister the red light that shone on its surface was. The eye of the devil.

'This interview is being tape recorded in an interview room in Shepherdess Walk, London. I am Frederick Crow, Detective Inspector at the Metropolitan Police Force. Miss Fernleigh, please state your full name and date of birth for the record.'

I froze. Tentacles of darkness were making steady progress out from the corner of the room now and slithered quickly across the ceiling, down the back wall, and over the floor. Snap. Something locked round my right heel. I leant back in the plastic chair slightly to watch as the black, snake-like creature licked at my leg. Wind whistled in my ears.

'In your own time,' the officer said sarcastically.

I heard his voice and forced myself to look up at the people surrounding me. Their pupils blinked back: the beer-bellied crow had his fingers locked together and rested his elbows on the table, a black worm slithering down his neck. The lawyer rubbed one side of his moustache repetitively, teasing the slime off it left by the slug crawling over his face. The spare officer sat back, neutral, untouched by the tendrils, like a dove in the darkness. I looked down again and noticed the floor beneath me had turned into a swirling pool of thick, black, tar. Shiny eels with razor teeth hissed as they swam in it, ready to pull us down into the sticky, suffocating trap below.

'It's OK, you can answer,' the lawyer encouraged, a bead of sweat appearing like a tiny magnifying glass on his forehead. 'Can we get the young lady a drink of water, please?'

That small display of kindness sent the darkness away and, as quickly as it had gone, the room lit up again, the black mass retreating, confined to the corner once more. The dove flew out of the room. I shook my head, trying to forget what I'd just seen.

'My full name is, um, Jade Iris Fernleigh. My date of birth is the 3rd of December, 1984.'

The lawyer spoke. 'I'm Nick Jones, solicitor.' His voice was meek and I debated whether he was up to the job of defending me.

The door swung open and the female officer placed a plastic glass half-full with water in front of me. Bubbles formed at the top. Water shouldn't look like that.

'I'm Police Constable Katherine Rice.'

The fat crow bustled through some more police admin: times, dates, ranks.

'At ten past seven in the evening, Miss Ava Wells left her home voluntarily and drove west out of London. She was reported missing by her partner Mr Joshua Stein the next morning. Miss Fernleigh, members of the public have made specific allegations against you in relation to Miss Wells' disappearance. First, we'd like to know where you were that night.'

The lawyer looked at me.

'I was at home.'

The lawyer interrupted, 'I can't tell you what to do in this interview, Jade, but you have the right to enter a no comment answer.' The whites of his eyes shone.

'Were you alone?' the podgy policeman asked.

'Olivia was—' I changed my mind. 'I was alone.'

'Who's Olivia?' The crow had found a worm and was plucking it from its hole.

'No one.'

The questions were quick-fire and it didn't take him long to settle into a pattern of rattling off the next one before I had time to process the previous. In my peripheral vision I was aware of the dark matter building in the corner of the room again, metamorphosing from the snakey creatures with dark, glistening trails to something all the more sinister: tall, thin and tree-like, with long, probing branches for fingers and broken-off bark for teeth.

'So, you were alone that night. Did you call anyone, text anyone, can anyone corroborate your story?' His questions were all delivered in the same matter-of-fact monotone.

I kept my eye on the figure. 'No.'

'Did you have anything to do with Miss Wells' disappearance?' he probed.

It grew to its full height. 'No.'

'Do you know anyone who does?' It stretched out a hand towards the neutral officer.

'No.'

'Tell me about Olivia, who is she?'

I answered without thinking, my concentration on the tree-man. 'I killed her.'

The officers exchanged a glance. I heard my words too late and tried to pull my attention back to the room. I was saying all the wrong things, my head so thick with webs I couldn't remember the truth, let alone weave a narrative round the lie.

'We contacted your counsellor, she told us you haven't been to a session for several weeks now, is that right?'

'Yes.'

My throat was dry, I wished I could drink the water.

'Could you tell us when you last attended a session?'

'I can't remember, exactly,' I rasped.

'Could you confirm for the recording which medications you're currently taking?'

'No comment.'

A huff of mock-surprise escaped from the lawyer as I croaked out my answer. What they didn't know was that I'd been taking my pills regularly, more often than I should probably, but they weren't keeping the old me at bay, they weren't working, and now there was nothing I could do to stop the voices and the creatures from coming. The tree-woman moved quickly from the corner to behind me, casting a dark shadow round my seat.

You remember killing me, don't you? Snatching the air from my body, taking my life, covering it up.

It speaks with Olivia's voice, her acidic tongue lashing against my back.

The dove lady, with round, alabaster cheeks, spoke to me in a warm Scottish accent.

'Do you need to take a break, Jade?'

I could hear someone muttering.

'It was your own fault, Olivia'.

I watched as the officer's full-moon face turned thick with alarm and listened as the muttering grew louder and louder – it was speaking with my voice. The blackness began again, seeping out from the walls and churning, faster, towards me. I had to get to higher ground, that way it would take the others before it took me. I bolted, scrambling up onto the table accompanied by a cacophony of noise as my plastic chair hit the floor, voices cried out and limbs intertwined as they tried to bring me back down. There was a chill in the room and I curled up into a ball, evading capture, making it as hard as possible to be taken into the blackness by the figure.

'Why did you do it? Why didn't you help me?'

The fat officer and my useless lawyer fled the room, leaving the Scottish woman standing in the tar, refusing to give in to its menace.

'You're OK, love, you're doing fine,' she said repetitively, holding my arm.

'I knew I'd be blamed for it,' I sobbed through the pain of the memory.

'Where have you taken her?'

She gripped my arm tighter, the prolific reach of the

viscous darkness now binding us together. Her face started to change, shifting into someone else altogether.

I reacted instinctively, thrashing my arms out before firing myself towards her, palms first. Her skin collected under my fingernails as I scratched back the mask she was wearing. Who was really under there? She screamed as I knocked us both off-balance, falling into the pit, drowning together in the bubbling, boiling blackness.

An alarm rang out, but I barely heard it. Moments later, I felt a colossal blow to my forehead, then nothing.

47

You haven't fed her properly yet, you've barely given her anything to drink. I guess they'd call you a monster. A cold-hearted, dead-all-the-way-through, psychopath. But you hadn't always been this way, had you? They'd probably write a film about you, about this, that is, they *would* if they ever found out what you'd done, what you'd pulled off. But they never would, so your story would never be told. What a shame.

You watch her through the screen via the camera, as she tries to get up. She's chained to the bed; you want her to know how much she hurt you. The ties are a show of force, really. She can't escape and no one would hear her if she tried to scream. You might feed her today, take off her ties – you want her to suffer, to think there's a chance of survival, then take it away. She betrayed you: now it's your turn to show her how much it hurts.

48

Jade

Olivia smiled at me from down the corridor as a cross-eyed guard dragged me towards a cell. The prison reminded me of a museum, an ancient relic of a bygone time where they might have once held sailors and drunks, centuries ago, for misdemeanour crimes, but not a maximum-security prison in this day and age. The paintwork was haphazard, mismatched, much of the finish an untreated concrete, the walls so wet I could smell them. I looked at the water dribbling down, furry pockets of moss growing opportunistically along the walls. I listened to the consistent pendulum swing of each of my steps and started counting them as we walked. It helped to block out the sound of Olivia talking animatedly alongside me.

'You got away with what you did to me, but how will you get yourself out of this? You're going down. Down, down, down!'

She screamed the last three words twisting and turning, somersaulting and cartwheeling. She was dressed as a circus ringleader in bright coloured clothes that didn't fit her, dramatic make-up round her eyes and mouth, handing out tickets to imaginary people.

'Roll up, roll up to say your goodbyes – this witch will hang!'

The door slammed shut behind me and I was alone. Distant cries bounced off the cream-coloured breezeblock walls. A stainless-steel sink and toilet lurked in the corner, rusting round the edges, tired from years of use. A bed ran the length of the back wall. I couldn't focus on anything except how utterly wretched and sick I felt. My whole body hurt and I watched as my hands took on a life of their own, involuntary movements forcing them to shake uncontrollably. I tried sitting on them, then lying on them, sweat poured from my body and I felt as though my blood would boil, I was so hot. I urgently peeled my sweat-stained clothes from my skin, shivering and steaming simultaneously and threw them on the floor. I sat cross-legged on the bed, shifting to find a spot without a spring protruding through the cardboard mattress, and willed myself to survive.

I let the night engulf me, my mind diving to dangerous depths, in free-fall now and completely out of control. My dreams were violent and suicidal and I woke with a shock trying to peel a run of thick rope from round my neck.

Olivia was bending over me.

'Jade, darling, wake up, we have to act fast, there isn't long.' The bright whites of her eyes were full of fear.

'What's happening, where am I?' I stammered.

'You're in jail. But, don't worry, I have a plan.'

'Why are you helping me?' I lifted my body to seated, rubbing my eyes with my hands, willing away my slumber.

'Because I know you didn't mean to kill me.' Her words were firm.

I nodded an agreement and listened to the plan.

'They think you're guilty. They're probably getting the evidence now to say you took Ava. Sooner or later they're going to realise what you did to me, too.'

I nodded again, mechanically. I heard her words and accepted their truth.

'But they haven't proven anything yet, have they?'

No, they hadn't, there was still time.

'What do I need to do?' I was ready for anything.

'You need to get rid of your hair, of course. It contains too much DNA, it knows all of your secrets. They can match your hair to any crime, Jade.'

'There's nothing here, no scissors, no razor, there's no way.'

'Oh, Jade, there's always a way... pluck it, pull it, rip it, tear it. Do what you have to do, you want to survive don't you? You want to go home, don't you?' The wicked twist of her head made me feel uneasy but I did, I did want to go home.

I pulled myself together, closed my eyes, ran my hands through my hair, built up to the moment.

I feverishly plucked away at my scalp, beginning with the baby hair round my temples, pulling single strands at first then upgrading to clumps, then fistfuls, as I got used to the burning and the ripping. The concrete in front of me filled with thick tangles of my knotted mane, flecks of blood, chunks of skin. I started to feel better. I was gaining back control. One, two, pull. One, two, pull. I was in a rhythm when I heard a voice outside the cell. A movement. A scratch.

'Hello?' My voice was tiny.

No one answered and the noises stopped.

I sat still. Eyes ablaze, mouth ajar, one hand ready to pull the next fistful from my crown, listening out, smelling blood.

I must have imagined them, the noises, because there was nothing, no one was coming to help me.

I looked at the floor again, covered in parts of me, and felt the weight of regret. I raised my hand to my head, my fingers unused to feeling vast bald patches interspersed with tufts of hair and pockets of blood. Olivia was in the corner, playing with her long blonde locks, twisting them round her finger.

'Now you have to get rid of it.'

'What do you mean?'

She jumped from the corner of the room to within an inch of my face, our foreheads touching, her spit on my eyelashes.

'Eat it.'

'What?'

'That's the only way to get rid of it! They'll find it anywhere else!'

I frantically grabbed at the hair on the floor and tried to ram fistfuls down my throat, not bothering to chew, just doggedly swallowing the dried, dead, evidence. The strands were thick and knotted and covered in skin, I felt a ball forming in my throat as I wretchedly shoved more of it down. It was useless. I vomited. Strands and strands emerged from my mouth, the smell of blood and bile mixed and hit the floor. I dipped my fingers in the mixture, disgusting and dense, and watched Olivia out of the corner of my eye as she honed in on me once more. She took a puke-laced strand, tipped her head back, and swallowed. She stared at me. I had to do the same. She knew what was best for me, she was here to help, she was my friend.

As the clump built up once more in my throat, my stomach churned and swirled. I knew something wasn't right and I began to choke as sick rose from my gut, searching for the light like a fast-growing plant. A second wave surged, much stronger than the first, as it too sought an exit. But its progress was swiftly halted, repressed by the mound of hair in the way.

I blacked out as my lungs screamed for air.

'Sir! I need some assistance in here!'

'Jesus Christ. What did she do—'

49

Ava

I was aware of someone moving nearby, heard their footsteps across the carpet, felt the way the air moved out of the way as they walked.

He approached me and I cowered, bringing my knees up into my chest. I could hear myself whimpering.

'Stop,' he said.

Why was he doing this?

A hand wrapped round my ankle, then he cut the rope that bound them together. Next, he cut the ties round my wrists, and removed the guard from my mouth.

The feeling was incomparable. The freedom my body experienced, the way my skin came back to life. I wanted to hug him.

'I'll come back later.'

He'd left the run of chain round my neck.

With him gone, I tried again to get up. This time I was more successful as I used my newly independent limbs to bring myself to seated. I swayed as the blood rushed from my head and emptiness gnawed at my stomach.

The simple movement of rising to a seated position had awoken a variety of aches and pains and the skin on my back protested angrily at being pulled in a different direction. I became aware of how much the corners of my mouth hurt. I looked down at my ripped clothes. My body was a patchwork of purples, reds, blues and yellows. I had some cuts, they were fresh and they weren't that deep, but they were too numerous to count. I traced hand marks round my wrists and a lump on my head.

I didn't remember being in a fight.

I didn't remember much at all.

That had to change.

I closed my eyes and cast my mind back.

50

Jade

I blinked my eyes rapidly, the scene before me an incomplete mosaic. Eventually, the shapes sharpened and I saw a woman sat across from me. I sniffed the suffocating smell of antiseptic and, as I tried to move, became aware of a large needle embedded in my forearm. I was trapped in synthetic sheets full of static electricity, held down by a handcuff attached to a rail that surrounded all four sides of my bed. They were trying to kill me in my sleep. I thought how Olivia would appreciate the poetic justice of the situation.

A consistent, high-pitched pip repeated nearby and I turned my attention to the long tube of fluid attached to the needle in my arm. I was too drowsy to do anything about it, even though I knew it was poison, it was why my mouth tasted of chalk: they weren't letting me drink anything.

'Jade, hello, my name's Barbara.' She had bags under her eyes, fine lines on her forehead and wore crumpled clothes. She looked like she'd be a good mum. Had she been sleeping in that chair?

I tried to tell her 'hi' but my mouth didn't open and my head didn't nod.

'I wanted to check you were doing OK. We have you on some strong medication to help with those hallucinations, and you've had surgery to remove the hair from your stomach.'

Hallucinations.

She must already know about the way I see Olivia wherever I go and whatever I do.

'The dosage was a little high, so we'll be weaning you off it bit by bit. I've recommended a course of hypnotherapy, we can start tomorrow if you're feeling up to it.'

She squeezed my hand and I fell back to black.

'PSYCHOTIC' JADE FERNLEIGH CLEARED OF ALL CHARGES, DESPITE CONFESSION

In the latest shocking twist in the Ava Wells case, 'unstable and unpredictable' Jade Fernleigh has been cleared of all wrongdoing despite no alibi on the night of Ava's disappearance, a number of colleagues speaking out against her, and an obvious obsession with Ava herself. The charges have been dropped on the grounds of her mental health.

The police have released a statement:

'Proper protocol was not followed in the questioning of Miss Jade Fernleigh. She is being detained in a secure mental health facility and should not have been subjected to a police interrogation, or held in a solitary cell, without prior evaluation of her mental state. There will be a full and thorough review into these failings. No further evidence links Miss Fernleigh to Miss Wells' disappearance. She has been discounted from the investigation.'

51

Josh

You never know how close your world is to totally falling apart until it's too late. There's never a warning, a heads up, no softening of the blow. It just explodes. One minute you're eating your breakfast, checking your messages, the next someone calls you saying, *I need to tell you something. Are you sitting down?* I was on my way back to Olivia's flat from the supermarket – I'd been camped out here ever since Ava went missing – and walked by plain-faced people as they went about their everyday business. I looked directly into the eyes of every single person I passed, wondering if they knew how close they were to disaster, but the warm whip of summer meant the eyes and mouths I observed were all smiley and happy, incapable of pain, worlds away from understanding what it felt like to suffer. It told me something though: that none of them had just been dealt a blow, that none of their loved ones were missing, dead, or dying. My face, in contrast, was bare, an open book, chapter one, page one, of recent emotional disaster. Things like sun and rain and temperature become so irrelevant when someone you know is in danger. Worrying about the weather is a luxury reserved only for the content and, in fact, I'd have preferred it to be cold: the cold would have made me feel useful, the pain of it connecting me to her in some way.

My first experience with the life-altering-explosion-effect was with my parents. They were on holiday, I was at school. In the middle of a maths exam, actually. It was interesting how the memory began, right at that first sign of trauma, with David appearing at the door of my classroom. Even then, at that young age, I could tell immediately that something was terribly wrong. It was written all over him. I clearly remembered my overriding emotion at the time, too: embarrassment. Did he really have to draw this much attention to me in front of my friends? What if he was about to say something that would make me cry? David had appeared at the door and my first, powerful thought was that I really, really, wanted him to leave.

He hadn't, of course; he'd hurried in, slowing slightly as he'd entered the room, all eyes locked onto him, realising we were sitting an exam, a modicum of social awareness cutting through his urgency.

'Josh, can you?'

That was all he'd said.

I'd risen from my desk, head bowed, and left with him as quickly as possible. He'd wrapped his arm round my shoulders and again I'd felt an all-consuming embarrassment, sick with the knowledge that, for at least the rest of the week, I'd be called gay.

The finer details of being told, how much I was told, how I was told, were a little hazier. I'd been drip fed the truth over the years to the extent that all the memories have merged together and my childhood was now just a reflective blur of sadness and anger. Back then, I'd been absolutely hell-bent on my own self-destruction because *David* wasn't my dad, *he* couldn't tell me what to do. Olivia was probably the only person that had kept me from toppling over the edge. Like me, she was damaged, and it was the basis of our bond. Her mum was dead. Taken by an overdose when she was so young. Our stories were slightly different because her memory of her mother was almost nothing. She said she could only remember flashes and the picture she recalled most clearly was so depressing she didn't like to think about it often: Kate Watson passed out in the lounge, a cigarette in her hand burning a hole in the carpet. Olivia had been hungry, flapping round her mother like a young animal after a teat. Said she'd been there for a while. Limp. She wondered if that was the day she'd died. No screaming, no broken bones, no grand exit. Just a flaming cigarette and a life extinguished. The poor girl.

I really loved Olivia. And, with her as my almost-sister, things had started to make sense again. David, however, even though I hadn't liked him much back then, was responsible for pulling me back from the brink of addiction oblivion. He didn't have so much success with Olivia. David and I had started to make things work between us. I guess it was simply that I was growing up, could understand my emotions and realise that it wasn't David's fault my parents weren't alive any more and that, actually, he'd really helped me, looked out for me, brought me up as his own despite everything I'd thrown at him.

I started working for him when I was twenty-two and

the purpose of a career, prospects, being good at something for once, empowered me and kickstarted the process of welding my broken pieces back together again. Things were good, I was settled, I had my own place, I was dating, happy, and, a few years later, a new girl started at work who I was mad about.

Her name was Ava. She was a bit like a siren, I guess. A beautiful, bewitching, mythical creature too good to be true. I was so drawn to her, so intrigued by the thoughts in her head and the curves under her clothes. Even imagining her talk to me made my heart twinge. In the beginning we weren't close, but, when Olivia passed away, her siren call had been strong and we'd knotted together, bound to one another before either of us really knew how strongly we'd felt about the other. And now my siren was missing and it was like I was dealing with that and losing Olivia all over again, a bundle of sadness delivered in the same macabre package. I honestly didn't see the point of life any more if this was what was going to keep happening to everyone I ever loved.

I slotted the key into the lock as I approached the front door of the flat. I stopped for a moment and contemplated knocking, just to see if Ava would come running down the stairs to let me in, her brightness glowing through the doorway, the rush of her vanilla-scented skin as she bent in to kiss me. Even though Olivia had been an integral cog in my life for so many years, it was Ava who'd started to make me feel like someone new. The last dots of ash from the explosion of my parents' passing had finally started to drift away. I'd let someone love me. And now she was gone and I was questioning everything. Why did we get so close to just a handful of people? It was so risky, so fraught with problems. It just didn't make any sense, did it? You put all your hopes and dreams into a few select humans, built your future entirely on the premise that the people you selected would live through it with you, but, and here was the crux, you couldn't be with those people all the time; to tell them not to go near that cliff edge when taking a photo, to force them to get their chest pains looked at by a doctor, to warn them the lorry behind them was veering off-course, or that the aeroplane they were flying on had a terrible safety record.

And then, before long, one of them would die. And everything would fall apart, and it would be hideous. Because you'd invested so much of the rest of your life into them, you'd live forever with a handful of horrible questions. *What would we be doing now? ... How many kids would they have had? ... How would she have handled this situation? ... Would we still be together?... Would something have pushed us apart?* And, if it's a partner, you move on with someone else and you do it all over again. *Why?* I could tell you, having lost almost everyone I hold dear, that it was probably better to live alone, cut out your family and only let people into your life for a few months at a time, than axe them when things got heavy, so no ashes could build up, so that it was your decision not to continue with them and not that of the Universe, or God's so-called plan.

I'd resolved to stay in her flat until she was found. David knew all about Ava and I and – though he wasn't particularly pleased at the news – he was happy for me to be here now things were serious and she was missing. The police said she went willingly to Ireland, they showed me some grainy CCTV footage of a blonde woman in a baseball cap and massive sunglasses showing her boarding pass to an airport official. I'd told them emphatically at the time it wasn't her, but they treated my refusal to identify her and agree with them as if I was a blinded relative, acted as though the blurred footage of someone clearly posing as Ava was the same as her having left me a long goodbye note.

I'd told the police everything, how irrationally and erratically she was acting in the hours before her disappearance, how she'd fed me a story about her mum being ill, how she'd been hyper-emotional about leaving. How it had all been completely and utterly wrong. I wished that I'd followed her that night, the thought had actually crossed my mind at the time, which made swallowing the situation ever harder. I could have stopped this in its tracks.

I hovered in the kitchen doorway. I'd been to the supermarket to pick up bin bags as the food she'd left behind was going mouldy and suspicious smells were floating from the fridge. I had to deal with it, stop putting off the difficult jobs that I didn't want to do, but wouldn't let anyone else do in case they threw something important of hers away. Each cupboard took a lifetime as I held each item for a while, thinking, for example, that she'd picked this packet of spaghetti from the supermarket specifically, opened it with her elegant fingers and taken a little portion from within. I wondered what she'd had with it.

My mouth drooped at the corners as I cradled the packet for a little longer before putting it back in its place. When she got back, we'd eat Bolognese together. I'd cook. My eyes were foggy as I shuffled with the black bin liner to the next set of drawers. The top one was extraordinarily stiff, its handle reluctant to open fully, stuffed to the brim with paper. I couldn't explain why, but I just knew I had to get in there. It focused me and the tears that pricked the edges of my eyes evaporated as I inched my hand under the small gap in the drawer and pressed down on the stack of paper which was stopping it from opening properly. Inch by inch I coaxed it open. The writing was all the same, flashes of words standing out.

Bitch. Slut. Cheat.

All of them signed by the same author.

Charlie, Charlie, Charlie, Charlie, Charlie.

He must have sent at least fifty. There were no stamps, or envelopes, which meant they must have been posted directly through the letterbox. Why hadn't the police found these? My stomach dropped as I thought about her hiding them from me. Why would she do that? I knew what she was going through with Charlie, we went through it together, or at least I thought we had. I read the note at the top of the pile, the most recent:

I want you to wear white to my funeral. You were supposed to be my bride; it's poetic. Pick something out this week. It won't be long now. And, while you're standing in the pew, remembering me, I want you to know that the tears of those round you are all your fault. It didn't have to end this way. If only you'd

listened. In fact, wear red, Ava. It will match the blood
on your hands.
All my love,
Charlie.

An instant later, I was calling the police, ready to run them through the contents of the notes in my hands, the stack wobbling in my grip as I thought about how long I'd been sat right on top of the evidence I needed to get Ava back. How they'd failed to turn these up in their search, I didn't know. The phone rang once then was picked up with satisfying efficiency.

'Police, how can I help?' She was too cheery, her voice round and full and nowhere near officious enough.

'I'm calling about Ava Wells, missing person, I've found a stack of notes at her home. They're from her ex. I think he might have taken her.'

The line went quiet for a moment. 'Could you bring them down to the station? I'll make sure someone's free to meet you.'

The night was closing in, but I didn't hesitate before leaving, this was the way back to Ava, I could feel it.

My sad image was reflected back at me in the mirrored surfaces of the brightly lit station as I pushed my way past drunks and worried relatives to the front desk. I was wearing a khaki parka zipped up to my nose, my hair dishevelled and, if someone was describing me now, they'd say I had a beard. Not stubble. A full-on bushy monstrosity, an unkempt nest on my chin. Ava wasn't a fan of beards. I'd have to shave before I saw her again. Because I *would* see her again. I had to keep telling myself that. I thought about her hair, swishing round her shoulders in its iridescent shades of blonde. I thought about how soft it was to the touch, how my beard and her hair were the very antithesis of one another. What I wouldn't do to run my hands through those golden strands now, to stroke her skin and kiss her lips.

DI Frederick Crow greeted me. I'd met him a few times. We hadn't got off to a great start what with him insisting Ava had run away from me and me insisting that he and his team were a bunch of jobsworth idiots. He offered me a half-smile and a handshake, but the frown-line between his eyebrows gave him away. He wasn't pleased to see me, either. I was aware I must have appeared more aloof than normal because I completely ignored the first question he asked me, my attention distracted by a puce-faced busker who'd just danced into the station with an accordion blaring out 'We Wish You A Merry Shitmas'. The remix the world hadn't asked for. Especially not in the middle of summer.

'Mr Stein?'

'Yeah, sorry,' I grunted as I realised he'd already set off to our destination. He swiped us through the security doors and into what I guess they'd call the 'soft room'. This room wasn't for suspects: there were too many comfy furnishings, potted plants, black and white pictures in half-decent frames, an artificial smell supposed to remind me of fresh air. This was the kind of room where you're told your entire family has been killed and the police have no idea who did it. I'd been in a couple of them now. I took a seat and removed my parka. The T-shirt underneath had basically changed from blue to green I'd been wearing it so much. Fuck it, there were much bigger things to worry about than what I smelt like today.

'Tea? Coffee?' Crow asked.

I turned down his offer.

'These are for you.' I produced the stack of notes from my coat pocket and put them on the metal coffee table between us. I let out a deep breath. 'I already told you about Charlie, her ex.' I paused, I didn't want to antagonise him, so I kept my tone even and considered. 'But even *I* didn't know how bad things were. I had no idea he was sending these.'

Fred Crow snapped on a pair of gloves to sift through the evidence. Probably something I should have thought to do. His lips were pursed, expression dubious, and his eyes darted from letter to letter as he skim read each one.

A pulsing began at the top of my head, an urgency.

We don't really have time to read every single one, mate, we just need to put some more people on a team in charge of finding Charlie.

'OK,' Crow sighed and bowed his head. I heard him crack his knuckles against each other. He closed his eyes. 'We haven't been able to find Charlie yet.' He gripped the top of his nose with his thumb and forefinger.

Tension crept up through my spine and met at the pressure point at the top of my head. He'd told me this before, five days after she went missing.

We haven't been able to locate Mr Munk, yet, but, don't worry, our best guys are on it.

He was so fucking sexist on top of everything else.

'Guys', what about your 'gals', Crow? Don't let them work for the police yet, am I right? Too risky?

He continued, 'We've been trying to make contact with Mr Munk since the day Ava went missing. He's nowhere. No contact with his parents, no word to his friends, nothing. And if we can't find him, we can't question him, and if we can't question him, we can't ask him about these.' He picked up the notes. A thin layer of sweat glistened over his forehead. Crow was stressed out.

So was I.

'Isn't that a little bit more than suspicious in itself?'

'Not necessarily,' he replied, irritatingly diplomatically.

'Right.' I laid my palms flat on the table and steadied myself. 'I don't understand how both Ava and Charlie can just disappear off the face of the planet, no one have any clue where they are, and no one think it's suspicious enough to launch a full-scale search.'

'Well, as far as the evidence shows… Ava's in Ireland,' he interjected. He was always keen to wrap back to this shitty bit of investigative work, cradling the red herring they'd been given as bait, holding onto it as though it were the catch of the fucking day.

'She's not in Dublin. Like I've already told you, your images aren't of her,' I protested angrily, heat rising.

He kept his voice low, 'Mr Stein, even if it's not her, we need to figure out who it was and why someone would want to plant that kind of a diversion.'

'Isn't it pretty fucking obvious?' I was shaken up and watched as the DI mentally talked himself through his training protocols.

Don't get angry at the friends and family, Fred, it's a difficult time for them.

'In the meantime, Mr Stein, these are great; our next step

will be to figure out if Charlie has any Irish connections, associates, any previous trips, visas, that sort of thing. He might have created this diversion that you're so convinced about.' He lowered his gaze and made some notes.

'What the—?' I shouted, losing my cool. 'Charlie's Irish, you know that right. You *knew that already, right?*' I swore loudly at him and kicked the table.

'We have a team looking for him,' Crow replied, standing too, but clearly shaken.

'Well, get a bigger team, not just people fielding calls,' I shot back. I raised my voice again, I couldn't help it, this was too important not to emphasise.

'Listen, Mr Stein, we're the professionals here and you need to let us do our job. We'll decide how to handle the investigation. If we went chasing after every single lead that came in, we'd have officers all over the world and in every corner of the country looking into the madness that people report to us as fact. We need to be smart with our resources.'

Smart?

My blood was pumping hard. First, the investigation had ruled Ava a runaway. Case closed, no more questions please, stop the media coverage in its tracks, kill the story, kill the story, kill the story. Then, they'd gone after Jade Fernleigh purely down to media pressure, a woman so wrapped up in her own delusion she could barely function and they'd interviewed her to breaking point, to the level that she was now locked up in an asylum somewhere trying to recover from the ordeal. And now they were ignoring clear motive from her ex-boyfriend and hadn't even bothered to investigate, or tried very hard to find him. What was the point in a police force if I was just going to have to figure out where she was myself? I tried to regain my composure but my fists were in balls, jaw clenched, biceps and shoulders flexed, ready to fight.

'Do you think it's possible they ran away together?' Crow mused.

Was he goading me? I didn't answer and sat still emitting angry, fiery breaths from my nose.

'She'd hidden these notes from you, so perhaps there was something more to it? You know how some girls love the drama of a passionate relationship, the attention and all that—'

I couldn't stop the emotion as it hurtled up from my core and out of my body, bringing my arm with it, smashing my fist into the metal of the table between us, accompanied with a violent, primitive, roar and a numb pain. I looked down at the dent I'd made, wishing it had been Crow's face.

'You dumb fuck,' I hissed, picking up my jacket and slamming the door shut behind me. I called the papers on my way home.

POSSIBLE BREAKTHROUGH IN MISSING PERSONS CASE

Ava Wells' 'possessive and deranged' ex-boyfriend is yet to be located, or questioned, by police in a damning allegation from Miss Wells' current partner Joshua Stein.

The pair broke up acrimoniously earlier this year. Ava even gave a statement to police after a domestic incident at their address, and now there's new evidence to suggest Mr Munk was stalking her in the days before her disappearance, sending threatening notes to her address.

Ava's distraught partner, Josh Stein, spoke to us this morning. 'The police aren't even getting the basics right. What if he was on that flight with her? Has anyone even checked? Does anyone even know where he is?'

We reached out to lead investigator DI Crow this morning but he declined to comment.

52

Jade

I lay on top of the thin blue sheet. It was scratchy and I reached down to itch the backs of my bare legs, protesting against lying here for much longer. I was on so much medication that I couldn't think about the same thing for very long, still trying to piece together what had happened to me, when I felt up to it.

I knew time had passed because the sun was higher in the sky. A cold light defrosted the window at the end of the ward. I looked out of it, two beds away from me, and across the field beyond. In the far distance, I could make out a couple of early morning dog walkers. How wonderful it would be to wander out there, free, the country air so full of flavour. I thought of freshly cut grass, smelling sunflowers in strangers' gardens, running my hands through bunches of lavender...

I caught a glimmer of myself in the window and that brought my focus in closer, distracting me from the walkers beyond. It wasn't a full reflection, though, more like a black and white sketch. I could make out the short, unkempt dark hair that I recognised as mine, but black hollows stared back at me rather than the green eyes I was used to seeing. I ran my hands over my body to check it was definitely me. Ribs and hips jutted out during my inspection. I guess I hadn't noticed how much weight I'd lost. I looked down at my feet, the nails long, unpainted, my pale skin an off-purple, pulled tight over the bulging veins and bones.

Was that what these vultures were trying to do? Pick away at every bit of me until I was nothing but a corpse?

My secrets would be the only thing left, then they'd pluck those from me too. I called for the person on duty to take me to the bathroom. I sat on the bed, waiting patiently for the flip-flop, flip-flop, of turquoise Crocs on cheap lino. Seven-thirty, said the clock on the wall, tick-tock, tick-tock.

A woman came in. She had crooked teeth and lank hair. She took my arm and escorted me to the bathroom facilities. Thirty minutes from now the rest of the braindead would follow me in here, scrubbed and washed with soap so strong perhaps the authorities thought it was capable of bleaching away our deficiencies. An essential part of our rehabilitation. *Clean body, clean mind!* I relieved myself in the toilet. She turned slightly away from me and pretended she wasn't interested in what I was doing by sticking her finger in her ear and giving it a good wiggle. She didn't turn too far, though, just in case I shoved my head down the bowl and tried to drown myself in my own piss. She picked me up under the elbows when I refused to get up of my own accord. I smelt her earwax as she hoiked my underwear into position. She dragged me into the shower unit where she sprayed me down like a caged circus animal then escorted me back to my room. Breakfast next. I waited. I thought about nothing, my head empty, I watched the clock as the second hand meandered round the face, waiting, silently, for eight-thirty. That was all I could do, watch, wait, watch, wait.

I heard the familiar clunk of the lock mechanism opening and the psychiatrist tasked with fixing me poked her head round the ward door.

'Jade, how are you doing this morning?' Barbara's rosy complexion stretched into a cheery grin. 'I heard you were up early.'

The truth was, this morning felt different. I wanted to go outside, walk in that field I could see beyond the window, play with the dogs that ran through it. I didn't want to spend every single day for the rest of my life rolling through the same maddening routine. The endless cycles of hypnotherapy.

'I want to remember what happened,' I replied, honestly.

'That's fantastic, let's get you into the other room.'

She let me free and we walked side-by-side along the corridor to her office.

The room was bright, all the lights were on and I felt they would burn me if I stood too close.

'Can you switch those off?' I asked her, my eyes squinting as though someone was shining a torch directly at them.

I heard the material of her shoes, rubber-soled, squeak across the floor, the decisive flick of a light switch, followed immediately by relative darkness. I allowed my eyes to open a slither, taking in the room as though I was peering through a letterbox. I observed that, with the main light disabled, the task of illumination had been left to a small blue lamp on Barbara's desk, and it struggled to permeate the room with its dull lemon hue.

'Is that better, Jade?' Her voice was reassuring, firm. She cared about me.

Now that I could see more clearly, I let a full breath enter my lungs, opened my eyes, and took in my surroundings. White walls free from stimuli, her stark desk, my lonely chair, the blue lamp.

'Where do you want to begin, Jade?' Barbara asked, pen poised above her notepad, ready to scribble down my secrets.

'Can we just talk? No pens, no paper...'

She took a moment to digest the request, then placed her elegant fountain pen down on its side.

'Thank you,' I said. I looked down at my lap, trying to put into words what had been churning round in my mind. The ill-fitting canvas trousers I was wearing weren't mine, neither were the battered black trainers, plucked from a lost-property style basket of clothes from the hospital ward, each item approved for its absence of zips, buttons and unsuitability as a fashion-forward noose. 'I think the new medication is really helping me.'

'That's good, Jade, it's been quite a while since you last reported any hallucinations,' Barbara replied, upbeat.

I thought about Olivia for a second, trying to picture what she looked like. In my hallucination she didn't have any stand-out features, her presence wasn't so much a physical one as verbal. I could tell you the old Olivia had yellowy eyes and blonde hair, tanned limbs and a naughty smile. But the new Olivia didn't have much of a look at all, her voice was the same as the real her, though. At least I thought it was.

'How old would she be now?' I asked, pulling back a cuticle to distract from the emotional pain I felt.

'Olivia? Let's see…' Barbara flicked through some pages in her notebook, the paper scraping noisily against itself. 'Thirty.'

'Ah.' My voice broke.

'Do you blame yourself for what happened to her?' Barbara asked.

I slumped back into the chair, feeling the colossal weight of responsibility as she asked me that question. I'd always skated over the subject of what happened to Olivia and when I woke from the hypnotherapy, I would close myself off, careful not to give anything away. My eyes glossed over, the watery pools quickly breaking rank sending splashes onto my borrowed garments.

'Of course I do, I could have stopped it.'

Barbara's voice turned steely. 'Why don't you talk me through exactly what happened? I can't help you if I don't know.' She stood up from her chair and moved towards me, bending down at my side, her skin touching mine as she held my hands to stop them shaking.

'I should have helped, I was in there with her,' I blubbered through the words, knowing deep down that it wasn't my fault. 'It should have been me.' Barbara squeezed my hands tight but fear swelled in the void in my heart and my mind catapulted back to the night I wished I could forget ever happened.

53

Jade

One Year Ago

The nightclub was a heady mix of glitz and gutter. Repetitive beats reverberated off the black brick walls, the room dotted with beautiful twenty-somethings, their long limbs and lean muscles stretched out across velvet furnishings. They sipped triple-filtered vodka, snorted the purest class As.

Only the best for London's elite.

I was clad in black leather, red lipstick my only accessory. The world at my feet.

'Look what Charlie gave me,' Olivia said, smiling wickedly and nodding towards the ladies' toilets. 'It's the good stuff. Want to join?'

'No thanks, you go ahead,' I replied, out of my depth.

'Suit yourself. But don't tell Ava, I don't want her to know I'm having a moment of weakness. One tiny hit won't hurt, though. I can always start again tomorrow...'

Ava hadn't been at W&SP long but was already muscling

in on my territory. I'd been through a few detoxes with Liv, though none of them very successful. In a way I was happy that Ava's first attempt was going much the same as mine.

The music was loud and Olivia wanted to make sure I agreed.

'Promise you won't tell Ava?' she asked again, waiting for me to nod, before hurrying off. She was wearing a coal-coloured jacket that would cause anyone else to sweat to death in here, but she was thinner than a Bond Street mannequin and the heat didn't bother her.

I took out my phone and stared at the blank screen. I was desperate to text Josh, to ask if he wanted to join the group tonight, but I was hesitant... I'd nabbed his number from Olivia under the pretence of 'work' and was wary of appearing over-keen. We hardly knew each other despite working in the same building and, just as I was about to type something I'd regret, Charlie and Ava appeared with a tray of shots and saved me from myself. Despite Ava trying to overshadow me by helping Olivia with her addiction, I liked the girl. She was ambitious and determined and, from what I'd seen so far, a great person to have around on a night out. I couldn't say the same for her partner, however, who insisted on following her wherever she went like an angry stray.

'Vodka?' Ava offered.

I took one of the tiny glasses and threw my head back, wincing as the liquid carved a fleshy trail down my windpipe.

'Liv's in the toilet,' I said to Ava, betraying Olivia's wishes immediately, keen to let Ava know she'd failed in her attempt to help our friend. 'Charlie gave her something.'

Ava flashed him a look then shook her head.

'You gave her drugs? Charlie, she's six weeks clean, why would you do that?'

Ava stood up to face him and for the first time I noticed how thick the veins were that bulged down his forearms.

'I'm not the boss of Olivia, she can do what she fucking well wants.'

'You're not helping, though, are you?'

'God you're such a grandma, do you know that? Can't you just have fun? Let loose? Forget about it?'

He pulled her close and tried to get her to dance. She wriggled free and pushed him away, hard.

'Get off me.'

That was when he lost it. In the slow-motion seconds that followed he pulled his palm back behind him and, just as it was flying back towards Ava's face, a security guard stepped in and put his body between them. Charlie fought but he was smaller and drunker than the man who'd wrapped his arms round him and there was nothing he could do.

Ava turned her back to Charlie as he was dragged away, his grin flipped upside down. 'Don't dance with any of these dickheads! You'd better come home with me! Now!'

I looked away, embarrassed for Ava, her expression tight with frustration. Ava waited until he was gone to say anything, then she took another shot and spilled her heart to me.

'He's taking the move down here out on me. He knows I have a problem with him doing too many drugs, so he's taking them every night now, dealing them to Olivia, even. And she's been so good recently. I don't know how much longer I can go on while he's like this.'

Ava opening up to me was a big deal. I wasn't used to people asking for my help, but trying to navigate Ava through her problems with Charlie, with only a back catalogue of relationship failure to call on as experience, wasn't easy. I didn't have a clue what to say back.

Instead, I opted for a safe answer, 'I'm sure it's just a phase.' I suggested the only solution I could think of. 'Do you want to dance?'

I held out my hand and Ava took it, her skin soft. We danced together, diffusing the tension of the night by mouthing lyrics at each other and shifting our weight in time to the music. Ava moved much more naturally than I did, even her silky blonde locks kept the beat, and I was sure everyone in the room was watching Ava's beautiful body as it bopped up and down.

I bent in towards Ava's ear, smelt the vanilla scented mist she'd been spraying in her hair earlier, held her arm lightly in my hand and let her in on my heart's desire. 'I was about to text Josh. I really like him. Do you think I should?'

Ava shook her head and shouted back over the music to me. 'Absolutely not, it's...' She looked at her watch, shook it a couple of times. 'My watch is broken!' she cried over the music, laughing, throwing her hands up in the air. 'It's too late. It would be a booty-call! Unless that's what you want?'

'No. I want to do it properly. I want ...'

I stopped mid-sentence as I spotted a woman moving urgently towards us, eyeballs first.

'Quick. I think your friend took too much, maybe it was stronger than she thought, you have to get her home. She's in the third cubicle.'

We stood still, momentarily paralysed, each waiting for the other to take the lead.

'Move!'

The woman's face was red, blotched with white. Olivia probably wasn't the only one who'd taken too much.

First we saw her feet. They were sprawled out under the cubicle door, each one of her motionless sunshine-Shellaced toenails visible. I hurried towards her and tentatively pushed the door to the toilet open, its progress halted by Olivia's body on the other side. Through the gap, I could see Olivia's face smeared across the wall, legs apart, a flash of lace visible, powder on her top lip, the contents of her handbag dribbled on top of the black tiles.

'Take her arm,' I instructed Ava under my breath and we shuffled and squeezed into the cramped space together. A picture of a goddess with a finger to her lips hung on the toilet wall behind us. Under her gaze we counted to three. One, two...

In that moment I thought it was true what they said about moving dead bodies, even Olivia, who couldn't have been a pound above eight stone, weighed a tonne to manoeuvre and I broke a sweat just dragging her reluctant body from the floor and coercing her left arm over my shoulder. I felt Olivia's heart thundering rapidly against my side as we carried her out into the night.

'Don't you – get – let cook know,' she slurred nonsensically.

'You're not holding her high enough,' Ava puffed, out of breath, as we carried Olivia in through the front door. Ava had her legs and I held Olivia under her shoulders, but she was slipping down and out of our grip and now her peroxide blonde curls scraped along the floor. It was all wrong.

The taxi driver hadn't batted an eye as we'd carried her out of the car, thankful that he'd managed to get a paralytic passenger home without redecorating his back seats with vomit, probably, but I hoped no one was observing this charade as we hauled Olivia's body in over the threshold. This didn't look quite so innocent. I lost my grip, my fingers unable to hold her weight any longer and Olivia's upper body dropped like a sack of potatoes onto the marbled floor underfoot. A high-pitched crack followed as her skull made contact with the unforgiving surface.

'Oh God,' slurred Ava as blood started to drain from the back of Olivia's head.

I took a deep breath in, waterfalls of red running across the floor towards my high-heeled boots.

'Step back,' Ava said. Then she bent down next to Olivia and felt her pulse. 'It's rapid but it's there,' she said.

She had a pulse. That was good. I didn't need to hold my hand to Olivia's mouth to see that she was breathing. Her chest was moving up and down, urgent and shallow, but moving. That was good, too.

'Olivia?' Ava asked her. 'Is your head OK?'

Olivia's eyes rolled and she arched her back. 'Don't tell him, please,' she said again.

'Do you think she needs an ambulance?' I asked after Ava had finished her rudimentary assessments, my face flushed with worry.

'Honestly, I don't know,' Ava replied. 'But she's breathing, and talking, and she has a pulse, maybe we should just monitor her for a few hours…'

'What about her head?' I asked, feeling guilty for making things worse.

'It was just a knock. She didn't black out or anything. She'll be OK.'

'Do you think David would fire us for letting her get like this? What if he blames us? What if he thinks we did the drugs with her? What about Josh? Wouldn't he be mad, too? He's dead against Olivia taking this stuff.'

As I said the words, I knew these thoughts had more than crossed Ava's mind. She knew this could get us fired. If not fired then at least disciplined, a black mark against our names for as long as we worked in the industry. David and Josh knew about Olivia's habit but both abhorred it. Josh had been clean for years and, though neither Ava nor me knew David well, he was notorious for being fierce. How could we let something as stupid as this tarnish our reputations with him? Something that wasn't even our fault.

Ava nodded at me, then looked at Olivia and stroked her hair. Ava told Olivia everything was going to be fine.

'Shall we take her to bed?' Ava asked.

I looked towards the staircase. 'No chance.' Navigating thirty odd steps was out of the question, so we settled for lying her on the sofa in the living room instead. Then we sat in near silence watching Olivia fade in and out of sleep, listening quietly as Olivia's breathing stuttered and struggled.

I spoke again. 'What do we do now? I don't fancy staying the night here, do you?'

Ava looked torn. 'Charlie will flip if I don't get home.'

'She's going to be OK,' I said, trying to convince myself. 'David can't know about this.'

'Let's text him, from her phone. Say something like, Dad I'm sorry, I took too much of something tonight…'

'That way it's not on us.'

'Exactly.'

'At least we'll have told someone.'

'Should we tell Josh?'

We took her phone and sent the message, then laid her phone on the arm of the sofa so she could call for help if she needed it. Then we left her in that cold room, barely conscious, and hurried home. We abandoned her when she needed us the most. We let her die to save ourselves.

The next morning our worst fear came true: Olivia didn't turn up at the office and Ava and I had to plan a way out of what we'd done. We whispered in the ladies' toilets in the early morning. Neither of us had been able to sleep and my eyes were underlined with bright blue bags.

I started. 'We'll give her until half nine. If she doesn't turn up, you go to David and say you were meant to be meeting her.'

'And what do we say if she's…' Ava could hardly bring herself to say it. 'We have to tell the police exactly the same story.'

'We went out with Olivia, we got drunk, Liv had too much so we took her home – that way the taxi driver can't incriminate us – and, as soon as we'd got her inside, we left to go home. It's basically the truth.'

'We can't say that, David will flip that we left her.'

'OK, so we say we all got in the taxi and dropped her off on our way home.'

'All right.'

'What do we say about Charlie?' I asked.

'We have to leave him out of it. David will blame me by proxy if he knows it was Charlie's drugs that killed Olivia.'

'Fine. So we're agreed. And, you know, it's basically the truth.'

Ava nodded. It was. Apart from the fact that we could have helped Olivia sooner and actively chose not to. Apart from that, sure, it was the God's honest truth.

I took Ava's hands in mine. 'Promise me that no matter what happens this secret stays our secret. No matter what.'

'I promise.'

54

Ava

It was pitch black.

The room I was in seemed strangely familiar, as though I'd dreamt about it before, but I couldn't tell if that was the effect of whatever drugs I'd been given or an actual, tangible, memory.

I tried to sleep but my flashbacks were growing more and more powerful, pervading my thoughts and turning them into terrible nightmares, forcing me to live the horror all over again every time I closed my eyes.

My waking mind wasn't much better, determined to replay what had happened after I'd left Josh, trying to come up with a solution. How would I have escaped? What would I have done differently?

I allowed myself to travel back to that moment.

I sit in the car, those urgent, full beam headlights shining on my rear-view mirror. I have my foot on the accelerator, one hand ready to free my seatbelt, the other on the central locking. A figure moves towards me through the lights: tall, muscular. He comes to my window, he knocks, once. *Sheff.* I don't know his real name, he never told me, just wanted me to call him Sheff. Sheff the chef from Sheffield. Who looked more like a bodybuilder. Now I know why.

I lay on the bed in the same, ripped clothes I'd been living in since I was taken. My body might have been shutting down but my mind was still firing, tired and terrified, but sane. It was currently preoccupied with the thought of how long it would take me to die of water deprivation. I was sure I'd read that it killed you faster than starvation, but I had no idea how long I'd been here for and I didn't know if I'd been given anything to keep me alive whilst I had. I could have been out of it for weeks.

I focused on my breath. If I could breathe I was fine. I listened to my heart pumping away. It felt tired. Like it wanted to stop.

Then, through the stillness, a series of unfamiliar cracks and squeaks sounded.

The door opened.

It was a momentous occasion. And, even though I barely had the strength to angle my head towards it, my brain was crazy with questions. *Who was there, what did they want, why was I here, was this the end?*

Sheff stepped into my line of sight, his cold eyes surveying me.

I imagined running towards him, ambushing him and kicking him in the balls, flinging the door open as he sank in pain, and darting out into the world. I couldn't, though, of course. Not only had my body entirely stopped obeying my brain, it was so weak it couldn't have done anything about it even if the two were still linked.

He put down a sandwich and a glass of water on the floor in front of me.

Was it poisoned?

I considered the worst-case scenario: if it *was* poison, I'd rather die of that than a prolonged starvation.

It took every last drop of my energy to drag the meal towards me. I drank the water first, breathless between ravenous gulps, then ate the sandwich lying on my front, my hand reaching down from the bed to the ground to grab more when I was ready. At first, my mouth had forgotten how to chew and it took a while to get used to it again. Sheff's face was blank, his expression empty.

When I was finished I felt infinitely better, stronger, like my plight wasn't entirely doomed. If I could just get him talking, maybe I could work all this out.

'Who are you?' I asked through the cold silence, slightly surprised by the sound of my own voice.

He shot a nervous look towards the ceiling and I followed his stare to a small, black circle in the corner of the room. A camera. Someone was watching.

A crackling, then a clear command. 'No questions.'

I looked up, the sound was coming from some sort of intercom system, played into the room from somewhere else. The voice didn't sound immediately familiar through the distorted transmission.

Sheff leant down and picked up the plate, dropping crumbs onto the floor as he did. He left without a word.

I picked at the crumbs when I was alone again, lying on my front, thoughts whirring.

One particularly pertinent question stood out.

I'd never actually checked with David that he'd sent a chef for me, had I?

Who was this man?

55

Jade

Time passed in the most unusual way on the ward: minutes felt like hours, but, by the end of the day, I'd wonder where all the time had gone. I'd been moved to my own room now, so at least I wasn't a prisoner any more, but my surroundings were like a sad, soulless hotel room, or a boarding school for naughty teenagers, and I was angry with myself for my lack of progress. *Baby steps.* That's what Barbara would say. *Don't try and do everything at once, give yourself time.*

The walls surrounding me were cream and empty. A single bed with a blue and pink duvet lay along one side of the room, the opposite wall featuring a simple pine desk, a flimsy wardrobe at the back. I lay on my bed and thought about Ava. What had happened to her? I hadn't considered it fully, properly, meaningfully, until now. I thought back, maybe she *had* run away. I thought about her relationship with Josh. With David. Then, as though a lightbulb had just blown up inside my head, an image careered through my memory with such urgency I knew it couldn't be ignored. I grabbed my phone, which had only recently been returned to me, and somehow, amazingly, remembered the pincode. I scrolled into my camera roll. I studied the photo I'd taken of her at the summer party in David's country house, being carried into a room by him. The picture I'd tried to show Josh before he'd rejected me. I analysed it with a new intensity. Her arms were floppy by her sides, her head hung back in what I'd thought was laughter, but, looking closely now, perhaps better resembled a state of unconsciousness. And, just like that, I felt like I knew where she was. And who she was with.

56

Ava

I raised my hand to touch the tender bruise where the cuff made contact with my neck.

'Please take this thing off me. I'm not going anywhere, am I?' I pleaded with the man who lurked behind the camera who could see and hear everything I did.

'Absolutely not,' the voice answered.

I was feeling stronger thanks to the food Sheff had brought and I switched my attention to the rounded glass bowl, focusing on the flashing green light in the corner.

'So why not?' I retorted.

'You lied to me,' the voice replied.

I still wasn't sure who was behind the mask, the intonation was familiar but the tone was low and had been deliberately distorted to scare me. Outwardly, I remained impassive, but my insides ran riot. That revelation didn't narrow it down, I'd lied to so many people, about so many different things in order to survive. Any one of them could have led me to this place.

57

Jade

Josh had to see this picture. My motive for showing him was no longer revenge but genuine concern for Ava. We'd been so close before all this happened. I emailed him, reasoning it was the fastest way to get through.

> Josh, I took this the night of the summer party. This was the picture I wanted to show you. I thought she looked drunk but maybe she'd been drugged? Has David ever said anything about it? Why did he take her into that room?

I waited the rest of the day for a reply but none came and by nightfall I was growing concerned.

The windows were black, so I pulled the curtains to and got ready for bed. The other people that occupied the ward were winding down and late-night conversations were coming to a close. I waited until I'd counted all six bedroom doors shut. When I was sure no one was outside,

I tiptoed across to the toilet. I shuffled along the corridor, the walls stark and angular, the floor freezing underfoot.

The toilet seat was cold as I made contact with it, the window had been left open to air out someone else's stink, and I pushed as hard as I could to get the whole thing over with as quickly as possible. I heard a noise from beyond the door, light footsteps tracing their way towards me. I wiped quickly and stood up, not flushing, not wanting to alert any attention to my presence here. I pressed my ear against the door but the sound had subsided. Perhaps I'd imagined it, and, after a few more minutes of icy silence had passed, I decided it was safe enough to head back to my room. No one was there when I stuck my head out of the cubicle and looked up the length of the corridor, so I shuffled as quickly and quietly as I could back towards my bedroom door, shutting it gingerly behind me and jumped into bed, pulling the covers up over me to form my foamy fortress.

The door mechanism sounded with a sudden snap. I stopped breathing and heard the unmistakable sound of those same soft footsteps I'd heard earlier as they crept through the entranceway into my room. I was no longer alone. I pressed my body deep into the bed, praying it was someone who'd opened the wrong door and would run right back out again as soon as they realised. I wasn't sure whether to scream or play dead as the steps approached, drawing closer and closer. My eyes registered a shape in the darkness: a man.

He stood over me with a syringe in his hand, full of murky liquid. He was surprised to find me awake and didn't have much time to cover my mouth as my lungs screamed into action. I struck his neck and tried to rip the syringe from his grip.

'Help!' I cried out from between his fingers, crooked and weak. The word barely carried: my throat was constricted in shock, my call muffled by his grip. I swallowed and took a deeper breath, 'Help!' This time my cry was louder, and my plea bounced off the walls that surrounded us.

The man's face stirred with fury and he lunged with a renewed determination, pressing the syringe deep into my arm. I wriggled and wrestled under it, trying to swat it away, willing my body to form a barrier against it. I felt the prick of the needle and the plunge of the fluid as it transferred from the vial into my body. I stared into him, his fierce glare focused on the needle and nothing else, concerned only with finishing the task.

'They'll assume you overdosed. Poetic, don't you think?' he said, still focused on the needle.

Although part of me wanted to ask him why, with that line I knew exactly why he was here, what had happened, everything. It was crystal clear. This was revenge for what had happened to Olivia.

A piercing sound cut through the strangely intimate moment between us as the main alarm was activated. Someone had responded to my yell. The man looked up abruptly, roughly removed the needle from my bruised arm and sprinted towards the window. I tried to move to stop him, but the world became a thick, melted mess of shapes and colours as the drugs clouded my senses. I tried to scream again but only a drooling slur of sound came out. He was fiddling with the window as voices neared. My neighbours, the people I'd gone out of my way to ignore, were now my only chance of survival. He managed to prise the clasp open. His gloved fingers clawed at the windowsill then he pulled himself up onto it, using the desk nearby as a leg up.

'In here!' a voice said.

His body slid out through the frame and disappeared into the darkness.

The last thing I remembered were the way his eyes caught the light as he fled.

58

Josh

My heels pounded the streets as I made my way to the flat, my heart pumping hard as I thundered in through the doorway. Part of me was terrified that Crow was right about Ava. Why *had* she hidden the notes from me? What if he was right and she'd run away with Charlie? Would that be more difficult to recover from? At least the papers were applying some pressure to the investigation, a few reporters had even been in touch to let me know they were putting detectives of their own on the ground in Dublin to track Charlie down. I'd learnt a lot about their relationship since the news about him broke: the abuse he subjected her to, the way she'd felt trapped in her own home by him, that she felt she hadn't any choice but to accept David's offer of helping her out. I wish she'd let me in back then. I could have helped...

I logged into my work emails sitting at the kitchen island, ignoring the 890 that were unread since I last logged in weeks ago. But one caught my attention. The one on top of the pile.

From: Jade Fernleigh RE: Josh, what do you make of this photo?

I clicked into the attachment. This must have been the photo she'd tried to show me the night she'd turned up here looking like Edward Scissorhands. I shook as I craned my neck in closer to the screen, even though I wanted to recoil from what I was seeing. My first impression was that Ava looked drunk, passed out, maybe, that it looked as though David was carrying her to safety. But, on closer inspection, there were obvious red flags, really clear reasons why that wasn't the case. Her skin was almost yellow, for starters, and David was taking her into a room that had a number of bolts on the door frame. His hands were gripped round her, like she had no control of her own body, and neither one of them was smiling. It was clear she was really unwell.

Where did Jade find this? When was it taken? Why hadn't Ava or David told me about this?

These past few weeks had been a rollercoaster I couldn't get off. First Charlie, then David and now Ava – did I know her at all? All these secrets she was keeping from me didn't look good. I replied to Jade straight away. I noticed she'd sent it from her personal account, not much chance of her making it back to W&SP after the mess she made of everything on the AthLuxe account, I guess...

Jade, when did you take this?

As I pressed send I realised something, a penny dropped, Ava had told me about a gold dress she'd bought to wear to the summer party. So, this was David's country house then, maybe; the carpet looked right, the surroundings.

I chewed my fingernail as I felt out my next move.

I should call David.

Get some answers.

59

Ava

'Who are you?' I asked, letting the words ring in my ear.

The intercom fell silent and I waited, standing stock still in the same ripped clothes I'd been taken in, the same chain round my neck. The familiar sounds of the door locks opening whirred into action, the clunks and squeaks which were always followed by food being delivered by Sheff. I started salivating, like a dog trained to associate a certain sound with an immediate action. The analogy wasn't lost on me. I was his bitch: trapped in a cage, begging for food, howling for freedom. I could tell the door was heavy by the dull sound it made when it opened. It was probably reinforced with metal, bulletproof, even. There were a few scratches down its length and it crossed my mind that I might not have been the first person trapped behind it. The crack of light to the outside world widened as the door opened and the intoxicating fresh air of the hallway beyond flew in and hit my dirty face. The lithe silhouette in the frame wasn't Sheff's, though, and it took me a second to digest who was standing in its path with his yellow irises and cavernous face.

David Stein.

I pictured his face all those weeks ago when he'd convinced me to break up with Charlie, move into his house, live under his rules. His sad eyes, his persuasive mouth. The thought sent a stitch through my heart. I'd been played from the very beginning. *He knows what I did.* I retreated from my position in front of the camera and took small stumbling steps backward toward the bed. *He knows about Olivia and I am here to pay for my mistake.* His phone vibrated. He snatched it from his pocket and turned it off.

Just the two of us.

Just like the summer party.

I tried my hardest to push the painful and grotesque memories I had from that night back where they came from, instead shifting my attention to the tiny window opposite the bed. It was drizzling in the world beyond these walls. Light rain hit the glass, painting the room a dismal grey. *If only I could go back to that night.*

His face scrunched up as he breathed in the smell of me, disgusted and delighted in equal measure by the filth he'd forced me to survive in.

'Ava,' he leered in my direction. 'I assume you've already worked out why you're here?'

I said nothing. *He knows.*

He kept his volume low but changed his tone. 'I don't suppose that's what you want to talk about, though. You're probably wondering why you're *still* here, why I've kept you alive?' He rubbed his chin with his bony fingers. 'Am I right, darling?'

More nothing.

'Ah, you had so much confidence a few moments ago! What a shame. Cat got your tongue?'

His feline features dazzled me as he slammed the door shut and fastened the locks. Then he approached.

The sudden movement was enough to shock me. The heavy thud of his footsteps and the sway in his shoulders. He looked bigger, somehow, as he drew nearer. The tarantula hawk of the wasp world. To think I'd spent the past year accepting help from this man. His palm raised in a rush of motion and he clattered it in one heavy blow across my cheek, sending my head into a spin, my body from seated to flat across the bed in a matter of milliseconds. Searing pain scorched down the side of my face, his hand like a whip, and every word, plea and protestation, was knocked clean out of me.

'I've been wanting to do that for a while,' he growled, and roughly tied my wrists together in thick winds of plastic, tight enough to dig into my flesh. I stifled a cry of pain, not wanting to give him the satisfaction.

I didn't move an inch, my eyes only open a fraction, an unhealthy tension buzzing between us. I could only see the lower half of his body from where I lay. His shoes were pristine, perfect creases in his pinstripe suit trousers. But even though his outward appearance was spotless I could tell inside was a different story as he tied a knot in the plastic then started to pace away from me, rubbing his hands together, muttering to himself. Scum lay beneath that polished exterior.

'There have been too many lies, Ava. First Olivia—'

This was it: I had to talk. If I wanted to stay alive, to plead my case, I had to speak up. Now.

'I didn't murder Olivia,' I managed to croak.

I lifted my head slightly from the bed, only his torso in view, my voice raspy and frail.

He stopped and his hands fell to his sides. I angled my eyes upward. His chin turned first, pointing down, eyebrow raised, then the rest of his body followed as he pivoted towards me.

'I know that, Ava.' A smirk flashed across his face and he drew in closer once again. 'Because I did. I killed Olivia.'

'*What?*' I was confused. Wasn't that why I was here? Because Jade and I had abandoned her? Murder by inaction, or whatever you wanted to call it.

'She disobeyed me, Ava. I'd told her she'd exhausted her final chance and that if she relapsed again that would be it. I cannot stand betrayal. I'd done so much for that girl and she just kicked it back in my face, much like her mother. I had Sheff monitoring her, just as I had him monitoring you, but it wasn't Sheff who'd alerted me to her deceit that night. I think that person might have been you.'

I still couldn't pave a way towards his words making sense and my mouth took over, working on autopilot, going through the motions. The words tumbled out of my mouth before I could stop them.

'She overdosed.'

'She'd taken too much, certainly. And that low-life ex-boyfriend of yours had given her something cheap and nasty. But it wasn't enough to kill her. I went there that night, after someone, you, took her phone, sent that message asking for me, and helped me put an end to the maddening cycles of betrayal and dishonesty. I just gave her enough to finish the job.'

My eyes widened with horror. Jade and I had killed Olivia all right, but not with our inaction: with our action, by sending that message to David. If we hadn't done that, she might have survived.

Something in David's demeanour changed then, in the tone of his breathing and the set of his jaw, and he paced the floor with renewed intensity, the memory of killing Olivia bringing that different side of him to the fore.

'Rules are set by the powerful for the weak for a reason: they need to listen, they need to learn. First my wife, then Olivia, and now you. Because *none* of you understood, none of you *listened*, none of you realised how *serious* I was.'

He grabbed my neck and tore me from the bed, pushing my body back against the wall, the force of his weight against mine, knocking the wind out of me once again.

'You're the worst of the lot, though. I hope you know that. You made me believe you loved me, that you wanted to be with me.'

Stars lit up my vision as my head cracked into the plaster behind. Blood flowed from my nose and I tried to shake myself free.

'Stop, please, just—'

He cut me off. 'You used me, Ava. First, you came to me for help with Charlie, you let me in, you let me take care of you, made me fall for you and your sob story and your vulnerability. Only later did I realise what your true intentions had been: to get what you wanted out of me then stab me in the back.'

'You offered to help, David, I didn't force you to do anything.'

'You knew *exactly* what you were doing, Ava, don't play stupid. It's far too late for that. I thought you just needed space, so I gave it to you, but the whole time you were in a relationship with Josh! Right under my nose! Such a reckless girl.' He spat out the words, his saliva coating my eyelashes.

His eyes were burning into mine, wide and furious, daring me to scream. I kept quiet, avoided his glare, and observed him only through my peripheral vision. I noticed that, during our tussle, a chunk of his dark hair had come loose from its gelled-back position and hung limply over his left eye. I'd never seen him lose control before, hadn't thought it was possible for his hair to be in any other position than slicked-back perfection and, with his mask down, I saw for the first time how much he hated me, how much he hated everyone, how deep his need for revenge and control and order ran.

'I took your phone, Ava, the night after you moved into Olivia's. I wanted to make sure you'd been telling the truth about Charlie. I went through it in minute detail, every conversation, every email, every confession. I trusted you after that. I started to let you in.'

His sentences were speeding up, his words quick-fire.

'So I rewarded you: I sent Sheff to kill him.'

I couldn't look at him.

'When I told you what I'd done – that I'd dealt with him and you'd never have to worry about Charlie again – I admired you for your reaction. I saw myself in you. Someone you loved had betrayed your trust and so they had to go. You understood that. You barely reacted. It was just the same with Olivia and her mother. I thought we had an understanding, you and me. A connection. So maybe you already understand why you're here. Imagine if it were the other way round.'

My stomach felt as though it was laden with quicksand.

'And to think: things could have been so different.'

I was starting to suffocate against the wall, the cuff round my bruised neck crushing even deeper with the force David was applying.

'I wanted to keep you safe. I had you monitored and surveilled to make sure you felt loved. And then things started to change...'

He pressed harder.

'I uncovered your first betrayal: Charlie had proposed to you and you hadn't told me.'

Why was he still angry about that?

'But you managed to talk me round. I believed it was meaningless, now I'm not so sure: now I wonder if I feel rather sorry for Charlie. Back then I had no idea what you were capable of.'

'I wasn't lying,' I tried to say. 'That proposal was nothing.'

He barrelled on without acknowledging me. 'Then I found out *something* had happened the night of Olivia's death – something you clearly still felt guilty for – and I wanted you to tell me, Ava. I really did. I gave you so many opportunities to let me know the truth.'

I groaned in pain as I tried to breathe against his force.

'I didn't want to ask you outright: I wanted you to tell me. There's a big difference, you see. But you wouldn't crack. Even after everything I put you through to try and pressure you into it: keeping you in Olivia's house when I found out you were there the night of her death, making you wear her clothes, writing little love notes from Charlie and pushing them through the front door every night…' He laughed when my expression dropped, my brain just about alive enough to register what he was saying and what it meant. 'I like writing letters.'

I thought back to the break-up note we'd written all those nights ago. I should have known. Charlie would never have had the patience to write.

'I thought you'd ask me to look after you, to stay with you, that's what I was hoping for. Then, when we were close enough, you'd tell me the truth about your part in my daughter's final night. But you didn't. Which was OK at first. I was waiting, I understood I couldn't rush you: you'd just got out of a relationship and you didn't want me to get the wrong impression. So you stayed there alone and I watched you closing the door to the lounge, trying not to think about her. To be honest, you dealt with it very well, I thought that might have been more difficult for you than it was. In a way it made me like you even more, Ava. You're cold. Just like me.'

The lack of oxygen was starting to cut the images in front of me and I thought he looked almost impressed as the grey of the room started to swallow me up.

'And then you seduced me the night of the summer party and I was *elated*. Things were moving in the right direction, at last! But I didn't want to force it, so I let you go when you changed your mind. And then you decided you wanted nothing to do with me. I couldn't understand it. Why would you act so hot and then blow so cold? I thought you loved me. I thought we had an understanding.'

My body started twitching uncontrollably and he loosened his grip, dropping me like a stone to the floor.

I rushed to wrap my hands round my neck to quell the pain, taking huge, sharp, noisy breaths in, filling my deflated lungs with the sour air that surrounded me.

'I sent in Sheff to make sure you weren't seeing anyone else. He used to do the same job for me with Olivia. Part bodyguard part cook. He has a very particular set of skills...'

I quivered and cowered in a heap on the floor. He was clearly so proud of himself and took great pleasure in running me through the lengths he'd gone to, to find me out. If only I'd had the foresight to ask to look at the CCTV system David had been so keen to install. Not that he would have shared the incriminating images of himself dropping letters through my door in Charlie's name every night, but he would have refused to show me: and that might have helped me realise David wasn't what he seemed. As it was, I'd rolled straight into his trap, causing him no hassle whatsoever.

He eyed me up. 'Why do those you love the most always let you down so spectacularly?'

I shook my head.

'Why did you lie to me Ava? Why did you betray me? Why did you use me?'

There was nothing I could say.

'Answer!'

He kicked me in the ribs and all the wrong words spilled out of me. 'We were never together, we were never anything.'

'We slept together! You were living in my daughter's home! I filled it with clothes and food for you. How can you say *we were never in a relationship*?'

His furious temper, which bubbled unbelievably close to the surface, terrified me. 'Perhaps this was a lucky escape.'

I started to cry. I was backed into a corner.

'Pathetic.' He blinked a few times and sighed.

David smoothed back the frazzled pieces of hair that had fallen free during his outburst to their usual position. He regained his composure and stood tall again, straightened out the suit jacket he was wearing.

'Does Josh know?' I bleated.

I looked at him for a long second, daring him to tell me that Josh was involved, daring him to break my heart with the word yes.

'Look at those puppy dog eyes, Ava, honestly! Josh is far too weak for this, this is the big league, darling.'

My heartbeat steadied as that tiny silver lining covered me.

'But he knows something's up, I'm afraid. It turns out that Jade Fernleigh, despite being the world's most useless employee, had a final trick up her sleeve. She followed me the night of the summer party and took a picture of us about to spend the night together.'

I recalled her telling me about this photo weeks ago in the office. If only I'd realised back then it would be my only hope now. If only I'd asked to see it.

'She sent it to Josh earlier – I intercept all office emails that contain my name, just in case – so now he keeps ringing me… I'll have to talk to him tomorrow once I've figured out what to say.'

He looked away, thinking, then continued his stream of consciousness.

'So she's dead now, I'm afraid. Collateral damage. Though it's not as if she was very useful to me, or to anyone else, given the state she was in by the end.'

The abrupt way he delivered the news was so shocking, I couldn't believe the words he was saying.

'What?' I mouthed.

'She crossed me by taking that photo. That night was private, she had no business being up there with us. *Our first night together.*'

He leered. I stayed still.

'Sheff will have dispatched her by now. Overdose. A very high number of people in mental health institutions commit suicide. They get drugs smuggled in. Oh God, that reminds me, I should probably do some sort of statement for the press tomorrow morning. *She was a valuable member of our team, blah, blah, blah…*' His voice trailed off.

'Are you going to kill Josh, too?'

He sighed, a different emotion registering on his face.

'Poor Josh. When you came to tell me you and he were together I had to refocus. Josh hadn't known what we shared, or the feelings I had for you, this wasn't his fault: it was yours.'

He drew in close enough that I could smell his breath as it blew against my face. I tried to push myself as far back into the wall as I could. He drew in closer, crouched down towards me and assaulted my neck; gripping my skin with his teeth. I tried to make myself as small as possible, closing the gap between my shoulder and my jaw as much as I could, desperate to get away. But he held me in place, then, when he was done, stood back up, wiping away the moisture that surrounded his mouth.

'You liked that the other night,' he sneered.

I felt the dents of his teeth as I ran my fingers over my neck, tears falling down my face, mingling with the wetness he'd left behind. I wanted to spit at him. Crack his head off the wall. Tear chunks from his face. I dug my nails into the little grooves in the palms of my hands I'd already carved to make me feel alive, like I had some fight in me.

'Josh called me when you ran off that night. I knew you'd do that, of course; Sheff was waiting in his Range Rover outside for you, he tailed you the entire way.'

I pressed my fingers into my forehead, suppressing the *if only*, the near miss. I'd never really paid attention to the car Sheff drove.

'And you don't know much about the police investigation, do you? It's been quite the saga, darling, really, the media were furious that I'd given the police such a neat trail to follow. Though the police were convinced you'd run away, the media wanted more. I should have known, really: young blonde women always capture the imagination of the right wing tabloids, don't they? The detective in charge just wanted an easy life, he had the evidence and anything to the contrary he basically just ignored. Oxana rode in the car with Sheff, drove your car to Heathrow once he'd taken you, she found your passport in your bag and posed as you, boarding the flight to Ireland I'd booked hours earlier, she took out some Euros with your bank card and, well, you did the rest with your erratic disappearing act in front of Josh, texting your parents that strange goodbye, so that was that really. I had to adapt a few times, change the direction of the media stories so they couldn't focus on Josh or me. I convinced Georgette to speak out against Jade then, when she was exonerated, pulled my ace: Charlie. The reason I'd sent Oxana to Ireland was because *he* was from there. Did you know he went back after you broke up? That's where

Sheff found him: just outside Cork. Josh found the notes, which was helpful, it stopped me having to call in another anonymous tip. And now we're here! The grand finale. Where justice will finally be served.'

He announced the milestone grandiosely to an invisible audience.

I met his bold stare and held it, strong and unflinching. His shoulders twitched and a glint of hard silver flashed from his belt, but it wasn't a buckle that had caught my attention.

He was carrying a blade.

It looked like it was about ten inches long, pristine and razor-sharp.

He flicked his suit jacket open with a quick turn of his hand and the corners flew up behind him. The rise and fall reminded me of a matador's cape, the bullfighter playing with its prey, distracting it from his weapons with the movement of the material.

The jacket open, he slid his hand round the blade's handle, smiling as he pulled it from its shield. The tip was serrated. He held it low.

'Sit,' he said, as though he were talking to an animal. He was brusque now, and businesslike; he was in control again. I shuffled up to a seated position, compliant in the face of a weapon.

He squeezed the base of my jaw to open my mouth, took a large, white pill from his pocket, and slid his fingers into my mouth, between my teeth. He tasted metallic, like petrol, and his skin was rough.

'Swallow,' he instructed, pressing my mouth shut with his hand, the other still wrapped round the blade.

I gulped obediently

60

Josh

No answer. The cold buzz in the room amplified each of the three tones as they sounded out in quick succession, indicating that David had hung up the call. It felt as if time had stopped, that it was impossible that anything else was happening in the world, that it was totally out of the question for another event to register as even remotely important at this moment, that all efforts and all eyes should be focused on finding David. I rose from my position on the sofa, abandoning my search for Charlie, both buoyed and broken by Jade's email. What had happened the night of the summer party and why hadn't David, or Ava, told me about it?

I realised I didn't have much of a plan as I left the city on nothing but a horrible hunch. The truth was, David had always been something of an enigma: despite his kindness in taking me in when my parents died, I would hesitate before describing the man himself as kind. Truth be told, I'd always felt he adopted me when my parents passed away because it was the right thing to do for his reputation, rather than the right thing to do for me. Living in David's house hadn't been exactly loving, or warm, and without Olivia to talk to and confide in, I wasn't sure what would have become of me.

After university, Olivia went straight into a job at W&SP – her future had already been chosen for her – and David bought her a place of her own. It was at uni that she'd had her first taste of freedom and, along with that, her first taste of poor decision making. I was younger than Olivia so I still lived with David when her addictions started but, when I went to visit her, we'd veer off the rails together, probably in response to years of living under strict curfews and rules and regulations and, at first, David hadn't known anything about her hedonistic lifestyle. She'd been good at hiding it. Then, when she moved to London and started at W&SP, she got lazy and sloppy, and her actions started sparking negative news coverage. David responded with a show of force, putting her on medical leave from her position and sending her to rehab. But still she persisted.

When I moved down to the city and into my own place, I spent the majority of my first months in London with Olivia and her jacked-up pals. I flitted from job to job, my life running away from me, and, it was only when I was pictured drugged-up and out-of-it alongside Olivia, dubbed 'a bad influence', that David had ever been outright nasty to me. He told me that I wouldn't be left with any family, at all, if he ever saw another picture like that. I'd stopped the drugs then and there and David forgave me by offering me a position at W&SP. I'd gladly accepted and the job had been the best thing that ever happened to me: I had a steady income, independence, a purpose. Olivia, however, had battled against his wishes, her addiction growing stronger the more David told her no. When she continued to disobey him his treatment became ferocious. He'd wheel her off to institution after institution.

'Fix my daughter,' he'd demand, not realising all she'd really needed all this time was for her dad to look after her.

I worried for Ava: had she done something to provoke him? My mind was full of the possibilities as I pulled off the main road, dropping my speed on the winding country lanes towards Taften Manor. My wheels bounced over rocks and dipped into ruts, testing the suspension of my sporty two-seater.

I noticed the bright orange flash of an indicator behind me and a large car lumbered into the rear-view mirror. I slowed my pace, it followed suit, I drove faster, it kept up, I took a few wrong turns, it took them with me and, as I idled up the green lane towards the property, I started to think the worst. I had a tail. But I had an advantage. I knew these roads and I knew there was a dirt track to the side of the property barely visible from the main approach. I increased my speed, each twisting turn throwing my body uncomfortably from right to left in the driving seat, but it was working: the larger vehicle behind couldn't match my pace. Then I turned off my lights and screeched a hard right into the darkened track, high hedgerows on either side, nothing before me to illuminate my path in the darkness except the glow of the moon.

Something in me told me to stop, that driving up to the gates was a bad idea, so I pulled into a slight gap in the hedges and took a moment to compose myself. Satisfied

I'd shaken whoever was following me, for the moment at least, I propelled myself from the safety of the car and out into the dark. The muggy night formed beads of sweat on my brow and tree branches knotted together overhead, blocking the moonlight from reaching me.

The imposing building came into view a few minutes later, like a threat at the trail's end, and I marched purposefully towards my destination, clouds of foggy condensation erupting from my nose and mouth as the adrenaline pumped through me, pushing me to walk faster. Out of the cover of the trees and onto the exposed driveway, the sight of the building floored me, lit by the blue of the moon it looked like a sinister Disney castle, a spectacular and majestic gem, complete with turrets and gargoyles and a partial moat that encased the back of the house. The dark grey stone hinted at its ancient past, the sparkling flecks in the granite mimicking the stars of the night sky, the perfectly manicured hedges that lined the long, unlit lane to the front drive assuring its visitors that this was no stately home in trouble. I broke into a jog, my legs a little shaky as the building's menacing exterior drew closer. I was terrified. I prayed Ava wasn't here. God knows how she felt if she was. I snaked down the side of the house, thankful for the blackness round me. There were a few lights on in the upper floors but the downstairs was dead. Two cars were parked in the driveway: A Range Rover and a McLaren. David's was the McLaren. Whose was the other? Had that been what was following me?

I stopped for a moment and considered what to do next, but the various permutations of the next hour were too many to consider in full. I had to rely on instinct. If I knocked on the front door it would give David time to cover up what he might be doing. If I wanted to catch him I'd have to sneak in and get him red-handed. I selected a stone from the driveway. It was jagged and heavy and I stalked round the perimeter with it like a panther. There was a gate about twenty yards from the front of the building which led to the back gardens; it was closed and padlocked, but scaleable. I reached the metal posts and hoisted myself up and over the gate in one flowing movement, wincing as the spikes took my weight. Once over, I carried on, hurrying through the back garden to find a suitable entry point. A long, single-paned French door came into view. I tried the handle. Locked.

I pressed my face up against the glass first, my nose leaving a smudge on the pane, and checked what I was about to burst into. It was one of the little-used drawing rooms: elegant sofas, goose-down cushions, a gilded fireplace. I took the rock and smashed it against the handle, which dutifully fell to the floor, and stuck my fingers into the mechanism within, as though I knew anything about unpicking locks. Nothing gave way, so I forced my body weight into the door instead, trying to barge it open. Nada. Time was of the essence. I had to make a decision. I knew there weren't burglar alarms here, and the house was vast; what were the chances he'd hear me if I smashed the glass open? On the other hand, if he did hear, my element of surprise would be ruined.

I decided I didn't have a choice.

What use was surprise if she was already dead?

I hurled the rock as hard as I could at the glass pane. A crash cut through the air and I backed away as it made contact. It smashed immediately, shards exploding as though the stone had been a bomb, the reflective splinters falling haphazardly round their former home. I took a breath, the view to the room beyond was visible and I stepped carefully over the sharp edges and forced my body through the gap I'd created. My heart was thumping now, a new surge of adrenaline pumping ferociously through me, and I ran as quickly and quietly as I could through the room and along the corridor it linked to.

61

David

There's been an unexpected interruption.

A noise from downstairs.

An intruder?

You will have to adapt fast, you will be tested now.

You need to make a decision: leave the girl and investigate, or stay and chance that the sound was insignificant?

You cannot leave things to chance, cannot trust that Sheff will act on the threat without your say so. You can't just leave it. You change the direction of the knife and head out of the room.

62

Josh

I glanced down at the expensive watch on my wrist. A present from David for my 21st birthday. My heart twinged as I remembered the look on his face as he'd presented it to me.

'It used to be your dad's,' he'd told me.

What if I was wrong about this? What if he wasn't the evil megalomaniac I'd convinced myself he was on the drive up here? He'd be furious. I'd lose my job, certainly, and him. As well as Olivia and Ava. I'd have no family left. I tried hard to remove the emotion from the situation, thinking only of the possibility of finding Ava here, however small, and carried on tracing my way through the corridors. I didn't know the place well, had only been here once or twice, so I let my gut instinct guide me, allowed it to turn me left down the corridor and towards a lift.

I went to press the call button, but my body froze as it illuminated before I could make contact. Somebody else had pressed it. I watched the numbers above the lift climb and stop at level five. I heard a robotic voice telling the passenger the doors were opening.

Shit.

I had to hide.

There was a doorway about fifty feet away. I raced towards it.

I could hear the lift mechanisms working and thanked God that David hadn't upgraded it since my last visit. I had time to get there.

I hurtled into an industrial-sized kitchen, presumably where the catering team would come ahead of events like the summer party, comprised entirely of stainless steel and overhead racks hung heavy with a variety of pots and pans. The force of my momentum brought me to my knees as I attempted to stop. I shuffled behind the door, leaving it open a crack.

I wanted to poke my head out of it, to look down the hallway, but I knew I couldn't take any chances. He'd be on the prowl, his senses heightened.

Instead, I took a particularly shiny pan from the rack and angled half of it towards me, the other half down the corridor.

I watched in its blurred reflection as an enormous man exited the lift and looked right. It wasn't David.

His fists were like barrels.

Biceps like boulders.

Fury on his face.

I turned to ice.

I realised then I'd just run willingly into mortal danger and my head spun. I'd made a mistake coming here: it was rash and impulsive and stupid. I should have told someone, the police, DI Crow, anyone.

I put the pan down on the floor silently and shuffled on my hands and knees towards the back of the kitchen; I had to hide properly. Was this who had been on my tail? Was his the Range Rover?

I could hear the sound of his footsteps drawing nearer, they crescendoed and reached a fever pitch as his heels struck the rubber lino of the kitchen floor. *Easy to clean.* That's what he'd be thinking. Although, maybe he was one of those ex-SAS types capable of killing me with two fingers. No blood, guts or gore.

At least make it difficult for him, Josh; at least make yourself a nuisance. I felt him draw closer. He was barely breathing, but mine was fast and frantic, and, if I could hear it, he would too. I crouched down behind the set of counters that lined the left side of the room, and, judging from sound alone, he was inspecting the cupboards round the kitchen island, moving towards the back. Towards me. I had to move. One more step that way and I'd, probably, with the element of surprise on my side, be able to reach the door before him.

Three, two, one!

And, with that countdown, I lunged, moving with the explosivity of a sprinter out of the blocks, towards the door.

He shouted out but I barely heard him, my attention completely focused on the exit.

Something else cut through the air and a pocket knife thwacked into the wood of the door frame, missing my head by inches, his shouts building louder as he realised he'd missed.

My palm latched round the door handle and I flung it open, propelling myself through the threshold and down the corridor.

It wouldn't take long for him to extract the knife and chase me.

The lift.

The lift was right ahead.

I sprinted as fast as possible and jabbed the call button, using the lift frame to stop the momentum of my body. It opened instantly and I clambered inside. I heard his footsteps pounding the floor towards me.

I pressed for level five.

If he reached the lift before the doors closed, I was a goner.

If he managed to get a fingertip into the doors before they closed, would they reopen?

Hurry, hurry, hurry.

I felt sick.

I'd made the wrong decision.

Why would I risk the lift when I knew how old and cranky it was?

The doors were closing, inching closer together, teasing me with how slowly they were moving.

I rapidly fired my finger over the 'close doors' button.

His gravelly voice echoed off the walls as he drew level.

The doors closed.

I heard his finger depress the button outside, calling the lift, I heard his knife scrape through the door, saw the tip of its blade as I ascended away from him.

Mercifully, the doors stayed shut.

But, he knew I was going to floor five and he'd probably beat me up the stairs.

The lift doors creaked open at level five just as the doors to the stairwell directly opposite were ripped apart by the giant man pursuing me. I didn't have time to think about what to do, it just felt obvious: attack is the best form of defence. I careered towards him, bellowing, a guttural, primal sound accompanying my action, borne out of a desire to protect Ava, channelling all my pent-up frustration in not having found her on this man. He looked surprised, the speed of my approach disarming him for a split-second long enough to have an effect. I wrapped my arms as far round his thick waist as I could and my head thumped him square in the ribs. He grunted, and bent double, as we fell through the doorway together. He retaliated fast, swinging his fists in wide arcs, raining blows on either side of my head. An impending concussion drove me to act faster, forcing all my might against him, still at an advantage as long as momentum was with me. I pushed him toward the stairs, then roared mightily as I gave him another shove off the edge. His last punch, sure to knock me out, missed my temple by inches, and he stumbled backward on the top stair, forced to retract his arms and use them as balancers. I wrestled my own arms from round his waist and, when he linked his hand round my forearm, took my inspiration from him and unleashed a lunging left hook to the side of his face. His eyes widened. My fist made contact with his skull. Spit and blood sprayed out, covering us both. His grip loosened and his legs crumpled under him as he fell backwards down the steep, iron staircase, his head cracking open as it made a catastrophic impact with the metal below.

He lay there, convulsing.

'Holy shit,' I said out loud, my legs shaking. My stomach lurched at the sight of blood and brain matter expanding beneath his head.

63

David

Josh.

Of all people.

After everything you've done for him.

You watch him from the end of the corridor as he staggers out of the stairwell, face as white as chalk. Your likeness reflected in the various bones of his face. Your family.

You'd gathered from the shouts and crashes that he'd dispatched of your bodyguard. Part of you was impressed, your own flesh and blood physically out-matching Sheff was no mean feat.

You don't want to kill him. But you're wary.

You can't take too many chances. You keep the knife in your grip and unlock the door to Ava's room. You have to neutralise him, then you can explain. Once you tell him what she's done, the way she betrayed you both, Josh would have to understand.

64

Josh

I hurtled towards the door ahead and my stomach flipped in on itself as I bent over, dry-gagging as the revolting props that lined the walls wriggled their way into my consciousness. It was a sight I'd never be able to erase. The room I was stood in was covered in torture devices, laid out like a museum, as if they should have little tags next to them telling visitors what they were used for and where they were found. There were clubs and spikes and pliers and clips… There were words too, the same six repeated over and over again in big angry scribbles:

Betrayal, Disloyalty, Lies. Revenge, Retaliation, Demise.

A large screen sat on a white desk in the middle of the room and played an image of a girl, skin and bones and blonde hair, heaped on the floor. It took me a second to know for sure, but it was her, it was Ava. I gasped. Ava had a chain round her neck and lay motionless on the floor, foam round her mouth.

Was I too late?

I ran up to the screen and locked my hands round it, wanting to be close to her. A metal loop with a set of heavy-duty keys lay on the desk next to the screen, the only thing in here out of perfect alignment. I picked them up and looked round. On the right side of the white surveillance room was a door, even more secure than the one I'd just entered through, the keys clearly designed for it. I rushed towards it, my only focus on getting to her. She was so close. There were five locks but, as I fit what was clearly the largest key into the main central lock, I discovered they were all open.

Dread swamped me.

This was a trap.

65

David

You hear Josh fit the key into the lock and can almost taste his uncertainty as the door opens excruciatingly slowly. Of course he wasn't going to run away once he'd seen her, you know him well, you can predict him, which is why you know this will be difficult. You hear the creak of the floorboard underfoot as he shifts his weight forward, ready to rush towards his girl. He takes his first step into the room and, as though he'd put his foot into a bear trap, you snatch him. You lock your arm round his neck and force your knife up against his windpipe. He opens his mouth and starts to shout. Or croak, rather. The force you have round his windpipe is crushing his voicebox.

'Don't fight, Josh,' you demand.

His eyes are glued on the girl. The life left in her body is duelling with death. The pill you'd made her take is a lethal dose of cocaine mixed with a powerful horse tranquiliser. A truly toxic and yet wonderfully tidy way to exact the justice you deserve. Just because the world wouldn't believe someone like Ava would take an overdose doesn't mean you can't kill her in the way you've become so fond of! You love to watch the drugs take hold: the slow demise, the futile struggle.

'David, let me help her, whatever you've done, it's forgiven, we have to save her before it's too—'

You bring your arm tighter round his throat and kick the back of his knees in so he falls to the floor.

'That girl.' You bring the knife away from his throat and point it at Ava, sending an invisible beam between his line of sight and her frail body. 'Betrayed us both.'

You feel him relax, the tension in him not so palpable.

'She's a snake, Josh, she used us… Listen, Ava and I slept together the night of the summer party. We were *in a relationship*. But it was all a lie, an act to get Olivia's house, to get ahead at work, to live off my money, my kindness, my generosity. And, all the while, she was seeing you behind my back. You don't know this woman, you don't know the first thing about her.'

'What?' Josh stumbles and stutters, you can hear the cogs in his brain whirring.

'It happened in this very building, our first night together.'

He's foaming at the mouth, angry despite the truth you've told him.

'You sent me away that night, the night of the summer party, you planned to do something, you wanted me gone. I think you were to blame, not Ava, I think you forced yourself on her.'

'She didn't tell you about it though, did she?' You're goading him. You're hitting him where it hurts. 'If you're so convinced it was my fault then why didn't she say something? Why did she keep working for me?'

'Why didn't *you* say anything?'

'I didn't want to tell you because I didn't want to break your heart.' Your voice is soft and calm and, gently, you release your grip, moving your arm from a choke hold to a comforting grip round his shoulder. It won't be easy for him to understand.

What happens next you don't expect: in one swift motion, Josh's elbow expels the air from your lungs as it connects with your chest, crushing you. You can't stand upright, you think maybe he's broken one of your ribs. Your fury intensifies. He wriggles free and heads towards the girl.

'Did you know she was engaged to Charlie?' You rattle out, wheezing through the pain.

His face falls as he unties her knots.

'No—'

'There's a lot you don't know about her.'

Josh scowls, but brings her onto her back anyhow, pumping her chest with his hands, trying to conjure life from thin air.

'It's done,' you rasp. He hurls himself at you, screaming like a banshee, but you're too quick and you grab the knife from your belt. As he approaches you, you stab him instinctively, piercing him deep in the gut. You intended it as a flesh wound, but his howl and the way his hands scramble to stem the blood bursting from it, tell you you've inflicted real damage.

You retreat, watching him writhe in pain, clutching his middle. Regret. You don't want to kill him, you just want him to understand.

The look he gives you communicates that you have failed.

He slumps back against the wall and thick, dirty blood spills from his middle. Your blood. You have to put the regret to one side. The plan has changed so you must change with it.

You stagger away from him just as a cacophony of sound clatters into the tiny room, a rush of voices and noises and boots on the ground.

'Freeze! Hands up! Get up! Now!'

A police officer points a weapon directly between your eyes. They'd approached silently and now there was no way out.

Josh must have led them here. Or picked up a tail. They probably had a whole unit on him with instructions to follow wherever he went: just in case he led them to her.

Think.

You lunge for the lights in the room and smash a hand against their switches, casting the room into darkness. Josh cries out like he's been shot and something fires that sounds more like a starter pistol than a gun. These noises mix with the darkness and trigger chaos and violence which immediately engulf the room. You feel another person barging in, weapons drawn, but take advantage of the confusion by dropping to your hands and knees, heading for the doorway you'd entered through, the one that leads to the surveillance room – the only way out.

You make it into the second room and out into the corridor.

You climb to your feet, stealing a glance behind you as a voice cries out.

'Stop or I'll shoot.' The warning was fierce and final. You'd rather take the chance than face the rest of your life behind bars.

You don't stop.

Three more steps.

Two.

On—

Bullets pierce your torso.

Crimson spreads across your shirt.

You'd been stunned by the sound and speed of the gunfire, breathless from its impact, too shocked to register pain.

You fall to your knees, your patellas taking the impact as they smash to the floor, clutching your chest, your face twisted in hate.

Maybe people will write about you, after all.

One Week Later

THE WASP'S NEST

Ava Wells, a missing person presumed runaway – now in intensive care – was freed from her captor last week in a dramatic rescue operation. But a botched police investigation and a trudge of fake news hampered her recovery and only now is the truth starting to emerge. In an attempt to better understand the events surrounding Ava's abduction, we'll bring together the evidence that has come to light and begin to explain how Ava's captor was able to evade authorities for so long.

David Stein, infamous PR guru behind Watson & Stein Partners, had access to a huge network of media contacts: this was the single most effective tool at Mr Stein's disposal for hiding in plain sight. In fact, when revisiting reports of Ava's disappearance Mr Stein is conspicuous in his absence, but his office was behind almost all of the 'evidence' that linked to Ava's disappearance. W&SP were responsible for leaking Ava's supposed trail to Ireland – perhaps David believed once the media had reported on the direction the investigation was taking, police would be reluctant to backtrack and admit they were chasing a red herring. Ava's plane ticket was paid for by a company card, which David applied for. The woman who boarded the aircraft with Ava's passport, wearing thick sunglasses and a baseball cap to alter her appearance, is rumoured to go by the name of Oxana, a woman David pays for consultancy at his PR offices. The CCTV network in the house Ava was living in before she was taken was owned by David and yet the footage was never recovered by police, with Mr Stein managing to convince investigators the cameras had been inactive for a number of months. In addition, Georgette Giani has come forward to say she was 'pressured' by David to speak out against Jade Fernleigh in what she believes now was a textbook smear campaign. When Jade was exonerated, W&SP sources pointed the finger next at Ava's ex-partner Charlie Munk. Police are yet to locate Charlie, but it seems the more we tug on the threads associated with David Stein, the more bodies we uncover. Perhaps Charlie has met a similar fate.

Diving deeper into the tale, David Stein's pattern of abuse may have started many years ago. His former wife, Kate Watson, and their daughter Olivia both died of apparent overdoses brought on by years of addiction. Neither death was treated as suspicious at the time, however, David's actions have put the cases back under the spotlight and investigations into both may yet reopen. Adding weight to the serial-killer theory, Ava Wells was poisoned by a similar cocktail of drugs that ended the lives of both Kate and Olivia, and former partners of David Stein have come forward in the aftermath of this tragedy to support the idea that Ava wasn't his first victim. One woman, who did not want to be named, stated, 'He never showed any genuine sadness after Kate died. He moved on with me very quickly and refused to talk about her. I put it down to the different ways people deal with grief but now I think it's because he was culpable.'

Another victim in this saga was Jade Fernleigh, colleague of Ava's and one-time suspect in her disappearance as orchestrated behind the scenes by David Stein, but, in a rapid turn of events, Jade appears to have set the wheels in motion that led Josh, Ava's boyfriend and Stein's adopted son, to David's country house and to Ava's subsequent rescue. Jade was murdered with near-identical amounts of cocaine and tranquiliser in her system as Ava was given, however, police believe a different man: a contract killer nicknamed Sheff, who'd worked with David for a number of years, was responsible for Jade's death. Which begs the question: just how many people had David instructed this professional to assassinate over the years?

Ava was drugged and beaten by Stein during her abduction and, when she arrived at hospital, doctors said she was 'minutes from death'. Details into the full extent of her injuries have not yet been released. Sadly, Josh Stein died at the scene: killed by a single stab wound inflicted by his adopted father shortly before officers arrived. David Stein and his contract killer Sheff were also killed during the raid.

Ava's family have released a short statement. 'We ask only for privacy whilst we try to heal from this experience.' Sources close to the investigation say Ava herself is 'distraught' and 'devastated'.

The case, increasingly referred to as The Wasp's Nest, has highlighted serious shortcomings in a number of ways this case was handled, from our own media coverage down to the police handling of the disappearance, from start to finish. Both our paper and the police are planning 'major' investigations into what went wrong. We'll bring you more on Ava's recovery as we get it.

66

Ava

The doctor told me I died in that room. My heart stopped and, if the police hadn't started CPR when they did, I would never have woken up from the brain damage I would have sustained. When I came round the first person I asked for was Josh.

'Josh isn't with us, he didn't make it.'

That news made me wish I was still asleep. I'd died in that room with him and part of me would never understand how I was brought back to life when he wasn't.

A nurse gave me a few newspapers one morning, the ones with more measured reports of what had happened, to help me understand what I'd been through. David was being branded a serial killer, a maniacal egomaniac with a God-complex and pathological desire for control. They raided the W&SP offices: the entire place was rigged up with cameras and surveillance. Stories came out about bribes and blackmail. It seemed it wasn't just Olivia, or me, who he'd wanted to control but numerous members of staff, rivals and girlfriends, over the years.

In the raid on Olivia's flat they'd found video footage of David entering and leaving Olivia's apartment the night of her death – he hadn't set up CCTV especially for me, he'd had cameras there all along – and this footage, along with the diversions the force had found – the ticket to Ireland, the cash withdrawal, Oxana posing as me – had all led back to David. These pieces of evidence were enough to have the public convinced he'd killed his only daughter and, as it had been almost twenty years to the day that his wife had died, there wasn't anyone who didn't believe he hadn't done that, too.

Sheff had died of blunt force trauma to the head and a single hair, dropped from his arm, had tied him to Jade's ward room. He'd paid a cleaner to let him in after visiting hours and had administered her a lethal cocktail of drugs. The papers said she only died because of the picture she'd taken and sent to Josh. She'd cracked the case. She'd worked out all roads lead to David and had put Josh onto him. If she hadn't sent the picture to Josh's work email account – David intercepted any messages with his name in them – she might have survived. But, as soon as David realised Jade knew more than she should, he'd sent his trusty bodyguard to despatch of her. Presumably he'd hoped he could talk Josh into believing I was a willing participant in our 'relationship'. I will never know for sure what Josh died believing but I hope, with all that I have left, that he didn't spend his final moments doubting that I loved him. Because I did, I do, and will always.

One Year Later

67

Ava

The salty sea air dances round me as I lie on the balcony of my new seaside home. The sun drenches me in its rays, the cool breeze a welcome relief. You could say I've run away from my problems by moving down to the coast and away from the city, and I suppose that would be true, but no matter how far I travel from London the nightmares follow.

I think about Jade the most. I regret pushing her away after Olivia died and building walls between us instead of bridges. I regret everything about the night Olivia died. I regret ever asking David Stein for help. I regret putting my career before my happiness and my health. I had such a one-track mind about working there, it's only now I realise there's no point in a 'dream job' if it turns the rest of your life into a nightmare.

I hope one day I will be happy again and that, if I can't ever move on, at least be able to make peace with the fact that I survived when so many others died.

I watch as a noisy seagull lands on a wooden post on the

beach beyond. The bird squawks and yelps as if in danger, or in pain, and the sound fills the sky. Soon enough, another gull flies past and the pair wail over each other in dissonant, ghastly melodies. I decide to head inside and fold up the single wooden chair I keep on the deck of my tiny suntrap.

I live in a glass-fronted block of new-build apartments and am surrounded by units exactly like mine. I find there's a certain security in the similarity of it all. *Safety in numbers*, as they say. Because why would anyone head to the fifteenth floor to break into my flat, when there are hundreds of identical ones that line the easily-accessed ground and first floors? But, if anyone did scale the outside to take a look through my windows, they'd be disappointed: my tastes veered towards the incredibly boring and minimalistic, the only thing of value in this place a secondhand flat-screen in the bedroom.

But I didn't choose to live here just for the high-floor number. This complex also boasts a twenty-four-hour security guard, anti-climb gates, a keycode entry system, and CCTV along every corridor. In my own apartment I've installed motion-detection cameras and a geo-fence that alerts me if anything moves whilst I'm away. I check the footage obsessively throughout the day. I've become awfully paranoid since everything happened. But at least I'm still here. Small step though this might seem, moving to an apartment by myself has been a giant leap forward for me.

I'm wrapped up in a dressing gown stuck into a love story set in Ancient Rome, my eyelids heavy, ready for bed. My tongue tastes of the hot chocolate I've been sipping and the flat is warm and cosy, a candle burning over the mantle.

And then there is a knock at the door and it's as though someone has poured ice over my haven. My ears prick, the hair on my arms stand on end and I silently place the book down on the coffee table in front of me. Keeping my breath light, I tiptoe over to the door just as another series of raps fire out.

I pause, every inch of me alert and tense.

I hear shuffling and movement from outside and I press forward until I reach the door.

'I've moved in next door, just wanted to introduce myself,' shouts the voice.

But I don't let that disarm me. What kind of self-respecting neighbour introduces themselves after dark?

I move my eye in line with the peep hole and spot a man, back to the spy-hole, standing at my door. *Who is he?*

Hands up against the wood I keep watch as he makes a move to leave and then changes his mind, turning fully towards me and knocking once again. The thuds hit me as I lean into the barrier that separates us, each vibration running the length of my body. I am frozen, unable to move, because now I have seen his face: the angry vein that pulses over his forehead, the irritated scowl on his lips, the raven-coloured hair that sits on top of his head, and the hand clenched to a fist as he raises it once again to lure me into opening up.

Bang bang bang.

'We need to talk.'

Acknowledgments

I want to start by thanking my agent, Kate Nash, for her belief, unparalleled work ethic and enthusiasm. Thank you for making my dream a reality. Many thanks too to my editor, Hannah Smith, for holding my hand through the first-book wilderness! I am so grateful to have found you. Thanks also to the team at Aria, to Vicky, and the wider Head of Zeus family.

Special thank you to my mum and my sister for reading, re-reading and re-re-reading version upon version of this book (and others!) Your help has been immense and I appreciate it so much.

Thanks to my amazing dad for always encouraging me to be creative. To my brother: *grazie*. To Nana and Pompa, for being such wonderful grandparents. To my enormous family in Jersey and beyond. To my dear Nanny, who I'm sorry didn't get to see me achieve this particular goal.

Thank you to my wonderful friends, a few of whom endured a very early version of this story: Georgie, Abby and Katie. To Fiona, for having faith in me from the beginning, long before I had any in myself. To Sophie and Emily, for always being so encouraging. And to the girls in Jersey who will be glad my wild storytelling has found an outlet!

Heartfelt thanks to the outstanding women I have worked with over the years, who firmly disprove the existence of toxic female rivalries. Especially Eli, for being such an inspiration to everyone she works with. Thanks to those who have been toxic, too.

Above all, thanks to Colin. Without your kindness and support I wouldn't have written this book. I hope you're ready for a few more brainstorms.